VERDUN

VERDUN

JULES ROMAINS

translated from the French by
GERARD HOPKINS

PRION

This edition published in 2000 by
Prion Books Limited, Imperial Works,
Perren Street, London NW5 3ED

Reprinted 2000 (twice) and 2001

First published in French by Flammarion
Copyright © 1938 by Ernest Flammarion

This English translation was previously published by
Souvenir Press Ltd.

ISBN 1-85375-358-0

Cover design by Bob Eames
Cover image courtesy of Hulton Getty

Printed and bound in Great Britain
by Bookmarque Limited, Croydon, Surrey

CONTENTS

PART ONE: THE PRELUDE

PART TWO: THE BATTLE

VERDUN

PART ONE

THE PRELUDE

CHAPTER ONE

"One Grand Sweet Song"

Never before in the world's history had so many men, at one and the same time, said good-bye to their homes and families preparatory to cutting one another's throats. Never before had such crowds of soldiers marched to war so firmly convinced that the "cause" for which they were to fight was personal to each one of them.

Not all rejoiced. Not all festooned the trains with flowers or scribbled joking mottoes on them. Many there were who were made thoughtful by the sight of country-folk along the railway tracks strangely unresponsive to the boastful jests of the troops on the move, a shade too solemn in their salutation of the packed truck-loads of noisy warriors. But the feeling abroad was, generally speaking, one almost of relief. Most of the men seemed grateful to destiny for having forced their hands, for having taken from the individual all power of hesitation or of choice. Brutal her methods were, no doubt, but the victims might well live to thank her. She was behaving, on the whole, rather like the swimming-instructor who teaches the reluctant child to swim by pitching him head-first into the water.

No one doubted that, sooner or later, the whole world would be involved in this business of fighting. Already a good part of it was caught in the toils. But, true to tradition, scrupulously observant of all due rights of priority, the thing had begun as an affair of Frenchmen and Germans before spreading to the rest of the inhabited globe.

Each of the two nations had prepared for hostilities by conjuring up as thrilling a vision as possible of the nature of war. The Germans found stimulus in the belief that they were entering on a new stage of some old and epic struggle, that they were responding to the call of the knights and emperors of the Middle Ages, who stood pointing out the path of duty with outstretched swords. Nay, more, for behind these heroic figures, in a still mistier past, stood the ranked hordes of Arminius and of those other ancient leaders whose men had been slaughtered in the deep German forests by the legions of Rome, and now called upon their lineal descendants to seek a belated vengeance. The immediate object must be to win glory for the Teutonic race, to make its name a terror through the Continent, to crush the machinations of its envious neighbours, who, outraged by its wealth and greatness, had plotted with the rest of Europe in the hope of hemming in its power and bringing it low.

The French, on the other hand, professed to see themselves as the champions of humanity. Civilization, conscious now, not for the first time, that its future could be secured only at the cost of much savage blood-letting, had, so they felt, made choice of France to hold its banner high. Not but what the sacred motherland, too, was in question, not but what the hope of winning back the two lost provinces played some part in the decision; but the really important thing was to prove to mankind that the spirit of the Revolution was still alive. The French must show once more that they were still the same people who, since the days of the Crusades, had never taken up arms save in the interests of the race, who had ever willed that her neighbours, even though they asked it not, should have their part in that excellent way of life which the Gallic genius had shaped and brought to perfection.

But in addition to all this, the men of both sides were worked upon by the thought that they were setting off for a noisy, bustling, rough sort of holiday, a real schoolboy expedition. The very time of year, the fine, long days, contributed to strengthen the illusion. War would be a happy change from peace, with its host of irksome duties which modern life has served but to multiply and complicate. Even the amenities of daily life, all those things that go with comfort and prosperity, act in the long run as checks on freedom. Contemporary man is so hedged about with brittle, precious "properties" that the very caution needed to save them all from breakage becomes at last a weariness. A truce to such things! Here was a chance to live care-free for a while and irresponsibly to stretch the limbs in an orgy of crude action with never a thought for brittle things that might be broken. Life would be the better for some such "primitive" cure, for relapsing into simple ways, for losing touch with the manners of refinement. For the really young, for those in the full flower of adolescent health, the prospect was particularly entrancing—all the more so because, obviously, the interlude would be short.

Naturally, only a fool would go blissfully ahead without making allowances for the unexpected in this matter of duration as in other things. But even those who thought it wise to reckon on a three-months campaign (making allowances for all the inevitable haggling and play-acting that would inevitably be associated with the peace conference, the business might drag out till Christmas. What a wonderful Christmas, what a wonderful New Year, it would be—nothing like it ever before! What fun to relapse, a little weary, into the complications of peace!), even they did not exclude the possibility of a lightning victory in three weeks. There'd be hardly time to get used to the new conditions. It would all be rather like one of those sudden storms that mark a summer afternoon: peals of thunder, and then on the very heels of the pandemonium a renewed vision of blue skies; or like one of those typhoons told of by travellers; or, again, like a quick burst of temper, some wild crisis of drunkenness or passion. Nor could cool reason find the analogy at fault. This modern war, different from any previous war, would employ so vast an accumulation of technical equipment that obstacles and defences which in the old days must have been reduced by a slow process of nibbling would be carried at a bound. Any increase in the force employed must, surely, in any operation, result in increased speed?

For Germany, and for her Austro-Hungarian allies, any quick stroke capable of deciding the war in the first few weeks must take the form of defeating France before England—always assuming her willingness to come to the rescue—should be in a position to move. That done, they could deal with Russia, which by that time would be just about ready to take a hand, and confront her with the alternatives of complete destruction or immediate peace.

The French plan was to make a drive towards the Rhine and, by means of two or three swift successes achieved by reliance on the bayonet, the '75, and the offensive spirit, to dislocate the heavy German machine. The weight of the latter, its rigid organization, and the fact that the rather slow-witted men in charge would be taken by surprise offered a rational basis for the belief that it would be lacking in efficiency and decidedly vulnerable during the opening weeks of the campaign.

The French General Staff, however, as a further stimulus to its ingenuity, had not omitted to consider the possibility of a breach of Belgian neutrality by the foe, and the consequent risk of an outflanking movement from that direction. But it was clear from studying the map that such a movement could be developed only on the right bank of the Meuse, in which case the French armies, instead of confining their offensive to the centre and the right wing, would merely have to extend the field of their operations along the whole front between the Meuse and the Vosges to check successfully any attempt at a forward movement by the enemy in Belgium. In order, therefore, to retain until the last moment, complete liberty of action in throwing the main weight of its thrust in one of several directions, the High Command, deploying the forces at its disposition, had echeloned the IVth Army slightly to the rear, so as to give it, as it were, the advantage of being on a turntable.

But Joffre had made the mistake of underestimating both the enemy's effectives and the degree of his adventurousness. Moreover, several considerations which had nothing to do with pure strategy had weight with him. Even if "offensive" had not happened to be the fashionable jargon of the moment in military circles, it would still have had the great merit, in his eyes, of committing the nation once and for all to the campaign, of making the situation irrevocable, and of strengthening patriotism by a dash of self-confidence. It was Joffre's view that some early success in the field, however devoid of real value it might be, was absolutely essential. The anti-militaristic spirit in France might well be but momentarily numbed by emotionalism, and there was always the danger that it might once more get the upper hand. The nation must be given a quick and heady draught of victory. The army's stock would soar; there would be no turning back.

Further, victory must be connected in men's minds with Alsace-Lorraine. Not the name of the tiniest village in the lost provinces but for French ears was loud with the overtones of history. The least decisive of successes on such a battlefield would seem like a pledge forced from the hands of fate.

The better to ensure success, each of the two High Commands had taken the field with a whole dossier of formulas guaranteed to be infallible by such experts as Napoleon or Moltke and perfected by generations of professors in the military art.

All this printed accumulation of tactical genius, which ought to have ensured victory in three weeks, turned out to be no less productive of almost immediate defeat—though not carried to extremes, and, on the whole, pretty equally divided between the combatants. The French were beaten at Morhange and at Charleroi, the Germans on the Marne.

Whereupon the latter beat a hurried retreat and seemed so obviously headed for home that it looked as though a little hustling would get rid of them for good and all. No sooner, however, had they reached the fortified line prepared by their back-area troops to meet just such an emergency than they stopped, and, by dint of setting every available man to dig, produced in next to no time a line of trenches covering the whole length of their deployment, after which they turned on their pursuers, brought them to a standstill with concentrated machine-gun fire, and proceeded to install themselves in their new position, from which they appeared to be fully determined not to move.

Certain truths began now to emerge from a study of the

operations and had upon the leaders of both sides a more sobering, because less expected, effect even than the stench of decaying corpses. It became clear that there could no longer be any question for either side of striking a decisive blow or of carrying out brilliant tactical movements. It was equally impossible to break the enemy's centre or to envelop his flanks.

The romantic view of war which had done so much to keep men's hearts high in the early days, had received a stab in the back from which it never really recovered. War played a dirty trick on the warriors by turning out to be quite unlike what they had expected. The journalists and orators behind the front did not at first realize what had happened, or, if they did, they set about doing everything they could to hide the fact. The men in the line, however, had no illusions on the subject; nor had their leaders, nor even the political heads of the combatant nations. It was not yet obvious that the war would bring misery to the whole world, but it seemed probable that it would do no one any good—except the contractors. At best it would be a costly, difficult, and wearisome business. As a result, the governments in question began to take the line that they had done nothing to provoke it. How could anyone, they argued, have embarked light-heartedly on such a questionable adventure? They had no difficulty in persuading themselves that responsibility lay with the fellow opposite.

As to the generals, nervously fumbling in this strange new world, biting their lips to make sure that they were not dreaming, they gradually awoke to the fact that what they had so leisurely prepared, without ever clearly seeing the upshot, was something that had turned out to be utterly unpredictable—a war of millions.

They discovered that the physical properties of men reckoned by millions made up an element that conditioned and neutralized all considerations of mere strategy. Armies of so vast a size were found to possess an unexpected fluidity, a tendency to flow into, and fill up, any holes that might be made in their compact body, to envelop, impede, and turn the point of any opposing thrust; to give beneath a blow, to bend without breaking, to seep outwards from the flanks, covering more and more ground with an ever-active, ever-shifting front, growing to such a size that the forces involved could be regarded as nothing less than nations in arms, obstinately clinging to the ground they covered, adapting themselves to the accidents of its surface, tracing, almost instantaneously, with millions of pairs of arms, a continuous scratch over which they formed like a scab and at every point of which they faced the opposing lines with a ceaseless crackling of fire, a lethal trembling, as though something tormented, burning, and unapproachable had become installed as a natural feature of the landscape. In such circumstances the leaders could do little more than feed all the ramifications of their ranked multitudes, as best they could, with food, ammunition, orders of the most elementary kind, and reserves of men to fill the gaps which there was no difficulty in determining.

They discovered other truths as well. For instance, that the technical equipment which they had devised, and produced in enormous quantities, with the sole object of achieving with as little delay as possible a breach in the enemy's positions and the crushing and routing of his effectives, developed a power of resistance greater even than its power of attack. It was found that quick-firing artillery and machine-guns could do little against trenches thrown up in the course of a mere twenty-four hours. But they could, with deadly efficiency, break up any attack and, in a few minutes, cover the intervening no man's land with corpses, tiring far less rapidly than the advancing troops, no matter how often their assaults were repeated.

Another truth that was borne in on the military mind was that, whereas for an attack to stand any chance of success it must avail itself of every novelty of equipment, that it could never have too much, could never have enough, of technical resources, a defence could be conducted to perfection by employing the simplest materials, the trivialities of daily use, tricks as old as the human race, odds and ends of the most humiliating ordinariness: earth just thrown up with the spade, bags and boxes filled with soil or stones; wattle of twigs and clay; the kind of barbed wire that is commonly employed by gardeners.

But for some time the generals could not reconcile themselves to drawing the logical conclusion. They argued that the trouble in the opening phases of the campaign had been that they were not quick enough in delivering the knock-out blow, that they had been faced by completely new problems, the full extent of which they had not grasped. Provided, however, they kept doggedly at the job, open warfare would be bound to return, emerging from the slough in which it had got caught almost from the beginning, and then the methods of the Staff College would come again into their own. The Germans, who had taken the lead in this game of digging in and had covered hundreds of kilometres with an unapproachable firing line, had perceived that beyond their extreme right, in the direction of the sea, there was still a considerable stretch of free country, a whole plain across which there was no barrier of armed men, and that they still had sufficient "millions" in reserve to pour into this gap and so start a flanking movement on the enemy's left, without in any way weakening the continuous line of their main defences. Since they wished to carry out this operation without having to trouble about diversions, they were at pains to give the Russian bear a sharp rap on the snout, far away on the distant eastern frontier of Germany, in the hope of forcing the mammoth Empire to stay quiet and so give them the necessary respite.

But the spirit of the French Army was far from being dead, and it had no intention of allowing its flank to be turned. Reinforced, as it now was, with a considerable number of English troops, it found itself with a sufficient number of men to undertake a parallel movement towards the north coast. Straightaway there began to develop what the military experts, true to their old longing for a war of movement and the grand gesture, called the "race to the sea," but what in reality was nothing but one demonstration the more of the peculiar physical properties of these "armed millions," these two sluggish oozings, mutually conditioned in their origin and direction, both engaged in slowly eating up the few free miles that still lay open between them, and needing but to make contact to relapse once more into a condition of stagnation.

Then was to be seen a sight which had no precedent in history: two immense armies confronting each other along the whole length of their front, longing to come to a decision, yet incapable of making a single movement.

At most, the energy that was lacking to neither side, and was constantly renewed, did succeed in developing momentary bouts of pressure which were neutralized as soon as established, spasmodic efforts, exhibitions of muscle strained to muscle, such as may be seen in wrestling-matches when the bodies of the combatants seem fixed in a furious immobility. True, here it was no case of the contact of two naked bodies, but of two dehumanized surfaces prickly with steel points, sweating fire and corruption—a paradoxical conflict in which the main difficulty was to establish any kind of contact. Each of the two champions threw his weight against the other without ever being able to come to grips, let alone make his adversary give ground. There were certain modifications, however, to be noted even in this condition of stationary tension: feints, deceptive slackenings, attempted surprises; moments when one of the combatants was suddenly made aware that the muscle in his grip had gone soft, and was filled with a sudden hope that he had forced the enemy to the breaking-point.

At times, too, one of the two armies would assume an air of indifference: "You're quite happy where you are? You're in no hurry? Well, neither are we. We don't mind how long it goes on. We've no intention of exhausting ourselves for nothing. When you've had enough, say so." But there were also sudden stiffenings; little thrusts at unexpected points, delivered not so much in the hope of producing any marked effect as of testing the enemy's defences, of surprising him in a momentary but significant slackness; or even, by forcing him to a slight retirement, of making him take up a new position a shade less advantageous than the previous one had been.

Then a day would come when, after a long-prepared and

prodigal accumulation of effectives, a mass attack would be delivered against some carefully chosen point in the enemy line. Before each such forward movement the authorities told themselves with conviction that a "decisive blow" was still possible; that the reason previous blows had not been decisive was that the operations had been confined to too narrow a front; that the best proof of the soundness of the argument was that, in spite of shrapnel, machine-guns, and wire entanglements, the thing would undoubtedly come off this time. And when the attempt had once more failed, when the assaulting waves had withered under the fire of the defence, there was always comfort in the thought that the scale of the attack had still been too small, that someone had blundered, that there must be another attempt later, and that next time everything would be all right.

But, though no one dared admit it, the fact remained that each failure helped to weaken the general belief in the possibility of ever delivering a "decisive blow." It was known, of course, by this time, that there was no such thing in modern warfare as the initial "knockout"; but was there, after all, such a thing as a "knock-out" at all, even at the second or third attempt? Was there any room, under contemporary conditions, for the kind of "victory" men used to talk about, or for the plans and assumptions that had, of old, made such a victory possible? Mightn't it be that the whole problem of the military art had been reduced to one of simple endurance?

At such moments of anxious wondering the minds of the High Commands would resemble those little toys that tell the weather—the idea of the leader with dash and initiative would recede into the wooden house, and that of patience would emerge complete with umbrella.

And so men began to fall back on the thought of "hanging on" much as a sick man will turn his mind to old country remedies when the drugs of the medical faculty have been proved to be useless. "The war will be won by the side that can last fifteen minutes longer than the other." With quiet stealth there grew in men's minds a tendency to substitute for the conception of the "knock-out blow" that of the extra fifteen minutes. No one knew at what precise point in the future those last fifteen minutes would be found to be situated, but on either side their favour began to be eagerly canvassed. Men thought of them with ingratiating respect. They became, as it were, the rich uncle who is cosseted by the hopeful heir.

Was it due to the possibility of a knock-out or to the necessity of making sure of those extra fifteen minutes that the lines were organized so methodically? Trenches became deeper, stronger, multiplied in number; were linked by a system of covered communications and furnished with dug-outs. Artillery and machine-guns were housed in concrete emplacements. Observation posts were established at jealously guarded points, and served for the detailed mapping of the areas they commanded. A network of telephone lines, rivalling in complexity the system of any peace-time city, linked the various headquarters with an efficient completeness worthy of a group of co-ordinated factories. The ration carts followed the same route every night, and the horses, like those of the old mail-coaches, could be trusted to find the way by themselves. The situation of troops in the field was kept up to date in the various offices, where the clerks became as accustomed to having the details of the different formations at their fingertips as a prefect his different communes. In their eyes the men in the line were just so many items to be dealt with.

But behind the front this idea of the "last fifteen minutes" took on terrifying proportions. The "duration" began to be reckoned in ever increasing lengths of time; foundation stones were laid of buildings intended for war production; orders for munition plants were given abroad—at first the machinery had to be made outside the country—much as trade agreements are signed for long-term deliveries; financial transactions were set on foot with the slow deliberation usual in the building up of political alliances or the plotting of international treacheries, the benefit of which will not be felt for several years, or in the methodical dissemination of ideas among distant peoples, which can lead to action only after much patient waiting. In this way, slowly and piecemeal, the whole world was gradually caught up in the chaos of war.

It might be legitimate at times to wonder whether all this preparation for hanging on would not ultimately have a deleterious effect upon the will to victory. The war could be "won," in the old military sense, only by dint of pouring out men, material, and money like water. "Hanging on" meant a careful husbanding of resources. Mightn't it be argued that each attempt to force an issue weakened by so much the power of resistance of the side that made it? That every increase in the preparations for holding out by so much undermined the offensive spirit? Meanwhile the High Command on either side seemed to have made up its mind to play the war game according to two different and simultaneous systems, to be so frightened of losing if it stuck to one that it preferred to give up all idea of winning rather than make a definite choice between them.

In this mood the two peoples entered upon the first winter of the war, saw come and go, unmarked and uneloquent, the Christmas that was to have sounded the carillon of victory, saw 1915 dawn with little prospect of a decision.

CHAPTER TWO

The Wall

Through force of circumstance, the two adversaries strongly resembled each other in outward appearance. Their secret thoughts, however, were very different.

Fundamentally, the Germans still clung to their original dream: to keep the campaigns in east and west entirely distinct; to shift, thanks to their interior lines, the main mass of their effectives rapidly, and as occasion demanded, from front to front; to settle with one opponent before taking on the other. But experience had shown them that the business would be slower than they had anticipated, and that it would be wiser to come to grips with Russia first. They must try to crush her by delivering a "knock-out blow," which would be the easier to do since, though there was no limit to her reserves, she could not make full use of her available millions owing to the fact that they could establish no hard and fast position, but tended to move freely and rather aimlessly in an excess of elbow-room, with the result that they left a number of gaps in which liberty of manœuvre would still be possible.

While waiting for a decision in the east, the Germans contented themselves with maintaining intact—subject to a few local rectifications—the wall which they had erected against the French and their British and Belgian allies. Once the right moment had come, it would be easy to launch their full might against the opposing wall—lying but a street's width away—and, since their hands would be free elsewhere, to smash it to pieces.

The French, always assuming that they would not resign themselves for ever to the "hanging on" policy, had this advantage: that they could concentrate on a more limited objective—namely, the breaching of one section of the enemy wall; which done, they would be in a position to attack some vital point on the lines of communication, to roll up the human barrier on both sides of the gap thus made, and then, having regrouped their forces into genuine "armies," over-whelm the foe in open fighting.

They could endure anything rather than the thought of this wall that had been erected so insolently on their native soil, that had the effect of advancing the frontier so many miles nearer the heart of the country, that cut off within it so many French provinces.

All the normal dangers of war they would face willingly— but not the thought of this wall.

After a period of elaborate preparation, after careful selec-tion of the point to be attacked, they gathered themselves for a supreme effort and once again struck hard. The wall remained scarred but unbroken. Once again they were shaken to the depths of their being. War may be abominable, but, surely, even war has its rules? Certain things ought not to be possible; a wall such as this ought not to be possible.

Fiercely they refused to give up hope. There must be some way of achieving a still more formidable concentration, of striking still harder. The universe could not be so badly ordered that such efforts as they had made could go unre-warded.

At times they felt like men buried alive, like men guilty of the mad absurdity of trying to tear down a wall of squared masonry with their fingernails.

Where were those battles for freedom which begin with the sounding of the "charge" and end with cheering and the song of victory? The people of France almost blushed to think that they had ever believed in such things. Still, illusory though they might have been, they had been productive of a moral fervour which must not be allowed to seep away.

To have the material means of carrying on is not enough. A man must be able to tell himself that carrying on is a ratio-nal mode of behaviour, is worth the efforts it demands. If he is to see his friends fall, if he is to go on risking his life and suffering untold hardship, if he is to waste his best years in muddy shell-holes, he must have the necessity adequately explained to him.

The average soldier had, at first, been to a certain extent deceived, but not entirely. God knows he had had no love for war, but he had, to some extent, believed in it. Now he could no longer be in two minds about it. He could see that war was something positively evil, an enterprise of sheer stupidity. Its benefits were as nothing compared to its cost. Nothing in the world could be worth a war, unless it was the destruction of war itself, its suppression for ever, its deletion from the pages of history.

That, and that alone, must be the object of *this* war. There should never be another. With that end in view, and that only, it was being waged. For that reason it must be fought to the bitter end. The fellows opposite were not yet in the mood to understand such reasoning. If they were offered peace now, they were slavish enough, credulous enough, to believe their rulers when they told them (as they would tell them): "There, you see, they're giving in; you've won!" and demanded (as they would demand) impossible terms. They would understand only when they were beaten or too much exhausted to go on fighting. When that happened, they could be invited, to an accompaniment, if necessary, of a few kicks, to join with France in the establishment of a permanent peace for the whole world. It was just as well, perhaps, that this war should be so horrible, so dismal, so lacking in all the heady joys to be found in books. At least nobody now would have the effrontery to call it "fine." Nobody, however worked up emotionally, would be able to regret that there would never be another. Courage, then, must be the order of the day. Never had there been a burden of pain comparable to this, nor sacrifices more devastating. But then, never had there been a finer cause to fight for. The end of war in the history of mankind? No date since the beginning of recorded time had ever been so important. One might almost call it the birthday of civilization.

But this noble thought was quickly followed by another

that seemed to cling to it like a shadow: "Whatever happens, it must end this year." The year 1915 must be the greatest date in the story of humanity. Why not? The years ending in 15 had often, through the centuries, been strongly marked for good or evil. The foundation of universal peace would be a worthy centenary of the Battle of Waterloo.

To let it go beyond that point, drag on still further, to permit such an enormity as the second year of such a struggle, would be inconceivable.

But those whose duty it was to prepare for a long war, the specialists in "duration," the men responsible for ensuring that the "last fifteen minutes" should be to the advantage of France, comforted themselves with the reflection that their long-term reckonings might have the same sort of purely theoretical validity as the "calculations of strain" employed by constructional engineers, and that almost certainly the whole horrid business would perish of inanition long before it reached those terrible stages in forward time which it was their job to anticipate.

Over and over again the thought of the High Command took the following form: "We must forget everything we thought we had learned. There must be no useless regrets, no considerations of personal pride. We have got to see this war as it is, to deal with it as a fact. At all costs we must devise means of achieving not just victory in the void, but victory under these particular conditions."

With genuine compunction it reckoned its misdeeds and each day urged itself to greater efforts, to a manifestation of real military genius (the kind of genius it had always assumed would be ready at call). It must ensure the safety of the country—a matter of real concern to it—must deserve the confidence of the nation, of which rather too easily, rather too soon, it had thought itself to be worthy; must make its own both the glory and the accompanying rewards which would fall to the lot of anyone who should win so great a struggle, free the occupied territories, and win back the lost provinces; glory and rewards which, like the war that had occasioned them and the agonies that must be the prerequisites of victory, would be without precedent in the annals of mankind.

But it found another motive, too, in the excitement, the application, the pride, of the expert, deriving stimulus from the necessity, known by every worker in a technical field, of finding, at all costs, the answer to the particular problem of facing the incredible difficulties presented by something absolutely new to experience. What it had to do was analogous to the task that confronts the engineer who has to pierce a range of rocks which so far have turned the edge of all the usual tools, or the doctor who seeks to master and reduce in his patient a fever the causes of which he cannot understand.

Ever since the beginning of the winter, its head clutched in its hands, the High Command had tried to face the problem squarely. "For the present at least, this war must be regarded as one of position, in which equipment counts for everything; as nothing less than a siege on a grand scale. So far so good. The particular problem to be solved is how, given the necessary material, we can make a breach and then, by throwing in troops, widen it. The first step must be to break down by assault a given section of the wall. There is surely some definite degree of pressure before which a limited section of any given wall is bound to yield. The great thing is to free our minds of all preconceived ideas of scale, to have the courage to think coolly in terms of quantities which seem to us enormous. The breach once made must be occupied without the loss of a minute, before the enemy has time to react. To achieve this we shall have to forget all the customary conditions of open warfare, such as attacking over long distances with the bayonet, at the double, in close order, and under withering fire. The shortness of the intervening space to be covered will be the essential factor. What then? We shall have to throw into the gap as many men as possible and spread out in the enemy's rear so as to ensure the rapid disorganization of his communications."

As a matter of fact, the later stages of the attack remained rather vague. But merely to achieve the initial success, to breach the enemy's defences, would represent no small victory.

Stimulated by it, the directing genius would surely be able to improvise the necessary sequel as circumstances might demand.

The two first and absolutely essential conditions of success must therefore be: the complete disintegration of the enemy organization over a given area by gunfire, and an assault delivered over the shortest possible distance, the latter to be managed by the use of assembly trenches dug at the last moment under cover of a continuous barrage.

The new method was tried in January in the Champagne. On a short length of the German trenches the High Command poured a hundred thousand shells in forty-eight hours. Meanwhile assembly trenches were dug close up to the enemy front line. At the last moment, just as the assault troops were preparing to swarm over the parapet, a completely new device was employed—that of rolling, or drum, fire, a sudden acceleration by every battery engaged, on the point to be attacked. The object of this was to give to the few men still remaining alive in the opposite trenches, the handful who had survived the rain of a hundred thousand shells, the impression that this time the very heavens were falling on their heads, that the world was collapsing upon them in a torment of flame, that a vast hand of earth and steel armed with a million clutching fingers was about to crush them finally, and that it would be sheer childish folly to try to escape this ultimate hurricane of death. The final convincing touch was given to the picture by the detonation of a number of mines which turned communication trenches, front line, and parapet into one huge crater and hurled into the air fragments of dismembered men.

At this precise moment the assaulting waves moved forward, a screen of skirmishers covering the main bodies, across the short distance separating them from their objective.

The High Command waited for the results of this preliminary attack before engaging its reserves. It was even holding in readiness, a little farther back, a force of cavalry which should move forward into the gap as soon as the infantry had cleared a passage for it. The task of this mobile body was to reach with the minimum of delay the most vulnerable points of the enemy communications, threaten with envelopment such formations in the neighbourhood of the gap as had not quickly extricated themselves, spread panic in the back areas by the mere fact of its presence, and carry out a series of spectacular raids on the flanks of the advancing troops.

A portion of the wall did crumble, but only partially. The hundred thousand shells had not been enough to flatten out everything. A few centres of resistance still remained. Speaking generally, however, it was true to say that the enemy was forced to evacuate the area of destruction, which was occupied by the assaulting waves without much difficulty. The new method, therefore, subject to certain modifications, had so far proved successful. But scarcely had the attackers occupied the objective and settled down to wait for the reserves who were to exploit the initial success than they found themselves in their turn the target for a storm of shells. This came from the enemy artillery which, lying outside the delimited zone, had not been destroyed. At the same time the German infantry launched a series of counter-attacks which they conducted by means of a pretty little gadget adapted from former wars—the hand-grenade.

The long-expected reserves had started from too far back to arrive in time. But this was not all, for they were themselves caught in open ground by the enemy artillery, which not only inflicted heavy losses, but broke their formations, damped their ardour, and checked their rate of progress.

The French gunners had no idea what to do. Being ill informed as to the whereabouts of the infantry, they hesitated to fire for fear of hitting their own men.

The troops who had occupied the gap were forced to withdraw. A few units managed with great difficulty to maintain their positions. At these points the enemy wall was indeed demolished, but only to be re-established rather farther to the rear, where it stood, no less solid, no less exasperating. A salient had become a re-entrant angle. That was the sum total of so much effort.

Not content with having repulsed an attack, the enemy turned his attention to the peril from which he had just emerged, and set himself to evolve a new technique of reprisal which, during the next few weeks, he found several opportunities of testing.

He conceived the idea, as soon as concentrated fire on a limited area warned him of an impending offensive, of opening up with his own guns on the assault trenches, the position of which it was not difficult to determine, since the opposing barrage was carefully calculated to fall just in front of them. Now, waiting to go over the top is never a comfortable experience for troops, and if it has to be gone through to an accompaniment of deadly artillery fire, the offensive spirit is very soon as badly decimated as the ranks of the expectant attackers. Under such conditions who will succeed in getting them out into the open? This method, known to military circles as "counter-preparation," was based on sound good sense and very soon proved its efficacy.

The French High Command learned this new lesson, which it combined in imagination with those taught by the failure of its efforts in January. Its motto was: "Have an open mind for everything except discouragement. If you don't at first succeed, try, try again."

Thus encouraged, it proceeded to argue as follows: "If a hundred thousand shells in forty-eight hours are not enough to flatten out even a small portion of the enemy positions, if, in spite of them, centres of resistance can still survive—concrete dug-outs, machine-gun nests—we must strike harder, pound to a finer dust. What we need is more guns and more shells, particularly shells with a steep angle of descent, of the aerial torpedo type. Once the assault has started, we must have certain men specially told off to 'mop up' any centre that still looks like showing fight, while the main waves of the attack are left free to push on.

"To neutralize the danger of reserves arriving too late and suffering serious losses on the way up, we must mass them much nearer the original point of departure, in positions carefully reconnoitred and arranged beforehand. Special communication trenches must be provided so that they can be got right into the front line in comparative safety and as they are wanted.

"Since the enemy batteries defeat the initial success achieved by our attacks by making it impossible for the assaulting troops to hold on to their objectives, since they make any forward movement of our reserves difficult, and since, as a last straw, they have developed this damned business of counter-preparation, our own artillery must pay them special attention during the preliminary bombardment. Continual aerial photography will enable us to plot the positions of their emplacements at leisure, and special care must be paid to counter-battery work, which must be made to extend as far as possible behind the enemy lines.

"Since our own gunners complain that, once zero hour has come, they can be of very little use, because they are out of touch with the movement of the troops, we must see that observers are detailed to serve in the front line, we must move up headquarters positions closer to the battle zone, and we must see that the system of communications to be used during the course of the action is perfected."

At this point the thoughts of the soldier took a homeward course:

"If you want us to win, you must give us the means to do so. Turn out the stuff we need, or buy it from abroad. We must have more guns—especially heavy guns. (There was a time when we didn't believe in them, but those days are dead and done with.) Give us more shells of all calibres (try to send us as few as possible of the sort that will cause prematures in the gun-barrels). Machine-guns; aerial torpedoes; grenades. Aeroplanes, observation and pursuit machines alike. Barbed wire for holding up attacks; steel plates for making trench loopholes; metal sheets for dug-out roofing. Sandbags for parapets, for communication trenches and assembly points. Pit-props. Logs to use for roads across the mud. Trench-boots, so that the men can carry on when the water's above their ankles. Steel helmets for them to wear as a protection against shell-splinters...."

In Parliament the Army Commission, far from finding these demands excessive and pleading the country's inability to meet them, never ceased saying: "They're not asking for enough; they're too optimistic. They still think the war can be won with bayonets."

The improved methods were put to a practical test during the month of May, in Artois. Pétain was chosen to take charge of the operations, because he was known to be clear-sighted, with a strong sense of the difficulties to be surmounted, and the kind of soldier who, once he'd got his teeth in, would not be likely to let go.

The preliminary reconnaissance was a much more detailed affair than any so far undertaken. A far larger number of shells than in any previous bombardment was sent over in a far shorter period of time, and the enemy batteries were reached that aeroplanes had spotted. Seventeen mines were detonated simultaneously—the sign for the gunners to lengthen their range and for the infantry to move forward to the assault. The men had been told to get as far as possible and not to let themselves be held up by minor obstacles. Everything possible had been done to ensure the maintenance of communications during the battle. The troops had been issued with small flags for signalling their progress; telephonists were to follow the first waves and lay land lines; a number of artillery observers had been told off to keep in close touch with developments. Instead of wasting time in reducing the few remaining centres of resistance, the main body of assaulting troops was to press forward, leaving to specially detailed bodies the task of mopping up or masking such isolated strongpoints.

As on previous occasions, the general in command had issued to the tens of thousands of soldiers who were to bear the brunt of the attack, to the hundreds of thousands in reserve who, it was hoped, would exploit the initial advantage, to all the nation in arms waiting to take its turn in the line, an order of the day couched in the most solemn terms: "Keep your spirits up. This is our great effort. The enemy will be swept from French soil. The hour of victory is at hand."

No doubt he believed most of what he said—believed it in the same sense that a gambler can only go on playing if he believes that his next coup is going to come off, in the same sense that a runner can get the most out of his body only by imagining himself first at the tape. But he also intended his words to bolster the illusion of success, to act as an extra fillip, to provide just the additional kick necessary to the heady draught of enthusiasm that would make the difference. After all, what he promised was bound to be true some time; why not now? Why not ensure success by assuming it to be at hand?

The May offensive in Artois was a brilliant affair, and highly flattering to those who had planned it. But it was far from resulting in a definite break-through. So disappointing, indeed, were the gains registered that it seemed best to the authorities to represent it as nothing but a tryout of new methods, and, as such, auguring well for future attempts.

Unfortunately that "extra fillip" had left in the mouths of the soldiers engaged a nasty "hang-over" which could not be cleared up by the issue of discreet communiqués. Each failure to obtain full results from an offensive had an increasingly bad effect on the morale of the troops. The men found themselves back in the trenches with considerably fewer comrades and considerably greater doubts.

What worried them most and most shook their nerve was the series of silly local actions which filled in the intervals between the full-dress and inconclusive offensives. They could not understand the point of them. They were perfectly willing to admit that the High Command had been wrong in hoping to achieve a break-through by dint of an effort about the gigantic nature of which they were themselves under no illusion. But could anyone seriously imagine that the desired end could be achieved by hurling a few thousand men against one little section of the line? Was the gain of a few hundred yards of trench—always assuming that the counter-attack failed—really worth the lives of two thousand soldiers? These small-scale massacres set the men brooding. The more they thought the thing out, the more bitter did their reflections become: "The truth is they want to leave us lying out there; they want to get rid of us. That's what's really behind it."

They could not help guessing too that the motive for much of this minor slaughter lay in the personal ambition of some local commander. It might be that a brigadier was impatient for his third star. In such a case he would not hesitate to argue that the capture of a strong-point would advance him with his friends at headquarters. Since he was not naturally cruel, he carefully avoided considering the fact that his promotion would be obtained at the cost of a hundred killed, eighty "missing," and three hundred wounded. A divisional general's expectations were pitched higher; a corps commander's higher still. A strong-point would not be enough. The enterprise must be planned on a bigger scale—and so, too, the losses (but it didn't do to think about that). Such a line of argument very soon came to envisage hundreds of yards of trenches and thousands of casualties.

But quite often these small-scale attacks owed their inspiration to General Headquarters itself, whence they filtered down through the various degrees of the military hierarchy. Now, if General Headquarters wanted, quite naturally, to put a feather in its own cap, small local operations certainly would not do the trick. Nothing really was of any use short of a major offensive with a casualty list running into tens of thousands killed. There must, therefore, be some reason for its encouragement of any enterprise less extensive.

This was sometimes traceable to perfectly respectable motives. A position which, in the eyes of the private soldier, seemed quite without value might in fact command a fine field of view over part of the enemy line, might offer an ideal site for an artillery observation post. Alternatively, it might serve as a jumping-off place, or a good base of support, for some future general offensive. It might dominate some future battlefield. There was always the need, too, of harassing the enemy and inflicting losses on him (this, however, was apt to be rather a boomerang consideration); of occupying his attention and so preventing him from launching his own offensives against other parts of the French or Allied front; of sapping his morale by giving proof that the troops facing him were as strong as ever. In general terms, it was important to maintain what the psychologists on the Staff were pleased to call moral superiority and initiative.

Other motives there were, however, which the authorities were less anxious to acknowledge—partly because they had a rather nasty smell of complicity between the opposing Commands; such, for instance, as a peace move having its origin in the ranks, not authorized from the top. This line of thought was apt to develop as follows: Suppose the gangrene set up by the fretting of the front lines were, unfortunately, to find a cure for itself; suppose the men in the trenches got used to long periods of quiet, to fewer and fewer risks, and, ultimately, to none at all, to hanging on resignedly and ingloriously in their mud-holes; suppose they got rid of the idea that "the fellow on the other side" was someone to be killed or to kill, began to think that, after all, he was just a poor devil like themselves; suppose a tacit understanding grew up to do as little damage as possible, to leave one another in peace; suppose, what would be far worse, that the two armies began to exchange jokes, to walk about between the lines, to fraternize. Such beginnings might have terrible results. The men, French and German in collaboration, might make some very awkward discoveries; might, in so many words, say to one another: "What are we doing here? Shouldn't we all be better off if we just went home?"

Methods were found in the daily routine of trench life of neutralizing dangers of this kind. To prevent all these civilians in uniform from sniffing round the forbidden subject of peace, to keep the two nations in a constant state of sore irritation, it was only necessary—without making any appeal to enthusiasm or heroism—to play on the individual's craving for distraction, on his pride of skill, on his love of hunting, on his liking for adventure, on the fairly harmless schoolboy brutality that lurks in most of us. It was easy to find men to act as snipers—the job was popular—to pick off the first man

who showed his head above the opposite parapet; to get volunteers to crawl out and lob a grenade into a listening-post,
or to go on patrol with the object of capturing or killing a
few sentries. Reprisals always followed, so there was no fear of
the spirit of hostility dying down. Even if the feelings aroused
were no more than resentment at a neighbour's dirty trick, if
it could be exaggerated into "hatred of the enemy" only by
voluble colonels addressing their troops, it was enough to prevent even the humblest private from falling into the error of
confusing the "men opposite" with men in general.

But there were times when this daily course of blood-letting became a habit like any other—even wretched horses
grow used to the harness that irks them—and then recourse
had to be made to small combined operations, which plunged
all the men of a given formation into danger, into the corrosive bath of death, and had the added advantage of provoking
large-scale reprisals. This was what General Headquarters on
either side called "maintaining the offensive spirit of the
troops." But it was something that the troops themselves had
the greatest difficulty in grasping. They insisted on seeing only
the growing total of killed and wounded, the insignificance of
the material gains. The survivors shrugged their shoulders
when they heard that the Staff, telling over its modest rosary
of losses, was boasting of having "nibbled" at the enemy positions. It never occurred to them—and no one had the courage to explain the simple fact—that they were nothing but a
lot of animals trained to slaughter, and that those in command
had got to treat them as such by employing quite simple
means to revive a spirit of pugnacity which, left to itself,
would have been happy enough to go to sleep. Still less were
they capable of understanding that the Staffs, having entered
the war with a religious belief in the efficacy of the Offensive,
felt themselves to be guilty of a lack of faith in sitting still and
whining, and were constantly on guard against the temptation
of proving false to their dogma. The Staffs were rather like
professed Christians forced by circumstances to keep a check
on their enthusiasm. But whenever they found it possible to
do so, they offered to their God a little, almost furtive sacri-

fice, just to keep the principle alive while waiting for better times. Local attacks served as the pigeon whose throat is cut upon the altar of fortune to keep the idol in countenance until the time comes for the solemn immolation of the ox.

Not that the business hadn't, of course, to be conducted sensibly and every reasonable precaution taken against useless bloodshed. The general rule was always to do better than one's best.

Once again those in authority registered a solemn oath to take everything into consideration, to neglect no lesson of experience, to be guilty of no mistake. If, under such circumstances, fortune failed to play her part, she would be a sorry jade indeed.

The May offensive in Artois had come to nothing, and preparations were made to stage another, during the late summer, in Champagne. All the fairies were summoned to its cradle that they might load it with their gifts.

The most important of these would be the power of development over a wide front. Until now there had been an excessive tendency to confine attacks within over-narrow limits, the professed reason being the necessity of bringing a greater weight of gunfire to bear on the target. The trouble about this method was that it enabled the enemy to localize the threat well in advance of zero hour, and, when the breach in their line had been made, to find at once sufficient reserves to plug it successfully. The larger the gap, the less easily could it be stopped, and the greater the time at the disposal of the attackers for exploiting their initial advantage.

A sufficiently wide front having been chosen, the necessary preparations and reconnaissances could be made at leisure. They were put in hand, as a matter of fact, at more than one point, in order to confuse the enemy, and in order to leave a large margin of choice available to the High Command up to the very last moment. All that remained to do was to dig the assault trenches, and these would be left till the eleventh hour when the locale of the operations should have been finally determined.

On the last occasion the reserves had still been massed too far back. The reason for this had been the desire of Head-quarters to keep them under its hand as the battle developed and to be free to throw them, fanwise, in any one of several directions. This time they were to move, as it were, hard on the heels of the front-line troops. General instructions would be of the simplest—to keep moving straight ahead. Once the word "Go!" had been given, every man would know precise-ly what to do.

On the 9th of May the preliminary bombardment had been too short. In spite of its violence it had failed to achieve com-plete destruction. Next time, it was decided, it should be no less intense but much more protracted. It must last for several days. The necessary munition dumps were arranged for, and since during the intervening months there had been a marked increase in heavy guns, as a result, partly, of borrowings from fortresses and ships, partly of increased industrial output, the proportion of large-calibre shells was high. It was hoped that the artillery preparation would be far more efficient than ever before. The attacking waves would find everything flattened out in their path, would be faced by an enemy reduced to the last stage of material and moral disintegration, odds and ends of shell-shocked formations, a few poor wretches whom four days of continuous bombardment, without sleep and proba-bly without food, would have sent mad.

So far as the assault troops themselves were concerned, there was to be complete abandonment of all the old forma-tions. No more moving in close order across no man's land, but thin, widely spaced lines of skirmishers offering the small-est possible target to machine-gun fire. Each division engaged would be responsible for no more than a very restricted sec-tor, moving forward on a front of three regiments working in close contact and with reduced intervals. Every formation was to be organized in depth, the object being so to arrange mat-ters that the advance troops would have to depend for the passing of messages and orders, for support, and for reinforce-ment on their own people, on a machine whose well-oiled wheels had grown to function efficiently. Experience had shown that the principal cause of attacks being slowed down and brought to a standstill was the confusion for the units engaged resulting from a tendency to extend over too wide a front in the course of an advance. Lateral communications had a way of thinning out to either flank and ultimately of breaking down altogether from lack of concentration, while those from front to rear, more than ever essential on such occasions, as like as not had to depend upon an improvised system and suffered from the confusion of different formations and the good or bad will of individuals. Under the new arrangement each wave of the assault would have behind it a wave composed of men of the same unit, of the same regimental flesh and blood, used to passing on instructions to one another. Each unit would operate in the manner of a tentacle feeling its way forward in a series of undulatory movements, in close co-operation with others, but safe from becoming tangled or confused with them, since they would be in actual contact only at their rear ends.

The orders given to each unit were to get as far forward as possible without bothering too much about what was happening to their neighbours or about the intervals that might develop between the various thrusts. Lateral communications, chief factor in slowing down an advance, are useful mainly in defence or retreat. They matter far less while troops are going forward. They may even become a nuisance. The general direction of the movement would be assured by the flanks, the whole operation being controlled by the scheme laid down and by the alignment of the objectives.

The waves were so spaced as to avoid, as far as possible, the confusion inseparable from a battlefield, and everything conceivable was done to make full use of the purely material aspects of modern warfare.

Not only was an enormous expenditure of artillery ammunition carefully foreseen. It was decided to make use of all the new weapons, each one of which represented progress in the field of specialized technique: aerial torpedoes, grenades, gas.

Behind the front in Champagne—the district which the High Command seemed more and more to favour as the

moment for launching the offensive approached—a network
of railways was constructed along the valley of the Suippe.
New camps and depots were built. To facilitate the moving up
of reserve troops a number of wide communication trenches
were dug in solid earth, with clean-cut walls (the natural
cleanliness of the local soil made this easy); approximately one
every three hundred yards, and each reserved for a particular
type of traffic: troops moving up, troops moving down, runners. Those designed for the use of the last were sufficiently
wide to permit the passage of bicycles. Special military police
were detailed to control all this activity.

Immediately behind the front, huge assembly places were
prepared and carefully screened. The troops concentrated in
them presented a fresh, almost gay appearance: the men in
high spirits after a long period of rest, well fed, well disci-
plined, and equipped with brand-new horizon-blue uniforms
and newly issued steel helmets.

The sky was full of aeroplanes busily engaged in photo-
graphing the lines. The Army staffs exchanged information
about the results thus obtained and compared the evidence
with what they already had, marking their maps with points
and figures, drawing in red and blue lines, elaborating trench
systems with dots and cross-hatching, calculating angles and
distances, noting landmarks, bringing range-tables up to date,
and setting out barrage lines.

The enemy on his side made every effort to discover what
was going on. To add to his confusion and weaken his power
of resistance, similar offensives were prepared in Artois and on
the British front.

The event to which all this elaboration was leading up
would be a sort of combination of large-scale industry and
sport. The battle was going to be a game based on material
equipment comparable to that employed by great blast-furnaces
and giant factories. A game in which the balls would be made
of steel and explosives and would weigh anything from half a
pound to half a ton; in which the teams would be composed
of three hundred thousand men; in which scattered brains and
torn guts in abundance would take the place of falls and

sprained ankles; in which the winning-post would be represented by the church towers of Quesnoy, of Nouvion, of
Sedan, standing sixty miles or so from the starting-point.

CHAPTER THREE

The Attrition Factory

But for all its vastness, for all the care that had gone to its preparation, for all the crowding of men and material, the chosen stage was still too small to accommodate the tragedy to be performed. The battle was no more than one focal point of the war, this new offensive on the western front but a passing cynosure. Its occurrence relieved neither the General Staffs nor the Governments of the countries concerned of the necessity of planning other enterprises.

The search for new allies went on unceasingly. Almost from the beginning the Central Powers had succeeded in getting Turkey into the fold, and they were now trying to make the Bulgarians follow suit. Meanwhile the Allies were doing their best to seduce Italy, and both sides were having a fling at Rumania and Greece. In matters of this kind, pressure, corruption, blackmail, lies, and treachery of every description are held to be legitimate weapons, the use of which casts no slur on a nation's honour. The foulest trick of diplomacy looks clean beside the effect of a steel splinter on the human body.

The Central Powers were beginning to find it difficult to breathe, so closely were they held in the clutches of the blockade which was hemming them in, despite the outlets they had contrived through the neutral countries. They set themselves, therefore, to draw around the besiegers another kind of blockade, intangible and furtive. They, too, were trying to cut their foes off from the outer world, were bringing the art of submarine warfare to perfection. They sent to the bottom the ships that were bringing food to the Allies. Instead of the besieged they strove to become besiegers in their turn. In this way there developed two concentric systems of investment, the second on so huge a scale that one whole section of the globe was its considered object. It would be a wonder indeed if those conducting it could manage to achieve their end without bringing suffering upon mankind at large.

Indeed, since its very beginning this war had caught up in its toils such huge masses of men and material that it was almost inevitably fated to become universal. The whirlpool which it had set in motion exercised a force of attraction that was irresistible, if slow. Gradually the nations drew one another on; some unforeseen incident would occur which tipped the balance. Those who wished to resist the influence found that their arguments were too weak to be effective. Men in the antipodes spoke of the war's horrors, but since no one had experienced them, they found them difficult to imagine. The tearing gale, echoes of which reached those distant lands, inspired men with a desire to see for themselves rather than to flee its onset, to feel in their own persons the terrible attraction of the pit.

But this war was fated to become universal in another sense as well. From its very first days it had shown that it was not an affair of the specialists in one field alone, of the professional soldiers. It had enlisted in its service a vast quantity of human activities; little by little it left none unused. Here, too, one thing led to another, and the close bonds that had united them in peace were only made firmer by the necessities of war. War under modern conditions has need of everything that man produces, of everything he can manage to produce, though its avowed end is nothing but destruction. Even the activities of pure thought are mobilized. God was called in to play His part, not as a judge between the opposing causes, but as a supporter and champion of both sides alike, to the extent of taking a hand Himself in the carnage.

Nowhere either in Artois or in Champagne was there a hill sufficiently high to enable the commander to get an all-embracing view of the battlefield. He had to piece it together laboriously—and at leisure—in the drawing-room of a provincial villa converted temporarily into an office, with the

help of a great map pinned to the wall and a number of tele-
graphic summaries laid by an officer, from time to time, on a
table, each one of which might contain at least a single error no
less damaging than the maggot concealed in an ear of wheat.

That being so, what hope was there of finding a single brain
capable of envisaging the war as a whole, of seeing it steadily
through all its endless ramifications and under the many different forms it took, whether on the chalky uplands of
Champagne, on a Turkish peninsula, in a submarine cruising
below the North Sea, in the chancery of some Balkan state,
in a clearing-house for espionage in Bern, in the dockyards of
Philadelphia, or on the twelfth storey of a Wall Street bank?
Even minds highly trained and well placed for observation
could get but a sectional and indirect view of the whole, distorted by distance, with whole areas hidden in obscurity and
numerous details omitted from the calculation.

The connexion between these partial visions, their mutual
bearing, their composition, perhaps their mutually contradictory contributions, could be seen only by some watcher far
removed from humanity, by, for instance, the impersonal mind
of God, or in those dehumanized recesses of the universe
from which emerge the vast catastrophes of the stars, the slow
convulsions of the earth, where conscious Will is no longer
lord of all, but only Chance.

And if the directing conscience of the man in charge could
never grasp the scene in its entirety, so too it failed to see the
detail of the conflict, the ultimate elements, the fact of the war
itself as, behind all the paraphernalia of telegrams and reports,
it was lived and experienced by the human agent. Looked at
from this point of view, it appeared as a chaos of tiny atoms
which were a constant source of anxiety to the general far
away in his headquarters. He had to believe that his was the
controlling hand—at least in the main—but in his heart of
hearts he could never be quite sure. The more violent grew
the fighting, the harder it became to know what was happening. Remote in his office, the commander knew well
enough that telegrams and reports could do no more than
prick his mind to awareness, then set him thinking along pre-

conceived lines, remembering lessons learned at the Staff
College, or incidents of his own past when he served as a
lieutenant in some colonial campaign. When he read: "At
4.15 the 124th regiment detailed two companies to carry out
an attack on strong-point 414. The operation is proceeding,"
what, despite himself, took form before his mind's eye was the
picture of a crowd of Legionaries advancing across sand to
rush a mud fort, bayonets flashing, men boasting and swearing, while the heady notes of the bugle hoarsely rent the air,
and the defending blacks fired away with their last remaining
cartridges. He could not but know that his control of the distant battle was confused and uncertain. "Hill 252 must be
held at all costs." As likely as not such instructions, by the time
they reached the line, had lost all significance. Hill 252 might
long ago have fallen to the enemy, or his own men might be
there indeed, but quite incapable of holding on, owing to the
fire of the German guns. In a confusion of dead and dying a
dozen or so of the defending troops might still be left alive
without captain or lieutenant to take charge, beyond caring
what the Army commander might be thinking of the situation, and completely out of touch. Headquarters might
launch an offensive, but that done, it was like a man who has
opened a huge sluice above a thickly populated valley, or who
has set fire to a barn standing in the centre of a village. The
battle once joined burns fiercely, crackling its way through
the dry wood, partly according to plan, partly as chance and
circumstance determine. Precisely where it is most violent it
is least under control. To save his face the general must go on
issuing orders, but, unless he is a fool, he can only face the
fact, can say no more than: "It depends on me no longer. I can
only hope to God that everything goes well!" If he is religious, he will probably pray.

At both ends of the scale, therefore, the indeterminate, the
unknown, the hand of chance, held sway: in the huge con-
vulsion of a world at war, and in the smoke-smothered hell of
the trenches where thousands of poor devils flew at one
another's throat. Alike through telescope and microscope the
affair must now be seen. Nobody could say with certainty

which of its innumerable details really conditioned the contest. There was no lack of eye-witnesses, but none of them
could get far enough away from the drama to see it as a
whole. Any knowledge they might have dwindled at twenty
paces till it seemed no more than the light of a lantern
glimpsed through fog. Nor, on the other hand, could anyone
even guess what vast and hideous face the thing might show
hanging like a flaming star athwart the night of Time—that
night which not only is the past but contains, as well, the
emptiness of eternity, across which, like a comet, History dri-
ves its incandescent way. No one man had a will sufficiently
strong to make its weight felt upon the whole complexity of
war, no man was clear-seeing enough, determined enough, to
envisage in a single glance the total magnitude of events and
the life of the soldier in the trenches.

The leaders alike of nations and of armies realized to the
full this double impotence, this condition without precedent
in history, at least on so vast a scale. They tried to limit the
sphere of its operation. So far as it touched the world at large,
on, as it were, its astronomic side, they did their best to confine the workings of mere chance, to bring the plans of politicians and of soldiers into some sort of co-ordination, to substitute planned contacts for coincidence and error, to leave as
small a margin as possible for the unintentional, the undi-
rected. Similarly, in its "molecular" aspects, in the war as seen
from the point of view of the actual combatants, they set
themselves to create a perfect machinery of intercommunica-
tion, a means of circulating orders and information to individuals and units; to keep all working parts clear of dirt, to
adjust the system to the needs of the moment, to make the
will of the commander felt in the most trivial incidents of
routine, both as a stimulus and as a constant presence.

It was with this intention, for instance, that the Western
Allies had laboured, since the winter, not only to perfect
communications by means of telephone, signalling, and aeroplanes equipped with wireless but also to make sure of the
entry of Italy into the war by the time the great offensive
should be launched.

On their side, the Central Powers, blind neither to the evidence of coming activity nor to the approaching intervention of Italy, did all they could to ensure that, when the moment came, they could be certain of having available the maximum quantity of troops and material. For the time being, therefore, they put Russia out of action by delivering a harder blow than ever before on the snout of the mammoth Empire, after which—the Allies having allowed them sufficient time to achieve their purpose—they transported almost all their effectives to the western front with the intention of buttressing the wall which their adversaries were so intent on breaching.

At last the French preparations for their offensive were complete, though later than had been intended; too late to coincide with the entry into the war of the Italians, who now, on the Isonzo, were serving their apprenticeship to modern warfare, and too late also to embarrass the Austro-Germans in their dealings with Russia. The workings of chance had not, as it turned out, been very successfully limited, with the result that Mackensen had beaten the Russians completely, without, however, destroying them as he had hoped to do at one moment, and that the French had now to face the prospect of finding in front of them, ready to absorb the impetus of their drive and to repair any breach they might happen to make, a "good million or so" of Austro-Germans who would be fully their equals.

Once more the High Command appealed to the nation in arms to make the one last effort necessary to win complete victory. The year was on the decline, and summer, season of battles, had already passed the line where the equinoctial gales stood ready to give it greeting.

The seventy-five hours' bombardment was loosed. More than a million shells of all calibres flattened the front-line system, demolished the communication trenches, smashed the strong-points, pounded the gun positions, blocked the highways, turned cross-roads into craters, tore up railway tracks, reduced stations to ruins, and harassed the distant camps.

The assaulting waves moved forward with the strong tide of reserves hard on their heels. Every movement was carried out according to the latest theories of offensive warfare.

Rapid progress was made despite the bad weather. At one or two points it was possible to register outstanding successes. Each man, carrying out the latest orders, pushed straight ahead without bothering about his neighbour. But the attack petered out on the German support line.

At certain points where everything had gone well, this vast offensive—triumph of mechanical equipment—could show a gain of two kilometres. The only thing at all in proportion to the efforts involved, the only thing that, in fact, exceeded expectation, was the sum total of dead, wounded, and missing.

Once again the High Command was left to brood over its failure and draw wise conclusions from the evidence of facts.

They had not yet found the solution to their problems; that was the plain truth of the matter, and the truth must be faced. Somehow or other, things had gone wrong. They had bitten off more than they could chew. No doubt it is perfectly sound to loose a terrific bombardment with the object of achieving the maximum of destruction and demoralization before the infantry moves forward. But if it is continued too long, it gives the enemy time to bring up fresh troops from a distance and to establish an impregnable second line which will be found to have been almost completely undamaged by gunfire. The attacking waves will come up against it already wearied by their ordeal and imperfectly supported by artillery hastily moved up to new positions.

What it came to was that the very completeness of the preparation had robbed the attack of the element of surprise.

Worse still, the preliminary expenditure of ammunition had left the batteries short when it came to covering the advance.

Easy enough now to see what ought to have been done! The initial bombardment should have been shorter and, that it might not lose in efficacy, should have been conducted with a higher proportion of heavy pieces with a rapid rate of fire, and with aerial torpedoes carrying a big bursting charge.

Before the infantry moved, the enemy should have been harassed along almost his whole front and induced to use up his reserves at many points, so as to be left without any fresh troops to fall back on.

Close objectives should have been chosen, attainable in a single bound, since where they were too distant the assault inevitably found itself held up by intermediate systems situated on reverse slopes and left undamaged by artillery fire. The objectives should have been strictly limited and within easy reach. Once they had been occupied, there should have been a fresh bombardment preliminary to a fresh advance. A sufficient reserve of shells should have been kept handy to deal with obstacles met with in the course of the advance and to smash counter-attacks.

Finally—for no point must be omitted—it was no use leaving considerations of season out of account; it must always be remembered that weather has its habits like everything else. Never stage a major offensive during the autumnal equinox, when there are almost certain to be westerly gales and rain, and consequently a churning up of the Champagne soil, so suitable at other times for the manoeuvring of troops.

Alas! too late now....The terrible evidence of facts could not be ignored!... And now the impossible had happened, the one thing that had been regarded as inconceivable, that the poor devils in the line had been told was inconceivable—a second winter of war. The tens of thousands who had fallen had taken comfort from the thought that this time the job would be finished and done with. But the truth had got to be faced. The days were growing shorter, the fine weather receding. It would take months to prepare fresh operations on such a scale. The factories would have to turn out masses of new material, especially heavy guns with a high rate of fire; new plants would have to be set going and worked to full capacity; new reserves of ammunition must be built up. Unless a new offensive was to find itself faced by an enemy with vigour unimpaired, he must first be worn out, exhausted, his reserves used up. Yes, there was nothing for it but to await the effects of attrition.

A war of attrition. The very word was a horror. The idea it

embodied was enough to frighten the bravest. Until then it had entered men's thoughts, if at all, superficially and with a certain furtive shame. But now it must be looked squarely in the face. Until then no one had been willing to admit that the war might go on indefinitely, still less to consider what would happen if it did. There had, of course, been talk about "hanging on"—in case decisive victory should be long delayed—and about "the last fifteen minutes." But the vision that such words had conjured up had not been particularly terrifying: Two wrestlers held interminably in a tense embrace. Suddenly one of them lets his muscles go slack. He has lost courage; he can't go on. Whereupon the other, who has not relaxed his hold, wins without having to make any further effort.

But a war of attrition! The very thought tears the guts out of a man. It means thinking of the enemy opposite as a dense layer made up of "millions of soldiers." No good now breaking through at a single point. The whole front has got to be nibbled away. Before anything else can be done, there must be complete certainty that it has nowhere retained its thickness, that it has become tenuous as a sheet of paper. It must be filed thin, scraped, worn down, must become no more than a wood shaving made up of "millions of men," dead men, mutilated men, men turned into so much sawdust. To produce such an effect will be the work of months, demanding the patience of a saint. If it is done at all it will be only to a ceaseless accompaniment of bloodshed. At times it seems as though the thickness of those lines opposite remains undiminished, as though they take a malicious pleasure in forming new layers as fast as the foremost ranks are thinned. It is the back areas that grow empty as every available man is moved up to repair the wastage. Sober thought alone keeps despair at bay. After all, the back areas are not inexhaustible. The men they can provide are far fewer than the number of those killed at the front. If only the work of destruction can be pushed forward fast enough, the end is certain. The war will be bound to end when the fellows opposite have come to the end of their resources.

Unfortunately, attrition demands tools, and the tools are

human bodies. Continuous work exhausts the tools. How quickly? That is the whole question, but it is serious enough, in all conscience.

At Chantilly, No.1 Bureau of General Headquarters works over the casualty lists rendered by the formations. It works out that during the first four months of the war the average of wastage has been at the rate of a hundred and eighty thousand men a month. To be sure, such a figure may be regarded as slightly abnormal, including as it does the losses incurred in the early battles when the war was still a war of movement, and the casualties consequently high, since no attempt had been made to husband resources, but only to force a decision. It is only the later figures that are really significant. A hundred and forty-five thousand a month for the first half of 1915. That makes a solid base for calculation, working out at five thousand men a day, just about the total provided by a town the size of Poitiers on mobilization, twice the total of Mâcon, four times the total of ordinary little prefectures like Guéret, Gap, Mende, or Draguignan. In other words, merely to feed the war machine on the French side alone, means must be found of shovelling in one whole Poitiers every twenty-four hours, a Mâcon every morning and every evening, a Guéret or a Draguignan four times a day. Drop below that figure and the engine will begin to knock. Facts such as these make a man think. No good, of course, exaggerating. Striking though the figures are, they don't all represent pure loss. A fairly high proportion of the men shown are only damaged, can be more or less repaired and used again later—say a third of the whole. The minimum actual wastage on which intelligent anticipation can be based is not much more than three thousand men a day, considerably over a million a year—that "million" which, simply regarded as a number, has changed the whole art of war, and congealed activity into a continuous and solid front. Not such a terrific business, then, after all, not beyond the wit of man to calculate pretty easily. But that raises another question. For once allow that this million, by reason of its very elasticity, has imposed on warfare its seemingly impossible aspect, how can the wheels be reversed when numbers begin to melt away like snow?

It is possible, of course, to go through the country with a small-tooth comb, to rout out the men with soft jobs at the depots and in the administrative services, lower the standards of the medical boards, diminish the number of noncombatants, call up and train the younger classes; in short, bring pressure to bear upon the civilian population in order to increase the number of front-line troops, of men capable of being killed—squeeze the country to its last drop. Unfortunately, such methods, when used on either side, soon reach the exhaustion point. The hope is that the enemy will reach it first, and it is always permissible to believe they will, short of conclusive evidence to the contrary. At any rate, the great thing is to kill as many of the "fellows opposite" as possible, even though to do so may serve no strategic end nor exploit any particular tactical theory. Just kill because the more dead there are, the fewer living will remain.

War of attrition carried to its maximum. Attrition of flesh and blood, but also of all that depends for its existence on flesh and blood, of all the work of men's hands, of everything he has accumulated and made.

The economists had argued that the war must be short, because all their calculations had been worked out on a basis of real money. If there had been nothing but that to fall back on, the available funds would have been exhausted ages ago. But the peoples of Europe had learned how to keep the war going on a diet of fictitious gold, of something they called credit. Just as in the old romantic tales gamblers fumbling in their empty pockets would say suddenly: "Ah, there's that ring of mine...that field...that house. Why shouldn't I stake them?" so now the nations, even while ruin stared them in the face, realized that they were richer than they had ever guessed, and that, having turned all their real money into guns and shells, they could transform into paper wealth the soil, the forests, the houses, the harbours, the railways, the lighting system, of their native land—and so produce still more guns and still more shells.

The Central Powers, however, already running short of necessities, and seeing the moment approach when they could get no more credit, made yet another discovery: that even the end of credit doesn't mean the end of everything. When the industry of a nation is all directed to the single end of keeping a war going, it is its own people that it is paying; how that payment is made, therefore, doesn't very much matter. There is no reason why the women, the children, and the aged shouldn't be mobilized for labour, as their husbands, their fathers, and their sons are mobilized for death. The essential thing is to force the soil to produce enough ore and enough foodstuffs to supply the army, while at the same time guaranteeing the civilian population against starvation. A country, provided it is large enough, can always produce more than is realized in times of peace, and things previously scorned can always be used as substitutes for unobtainable imports. Hunger and cold, especially among civilians who labour obscurely out of the limelight, can always be endured far beyond any point that would previously have been deemed possible.

But if victory is to be sure, attrition must not be confined to the enemy's armies. It must extend to his rear as well. The rapid destruction of his front-line troops is but one aspect of the problem. It is necessary to calculate also the progress made by cold and hunger among his civilian population, the exhaustion of the natural resources of his country.

This is so to such an extent that the "front," in all its ramifications, tends to become the locality where two national agglomerations devour one another without thought of economy, without keeping anything back. The whole life, down to its most secret resources, of the two warring groups becomes concentrated there, strung out along the open wound of the trenches, to be swallowed up in the blazing inferno which is common to both of them. The whole problem is reduced to knowing on which side the exhaustion will be most rapid, will produce in the foundations on which the life of a country rests the greatest number of cavities or perforations, the most virulent mortification, the most certain preliminaries of crumbling and collapse. Which of two stretched surfaces will be the first to tear and reveal the deepest holes, or will subside in consequence of the sudden liquefaction, so to speak, of the social structure?

Is it not for just such an end that the supreme commander on either side must wait in patience?—always hoping, of course, that the rot will work more quickly in the ranks opposite than in his own, doing everything he can to shorten the period of waiting, ever counting on some happy accident to hasten the process, neglecting no opportunity of snatching an unexpected chance of victory, trying to pretend all the while that he still believes in the Napoleonic myths which fed his spirit in the early days—the crushing or envelopment of the enemy in the open field, the war of movement and manœuvre, in which the general becomes once more the chess-player with his flashes of genius, and is not merely the engineer-in-chief of an Attrition Factory.

One way out there might have been: peace—a fantastic mental aberration in the minds of the peoples concerned which might lead them to say to themselves: "Is it absolutely essential that we fight this business out to its bitter end? War is not now, even if it ever was, what we thought it would be. Since it is obvious that neither side can succeed in exhausting the other without at the same time exhausting itself almost as much, and since the distinguishing characteristic of modern warfare seems to be that it will never come to an end of itself, why shouldn't we look for some other solution? Even a bad peace would be an untold blessing for the world at large."

However sensible such a line of argument, it was impossible. Each of the two combatants turned it over in the secret recesses of his own mind, but only to put it from him as unthinkable. The cost of the war had already been too high in human lives and in treasure. Only victory, even if it brought ruin in its train, could offer a real, if incalculable, compensation. Besides, the two nations, through the mouths of their governors, had sworn too often that they would never desist until the enemy was brought to his knees. If, after the slaughter of so many hundreds of thousands of men, the destruction of so much territory, the wasting of so much money, they were to find suddenly that there was after all a basis for talk, for discussion, for mutual settlement, what excuse could they plead for not having come to that conclusion sooner? The sense of absurdity in the whole affair would be intolerable. The responsible heads in particular would have to face too bad an awakening. Rather than that they would go on gambling to the end. Even if conversations could have been begun, the fear of facing the balance-sheet would have brought them to nothing. On neither side were the authorities big-minded enough to confess to their people that this war had been proved to be null and void. On neither side were they willing to renounce the ends for which they had begun the struggle (if only because they had got to find some means of paying the allies they had enlisted by the way, who wouldn't be too pleased to think that they had been inconvenienced for nothing).

It would be difficult enough even to sit down at a table and find a formula for discussion. "First evacuate our territory, and then we can talk." "No, I can't give up what I've got; it's my only security." Each negotiator would insist, if only to satisfy public opinion at home, on behaving as if, after all, he had won the war. Only too soon they'd be at it hammer and tongs, like a lot of children or high-strung women.

Nothing for it but to begin fighting all over again. But meanwhile weariness, disillusion, a reawakening of the critical faculty, would have been at work among the soldiers. It would be a difficult and dangerous job starting up once more a machine which had been got into good working order, thanks to having routine and acquired habit at the wheel, thanks to that little dose of bureaucracy without which human beings cannot be governed at all.

The most energetic of the military chiefs said to themselves: "It's not the sort of responsibility I'm inclined to shoulder," and the politicians at home saw in imagination rifle-butts held high in mutiny and a flutter of red flags.

For it must always be remembered that the adventure of '14

can be partly accounted for as a tacit choice made by humanity between war and revolution. Nowhere had that truth been seen more clearly, or the decision been more deliberately taken, than among the governing classes. "Only at the price of war, heavy though it may be, only by the re-establishment of discipline and by the safety-valve to passions which it will provide, can we hope to maintain the present social order." Among the workers the feeling had been more passive, less articulate: "If we are still to live at peace, we shall have no excuse to put off indefinitely our settling of accounts with the upholders of privilege. Whatever you may say, that'll be a big job. Perhaps it would be less trouble just to obey. War's a damn fine excuse. In a manner of speaking, it's a case of Hobson's choice."

Besides, it's an ill wind that blows nobody good. The war contractors were making a nice lot of money. Fortunes were springing from the ground of national disaster like a crop of obscene toadstools. Village blacksmiths were turning out shells and becoming millionaires in the process. Rag-pickers who had made big contracts with the Ordnance Department were now in a position to give their wives ropes of pearls. In the back areas pot-bellied provincials, resplendent in their captain's uniforms and freed from the tyranny of nagging wives, were revelling in the unaccustomed delight of being obeyed, every hour of the day, "on the spot and without a murmur," of being waited on hand and foot with no expense to themselves, of eating good meals in jolly company, of having all the mistresses they wanted—in short, of leading the kind of intoxicating and profligate lives they had read about in historical novels.

Here and there, at the heart, even, of the warring peoples, were conspirators who dreamed of remaking nations long since dead and vanished, seeing themselves, naturally, as their heads, but realizing that any such rebirth could be brought about only among the ruins of the old Europe. Many of them had no particular wish to see either side victorious, but what they wished to see least of all was a peace by agreement, or, as it was customary to say then, a "premature peace."

Lastly, the Neutrals—under which head could be grouped all those countries where the population, from factory hand to the owner of great estates, had become producers of the sinews of war—were, like their fellows all over the world, stuffing themselves with profits. The non-Europeans, once Europe's debtors, had paid back what they owed and were now, in their turn, creditors, and rather proud of the fact. The younger continents were losing their sense of respect, were breaking from the leading-strings held till now by a parent who had obviously gone mad. The coloured races watched with a smile their onetime masters and oppressors, the white men, busily at work massacring one another.

So there was to be another winter. The soldiers looked round at their trenches as at a place which they must reconcile themselves to inhabiting for a long time yet; trenches which were already relapsing into their bad-weather state. In the ditches of Flanders the water seeped up from below; in the trenches of Picardie the rain made a thin deposit of whitish mud; those of Champagne, with their walls of sand and chalk, remained clean longer than most, but a time came when they, too, fell in; those of the Argonne became filled gradually with a green-coloured, liquid marl; round Verdun continuous rains turned the ground into a cemetery of sticky clay which only waited for the dead to fall before closing over them; in the forests of the Vosges the mud was of a black leaf-mould which had rotted between the roots of trees.

CHAPTER FOUR

Jerphanion Returns to the Line

They saw with relief the two mounds of earth which marked the beginning of the communication trench. For the last half-hour they had been worried by heavy shells falling regularly some two or three hundred yards to their left. One had come even closer. But it had struck a small hillock at the foot of a fir-tree and must have buried itself in the loose earth, since, instead of a violent explosion and a rain of splinters all round, there had been nothing but a muffled thud and a little spout of mud away from them.

Fabre, who took great pride in his knowledge of calibres, maintained that they were 150's—"just the ordinary stuff." Jerphanion had said at first that he didn't recognize the noise they made and that they certainly weren't 150's, but later he was not so sure. The thought of admitting his error was distasteful to him, and still more so the thought that three months' absence should have been enough to make him uncertain of such elementary things, of things that he had learned during his time in the trenches. "What was the good of going through it all?" He didn't like admitting that in matters of this kind—as, too, in being able to distinguish various species of plants, or of styles in furniture and architecture—he had a worse memory or judgment than others. He preferred to assume that the Boches had been recently trying out a new gun of which Fabre knew no more than he did himself. He suggested that this might be so, but Fabre merely shrugged his shoulders.

Not much fun this coming back to the line. It wouldn't be so bad if things had changed a bit while one was away. A thing's no less filthy for being familiar; it only makes one feel that the whole business is more futile than ever.

Gradually the trench grew deeper, but not so quickly as one would have liked. In places, and for no apparent reason, the bottom rose for a space of several yards, the earth having "bubbled" automatically like a piece of parquet flooring. As the walker's foot was pressed upwards by this excrescence, his head, till then concealed, emerged inevitably above the parapet, so that he had time to see the flat plain all around, which looked like some desert region of the South. "Afric's sunny shores—I'm fed up with it. There's nothing to eat there but sand." The idea of sand came pat. He could see it in his mind's eye—pale yellow, the natural colour of the ground, carefully scraped together by a pastoral race and then pounded up to make a sort of crude pudding. A pastoral race, hiding from casual encounters; used to concealing itself and watching strangers from afar; very thin and bony, as might be expected with such food.

The trench was dug almost in a straight line. A shell could have enfiladed whole sections of it. Evidently they were still a good way from the line. It would have been hardly reasonable to expect the working parties that had made it to start zigzagging it so far back; besides, it would have made a much longer walk.

The composition of the soil was very curious: full of little white blotches set in a kind of sand; thin, sharp splinters of lustreless white, rather like the rubbish one finds lying about in a stone-cutter's work-shop. The sand was reddish, tending to yellow, with a hint of grey. The whole effect was less of real, unworked soil such as one sees in the countryside than of the stuff one finds in city embankments.

The sun was still warm though not very high in the heavens; a little too pale to be cheerful. There was a feeling of summer's end in the air. The scattered trees, mostly small firs, did not show the change of season.

The men moved without enthusiasm. The trench was broad enough to let them, with a little crowding, walk two abreast, but they seemed to prefer going in single file, to enjoy its relative guarantee of privacy. They spoke little. No one attempted to sing. Many of them drooped their heads forward more than was rendered strictly necessary by fatigue or by the weight of their packs. Their eyes, when they were visible, expressed a sort of assumed and ironic resignation. It was as though they were saying with a touch of mockery: "Well, here we are again; what more d'you want?"

Jerphanion said to Fabre:

"The men don't look any too good."

Behind them shells continued to fall every five or six minutes, always on the same spot. The sound of the explosions was much muffled. They didn't seem to have any real connexion with the moving column—for the moment at least. "What are they trying to get? There's no crossroads anywhere near, nor any guns or camps. Perhaps they're after the entrance to the trench."

Away in front, and on either side, like bubbles on a sluggish pond, detonations faintly disturbed the far horizon at irrregular intervals, coming from Heaven knew where, differing in intensity, yet with the kind of sameness that makes all the stars in the night sky resemble one another. The general impression was of something that had become habitual. No need to wonder what was happening. It was all perfectly ordinary. Looking from one's open window in a great city and hearing the motor horns, one is spurred to no curiosity. If one lives in a great seaport, the sound of fog-horns seems normal. In a sense there is no sense in the message these things have to tell. The scattered noise of gunfire was nothing unusual, but merely one of the natural features of the landscape, one of the conditions of existence in such a place. Life could become like that—that was all there was to it. A faint report, then another a shade louder, a third rather less loud. All rather pointless, something to keep the world going, the world, in this connexion, meaning the war, since war had become the world's normal condition. Occasionally the explosion, far away to the rear, of a shell that had gone over one's head, just to remind one that this normal state of the world involves a rather abnormal amount of death and destruction.

They reached a point where the trench began to zigzag, then another where there was a trench junction. Fabre stopped to wait for the men of his company to come up. There was a sense of hidden life packed away in neighbouring trenches. Men coming from the other direction passed easily enough, owing to the width of the passageway. Jerphanion was not yet used to the look of the new steel helmet. The uniforms seemed cleaner, better kept, than formerly—more evidence that the war was becoming a routine affair.

The communication trench came to an end rather unexpectedly. One found oneself having to splash through the boggy outskirts of a small wood, the floor of which was composed of odds and ends of branches, twigs, and debris of all sorts, not excluding numerous small pieces of coal. The path led into the depths of the wood, which so far had suffered little damage. The trees still retained several yellow, or yellowing, leaves. One would have been inclined to say—but for the apparent absurdity of such an idea—that the leaves had been less touched by gunfire than the branches. Here and there in the undergrowth could be seen a number of crude huts looking not entirely out of place. The only surprising thing about them was their close proximity to the line.

Movement became very slow. Twice the column had to halt to give passage to working parties, and once to a party of stretcher-bearers with three wounded men.

A little farther on they crossed a makeshift bridge of half-submerged tree-trunks covered with partly smashed duckboards, which spanned a muddy rivulet, in colour something between pearl and mouse grey, which wound its way through the trees. At a little distance some soldiers were bathing in a creek.

Jerphanion heard one of the men behind him say:

"Whopping big cooties round here. Those blokes are busy drowning 'em."

Further on still, where the bank jutted out into the stream, a man was engaged in something that looked like fishing. The sound of the guns was more distinct now, but more sporadic. For the moment at least there seemed to be no shells passing overhead.

CHAPTER FIVE

One Kind of Fear

They emerged from the wood. The trench forked, and twenty yards farther on, the left-hand branch split once more into two. Everywhere the earth was remarkably clean. Only in a very few spots did the wall give any sign of having fallen in and been repaired. The conditions underfoot were not too bad. Only prolonged search would have revealed any evidence of fighting or of continuous occupation. One could almost have believed that one was in a section of the reserve system maintained by resting troops and kept scrupulously clean for the benefit of visiting notables. The sun was high enough to shine into these grooves cut in the earth, which seemed to bask in its warmth.

Suddenly there occurred two explosions, one on the heels of the other, neither of them very violent, but with a curiously heavy, muffled quality; the sound was close at hand and seemed to have been transmitted by the air rather than by the earth.

"Trench-mortars, eh?" said Jerphanion to his sergeant, Pilland.

"That's right, sir."

Jerphanion was conscious of a sudden change of mood, a special kind of shock which he had no difficulty in recognizing since it had happened to him before. It was as though he had been completely transported from one state of being to another. All his senses were equally affected, eyes, lungs, mind, and limbs. Nothing, within him or without, but was different from what it had been a moment before. Each nerve-end seemed suddenly conscious of a feeling of oppression, of something between excruciating pain and strangulation.

Every organ of his body felt as though it had been caught up
and constricted. He had a sensation of being tightly squeezed,
while at the same moment something seemed to click in his
brain. No doubt about what had happened. His head, his
hands, the stretched skin of his chest, the way his blood circulated through veins and arteries, his sense of the passage of
time, his anticipation of what the next moments would
bring—it was as though his whole conscious being had
become aware that it was set in a vice which some hand had
turned quite definitely, though quite gently. His body seemed
to contract within a narrowing sheath with an effect of tin-
gling. He could find relief only, as it were, by shrivelling up
inside himself, by making himself smaller. His eyes, on the
contrary, felt distended, as though they had been just noticeably pushed outwards from their orbits. Some stranger to this
place, meeting him suddenly, could not but have been struck
by his expression. His brain, too, as though in an effort to
escape, or as though subjected to some uprush from within,
felt like a living thing pressing heavily against the confining
skull made more rigid by the steel of his helmet. There was
nothing in the experience that could be called acute pain;
quite the contrary, nothing like a sudden shock to be followed
by an easing of the strain. What was happening seemed deliberately to avoid getting worse; rather, it appeared to be establishing itself as a chronic state. His mind might register what
had occurred like a singing in the ears, but only to resign itself
forthwith to the thing's continuance. "It's come. Incredible
though it may seem, it's come, as it came before."

Call it fear if you like, but not in the crude sense of the
word.

Until this moment—since he had started on this march up
to the line—Jerphanion had not been conscious of fear, of the
fear that was lying in wait for him. He had been aware of
nothing so much as of a feeling of irresponsibility mixed with
a vague access of moral self-satisfaction tinged with an equally vague sense of guilt. "I am returning to an area where,
nowadays, a man runs considerable risk of being killed and is
certain, meanwhile, of having to suffer a great many inconve-

niences, some of them particularly vile and meaningless. After all, I've been out of it all for a long time. I've nothing much to complain about, and no one's got anything against me."

He had not really been frightened, even when the 150's—the "ordinary stuff"—had fallen to their left while they were still in the open; or, if he had, it had been in a perfectly reasonable way which he knew how to deal with; the tiresomeness of having to face a danger which, without being deliberately aimed at him, might touch him accidentally, much as a runaway truck may crush a passing pedestrian, which merely meant that he couldn't just moon along with his head in the clouds, or chat absent-mindedly to his friend Fabre of the 10th company.

Nor had he been frightened hearing the distant thudding of the horizon draw nearer, or seeing it spread its arms to engulf him. The prospect had given him something unpleasant to think about; but that wasn't really fear.

It was the two trench-mortar bombs, the second accentuating the first, that had occasioned the particular little click in his brain. Till that moment Jerphanion had merely been renewing acquaintance with a danger area long familiar to him. Since then he had gone a step further: he was renewing acquaintance with fear. But with the sort of fear that may well pass unnoticed, since, far from trading on inexperience, it assumes familiarity and a discipline of resistance; a fear unaccompanied by any sense of shock or even by a noticeable trembling of the limbs, free of any merely episodic character or of those automatic reactions which might absorb and dissipate it, of anything, especially, that bore the remotest resemblance to a movement of flight; a sensation that was the concentrated essence of fear in its harshest form. The cup which it proffered him must be drained on the spot, must be drained secretly, and no sooner was it emptied than it became filled once more. It was, on the other hand, almost insensible to what might happen in the immediate future. Particular incidents, the flow and ebb of danger, might eventually add to it, but without much increasing the total or changing its fundamental nature. No period of calm would make it disappear so long as the human organism which it inhabited remained alive. It was fear because fear was indigenous to the place; fear was just the colour of life as it was lived in the front line, just a reminder that one was in the trenches and that one was still living.

Such fear colours everything, but the least little bit of self-respect enables a man to deny its existence with every appearance of sincerity. One can always get round it by calling it "involuntary reaction."

But why had the noise of two trench-mortar bombs been more unnerving than that of the 150's awhile back? Why had the "involuntary reaction" begun just at that moment, neither before nor after? Simply because it must begin some time. The 150's had fallen while they were still more or less in a back area. The world of danger has a way of subtly dividing itself into progressive zones, each one of which arouses special and more or less fixed emotions. "Trench fear" is a purely local product. Like the "trench louse" it thrives only in the front line.

Jerphanion thought back to the day in September 1914 when he had first come under fire in the marshes of Saint-Gond. Then, as now, he had heard the sound of gunfire come gradually closer. Fear had arrived much sooner then, but it had been pushed into the background by a curiosity so novel and so strong, by so violent an effort to show himself equal to the occasion, even by a self-searching interrogation so anxious and so prolonged, that, far from seeming an evil destined never to leave him more, it had neutralized itself in the very effort to treat the occurrence as a phenomenon of merely passing significance. He had, as it were, left it to look after itself, thrust it into the background of his conscience, so concerned had he been with the surge within himself of great waves of nervous excitement and exaltation.

But that phase was behind him now. No more excitement now, scarcely even curiosity about what had become so familiar—after all, there was not much room for either emotion in the limited field of action open to a second lieutenant (one spends months away from the front only to find the same old shells when one does get back). He was hardly curious any longer about his own reactions. One knows only too well what one can do and what one can put up with. One knows that courage has little effect on danger, and that no amount of determination can deflect a bullet by so much as a millimetre. One loses even the mystical respect for danger, so surely has one learned by experience that it is just a great hulking, stupid beast that goes on and on, and that no amount of worrying about it will keep one safe. On the contrary, it will probably increase one's chances of getting it in the neck. In short, the longer one associated with danger, the fewer illusions did one have left about it. No, this particular manifestation of fear had just got to be accepted as something quite simple, without frills, without variation, without even the power to develop, that went on and on.

CHAPTER SIX

In the Trenches

"Who said it was an old Boche trench?"

"I certainly didn't. You wouldn't ask such a damn fool question if you'd reconnoitred the sector yesterday as you ought to have done. Who was it had two men's work shoved onto him? Your old and valued friend. It's not in the least like an old Boche trench. No doubt in your innocence you've been looking forward to all the home comforts; well, you won't find 'em here. It's just one of the assault trenches they dug for the September offensive. And that's quite different. Not that you're missing much. Old Boche trenches have an uncomfortable way of being rather too close to the present Boche trenches, and that's too close for comfort. The chaps we're relieving have already started making things ship-shape, but there's the hell of a lot to do still. If you'll look at the handing-over papers, I've no doubt you'll find a nice lot of little schemes, complete with detailed instructions. Division wants to make this a show sector for the Modern War Exhibition, which, as you know, is to be opened in 1920. I'm going to be curator-in-chief in virtue of my wound-stripes.... There's a whole list of grand names being kept in readiness for all the fire and communication trenches they've planned. The troops'll want to stay here for ever.... You'll have to furnish a good deal more than your share of working parties."

"Well, they've got to leave me enough men to get my own line in order!" cried Jerphanion in a tone of despair.

"Isn't it good enough as it is? Have you ever seen a cleaner bit of line? Look here, it's as neat as a brick wall."

Fabre tapped the hard, sandy parapet, which was as vertical as though it had been dug with a plumb-line.

"Perhaps so, but there are no loop-holes, and hardly any fire step. There's a whole pile of steel plates in the corner of my dug-out that have got to be put in position. A nice little job for the trench-mortar fellows. And talking of dug-outs—have you seen 'em? Just take a squint at mine; yours is double the size."

"So it ought to be; it's got a much lower roof."

"The men have got practically nothing at all. Where did the fellows we've relieved pack in?"

"I expect they went home every night."

"There are a lot of orders too about wire. Why didn't they put it out themselves? It looks as though I've got to do in a week what they've failed to do in a month."

"You can always ask to stay in longer. Just you watch your step, my lad. I don't mind betting that if you'll go over the top on the 6th of October, they'll do your wiring for you. Even the poor devils lying out there'd come back if you gave 'em such a chance."

Jerphanion had gone back to his dug-out to take another look at its shortcomings and chew the cud of his grievance. He had to admit, however, that the floor was dry, the walls sound, the roof thick and apparently solid although there were no pit-props to support it. There was none of that clammy, subterranean moisture about the place which even the best dug-outs have. On the contrary, it was filled with a warm, almost astringent smell, which could not be altogether accounted for by the weather. The soil must have something to do with it.

Jerphanion caught sight of his quartermaster sergeant, a man with a pointed beard, called Baudefonds, who was writing on his knees. He had known him for only a short time and had never done a tour of duty with him in the line. Baudefonds was writing with an air of great concentration. The paper, though coarse, had an official look.

"What are you doing?"

"Making out my daily report, sir."

"*Your* daily report, eh?" Jerphanion burst out laughing.

"You've got a nerve, I must say!"

Baudefonds, quite unruffled, proceeded to explain:

"I like doing things ahead of time; I may not have a chance later."

Jerphanion leaned over to look at the paper. The first words: "Operations: nil," were followed by a detailed statement of work to be done: amount of wire to be put out (the precise number of yards); steel plates to be put in position (how many); work to be begun on shelters for the men (number of shelters). He admired the man's foresight, the modest total of his figures, and the philosophic way in which he linked past and future. But the sight had a significance which made him feel sick at heart. Didn't this kind of program imply that the war would go on for ever? Baudefonds was just writing: "Enemy works: nil. Signs of activity...."

Chuckling good-humouredly, Jerphanion pointed to the unfinished line:

"Nil? Suppose that between now and tomorrow they send over a dozen or so minnies?"

The quartermaster sergeant looked perplexed. He bit the end of his pen.

"Oh," he said, "I can always add. I leave blanks on purpose."

But he pondered the other's words, and without relaxing his serious expression, like a doctor writing out a prescription after examining a patient, wrote:

"About ten trench-mortar bombs came over between six and eight o'clock in the evening. All fell short."

Half an hour later Jerphanion was in Fabre's dug-out, when they heard a violent explosion quite close at hand, followed most immediately by another. Then there was silence.

Jerphanion poked his head out of the dug-out.

"Trench-mortars," he said; "and on my lot."

He had recognized the smell, that unmistakable mixture of acetylene, dish-water, and a drain in hot weather. Even that hadn't changed. Nor the yellowish smoke which he saw beginning to blow over from the left.

"I must go and see."

He wondered whether he would have time to reach his own dug-out before the next burst, but he was anxious to find out whether the first two had done any damage.

The first men he met, who belonged to Fabre's company, the 10th, reassured him:

"They fell your way all right, sir; but nobody copped nothing."

His own sector consisted of two diverging trenches which joined at their two extremities like the branches of a stream and enclosed between them an island of slightly rising ground. One of these had been an old assembly trench, while the other had been dug farther to the rear since the September offensive.

He found his men in rather an excited state.

"We were just trying to make a good job of our shelters," they said: and, indeed, many had spades in their hands; but they had stopped working.

"Where exactly did it fall?"

"The first over on the left, out in the open, just over by the light infantry; the second about fifteen yards out in our wire. Not that it did any harm to the wire, because there isn't any."

Other voices confirmed this information, and somebody added:

"Giving us a welcome, sir."

At the entrance to his dug-out he found Sergeant Pilland. "Just coming to look for you, lieutenant. No harm done. We'll give them back their own medicine in a hurry. I'm off to find the trench-mortar men."

Jerphanion stopped him. "Stay where you are."

"Don't you want me to, sir?"

Pilland looked thoroughly disappointed.

"No, they'll only retaliate, and next time somebody may get killed. It's quite pointless."

"But they'll think we've got no guts, that they needn't bother about us, sir."

"They can think what they like."

"Yes, sir."

Pilland departed. Jerphanion was seized by a sudden fear.

"Tell the corporal of the 58th that he's not to fire under any circumstances without orders. If he does, tell him he'll have to have it out with me. He's only to fire on my personal orders. See he understands. I shall hold you responsible....Where is Lieutenant Cotin? Have you seen him?"

"Yes, sir; he was at the far end of the fire trench when the minnies fell."

"Good. Pass on those orders to him on your way back."

They heard three rifle-shots which someone had let off at random to ease his nerves.

"No rifle-fire either. Those are my orders. They can't possibly hit anything....Just damn foolishness."

Jerphanion spent the last half-hour of daylight in a small salient made by the trench close to his dug-out. He was seated on the fire-step, his back against the rough sandstone, which felt not uncomfortable, smoking his pipe. He let his thoughts wander. The light was particularly beautiful, with something in it of an autumn dusk. It was his first evening in the line for many months.

Here he was in the trenches again, with every prospect of remaining there indefinitely. That such a thing should be possible, that this was his, Jerphanion's, own little niche in this immense, stationary, or almost stationary, war, gave him sufficient food for thought. The German minnies had not begun their little game again. The sound of gunfire had grown less and less frequent, so that as much as ten minutes went by without a single thud from the distant horizon. His ears had become once more attuned to the small sounds of the trenches, which were almost like those of a village. Fear (not to be admitted, not to be named) had now no reason to show its head. At the present moment there was no excuse for feeling afraid. To all appearance, his mind worked peacefully as though there had never been any question of fear. For the time being, it could lie still, deep down in his spirit, in all its furtive purity.

Someone tapped him on the shoulder.

"Fed up?"

It was Fabre. Possibly he was fed up himself, but he had presumably decided to hide his melancholy behind a mask of gaiety.

"We're not too badly off, you know. Think of all the poor devils standing ankle-deep in mud. So long as I'm dry…"

"Wait till it rains."

"Rains! Everything's relative. This ground'll absorb rain quicker than most. You may get a couple of inches of mud under your feet, but elsewhere they'll be splashing about up to their knees. Besides, don't you like a place like this where one can get a good view over the countryside?"

"A lot of good it does one! There's not an inch of parapet where one can risk showing one's nose."

"That's just where you're wrong. There's a spot I know, about two hundred yards to the rear, where the wood makes an angle…. There's a trench there that leads nowhere, and a little rise in the under-growth; you can sit there and see everything."

"Don't they drop stuff on it?"

"Not specially. The Boche knows it can't be used as an observation post because the field of view's too short. They don't bother about it—and they won't, unless some fool thinks of putting a machine-gun there….Another advantage about this place, especially in our sector—it's different farther over to the right, beyond point 432 just opposite Domremy alley—is that the enemy's lines are so far off. We don't get any of that damned bombing, and there's so little cover in the open that there's precious little chance of anyone crawling up and dropping grenades over the parapet, or taking a pot-shot at one from up a tree. You know all about that sort of thing. Admit there are points about living here."

Jerphanion admitted it, but maintained, on the other hand, that being dropped down in an open plain and plopped into a lot of ditches that bore no relation to the lie of the land, without any support or protection from natural features, merely accentuated for him the arbitrariness, the absurdity, the claustrophobic nature of the life they were condemned to lead. "One's here because one's been put here, and that's all there is about it." On a wooded hillside, on the other hand, though one may run greater risks, one's conscious of a sort of primitive instinct; one sees why one's there, one approves the choice of site.

"I feel here as I should feel if I was asked to sleep in a bed that had been plunked down in the middle of a huge room, beneath a dome."

He added that it wasn't simply a matter of instinct. This stretch of front, with no apparent reason for being where it was, gave him no feeling of stability. Its very existence must be a constant temptation to the Staff. "Offensive action" stuck out all over it.

CHAPTER SEVEN

A Spot with a Nice View

By the time they had finished their evening meal, the moon was shining brightly. Fabre suggested to Jerphanion that he should show him the spot from which there was a view.

"You can see for yourself—and there's absolutely no danger."

On their way Jerphanion went on with what he had been saying before:

"I can't help wondering what they're going to do with us.... Winter's coming on. Can they really resign themselves patiently to wait for next year and then stage another full-dress show? There are such things as winter offensives, as we know to our cost. Should such an idea occur to them, I'm afraid they might regard this sector as ideal for the purpose, with its extended field of view, its wealth of open country, its good dry soil. Just think it over.... And then what about the Boches? I wouldn't put it past them to try something. What's your opinion?"

Fabre found the conversation becoming rather too serious.

"I prefer not to have one."

"So I gather," replied Jerphanion rather sulkily. "That's certainly one way of dealing with things, and for the moment it's as good as another. But you can't just stick your head in the sand for ever."

Fabre seemed suddenly indignant. "Don't be so damned unreasonable! Do you really want to know what I think?"

He had assumed the tone of an actor of melodrama or a fighting lawyer. It did not matter how loud he shouted. The Boches were far away, and there was no one but themselves in the trench. Every now and then the moon cast upon the white, almost phosphorescent wall of earth, the shadow of half or a third of their bodies, strangely deformed and fantastically shaped. Fabre's voice made them seem like two actors rehearsing the great scene of some play in which the hero is to be murdered in the castle moat.

Jerphanion, who had no idea what his companion was about, played up to him with something of a bad grace:

"Well, what do you think?"

"This," replied Fabre, lowering his voice slightly, but still speaking with an undertone of violence and striking at some unseen adversary with his clenched right hand: "that when the time comes, we shall charge the foe and let cold steel decide!"

Jerphanion burst out laughing. There was something excessive about his mirth as he guffawed away for several minutes. The unexpectedness of this joke—which he had completely forgotten—released in him a sense of the comic, too little exercised of late, alas, and the reaction did him good. It was no worse a joke for being old, and it belonged to a wholly admirable tradition. He remembered how often it had kept them all sane during those autumn days of 1914. It dated from the time when he had been serving in Foch's army—that is to say, from the end of August. A ranker called Masjan—nicknamed Majambe—had brought it with him from the depot where he had happened on it, by a stroke of good fortune, in a fairly recent article written by General Foch, formerly director of the Staff College, eminent instructor and inspirer of the High Command, pundit of strategy, and now in charge of their own Army. The original form of the sentence had been in the infinitive, and was intended, in its author's mind, to answer the following question: "How is a decision in the field to be obtained in the next war?" Simple enough: "Charge the foe," etc.... The saying had at once become current among the officers of the division. At that time the French infantry was experiencing for the first time the effect of machine-gun fire at a thousand yards, and of "coal-boxes" at six or eight thousand, and had discovered that the bayonet, so eloquently beloved of those who wrote about war, was not of much more use than a pocket-knife. The idea of somebody very naturally chafing at delay, charging the foe, and "letting cold steel decide" was irresistibly comic. The very words "cold steel" conjured up a whole chapter of pre-war stupidity, with its love of big words, its entire lack of imagination and intellectual honesty, its refusal to face facts, its inherent vulgarity— an attitude, in fact, that had been common to officials of every degree of eminence or obscurity. The juicy flavour of the ridiculous morsel was enhanced for those who, like Jerphanion and his companions, could reflect that they were actually serving under the orders of the man who had concocted it. What did he himself think of it now? Probably he had forgotten the whole episode. Doubtless, having learned by experience, though at considerably less cost than his men, he was now busily engaged in inventing phrases of a different kind, though no less false, with which to adorn his reports to General Headquarters. At that time, too, there were being passed from hand to hand, to the accompaniment sometimes of waggish comments, sometimes of angry oaths, the articles of Richepin, Lavedan, Barrès, and other hot-heads of the Academy, who had taken on themselves the duty of teaching the men at the front how to die, while assuring them that the enemy they had to face was wretchedly armed, half-witted, and partially starved.

To come out with the phrase at just the right moment before a lot of pals made up for a good deal. Like a puff of tobacco smoke, it softened the idiocies of mankind in a sort of philosophic haze. There were several ways of handling it, all equally popular. Not the least effective consisted in the speaker's assuming a phlegmatic tone, as of one summing up in a court of law. Jerphanion could see again, in particular, the edge of a small wood, could feel again the weariness of the hard day's end and remember the face of the man who had been at his side, Marchand, who commanded the next section to his own. They were outflanked both to right and to left; the company commander was dead; the colonel out of touch; all lines down. Enemy machine-gun fire was picking off the men at the rate of one a minute. Jerphanion, at his wits' end, had turned to Marchand, who was lying in the grass close at hand, and said: "What the hell are we going to do now?" and Marchand, in pauses of the deafening uproar, speaking quite calmly, like a man communicating a rather personal matter, had replied: "Charge the foe and let cold steel decide." At the same moment the Germans had sent over a particularly heavy instalment of high-explosive and shrapnel, to say nothing of the bullets that went whining overhead almost continuously. But "the Phrase" had done the trick as usual just as though nothing particular was going on. The immediate effect on Jerphanion had been to make him laugh, not silently, but with the full force of his lungs, lying there with his beard pressed into the earth. It was almost as though the eternal Spirit of Irony had drawn near to these two men where they grovelled amid the hellish din, had touched them on the shoulder and whispered: "Times are bad, but I'm here." Poor Marchand; he had his head blown to bits a few days later.

They reached the piece of dead-end trench which Fabre called "the Belvedere." He seemed to be expecting some sort of compliment. Jerphanion was inclined to admit that it might be worse. Although the slope of the ground had been barely noticeable as they walked, the view really was quite extensive, particularly towards the right. Auberive and the country lying off to the left were the only part that could not be seen. It was difficult to judge how safe the place would have seemed in broad daylight, but, as Fabre demonstrated, one could stand very nearly upright, with one's knees supported by a kind of prie-Dieu formed by a projection of earth low down in the parapet. Alternatively, one could press one's backside against the trench wall with one's feet against the parapet to prevent one slipping down. In either case one's head just showed above ground level between two clumps of brushwood. Close behind, the angle of the wood, with its margin of scrub, formed a background. The odds were that from a distance of several hundred yards the whole impression was one of blur, and that a human head, or a couple of heads, even if they moved about, even if their owners were smoking, would be invisible.

Jerphanion was surprised to find that the place had never been put to any use, but had been left free for anyone who wanted a quiet pipe and a place to think in comfort and look at the landscape. It wouldn't, probably, have been of much value as an artillery observation post, except during an attack. But surely it was an ideal spot for a machine-gun? He put the thought into words, to be rewarded with a pained look from Fabre. Was the only result of his showing old "Jerphat" his "Belvedere" to be that someone would turn the place into a machine-gun nest? Had the fellow, for all his "old soldier" airs, become as keen on his job as that?

Jerphanion hastened to reassure him:

"I was only joking. What sort of fool do you take me for? That kind of thing's not going to shorten the war by one minute...."

Fabre remarked that the angle of the wood had at one time been lousy with machine-guns. But the Boche had got wise to what was going on and had made the place too hot. The machine-guns had been moved; the Boche had stopped sniping it, and the Belvedere had been left in peace.

They gazed out over the moonlit countryside. The plain in its apparent flatness had a look of the sea. Since it gradually sloped upwards to the far distance, the impression of a marine horizon was increased. The only thing one forgot was that, had it really been the sea, the range of view would have been shorter.

Beneath the moon the plain had a white, starched look, diversified by a number of black depressions as of cultivated ground, which somehow accentuated its resemblance to an ocean surface. Here and there some projection whiter than the rest gave the illusion of a breaking wave. Gradually the eye noticed a series of long white scars, roughly parallel, which corresponded to the French trenches, and might, at a pinch, have been taken for lines of foam broken and contorted by rocks or by some submarine disturbance. The dark line of the woods swept forward from behind their backs and was continued on the right (on the left it completely blocked the view), becoming thinner and thinner until it ceased altogeth-

er, like a stretch of coastline dwindling away at the far side of
a bay. A few small noises rose from the French trenches, odd,
earthbound noises that the ear found difficulty in placing or
identifying. With the exercise of some imagination it was possible to fancy that they rose from some lower town huddled
round this milky sea. Surrendering to this fantasy, the watcher at once felt as though he himself were situated on a far
higher level. The Belvedere might, perhaps, be set on some
cliff or on the fortifications that dominated the lower town.
To hold the illusion it was necessary only to lower one's head
behind the parapet of earth so as to see no more than a limited segment of the white and foam-flecked scene.

Behind the German lines the two men could see, now and
again, little stabs of flame, or their reflection. These were the
flashes of guns. Most of them were very far away. They could
hear the muffled explosions, but owing to the distance there
seemed little if any connexion between the sound and the
flash. The latter might have been some signal lamp, or the
beam of a revolving light; the former some quite accidental
noise like the tail end of a thunder-storm. Or the two together might be the distant echo of a fleet at manœuvres
engaged in night firing.

One had to look hard in order to see the actual German
trenches. Here and there they were betrayed by the glint of
newly turned earth or the glow of some vague, moving light.
A candle, a lamp, shining in a dug-out incompletely curtained
by its canvas screen, or a stove suddenly lit in a shell-hole, was
enough to catch the eye. The surface of the ground reflected
light so readily that the least glint was caught up and made
visible.

After a while Jerphanion's eyes could make out between the
German and French lines, but rather nearer the former, a considerable number of dark, oddly shaped blotches. Clearly they
were not due to any accident of the ground, but he was not
sure what they were. He asked his friend.

"Don't you know what those are?" said Fabre. "Didn't you
notice them this afternoon? As a matter of fact, I'm not certain there are any opposite your bit of line."

"I think I know—but—" A troubled note had crept into Jerphanion's voice.

"You've got it; they're corpses."

"Ours?"

"Certainly."

"How long have they been there?"

"Since the big attack, the one on the 26th of September."

"Almost a month, then."

"Yes."

"How awful! They must stink like blazes!"

"There's a slight south-west breeze today, so the Boche is getting the benefit of them. When it's blowing from a different quarter, I don't know, but—well, probably...."

"Hasn't there been any attempt made to bring them in ?"

"Yes, I think so. I'm told there were a great many more of them. I know I saw heaps more after the 6th of October, when I was in front of redoubt 224....They'd have got in all those fellows out there, only the Boche swine thought it fun to pick off the stretcher-bearers...I'm only telling you what I've heard. Several volunteers for the job were killed. All that really matters is to collect the identification tags to send home....That's quicker than pulling in the bodies. Unfortunately the men don't much care about risking their lives for a thing like that. It's difficult to raise enough for anything as it is."

They spoke of the state of morale. Jerphanion, ever since his return to the front, had been much struck by the change he had noticed in the troops. He had stormed and threatened without much result. He had tried all sorts of methods. "Am I," he had wondered, "losing my touch?" On the occasions when he had scolded his men instead of punishing them, he had been met with a good deal of grumbling. For instance, one man had said: "It's all very well for you, sir; you didn't have to go over the top. You don't know what it was like."

"Yes," said Fabre; "their morale had never been higher than it was at the beginning of September. They had seen all the preparations being made, and thought them wonderful. They had to admit that for the first time they were going to be given a real chance instead of just being driven to the slaughter. I've seen them laughing for joy at the up-to-date com-munication trenches, the light railways, the ammunition dumps, at the famous 'Place de l'Opéra' with its piles of sand-bags. And they felt as though they themselves had been made over, with their new uniforms and their steel helmets. They were being well fed....But when the September offensive was held up, all that changed, and since most of them had to go through it all again at the beginning of October, they had all the guts taken out of them. Luckily the Boche didn't know."

He had taken part in two offensives at different points of the same sector. He wasn't much of a hand at telling a story. Besides, battle narratives soon come to look ridiculous and unnecessary to men sharing the same experiences, the kind of joke that soon loses its point. "Talk about the women you had on your last leave, if you like, but, for God's sake, don't start jawing about bombs and smashed heads." Fabre, too, with his affectation of frivolity, found it more difficult than most to relate epic tales.

But when he was with someone who knew the ropes, he could drop a number of pretty eloquent hints. He told one or two stories of men caught up on wire that had been official-ly destroyed, and quoted—as a not uninteresting detail—the number of casualties in his section and in the battalion gen-erally.

"The day before you got back we had a draft of chaps from the north. Before they came you could have put your com-pany in your pocket....That explains why there are so many strange faces, so many men who don't seem to know one another....Many of them are from the occupied territory and have left their families behind them. That doesn't make them feel any kinder towards the Boche; on the other hand, it does-n't much help to improve morale. Put yourself in their place. Most of them are wondering whether they've got a home at all, whether there's anything left to fight for or go back to when the war's over. They're like a lot of lost kids. They might make excellent Legionaries for some colonial expedition, but in a war like this, where most of the men exist on letters and parcels from home, and leave!...They're cut off from all that....They've nothing to look forward to but the sort of fun they can get in the back areas....Do you wonder that all this grousing and ill temper goes unchecked?"

There was nothing, thought Fabre, particularly mysterious about the demoralization which had set in after the double failure of the autumn. They had been told so often that this time they were going to finish the job, and all there was to show for it was another lot of lies. They'd be fools indeed if they went on believing what they were told. Then there were all the mistakes that had come to light in the course of the offensive; imperfect preparations: too much wire left unde-stroyed, too many machine-guns in concrete emplacements which the artillery had failed to silence, just in the very places where there oughtn't to have been any. But worst of all, and most detrimental to morale, was the fact that the men had seen with their own eyes—quite apart from what they had been told from above—all the detailed plans for the attack, had weighed everything in the balance of their own common sense, and had been convinced that this time they were going to succeed. The failure of the offensive had struck not so much at the efficiency of their leaders, but at themselves, had shaken their confidence in their own judgment. It had never before occurred to them that the fault might lie in their own powers. Now they preferred to conclude that if victory couldn't be achieved in conditions which they, in their ster-ling good sense, had regarded as almost perfect, then it could never be achieved at all. There was no reason why this unnatural war should ever stop, or rather it would only stop when everybody, on both sides, had been killed. There was going to be another winter, that was obvious; but one winter more or less wouldn't change matters. The soldiers were beginning to think that they were in for a life sentence. The end of the ordeal would come only with the end of their lives.

Fabre explained all this without departing much from his usual attitude of mocking detachment. There was an under-tone to his words that seemed to say: "Odd, isn't it? Poor dev-ils, it's not altogether their fault," just as though he were not personally concerned at all.

They went on to discuss Second Lieutenant Cotin.

"Do you know much about him?" asked Jerphanion.

"Next to nothing. He turned up a day or two before you, between the two attacks. Just out of hospital."

"Wounded?"

"No, sick."

"What was he in before—the 151st?"

"No; dragoons, I think; transferred at his own request."

"Keen for promotion?"

"Perhaps. But I rather think he's after the glory." Fabre spoke the word quite simply. "I gather he found the cavalry war a bit of a farce."

"Did he find the attack of the 6th a bit of a farce too?"

"He showed himself a pretty good soldier; always at his men for not having enough guts. He was quite ready to start again the next day. I don't mind betting he's bored stiff now. I expect he's beginning to find things a bit slow in the infantry."

"Odd. He's a little slip of a fellow too." Jerphanion busied himself for a while with his own thoughts; then: "One comes across curious chaps in this war. Men like Cotin rather frighten me...."

"Why?"

"Horrify me, I should say....He makes me think of a sickly sort of demon. He looks ordinary enough, but all the while what he would really enjoy would be to crush all human life to powder between a couple of stones, without meaning any harm, like a boy crushing a fly."

"What for?"

"Oh, I don't know what for. I may be wrong. I really don't know anything about him."

Over on their right, beyond the front line but not far from it, in an angle made by the fire trench opposite the next battalion, they saw the shadowy forms of men appear and start crawling about.

"A patrol? No; probably a working party."

"What are they doing—trying to bring in the dead?"

"I don't think so. They seem to be stopping this side. They're moving something. Putting up barbed wire, I should say, only it looks too big. There's more than one of whatever it is. Probably knife-rests. We ought to be doing it too, you know. But ours haven't come yet, which is a very good reason why we're not. They're great whopping things, as long as prehistoric monsters. It takes eight or ten men to carry one of 'em."

Jerphanion watched the shadowy forms moving in the moonlight.

"They're terribly visible," he said.

A moment later they saw one, then two, then three stabs of flame at the same point on the horizon. They had time to formulate, each without speaking, a number of more or less plausible hypotheses; to think:

"I believe I know...."

"Yes, that's it."

They heard a muffled bark, followed immediately by a "Boom!" then by two other "Booms!" Because they were looking at the working party, they didn't at first see where the shells had fallen, which was just opposite where they stood and some fifty yards in front of the line. Almost certainly 77's.

"If they're trying to get the working party, as I rather think they are, they'll have to alter their line. But the stuff may have been meant for us at that range. We look like having some pleasant nights in store for us!"

There were several more flashes.

"How about getting back?" they said simultaneously.

It wasn't that they thought their dug-outs would be safer than the "Belvedere." Their minds were working quite differently. "With our men so nervous, those 77's are going to play merry hell. We must be where they can see us."

The bombardment went on sporadically for another twenty minutes or so. At one moment it seemed to be coming from two different directions. All together about fifty shells were sent over. Jerphanion had no wounded in his company.

He heard that two men in the next-door working party had been hit, though they'd bolted for cover almost at once.

"This'll mean something extra for Baudefonds to put in his report. 'Brisk bombardment between so and so o'clock.'"

When all had been quiet again for some time and it looked as though the excitement was over, he decided to turn in. He was very tired and felt sucked dry. He put off writing to his wife until next day. He had been meaning to get a letter off to Jallez too for the last fortnight.

CHAPTER EIGHT

Reverie of a Lieutenant in the Autumn of 1915

He made up his bed, which consisted of a tolerable mattress, a pillow covered in coarse brown canvas, and two blankets, all of which were dry. Overhead six feet of good earth lay between him and possible shells. The thing he minded most was the enforced presence of Second Lieutenant Cotin at the other end of the dug-out. Not that he wasn't perfectly obliging and easy to get on with, but somehow those qualities did not recommend him. It would have been better, in a way, if he had been frankly detestable. For the moment, however, he was not to be seen. Doubtless he was showing commendable keenness elsewhere. It might be possible to get to sleep before he came back. Better leave a candle burning for him on a biscuit-box. (The tin lid in which it stood was large enough to remove any danger of fire.)

But it wasn't so easy to get to sleep. So perversely did Jerphanion's mind work that he could never manage to drop off when he was in the line without first inducing in himself an illusion of security. Luckily, it did not take much to achieve this end. It was enough, even in a wood peppered all night long by shrapnel, if he could count on a shelter of brushwood with a roof of canvas stretched on four poles, or a hole scooped out of a perpendicular wall of earth in a trench under shell-fire; or on even less. He was a good hand imitating the birds and could make a comfortable nest for himself out of the merest twigs of make-believe. In fact, the less he had to work with, the greater the satisfaction he got from exercising his ingenuity. The tiniest hint was sufficient foundation for his superstructures of fantasy. His illusion of safety could be successfully built up on ground that was no more than the barely perceptible difference between two contiguous degrees of the same danger. He might, for instance, find himself some night squeezed into the slightest of hollows, and yet, thanks to the way in which he had curled himself up, feel his head rather less exposed than his legs, his legs slightly better protected than if they were lying outside—not in relation to any definite peril, for, after all, a shell is not particularly discriminating, but rather to the simple and somewhat fantastic idea of peril in general.

Here, in his dug-out, where he could dispose of more elaborate resources, he felt that he had the right to be more exigent than usual. Stretched on his mattress, his head supported by the brown canvas pillow, his legs tucked comfortably into the two blankets, he set himself, by the light of the candle, to take stock of his quarters. The entrance was low and adequately masked. He had already got up once to adjust the curtain. Even allowing for the reflection of the chalk, there was very little chance of a flicker escaping of sufficient brightness to attract watchful eyes out there on the plain. Future arrivals would probably not be so careful as he had been, but by that time the odds were that he would be asleep and so beyond caring.

The whole dug-out seemed to have been excavated from solid rock, not perhaps of the hard, quarry type, but composed rather of a natural mixture of sand and limestone. The grains of the sand, clearly visible as they were in the candlelight, which threw them here and there into exaggerated relief, gave him some cause for anxiety. Earth of that texture might so easily crumble under impact or dissolve in water. He could imagine the whole roof being washed in on some stormy night and engulfing him in a sort of sodden, squelching mess. He would be suffocated, buried alive, in liquid sand. But a second thought came hard on the heels of the first to comfort him: "Chalk and sand." Limestone is the same as chalk. To say that anything is "built of chalk and sand" is to attribute to it a character of great solidity. He felt his security suddenly guaranteed by the authority of tradition. There must be *something* in popular sayings.

But he was worried by the absence of pit-props and frames. He was perfectly willing to believe that, in theory, an excavation of this kind— "chalk and sand"—didn't need them. Under peace conditions a similar cave might stand indefinitely. But war, it must always be remembered, has its own standards. What would happen if a shell fell bang on top? If it was a big enough shell, it was obvious what the result would be—total collapse. Better not to think of it. A small shell would do little more than dent the surface. But what about one of medium size? Would it bury itself sufficiently deep to burst inside the place? If it did, then the whole contraption would go up in dust and smoke. What was far more likely was that it would burst in the thickness of the roof and send the whole mass cascading down into the space beneath.

And that reminded him that he often had to reconcile two opposite tendencies in himself: a liking for underground shelters and the deep, muffled security which they promised, with his fear of being suffocated and entombed. One of the obsessions against which he had to fight most violently under these conditions of trench life came from the fear of being buried, or, worse still, of suffocating inch by inch in some narrow space that had been blocked by a fall of earth at the entrance.

He ended by assuring himself that the night was calm, that there was very little chance of a heavy bombardment starting before daybreak, and that, as things were, he could allow himself to indulge in a sense of security in this deep shelter that was little short of perfect (except, of course, for that one little involuntary tremor of nervousness which would persist no matter what he did or thought), a sense which was an admirable aid to inducing slumber. He decided, however, that as soon as it was daylight he would see about getting at least one frame and one pit-prop installed; the frame to be placed at the centre point of the roof, with the prop supporting it. Other improvements he could think about later.

He might, at this point, have gone to sleep without worrying further, had it not been for another idea that kept him wakeful, an idea which owed its origin to his conversation with Fabre, a composite idea which showed first one face, then another, of its multiple self; a regular polypus of an idea.

It began by sowing in his mind doubts about the men. He imagined them as demoralized, fed up, filled with a bitter grudge against their officers. He was an officer; a junior one to be sure, and his degree of responsibility in the eyes of the soldiers must be small, all the more so since he had taken part in the recent attacks. All the same, officers of every rank are bound together by the chains of a mysterious solidarity.... He would certainly never have sufficient moral courage to live in an atmosphere of general hostility. Least of all people could he subscribe to the saying: "*Oderint dum metuant.*" Not that he wanted to be adored. He would be perfectly content to feel that he was regarded with confidence and attachment....Without that assurance his job would be intolerable. Awful to know that his men were cowed, that he could keep them only by force in conditions that, if they were not faced with conscientious devotion to duty and a spirit of goodwill, must approximate to the worst conceivable types of penal servitude. Awful to know that they regarded him only as someone who doled out rations of misery and chances of getting killed. Far, far better to be one of them himself, to pull at the oars with the other galley-slaves.

Why had morale fallen to such a low pitch? Because the men felt that the lives of their comrades had been just thrown away wantonly (and who would say they were wrong?); and also because they had lost all faith in the war's ever ending (again, who would say they were wrong?). Absurd, childish, perhaps; yet not so absurd as might at first appear. What was much more absurd was the attempt to see this war in the light of arguments drawn from the lessons of earlier wars. All the wars of recent history of course had ended, had, as a matter of fact, been fairly short, including those of Napoleon. No doubt they had begun again almost at once, but they had ended. But the records of humanity did hold memory of wars that had practically been endless, practically, that is to say, when reckoned by the scale of human life. If this war was going on in ten years' time, it would, for those taking part in it, be to all intents and purposes eternal. Most of them would be dead. As to the rare survivors…well, the arguments in favour of a short war drawn from the deadliness of modern weapons, from considerations of economy and finance, had been shown to be worthless. After fifteen months of fighting didn't the prospects of peace seem just as far off as they had done on the day of mobilization? The nations of Europe were so fast caught in the toils of war that they no longer knew how to break free. The only thing they thought about now was how they might involve the few countries that had so far remained outside.

Gloomily brooding there in his dug-out, Jerphanion set himself to think out rationally what his men outside in the trenches were thinking in an access of despair. "The idea that a catastrophe cannot last for ever is a prejudice born of happy periods of peace. The shattering break-up of the Roman Empire went on indefinitely. We of the West know little of the history of China; but we find no difficulty in imagining the China of ancient days slowly dropping to pieces through two centuries of convulsive collapse. Our natural instincts are not revolted by the idea. If someone told us that modern China, torn by internal violence since the days of the Boxer risings, would not find peace again until the year 2000, should we be profoundly shocked? A catastrophe once started continues by dint of multiplying itself. A war of emperors and great stand-ing armies becomes finally a war of generals and robber bands."

If he was to get any sleep at all, he must find a grain of moral comfort somewhere. He needed more now than the illusion of his own personal security. He must create for him-self the further illusion that the world was somehow to remain habitable, that, in some way or other, it would be pos-sible to come to terms with it. Otherwise the human spirit, shaken and torn to its ultimate depths, would simply refuse to provide the minimum of vitality which human beings require if they are to remain animate at all, if they are even to sleep, since the act of sleeping implies the willingness to face tomorrow and the days that are to follow, assumes a degree of confidence sufficient to force the sleeper into the effort required by renewed wakefulness.

Jerphanion, therefore, began fumblingly to construct for himself a fantasy which, while taking into account the bitter truths which had formed the matter of his recent broodings, did, none the less, satisfy to some extent his craving. It was not unlike the kind of game played by poor children in the stinking back yard of some tenement: a game that makes no attempt to ignore the hideous background, but accepts it, uses it, even, as the decoration and material of its invented world, and thereby finds consolation all the less fragile for facing the facts and conditions of its existence.

It was an odd sort of dream if one stopped to consider the brain of the man who formulated it. And not the least strange thing about it was that he should have felt it necessary to place his fantasy in an actual future, that he should have thought of it as at least plausible if not probable, that he should have worked it out in all its curious details.

He saw, in imagination, the war going on and on…just as his men saw it—a succession of shocks, of offensives, conducted with weapons ever more numerous and more deadly, though never deadly enough to force it to an end, but only to keep it going. The roots of this war would drive ever deeper and deeper into the soil of the nations. There would be less and less reason why the fronts should ever move. And yet, in the end, this stagnant war would just rot away where it stood, involving the country lying behind in its own corruption. Gradually it would begin to show the passive symptoms of collapse. A moment would arrive when orders would cease to come up from the rear, when supplies would fail. The armies would break from their close embrace and dwindle away in shreds and patches. The men would begin to leave the front and wander off, without any definite objective, but simply to escape dying of starvation. They would set off in more or less large groups, for the old organization would still tend to be operative, and the soldiers would have lost the habit of living otherwise than with their comrades, have lost the sense of all other bonds, without family or country, with only the army. Naturally, they would take with them their weapons, and as much ammunition as they might have left. Then would begin for them a life of haphazard adventure. They would get their food where they could find it. They would spread over the countryside, intending no particular violence, wishing neither to pillage nor destroy. But they would have to live, and since they would still have a grudge against the people of the back areas who had so willingly allowed the front-line troops to stagnate and die for so long in the trenches, while they themselves had prospered in a world of contracts and supplies, they would not bother about putting on kid gloves when it came to requisitioning for their needs, would not mind hustling a few mayors of communes, and a few fat and prosperous farmers: "Where is your wheat?…Two cows and six sheep by the church in half an hour." And since the regions near the front would soon have been eaten bare by this swarm of locusts, they would tend naturally to move farther and farther afield, the formations separating so as not to impede one another in the search, the rule being that there must be no squabbling between bands. They would all have suffered too much in common to harm one another now. In this way the bands would proceed on and ever on, from one commune to another, following the roads, the line of the valleys, or their own instinctive sense of direction: "Those hills over there don't look too bad, eh?" or somebody might volunteer information: "I know a damn fine spot with plenty of poultry and plenty of cows, where no one's been yet…." Each band would retain its internal discipline without any trouble, so deeply engrained would habit have become, so often would the men have obeyed orders when it had been a matter of fulfilling duties far more distasteful. Each band would love its chief unquestioningly, almost tenderly. Ended would be that odious time when the leader had imposed upon his men hardship and death, without having to justify his orders in any way that they could accept, when, of necessity, they had regarded him as the warder in charge of a gang. It would be wonderful now for the leader to say to himself that his men counted blindly on him to supply their wants and ensure their safety, that no longer need he address them in terms of army orders, no longer use those grandiose words which had served of old but to put a mask on sacrifice, could speak to them directly, honestly, and in a way that they could understand.

Nor, of course, would they be forbidden to rest for a while, should the wish so take them. They might happen, for instance, on some little corner well sheltered by hills, rich in all things that men need, with its market town and its group of dependent villages. The band, with its leader at its head, would settle down there until further notice, quite in the feudal way. The men would learn a new tact, would so conduct themselves as to make the inhabitants receive them willingly, taxing the resources of the place to keep them in food and necessaries, making no effort to get rid of them, whether by forcible resistance or by enlisting other haphazard adventurers to stand their champions—for circumstances would breed soldiers of fortune like flies. There would have to be at least the rudiments of organization, sufficient discipline to guard against slackness and the effects of self-indulgence, to maintain the standards of "military virtue," for the men would have to learn that their true interest lay in remaining good soldiers.

Jerphanion, in imagination, wandered on and on, over many miles of country, always at the head of his band, of the men who, in the old war days, had been of his company. Neighbouring troops might, perhaps, cohere in still larger formations; some general, for instance, might put himself at the head of a division or even of an army, and so set forth to look for adventure. But it was unlikely to happen often thus. The generals in this war had lived too far from their men in that distant zone where suffering had tended to resolve itself into statistics, and battles to become no more than accumulations of reports. But however that might be, he, Jerphanion, would have set out with his company, with Fabre's probably added. He would be responsible to nobody but himself. After a lengthened odyssey, a time of wandering and adventure, a struggle against many temptations to settle somewhere on the way, he would bring his faithful followers at last to the land he knew well, the land of his birth and heritage. He would choose it partly, no doubt, because it was his own, but partly too because he knew its ways and could deal there successfully with competition, could hold for ever what his sword should win. There would be an initial period, long and dangerous, in which he would have to establish his authority, put it beyond challenge, overcome resistance and assaults from without, counter discontent and slackness from within. The great days of feudalism would come later. First there must be the years of migration and of settlement. For that reason, instead of taking possession at once of Saint-Julien-Chapteuil, which lay at the centre of the circling hills, he would occupy the forest of Meygal, with its fine defensive possibilities, and would organize it. To organize a place so situated would be child's play for men who had dug trenches and communications so often in the most unpromising circumstances. Nor would life in a forest be any hardship for them, since they would have all the time they needed for the construction of huts and comfortable shelters…for there would be no need to bother about shells. Caverns would have to be constructed in the rocks for the storage of what ammunition remained to them. The problem of ammunition would be difficult. It would have to be used with the greatest economy.

The establishment of outlying posts at Saint-Julien and elsewhere would present no difficulties. He knew already the villages he would pick for the purpose. The population would be treated as gently as possible, and friendly relations ensured. The former dwellers on the land would soon come to realize that these armed men would protect them from far more dangerous incursions, and they would derive confidence from the knowledge that the leader was native to their soil. Odette? She must come with them, for life without her was, for Jerphanion, inconceivable. The situation might become rather delicate; it must not be allowed to establish a precedent. Not, of course, that anyone would dare to see in it an infraction of the war-band's self-established rule. The lord's wife is the lord's wife. The men could satisfy their amorous propensities with the local women; that would be nobody's business but their own. After all those years of war, there would be no lack of unattached females.

The thought of his uncle Crouziols, known as Pierre de Lherm, took shape for a moment in Jerphanion's mind. Had his uncle been there before him, his nephew would never for a moment have dreamed of confiding to him such a fantasy. But so uncontrolled are the workings of the imagination that, in some odd way, it did but carry further another fantasy with which that same uncle had played one morning while he gathered sticks in his wood of Bès.

What most impressed itself on Jerphanion, as he lay with his eyes closed wooing sleep, was the marvellous richness of his dream. Detail after detail emerged into his consciousness. Problem after problem arose which it would need long hours to resolve. Episodes sprouted like buds from the main stem of his invention. He was free, if he liked, to go over the whole ground again from the beginning, or to concentrate on some particular part of its complexity. But somehow, no matter what horrors the actual war might have in keeping for the future, the dream insisted on remaining probable, convincing. So convincing, indeed, was the illusion it induced that, short of opening his eyes, he could not have said for certain whether he was lying in a chalk cave of Champagne or in a rocky strong-point of Meygal.

CHAPTER NINE

Clanricard at Vauquois

Clanricard…card card card card,
Call for what you want at the bar, bar, bar!
(to the tune of *Here Comes the Sergeant Major*)

It was only that ass Norestier (popularly known as Norestance) at one of his everlasting jokes. No offence meant, of course—he'd just as soon have substituted his own name when food was in the offing, making a jest of the remarkable size of his appetite:

> *Norestance… tance tance tance tance,*
> *One can see it's meant for you at a glance…etc.*

But somehow one's no more in the mood for that kind of childish facetiousness at meal-time than one is at reveille after a night in a ditch.

Clanricard straightened himself, got up from his bed-board, shook off the straw—odds and ends of old brown straw—that was sticking to him, buttoned his overcoat, fastened his belt, put on his helmet, was careful not to forget his gloves (he'd probably take them off again in a minute, but they were necessary to his moral comfort), and, bending double and tripping as usual on the same step of the short stairway, emerged from Eastern Tunnel.

He refused to let his mind work—just as one makes frantic efforts not to notice when the dentist starts in with his drill. He took a great gulp of the cold dawn air, and felt at once as though he had swallowed a mouthful of alcohol. The pure freshness seemed suddenly such a new thing that, for the moment, it was almost unpleasant (it didn't do to think too much of what the breeze had touched on its way hither!). He felt slightly sick. He reflected that a couple of mouthfuls of hot coffee would make all the difference to these early starts.

It ought not to tax his ingenuity too far to have some always ready. Easy to have a thermos handy, and he could share it with Norestier and the N.C.O. on duty. He fumbled in his overcoat pocket for a bar of chocolate and broke off a piece.

Not a sound from the Cheppy gun, the Boche's own particular pet, though it was about the time it usually woke up. The Cheppy gun kept regular hours, rather like an early-rising office-worker. Its fondness for method, its scrupulous attention to duty, always took the form of a "morning offering" made at the expense of the first man who put in an appearance in Eastern Alley. Had it occurred to Clanricard that the Cheppy gun was not yet ready, he would have taken Eastern Alley on his way out, and thus have avoided having to use it on the road back.

Suddenly it occurred to him that he couldn't feel his pipe in his pocket. He slapped himself all over. He had forgotten it. Like everyone else he had become a pipe-smoker, and his pipe—a light-coloured, speckled, and expensive English brier which Mathilde had sent him—was one of his most highly prized possessions. Could he have lost it? Surely not, and then, Heaven be praised, he remembered. It was in the haversack which he used as a pillow. He had been smoking it just before he fell asleep, and had slipped it into a corner of the haversack.

He retraced his footsteps, lifted the ground-sheet which hung over the entrance to the dug-out—an old tarpaulin inherited from God knows where, probably some old battalion limber—and came to a full stop as though he had run his head against a wall. Impossible to find words strong enough to describe the atmosphere down there. It stood up like something solid through which he'd got to force a way: "thick enough to cut with a knife." Every kind of foul vapour, everything least acceptable to nose and lungs, seemed to have been rolled and churned together into a substance just not heavy enough to clutch with his hands, yet impossible to designate as air. There was something of every kind in it—bad breath, wind, the smell of wet dog; reminders of a policeman's boots, of stale tobacco; even of the kind of fried-fish shop one comes across in the slums, and traces of suicide by charcoal fumes.

How could he have slept hour after hour with his living body sunk in this stagnant, rotting medium?

The gentle Clanricard felt the most outrageous oaths rise to his lips. He envied men who could invent violent obscenities on the spur of the moment. They would have eased his temper. As it was, he had to content himself with muttering: "Like the stink of a whore-house!" He fell back a pace, faced towards the outside, still keeping the ground-sheet lifted in his hand, took a deep breath of air, and then, compressing his lips and holding his nose, quickly ran down and across to where his bed stood, being careful to leave the curtain at the door as wide open as possible. He felt for his pipe and found it, keeping himself meanwhile, like a diver, from breathing, heard a voice say: "Who's the damn fool who's left the door open?" and once more hurried up to ground level.

He turned to the left. For the moment the rain was scarcely noticeable, but it must have been coming down hard all night, to judge from the greyish-brown mud which covered the bottom of the trench to a depth of several inches with a sort of glutinous sauce. Trench indeed!—the word, implying, as it did, a certain amount of expenditure of human labour, was hardly applicable to the zigzag track, the featureless pathway through a world of chaos, along which he now had to walk.

The only thing about it that in any way resembled a field-work was its serpentine nature and the fact that when a man of normal height stood in it with his feet sunk in the slime, his head was, except in places, slightly below the average ground level of the nameless accumulation of rubbish through which he made his way.

Refuse-heap, house-wrecker's yard, cesspool, common sewer…the place had something of all of them rolled together into a single entity and carried to its highest power. It stood out from the surrounding country like a truncated hill, and the visitor could not have helped wondering how, suppose the task to have been necessary, such an eminence could have been reconstituted from the bottom up. It would have been no easy job; the only possible solution would have been to imagine some megalomaniac, some slum-bred Nero, taking it in hand....He must have set men to work demolishing hundreds of shanties, with all the wretched sticks of furniture they contained, and sweeping the rubbish together into a heap mixed with strands of barbed wire from back yards and the iron frames of garden gates. Here and there in the course of their labours they must have torn down several houses of a more permanent type—stone, brick, rubble, plaster—two or three floors high, which as they fell had spewed forth their intestines of rusty metal and rotting planks. The whole, masonry and all, had then been raked together. To this had been added the contents of a few junk-stalls looted from a neighbouring fair, preferably those that specialized in weapons of every kind—bayonets, belt-buckles, rifle-barrels minus their stocks. From this material a huge mound of refuse had been raised. Still fearful of overlooking anything, its creators had added a fair-sized section of the Saint-Ouen cemetery, being careful to see that the trench should have a representative display of all there was—family tombs, thirty-year-old vaults, modest middle-class monuments, and paupers' graves still packed with corpses—an attention which had added to the mound, till then too exclusively composed of beam-ends, tarred paper, packing-cases, and other lightweight stuff, a few nobler elements, such as fine hewn stones gone green with age, heavy flagstones, lengths of wrought iron and steel, decorative metalwork, not forgetting a few examples of human bones and of bodies in that intermediate state of decomposition anterior to the skeleton stage, which, for all their pulpy, fluid state, still bulked large in the general scene. The whole conglomeration had then been gone over again and piled anew. That done, the result had been harrowed with a sort of giant's plough or mechanical excavator. Great fissures, drawn anyhow, had made their appearance, diversified with odd heaps and projections, a bewildered chaos of dilapidation which gave a kind of cross-section of all the combined wealth of material which had gone to make the whole. Various odds and ends projecting from the earth walls touched the passer-by no matter how eagerly he strove to avoid them: the top of a stake, the lip of a mess-tin, a scrap of leather, the neck of a bottle, the handle of a bayonet, a steel spike stuck crazily in a beam. Crowds of sacks there were too, in every kind of position, packed tight with something that was soft and black, stubby, paunchy sacks, puckered and crammed to bursting. At the last moment, just as the final touch had been given to the huge erection, a convoy of lorries filled with bags of manure must have been driven up to just beyond the "cemetery zone" and there overturned.

The only thing missing from this classic assortment of sewage-farm leavings was a chamber-pot. No single chamber-pot displayed its rounded paunch nor gaped with broken maw. But there were plenty of latrine pails, some showing signs of recent use. Paper soiled in no ambiguous fashion, fluttered above narrow excavations at the bottom of which was heaped a browner filth, while here and there, between two stones set high in the trench wall, oozed a trickle of black excrement, coming God knows whence, which the sun was no longer hot enough to dry, but which the swollen flies still found eminently to their taste.

Yes, the sewage was still fresh and living, fresh too the graveyard, and, in a sense, living too. Let but the mind dwell on the thought of it, and the smell, here faint, there dense and obsessive, became a permanent feature of the place. And it was difficult to remain detached where, at one point in the trench wall, a human hand stuck out, a thin sheath of black and sticky flesh—the colour of black flies—that barely hid the bone beneath, projecting from a torn coat-sleeve.

The hand had been there during the battalion's last stay in the sector, but then it had been an ordinary hand and of quite a different colour: whitish, like a dead and drooping flower. It was not a large object, but it was horribly suggestive. As one looked, one realized that the ploughshare turning up the mountainous rubbish-heap must have struck many such, and it was borne in on one that to walk here was like walking through the dense thickness of a vast pudding concocted of corpses.

The place appeared in the communiqués as the Butte de Vauquois. Clanricard had a temperamental dislike of exaggeration. His imagination was mild. He was not one of those men who, the better to face a hideous sight, conjure up in thought something three times as bad, finding in the exercise a certain comfort, since thus they are themselves the creators of what they fear. But neither was he of those who hide the truth behind a veil of foolish optimism and lying thoughts. Had the place been moderately depressing, Clanricard would have been perfectly contented (very little satisfied him) to regard it as moderately depressing. But the Butte de Vauquois was not moderately depressing. It was intolerable.

He had had experience—alas, too seldom!—of other sectors of the front. He had contemplated, with no weakening of his sense of indignation and of bitterness, the spectacle of a war which he would find no less hateful in ten years' time than he did now, assuming that it lasted ten years and that he was there to see it. But what he said to himself was: "It is as hateful as only war can be. It is not easy to see how it could very well be less hateful."

He was surprised sometimes to find himself regarding with a certain equanimity this return of the human spirit to the primitive conditions of the early world. "These hours of wakeful slumber in the open air, curled at the bottom of a hole smelling of earth and growing things. This sudden waking to a world of green leaves. This learning how to tell, from the call of birds, whether the clouds are messengers of rain or sun. This gathering of twigs to make a fire for coffee.…"

On the other hand, this Butte! This heap of ruins stuffed with dead men's bones!

Besides, there was no excuse. He knew, of course, the official version: "Strategic position of the greatest importance. Wide field of view over the surrounding country—all proved beyond doubt by the obstinacy with which the enemy has disputed its possession."

Which, if it proved anything, proved only that the enemy was as idiotic as we were ourselves. The strategic argument might have been valid once, but not now. Both sides clung to the position, nose to nose. It could be of no conceivable value to either save as a factory of death. If, by some miracle, and at the cost of enormous losses, one of the two adversaries should succeed in loosening the other's hold upon it, the victory would be but fleeting. The Butte, swept by every battery within a radius of five miles, a famous target for all the gunners of the vicinity, would be smashed to pieces by shells of all imaginable sizes. As things were at present, it was to some extent protected by the very nearness of the enemy lines. The Germans thought twice before sending over heavy stuff which, as like as not, would fall among their own men. Mutual destruction was carried out as far as possible at short range. The two savage beasts, cooped in the same cage, confined their activities to killing one another with bombs, trench-mortars, and mines.

The sensible thing would have been for both sides to give up the place simultaneously and withdraw; by a tacit agreement to leave the cursed spot as neutral ground. The instrumentalists in this symphony of death would have welcomed such a decision, but the conductors had grown to regard the place as a symbol of prestige.

Here and there in the chaotic maze sentries flattened themselves against the trench wall to let the officer pass. He said a few words to each, sometimes no more than a brief "Good morning," while sometimes he said nothing, but contented himself with giving them a friendly pat on the shoulder.

With Bruneau, who was a Parisian of the 11th arrondissement, he had a short conversation:

"How goes it? Not too wet?…Anything to report?"

"They sent over two or three minnies an hour back on White Knob. Didn't you hear 'em, sir?"

"No, I was asleep."

"Oh!" replied Bruneau good-naturedly, as though seeking an excuse for the other's inattention; "they weren't very loud….The wind wouldn't have carried the noise. It's blowing from the north this morning. That's why it's not raining harder."

Since he had come to the front, the fellow had developed
the weather wisdom of a peasant. To tell the sky had become
a real comfort to him, an occupation for the mind. He knew,
for instance, that at this season of the year a wind from the
west or south would have brought a more violent downpour.

"It's a sort of a sea mist," he added; "one doesn't feel it much
here, but in the Argonne it must be dripping off the trees like
the devil!…What's odd, in a way, is that it isn't colder."

Clanricard had turned his head to take a look at White
Knob and the Black Wood—names that had become mytho-
logical for the men in the Vauquois sector. From where he
stood one could see them almost too clearly; in fact, one
could see little else.

He thought of West Vauquois—where too he had been
often, for his sins!—of a spot lying beyond Western Alley, which
commanded a view over Boureuilles and the whole plain of
the Aire, a wide stretch of country with blue distances, and very
lovely. It was better than where they were now, for here White
Knob and the Black Wood were ever at their backs, seeming to
spur them on, to chide them for not going forward faster to
meet destruction; while on the flank they had always the wood
of Cheppy with its irking swarm of shells.…Fancy comparing
different parts of Vauquois and preferring one to another!
Things must have come to a pretty pass!

He asked Bruneau for news of the Cheppy gun (for thus
they had agreed to call it. Actually, this other Vauquois myth,
this plaguing demon, would be found, on examination, to
resolve itself into a plurality of imps, a travelling circus of
show guns). Apparently it had shown no signs of life as yet.

Clanricard continued his round, exchanging an occasional
word with the men, bending double to pass under bridges,
skirting the lips of craters, and making mental notes of places
where the poor excuses for parapet and loop-hole in this lost
land must at all costs be repaired. Now and then the sound of
rifle-fire, or of a distant gun, came to his ears. But nothing
much was happening; too little, perhaps, for this cursed
Vauquois, where not even peace and quiet could bear a smiling face.

When he had finished his tour, after a brief visit to Eastern Alley, where the Cheppy gun had so far left no unwelcome signs of its activity, he stopped in a corner that was rather less muddy, rather less hideous, than its neighbours, about twenty yards from one of the entrances to his dug-out, produced his pipe, stuffed the bowl with tobacco, lit it, and, with his back against the trench wall and his left foot resting on a large stone that served him for a stool, started to smoke, smiling to himself at the thought that his attitude would be interpreted (if they could see it) by the civilian fire-eaters away back at the rear as symbolic of the "thoughtful poilu."

Suddenly he felt a shock. There could be no doubt of its significance. Ten seconds were enough for him to identify it. It seemed to strike from all sides at once at his sense of equilibrium. Had it come from left or right, from in front or from behind? Difficult to be sure. He felt as though he had been shaken to the roots of his being, as though there were no stable point left in his universe, as though he were a solid mass of liquid flung into the trench by someone standing with a pail on the top of the parapet. Such a shock would be commonplace for people living in a country subject to earthquakes, but for the men of Vauquois it meant something out of the ordinary. It was followed, almost at once (and it was this that made it so characteristic) by a deep, reverberating rumble that appeared to reach his senses through the medium of the shuddering earth around and ended, not by dwindling away into silence, but by a stifled roar, like a thunder-clap deep in the bowels of the earth. Hard on its heels came other noises of creaks and crashes, of things falling to ruin that, in this hell of ruin, remained yet to be broken, of things thudding to the ground, hard things, soft things, things in a rain of atomized destruction; great solid lumps and tinkling fragments. He thought what he might have seen had he been better placed for seeing. But, for the moment, there was nothing for his eyes to note.

He rushed towards the dug-out. As he ran, stones and rubbish were falling all around. He was conscious of a wave of odour, not particularly unpleasant, made up of the smells of flint, acetylene, and leaf mould (anything was better than the stench of death and sewage). He elbowed his way past two sentries. Before he could lift the curtain over the entry it was lifted from within. Sergeant Vuiel stood before him, his eyes heavy with sleep, a dazed look on his face.

"What's happened, sir?"

Clanricard made no reply, but ran down two steps and shouted into the dug-out:

"Mine! Turn out! They'll attack in a minute. Issue grenades!"

"All right, all right," said Norestier with a weary yawn; "we all know it's a mine."

"Look after the grenades, then. I'm going up to the front line."

There was a heavy "boom"; then another, of the sort that Norestier, for obscure reasons, had christened "wardrobes." Trench-mortars starting. At the same moment the Cheppy gun began firing at top speed. Clanricard started up Eastern Alley, going as hard as the mud would let him. He banged his shoulder hard against a piece of projecting rock and, a second later, almost broke his ankle on a piece of knife-rest wire half hidden in the mud. But he was relieved to find that when one of the Cheppy gun's light shells burst four paces behind him, not a single splinter came his way, thanks to a bend in the trench. Away on his left he could hear the banging of a number of bombs, mingled with a few rifle-shots and the rattle of machine-guns. Still on the left, but farther down the slope, a few aerial torpedoes began to fall with a great deal of noise, apparently somewhere near Middle Alley. In the fire trench he found about ten men banging away more or less at random. Each time that a trench-mortar shell or aerial torpedo rose swishing into the air, they flattened themselves against the parapet.

"Do you know where the mine went up?"

"Over by the church, sir. I saw the stuff flying."

The speaker added in a superior tone:

"But it wasn't a very big one."

"All the same, they're attacking."

"So they say, but not on our front."

On "our front," in fact, no movement could be discerned in the enemy's line. For the moment, at least, there was a marked absence of either bombs or rifle-fire.

Over on the left a brisk action seemed to be in progress, but it was difficult to make out details. "If we're wanted," thought Clanricard, "we shall get orders from Battalion H.Q. Whatever fighting's going on must be round the crater, whether it's big or little."

He went as far as the last fire-bay. Through a loop-hole which faced east towards the re-entrant angle made by the French line, just where it was cut by what once had been the rue des Juifs, he got a hurried glimpse of a few German soldiers clambering up a bank and throwing grenades as they went. They must have come from the enemy positions known locally as the "trenches east of the church." There was a great deal of noise and a pungent smell of battle which was superimposed on the general smell of a wrecked slum, though it did not entirely smother it.

Clanricard went back to his men. To the first two he said:

"Quick. Man those two loop-holes. At those fellows jumping about out there, rapid fire! Jump to it, but aim carefully."

To the next two:

"Keep on passing clips up to your pals. Give 'em your own. Let 'em have your rifles when theirs get too hot. Yes, that's the best way; pass up your rifles ready loaded."

To the rest he said:

"Man the loop-holes, and keep your rifles ready. And don't lose sight of the Boche trenches opposite. Fire at the slightest movement. Got plenty of grenades? Good. Keep 'em for when they start coming over. I'll get some more up for you. But don't waste 'em."

He was afraid that the men might get rattled and throw their grenades too soon in the excitement of the moment, without waiting for the Boches to come within range. He set himself to provide an outlet for their impatience.

"Take a pot at their front line now and again, just to let 'em see we're up and doing. But not more than one a minute.

Those are your orders."

A sergeant appeared. Clanricard repeated his instructions; then:

"I'll just go and see whether the machine-gunners can enfilade the Boches as they come over on the left."

"They can't, sir. I've just come from there. They'll have to be moved."

"Not worth it."

"Jerry'd be over before you'd got 'em fixed."

"Yes. What are they doing with those grenades? They're the hell of a time getting 'em."

As he spoke, a number of men arrived carrying haversacks filled with grenades. Clanricard said to the sergeant:

"Carry on here. I must go and see whether there are any orders from the battalion."

One of the men who had just come up overheard what he said and chipped in:

"There weren't any, sir, when we started away with the grenades. But there's some wounded."

"Our fellows?"

"Yes, sir; two."

"Serious?"

"Pretty bad."

"Who are they?"

"Chap called Hesquin, sir, and Corporal Weinmann."

"Thanks; I'll go and have a look."

He started off along Eastern Alley. The Cheppy gun was firing now at a point much lower down the slope, obviously to stop reinforcements which could be seen, or were assumed to be, moving up from Cigalerie Farm. Oh well, it was all in the day's work. Too far to go round.

He got through without trouble. The "wardrobes" and other stuff were keeping up a merry din between the church and Central Alley. The latter spot was, for the moment, an island of calm surrounded—at no more than a hundred and fifty yards' distance—by pandemonium. It was odd that, in such circumstances, one should be aware—and the difference was not imaginary—of this tiny, fragile oasis of peace all around.

His first action on reaching the dug-out was to find out whether anything had come from the battalion. Orders had just arrived. The line was to be kept fully manned, but a small detachment with grenades was to be sent to the northern end of Cigalerie Farm Alley to support the men of the 7th in case they had to withdraw. Lieutenant Norestier had just started with the equivalent of a section.

He made inquiries about Weinmann and Hesquin. They were still there, lying on stretchers, ready to be moved. But they couldn't be got down the line while the flank of the Butte was under such heavy fire.

They had been wounded by an aerial torpedo, or, more precisely, by the effects of its explosion. The end of the sap where they happened to be, at the western extremity of the sector, had collapsed on top of them. Weinmann bore few outward signs of injury, but he was more or less in a coma. He had been badly bruised, and a beam had fallen across his back. It seemed likely that his spine had been broken.

Hesquin's wound was far more horrible: his left cheek had been carried away, the left side of his jaw fractured, and the upper part of his face so torn that his eye appeared to be on the point of falling out of its socket. He had lost a lot of blood, and was in considerable pain. But he was still conscious. The orderly seemed to think he might recover. What worried Clanricard was the thought that this frightful wound, which had gone so deep and lacerated so much flesh, had been made not by a comparatively clean shell-splinter, but by a fragment of dirty stone, and that the open gash had been plentifully sprinkled with rubbish and infected dirt. He was assured that the injury had been thoroughly washed, and that the bleeding had carried off a good deal of the poison. But his mind was far from being at ease. He would have given a lot if the wretched Hesquin, whose hand he took with a smile of affection, could have been got down to the dressing-station at once, properly attended to, and given an anti-tetanus injection.

He received the impression that the noise outside was diminishing in intensity. A runner arrived with a report that the attack seemed to have been held. The Boches had withdrawn to their own lines, though possession of the mine-crater was still in dispute. But it was small and didn't matter much.

"Were many of the 7th killed when the mine went up?" Clanricard asked.

"They don't know yet, sir. They've dug out two dead so far. But there are three or four fellows still underneath whom they can't get at. Pretty rough luck, that!…"

Clanricard had a momentary feeling of joy to think that the Butte de Vauquois—ridiculous and hateful though it might be—had not, this time at least, fallen into the enemy's hands.

CHAPTER TEN

Jerphanion's Letter to Odette:
Attila; Shock Troops

For the last few days I have been terribly lazy, or rather I have been preoccupied in a way that, alas, you know only too well. But this time you are going to have a really long letter. We are out in rest billets at B. Our cantonment is fairly comfortable. My men live in two huge barns, one belonging to a farm where I have managed to find a room. I have it entirely to myself, which is very important. To all intents and purposes we are never under fire. At this distance from the front one's liable to get shells of only the heaviest calibre, and it's most unlikely that they'll fall on our particular little cabbage patch. The risk is minute, though not entirely non-existent. The roof of my No. 2 barn shows traces of having been hit by a shell which must have done a good deal of damage. But that sort of thing we regard here more or less in the light of an accident.

The last stay in the line wasn't too bad. I had only one man killed (it was partly his own fault) and six wounded, four of them slightly. What most got us down, as I told you in my Tuesday's letter, were the working parties (putting up wire, knife-rests, etc.). The targets we offered must have been terribly tempting to the enemy; it's always as well to imagine oneself in his place. And then, you see, it's always frightfully hard to keep the men from uselessly worrying the chaps opposite whenever they get the chance, and producing retaliation. But the soldier's mind seems incapable of rational argument. He never stops grousing about the piecemeal dangers that beset him when the front's calm, but still less can he resist the chance of taking a pot-shot, as he says, at the other fellows when he sees them wandering about with canvas buckets or other implements of a similarly peaceable nature. (That's a bad example, because it so happens that on this bit of front no one moves in daylight over the top. But you understand what I mean.)

My trench-mortar section have been giving me the worst trouble. Thank Heaven, there's every likelihood of my getting rid of them soon. They are being grouped into regular batteries under the command of an artillery officer. I only hope he won't find them too big a handful. Meanwhile, it's not the slightest use my protesting. "The Boche is lying low," I say. "If you start tickling him, he's bound to answer back. Your weapon is designed for the express purpose of demolishing obstacles preparatory to an assault, or of helping to break up an enemy attack. Keep it till it's wanted." But they can always find some excuse for having fired. "There was obviously something doing over there, sir; they were getting ready to have a knock at us. There was no time to warn you; as you see, we've stopped their little game." Or, if they do warn me of their intentions, it's in some such words as these: "We can't let them finish that strong-point, sir, just as they like. Take my word for it, sir, they're working at something pretty big, with emplacements and all, a bit to the rear, between point 451 and 450....Just take a squint through your glasses, sir....What a chance!..." What can I say to talk like that? They'd only hold me responsible the next time some wretched machine-gun opened up from that direction and happened to kill one of our men....(They don't mind nearly so much about being the indirect cause of a great many more men being killed in the course of a retaliation. It's the same sort of reasoning as that of the High Command or of the politicians when confront-ed with certain "historic" responsibilities.) I suspect too that my second lieutenant Cotin gives them orders on the sly, or at least eggs them on....If I try to interfere, I merely get the reputation of being an inefficient officer for my pains. My doctrine of leaving well alone, you see, is rather heretical. The Staff sees things in the same light as the trench-mortar men. They call it "maintaining moral ascendancy." Not that they care two hoots about moral ascendancy, but they adore their wretched little mortar, which is really a bit of old iron no bigger than a toy. They regard me as the ill-tempered old codger who tries to stop them playing with it. You ought to see them. They get four or five of my chaps round the miserable thing and then start explaining, arguing, and showing how the damned contraption works. And so it goes on. They're never really happy until they have sent a shell over just for luck. That they get a hell of a lot back doesn't seem to worry them. They regard the two operations as entirely disconnected, as belonging to two different worlds. One of the most extraordinary things here in the trenches is the apparent inability of the soldier to imagine any connexion between the tiny movement necessary to release a projectile—whether it's a single bullet, a machine-gun belt, or a trench-mortar shell—a movement that's usually the result of sheer boredom or momentary nerves, and the effect caused at the other end of the trajectory in the shape of smashed heads or torn bodies. If he does let his imagination work, he certainly doesn't apply the results to himself. The torn bodies, being Boche, seem to him about as important as partridges or rabbits. They never really put two and two together. Oh, I know I'm being pretty obvious. If mankind in general could put two and two together, there'd be no more war.

At first sight this village of Baconnes is dull enough, in all conscience. It lies on the outskirts of the great camp of Châlons, that militarized Sahara, which I think must be one of the foulest places on the face of the earth. Even in peacetime merely to look at its pebbles and its stunted pines was to conjure up the vision of war. As things are today it makes even the front seem worse than it is by the picture it gives of what the country behind, to a depth of ten miles or so, looks like when the military have started in to organize things in preparation for an endless state of hostilities.

I've got to know the curé of Baconnes, or rather a curé who has to serve several parishes of which Baconnes is one, a jovial, sharp-witted man who sets off on a bicycle to make the round of his priestly sector and apparently takes no notice whatever of the shells he happens to meet with on the way.

He told me an extraordinary thing about the place. It seems that the village owes its origins to a portion of Attila's army which became separated from the main body after the rout of Châlons, and, not knowing where to go, happened on this spot, dug in, and stayed here. They intermarried with the inhabitants, and for centuries appear to have had scarcely anything to do with their neighbours, who in early days must have been few and far between. The curé assures me that they are of a perfectly distinct type, differing from other folk particularly in their temper and mental outlook. There seems to be a quite definite Baconnes mentality. I've been trying to discover its peculiarities. "They're a set of outrageous rogues," says the curé, "but very amusing. Their sense of fun is aggressive and extremely whimsical. They're always ready to play practical jokes on anyone." "Are you on good terms with them?" "Excellent." "Are they religious-minded?" "Not the least little bit. Even in the piping times of peace I never used to get more than five to come to Mass. But, for all that, they're as friendly as possible and always up to a bit of fun."

He showed me an earthwork, a mysterious sort of erection, which runs along the whole of one side of the village. It appears that this is still called "Attila's Wall," and has been for a long time. Originally it surrounded the whole site and was the limit of the primitive settlement. The curé maintains that the whole subject has been gone into by local antiquarians and established as historical fact.

I like the story. I study the faces of the few remaining inhabitants in the hope of discovering a few Mongoloid characteristics. So far, I must admit, the results of my investigation are few. But doubtless the climate has had an effect in the course of centuries....I've tried, too, to pick up a few examples of the Baconnes temperament. But circumstances are not very favourable to that kind of work. I amuse myself by imagining Attila's men in their modern guise—sly, caustic, essentially irreligious, talkative, and humorous, something half-way between Swift and Voltaire. Incidents of that kind must certainly have occurred here and there during the great migrations and tribal wars. Why not here? Once you admit the premise,

which is that the place was abnormally isolated—it's sufficiently cut off today, so what must it have been fifteen hundred years ago?—the rest follows with perfect plausibility.

You remember Caulet's wonderful theory about the
Beauce? I often find myself thinking of it. The curé's story
would fit in with it very well. I must tell him about it when
next we meet. By the way, what's happened to him? Always
being put back by medical boards, I suppose.

For the time being we're playing the part of Attila's army
here. It is quite possible that some day—if another period of
historic catastrophes really does descend upon the world—my
own company, an isolated, wandering fragment, may in their
turn settle down somewhere and found a village that will per-
petuate itself down the centuries. Don't worry. If that ever
happens, I'll see that you're in it too.

. . . .

There's a rumour going round—what we call here a
"kitchen draught." Whether it's false or true I don't know. In
any case, don't breathe a word to a soul. (As a matter of fact
it has been confirmed by Lieutenant X, you know whom I
mean, the one with an uncle in high places.)

It seems that the big-wigs are planning a change of method.
No more offensives until next year. Some time in the first
four months of '16 a really big-scale attack, but carried out in
a new way. I'll spare you the details. The essential point is the
employment of "shock troops." They don't want any longer to
carry out the break-through with ordinary formations made
up of whatever troops happen to be available, which is tanta-
mount to saying troops of average, or less than average, value
in discipline, training, morale, and individual courage, etc.
That's what's always been done hitherto, and it explains why
results have always fallen so far below the efforts made. The
new idea—not a bad one either, it seems to me, looked at
from a purely "war" point of view—is to build up a certain
number of units of all arms, which shall be marked by a high
degree of excellence. This will have to be done first by a careful picking of men and regiments, next by a period of highly
specialized training (something quite different from the tradi-

tional and half-alive idiocies with which our rest periods out of the line are made hideous). Only think what might be done with a regiment composed entirely of men who were intelligent, resourceful, brave, and trained in the use of the rifle, led by N.C.O.'s who were neither slackers nor bullies, and commanded by officers not one of whom would be a superannuated dodderer or a red-faced major. Think what such a body of men might become after even two months, if, instead of being "drilled" in the bad sense of the word, they were put through a series of intelligent experiments having some real relation to the conditions of modern warfare and to the equipment which is being used today. Suppose, too, that the men were treated decently, like a team of athletes instead of a load of potatoes for ever being banged about and irritated when they aren't left to bore themselves sick. A regiment I said, but what about a division?… I am quite convinced that a division of such quality would achieve more than three ordinary ones, might even win quite amazing successes, because to break the enemy front with certainty at a single point would be something entirely different from failing to break it at three points simultaneously.

And now about what concerns me personally. These shock troops will need officer instructors. These, presumably, will be best found among men of a certain level of intelligence who are capable of thinking about the war as they have seen it at close quarters. It looks as though, at first anyhow, there will not be an excess of candidates for the job. The attractions of the rear are not sufficient to overcome the unpleasing implications of the words "shock troops." At any rate, the difficulty is going to be to find the right sort of candidate. There are very few professional soldiers of the right sort to be found now among the junior ranks. Most of them are either dead or out of their minds. Among the holders of temporary commissions there are plenty of daredevils who'd jump at the chance, but their general level of intelligence is not high. It would be no bad thing to have a few of them in the actual shock formations, but only after careful selection and intensive training. They'd be no use as instructors. Now do you see what I'm after?…Don't get frightened too soon. Shock troops aren't made in a day. They'll have to be provided for and formed into a permanent reserve. It'll be a sort of school. If an officer instructor shows real ability at his work, I'm pretty sure that the directors of the school will want to hang on to him. It'll be a way of keeping out of the line, with the advantage of being highly respectable and even noble. The longer I live this cursed life, the more inclined do I become to snatch at anything good that comes my way. If I can have three months away from trench-mortars and field-guns, if I can escape the winter mud of the line and sleep in conditions that are almost human, as I'm doing here, that's so much gained. Meanwhile things may happen, the unhoped-for occur. For when the world has been turned topsyturvy, nothing is impossible, not even good luck.

Naturally, my dear Odette, I shall do nothing about all this without your express permission. I trust your instinct in such matters. Think over what I have told you. There's no hurry. It's only too probable that the pundits at G.H.Q. will take a long time before they can make up their minds to anything of the sort, so long, in fact, that the whole plan may be blown sky-high by some action on the part of the enemy.

CHAPTER ELEVEN

General Duroure at Home

At each repetition, the lieutenant-colonel's gesture was the same. He took the thin oblong of paper between the thumb and index-finger of his left hand with an air of distaste as though he were handling something quite unimportant and rather grubby; glanced at it casually through his single eyeglass in order to commit its contents to memory; and, that done, allowed a few words to fall from his lips:

"Lepetit reports artillery fire on point 245. Getting worked up, as usual, before there's really any need. Hm…ah…suggests a slight straightening of the line on the ground that one of his trenches is enfiladed."

Or:

"A small raid on the extreme eastern flank of Despois's division. Several yards of trench lost. Will be retaken, he says, at dawn today. Hm…ah….Wants you to have that section of 155's moved at once from south of Hill 285 to a point southeast of Marrieux Wood."

As soon as they were done with, the messages were dropped gently on a slowly growing pile. At a certain point in the procedure, however, he picked up a sheet of paper rather larger in size than its predecessors and, this time, condescended to bring into action two fingers of each hand.

"Here's something from Marie's division. They've got into position at last. Liaison officer's car broke down. Excuse not good enough. Apart from that…hm, ah…nothing to report. General situation…hm….Enemy activity…hm…. Work done, patrols, etc…. Artillery, hm…number of shells expended, 1,320. The devil there were! Not much to show for it. Condition of troops, hm….Casualties…" The "hm" which followed hard on the word "casualties" showed by its inflexion that the total was—save the mark!—reasonable; more reasonable than that of the shells expended. "Report on enemy works....Hm...same old stuff...."

General Duroure listened while debating inwardly whether he should or should not eat the last piece of toast. He noticed that it was a cold day.

He looked at his watch. Gracious! twenty-five past seven. In another minute or so his orderly officer would be round with the horses.

How time did fly! He had got up at six precisely, and been washed, shaved, and dressed by six thirty. Not too bad. Then he'd wasted a quarter of an hour doing nothing in particular —waiting for Ponche to finish laying the table and bring in breakfast (devilishly slow mover, Ponche), watching the fire burn in the grate; waiting for Radigué, who'd explained his delay by saying he hadn't got all the telephone messages transcribed—truth was the fellow didn't like being hurried any more than he did himself. After that, he'd been through the reports that had come in during the night—nothing much in 'em as a rule—and dictated a few odds and ends of instructions.

The general rose, wiped his mouth, and shook his Chief of Staff by the hand.

"So long."

He went out of the dining-room with its air of old-fashioned, prosperous comfort and descended the front steps. Captain Cabillaud was there with the horses, and Vichard and Juste, the grooms.

They'd been thoughtful enough to send round both Poucette and Gnafron so that he could choose which he'd take out. He chose Poucette, who hadn't had a gallop for two days. Vichard led Gnafron back to the stables, making a detour by the lower boulevard in order to give him a walk.

The morning ride was a piece of solemn ritual. General Duroure considered it absolutely essential to his health of mind and body at times such as these when he had to shoulder such heavy responsibilities. As a colonel, and lecturer at the Staff College, he had had to content himself at this hour of the morning with a ride in a motor-bus. Horse exercise had become a necessity for him only since he had held the rank of general officer. He was sincerely convinced, however, that he had always adored horses. It would not have needed much to persuade him that he had always been a general officer.

On taking over a new command and inspecting the H.Q. left him by his predecessor, or the arrangements made for him by his own billeting officer, one of the first questions he asked—often the very first—was: "What accommodation is there for the horses?" The point took precedence in his mind of all others, if not in importance, at least in time.

"Where are they going to put the horses?"

"Where are they going to put me?" came later. He insisted on having large stables, easy to keep clean, where the grooms could be accommodated, and not too far from his own quarters.

On these morning rides he could gladly have dispensed with the presence of Captain Cabillaud, his aide, a chubby little reservist, beautifully turned out, his hair perfectly brushed, the son of a rich pottery-manufacturer, rolling in money, from all accounts, who had attained the rank of captain by God knows what ingenuities of wire-pulling, a typical example of the resplendent shirker, destined beyond doubt to be decorated with the Croix de Guerre, and entirely lacking in conversation. The phrase that came most naturally to his lips was: "Why, yes, sir; of course, sir," followed by a sort of innocent giggle. But he had been recommended for the post by a Minister, and had several relations among the higher ranks of the hierarchy. He might be a fool, but he'd got to be treated tactfully. Besides, there was the question of prestige to be considered. When one is (to all intents and purposes) an army commander, one can't go about without an officer in attendance. It impresses people with one's importance, makes the morning ride a piece of official routine, saves it from being merely a "pleasure party." Little things like that are important when it's a matter of keeping up the morale of the civilian population near the front.

If these morning rides were sacred, the return from them

was not less so. At nine thirty Duroure seated himself at his
desk and offered Radigué a chair. The room which served
him as an office had formerly been the smoking-room of the
house. Most of the furniture had been removed to fit it for its
new duties. Plain wooden shelves covered one of the walls,
while another had been cleared to make room for a number
of maps. Duroure would not budge from the room until midday. In addition to Radigué, whom he kept almost constantly
within call, he liked to have available, together or separately,
according to the needs of the moment, Radigué's assistant,
Major Clédinger, and the heads or seconds-in-command of
his three departments. It was during this morning session that
he went through the various communications from General
Headquarters. He read personally all the documents which
Radigué told him were essential, and similarly gave his attention to anything of particular importance that might have
turned up in the mass of communications received from the
formations of his command. That done, he dictated his own
orders to Radigué, who never hesitated to offer his views on
the matters in question. Radigué's disapproval was conveyed
by a rather more disgusted expression than usual, which his
chief found extremely irritating.

Towards the end of the morning he received any visitors
who might wish to see him—generals, heads of formations or
administrative services, whom he might have summoned,
who might have asked for an interview, or who, sometimes,
turned up unexpectedly. He tried, as far as possible, to refuse
nobody. He held the view that a great leader must be
approachable if he is to command the confidence of his subordinates. But he had made a rule that the interviews were to
be kept very short. The understanding was that they should all
be fitted in between eleven thirty and twelve, at which hour
the general sat down to the midday meal with the members
of his personal staff: Colonel Radigué, Major Clédinger, and
Captain Cabillaud. It was a matter of pride with Duroure that
he had managed to regulate his own life at the front, and, by
force of example, the lives of his whole staff, according to a
fixed time-table. Unerring punctuality he regarded as a chal-

lenge to circumstance and as a sort of heroic discipline. In old days, when he had thought about the next war and the part he would play in it—those days when he had referred in lyrical terms to such things as the "uninterrupted advance" and the "initial shock"—he had never for a moment anticipated the peaceful office life, the comfortable, bourgeois existence, which would fall to the lot of the senior commanders and their staffs. He had naturally been inclined to see in imagination the leader carried forward by the "uninterrupted advance" and personally controlling it.

But circumstances had decreed otherwise, and Duroure had submitted without even a backward glance at imagined glories. In adapting himself to the necessity of the times, he had done no more than the other officers of his rank. The only difference was that he had managed to introduce into the routine a gift for generalized enthusiasm peculiar to himself, a tendency to get excited about ideas—without questioning too closely their nature or worrying about how long he had held them.

He had brought his rather violent imagination to bear on the conditions of modern warfare. He saw quite clearly that it was an organism made up of quite different activities. There was the actual front line, a place characterized by surprise strokes, by primitive violence, by catastrophes confined within fairly localized limits, by, in short, a confused activity in which chance, the unexpected, and the incalculable necessarily played a considerable part. But behind that lay a zone marked by totally different features, the zone of "command," where the matter of prime importance was to know what was happening, to foresee and, as far as possible, to determine what should happen. This division of functions had assumed in his eyes a sort of natural grandeur. It resembled the processes of nature as seen in animal tissues. It was right that there should be no diminution in the feverish activity of the actual front, that routine should not be allowed to deaden the fierce urge of violence; it would have seemed fatal to him to allow officers or men to get into too regular habits, or to attach an exaggerated value to personal safety. But it was no less right and proper that command should be exercised under conditions assured of adequate protection, where disturbance—in other words, danger—had been reduced to a minimum. To collect and collate items of information, to organize, to foresee, to issue orders—these things belonged to the realm of the intellect and should be marked by an almost scientific detachment. No man can think in the heat of battle. The good administrator surrounds himself with peace and quiet in order that his mind may work clearly. A laboratory is a place of quiet efficiency; a scholar is a man of habit, a fanatic for routine and regularity. It was no use complaining of the conditions of modern war, no use cursing and swearing and saying: "What a hell of a job this is! How much happier I'd be marching at the head of my men!" That wasn't the way great leaders were made. One didn't become a great leader by grousing about having to lead a miserable, sedentary life, but by developing to the last degree of perfection the qualities of regularity and stability, of astronomic imperturbability and detachment which were the *sine qua non* of the commander's functions and must be as far removed as could be from the healthy violence of the trenches and the battlefield.

Duroure had made this theory of his the subject of a highly topical article which had appeared in the *Revue des Deux Mondes* on the 15th of September (shortly before the Champagne offensive) over the signature "General X...."

At midday Duroure sat down to a square meal consisting of hors d'oeuvres, two meat dishes, or one of fish and one of meat, plenty of green vegetables, cheese and fruit, with red and white burgundy and coffee. No spirits were served. Breakfast, though taken in the English fashion with eggs, bacon, jam, etc., on the advice of Mme. Duroure, was almost forgotten. Close on two hours of horseback riding give one an appetite, which a morning of office work does nothing to allay. Duroure had never been so well. Never, so far as his physical health went, had he enjoyed such a sensation of vigorous maturity, or felt himself functioning more smoothly. More than once when he had been in the back areas and heard some civilian, some woman, perhaps, condoling with those who had to put up with the hard life of the front, he had been on the point of saying: "Of course it's hard, but look at me. Have you ever seen me in better form?" Only a sort of shamefaced modesty had kept him silent. His superb health had even roused in him certain sexual desires. He recognized them with a certain amount of pleasure, though he made no attempt to satisfy them. Now, less than ever, would he wish to be guilty of infidelity to his wife. War, in his eyes, was a school of virtue. Besides, it wouldn't have been easy to manage discreetly. If sacrifices were necessary, it was essential that he should give the example of sacrifice, and one must always remember that the men in the trenches couldn't have a woman when the fancy took them.

Today at luncheon he was expecting two stranger guests: two deputies who were making a short tour of the line. Duroure was not particularly fond of politicians in any case, and these two were quite undistinguished, although, apparently, they were members of the Army Commission. He must, however, make them welcome. Since they had been forced on him, there was nothing for it but to be polite and make as good an impression on them as possible. An army commander (to all intents and purposes) is so much in the public eye that he can't ignore the movements of opinion, especially of parliamentary opinion. He might, too, in the course of conversation, be able to hint at certain views of his own which he hoped to see realized some day. It wouldn't be a bad thing to prepare the way for them in influential quarters.

The meal would be just as it always was; liqueurs would be served afterwards. Nor would it last a moment longer than usual. At one thirty precisely, to a roll of drums, the general would give the sign to rise from table. The deputies would feel flattered at having to comply with the rigorous discipline of the front areas. The general would say to them: "Are you coming with me, gentlemen?" and would make his daily round in the car, exactly as usual. This meant paying a visit to one of the sectors of his front. In the course of it he called on various headquarters, had a look at one of the heavy batteries, saw with his own eyes the progress that was being made with certain reserve systems. He inspected camps, "watched" resting troops at their training, had an occasional word with the men. He usually arranged, when time permitted (at this time of year darkness fell early), after looking in at a brigade or battalion H.Q., to go on foot as far as the front line. Nothing was better for the morale of the troops than to see the great man trudging through the mud, or peeping through a loop-hole in no way different from the one where some poor fellow had been killed a week earlier. He made use of these trips to the line to verify points raised at the morning conference. As a rule, he chose a spot at which the daily intelligence report had noted "slight enemy activity" or "all quiet"; not that he was afraid of danger, but because it would have been absurd to expose a life on which so many other lives depended, when the same moral effect could be obtained with less risk.

For today's visit, however, Duroure had chosen a rather more active sector. A subtle intention lay behind this decision. The activity in question consisted, for the moment, in an intermittent artillery duel at long range between two medium batteries, one German, the other French, each of which was trying to prevent the other from establishing itself in an advantageous position. The shells—about a hundred a day from either side—passed high above the trenches and had, so far, not interfered much with the back areas, since the batteries concerned had so far concentrated their fire pretty accurately on the emplacements occupied, on a reverse slope, by their opposite number. But on a visitor strange to such scenes the effect would be considerable. The noise of the discharge, the swish of the shells, the crash of the explosions, would be bound to give him the impression that he was at the very heart of a battle. According to information received, this change of courtesies between the two batteries took place mainly between eight and nine o'clock and about sunset. It was to be hoped that, today of all days, there would be no slackening of the customary duel. That would be too disappointing.

There was a trace of mischief in Duroure's attitude towards

the two civilian politicians whom he had to cart round with him. They should see that a tour of the front was rather more than an amusing game. But the great thing was that they should take back with them a favourable impression of the way in which he, Duroure, carried out his duties. It might be—to judge by what one heard—that there were commanders who remained too constantly at a distance from personal danger. So much the worse for them if their behaviour suffered from comparison with his own. His theory that a general's job must be done methodically and in comparative peace did not forbid an occasional visit to the battle zone. But these visits must be part of the routine of his life, a fulfilment, not an infringement, of a self-imposed discipline.

This daily tour, which in October had lasted four and a half hours, had been reduced to four now that the days were shorter. It was made with two cars, to guard against the danger of a breakdown. They returned to H.Q. about half past five—that is to say, after dark. Occasionally an air-raid warning complicated matters, because it meant driving without lights. Up till now the general had never been more than ten minutes late, and had never driven at more than fifty miles an hour. A cup of tea was always waiting for him with a piece of one of Molard's, the confectioner's, cakes. After inquiring about any important communications which might have come in since midday, and looking over certain orders the drafts for which he had dictated that morning, he spent the time until half past seven reading the newspapers and any other information there might be about activity on the rest of the front and in the Allied sectors. At seven thirty he dined with his usual companions. The period from eight thirty to nine was given up to casual conversation by the fire in the big drawing-room. This interval was regarded as sacred to relaxation. The general made a point of being genial and of encouraging his staff to adopt towards himself a more intimate attitude than during the hours of duty. Sometimes Cabillaud would play the piano—his one and only talent.

At nine the general went upstairs again to his office and remained there until eleven, occupying the time with his personal correspondence, of which letters to his wife formed the most considerable item, though the entering up of his war-diary was a recurrent duty. At such times, too, he would work at an occasional article, or summarize the events of which he had been an eyewitness in a document which was not destined to be forwarded through official channels. Should an opportunity arise he would send these notes in a private letter to the Commander-in-Chief, one of the big-wigs on the General Staff, or even, with all due regard for necessary caution, to some highly placed civilian personage.

He turned in his saddle and summoned his aide.

"Cabillaud!"

"Sir?"

"Remind me when we get back to ring artillery headquarters at the Bois des Moines, just south of point 280. Don't forget now."

"Yes, sir; certainly, sir."

Duroure turned his horse into a forest clearing. The going was good. He broke into a trot. He smiled to himself at the thought of that telephone message. There must be nothing compromising about it. He must find some innocent formula. No harm in an occasional joke.

CHAPTER TWELVE

Two Deputies Go for a Drive

Meanwhile, in the intervals of being bumped about on the excessively hard springs of a car that was labouring its way along the uneven roads of the forward zone, the two Parliamentary gentlemen were busy interrogating Captain Halletin-Fauchères, the staff officer from G.H.Q. who had been detailed to take them to L—.

Although they had been warned that General Duroure would not be ready for them until shortly before midday, they had insisted on leaving Paris at a very early hour, in order to give themselves a good margin for what they supposed would be an extremely difficult journey. For no considerations in the world would they have kept their host waiting. Every fifteen minutes or so they asked the elegant and phlegmatic young captain whether he did not think that the last part of their journey would delay them.

They were trying, too, to pick up a few odds and ends of information about the great commander whose guests they were to be, for whom, it appeared, they already felt considerable respect.

"His war record has been exceptionally brilliant, has it not?" asked M. Audincourt.

The captain, with the slightly condescending smile of a young courtier who is no stranger to the great, who, living at the fountain-head of favours and appointments, knows better than mere outsiders about the odd freaks of fortune, replied with a drawl:

"I suppose you might put it like that...."

"They say that when war broke out he was just colonel of a line regiment."

"It is certainly true that he was mobilized as a colonel, but not"—he corrected his interlocutor with an air of long-suffering patience—"not of infantry....He is an artilleryman."

"Still, it's an inspiring thought, is it not, Mousson, that a man who, little more than a year ago, was a simple colonel, unknown outside his garrison town, is now—" M. Audincourt completed his sentence by making a vague gesture towards the landscape.

The captain, though under no illusion that he could make these laymen grasp the subtle distinctions obtaining in military matters, started to explain, accompanying his words with a commentary of smiles.

"Unknown is perhaps a shade excessive. He had been a lecturer at the Staff College, where, in a really quite remarkable course—it attracted a considerable amount of attention at the time—he expounded certain ideas about which he might not be perhaps quite so—er—dogmatic today....Which means, of course, that he was in constant touch with a number of influential officers, Foch among others, who, as you know, was at that time Commandant. A little later he contributed a number of articles to various periodicals...." (Here the speaker's tone betrayed a note of easy unconcern.) "He was more or less in the public eye, though he had the reputation rather of a theorist than of an active soldier. But as soon as he had a few achievements to his name on service, he, like a good many others, began to be noticed....He's not the kind of man to hide his light under a bushel."

The two civilians were rather surprised to hear a young captain speak so freely of a distinguished senior officer. Their ideas about the rigid hierarchy of the army suffered a slight shock. But M. Audincourt, with the obstinacy of a man who is out for instruction, continued the conversation:

"I have been led to understand that he was very successful in the field."

"I believe so."

M. Audincourt turned to his colleague and remarked, loud enough to be overheard by their guide:

"It's a pity, isn't it, that we forgot to ask for information about the principal stages of his career?"

"I have not, I fear, got them at my fingers' tips," replied the captain, stung to a mild protest. "It's not exactly my line…but I believe that when war broke out he was commanding the artillery of some division of the Vth Army, Lanrezac's…the kind of post a man with his record might expect to hold….During the Sambre battle the general in command of the corps artillery lost his head, I believe, and was superseded after the Charleroi business, with a lot of others, including the army commander. Duroure, who had made a better showing, succeeded, at least temporarily, to his duties….If I remember correctly, he was not given his brigade until after the Marne."

"Where, I think, he was mentioned in dispatches, too?"

"Quite likely….As a result, if I'm not wrong, he was appointed to Foch's staff in October….Foch had always had his eye on him since the Staff College days….Duroure served under him in Flanders during what was known as the Race to the Sea—you remember? After that, well, he made pretty rapid progress on the Champagne front. He was given a division, and then a corps….If you want to know precisely when he got his third star, I can easily find out for you….Just say the word and I'll ask one of my colleagues on the Staff….He played an important part in the September offensive….His corps was pretty roughly handled…and G.H.Q. sent him here…." In a deliberately expressionless tone the captain added: "He had hoped for something better."

"Better? But how could that be? Isn't he commanding an army? What more could he want than to be in command of an army at the end of '15 when he was nothing but a colonel in August 1914!"

"Scarcely an army," the captain corrected him. "I suppose he's got the equivalent of four or five divisions, plus a few details. We call that a 'group.'" The exact significance of the smile with which he made this announcement was difficult to interpret: "The Duroure group."

"Still, it amounts to a considerable number of men?"

"Oh—about eighty thousand, say a hundred thousand with the technical troops."

"That doesn't seem too bad to me."

"He was hoping for an army. There are a good many Territorials in his hundred thousand. And it's a very quiet sector. That's the reason for the Territorials...." The captain smiled. "You'll find him, I'm afraid, a man with a grievance."

CHAPTER THIRTEEN

A Great Commander in the Making

Completely satisfied Duroure most certainly was not. But to say that he had a grievance was, perhaps, an over-simplification of the matter. He had reached the stage of believing that he had been badly treated, and was fond of cursing the tricks of fortune and the injustice of men. It is only too easy to get into a habit, and he was inclined to forget that he had very little, in fact, to grumble about. But, as often in such cases, he was a good deal less disgruntled than his complaints might have led one to suppose. Even in his blackest moods the fact remained, fortunately for him, that deep down he was conscious of a sense of happiness and of unimpaired vitality. This mood had dominated him almost as soon as he was mobilized. He had, it is true, passed through a short period of anxiety: "I ought to be playing a great part in this adventure, but shall I, actually, be anything more than mediocre?" But that stage once past, his serenity had first increased, then become stable. Even in the worst days, even when his patriotic soul was appalled by the thought that France was tottering on the brink of ruin, he could not but admit that, black though his mood might be, he felt years younger.

Since the Marne, since, in particular, his spell of duty in Flanders, this sense of renewed youth had never once been shaken. How should he not feel young? What does youth mean if not the gift of being able to look forward? Only one disaster can deprive a man of this intoxicating consciousness of the future: a physical exhaustion or a breakdown in health so definite that to drink the future's brimming cup, to wave a welcoming hand to the years to come, seems a mockery. Duroure, who had never suffered from bodily ailments, needed but a confident outlook to ensure his physical well-being.

What had happened was indeed miraculous. He had been on the point of having to retire after fighting tooth and nail to postpone the moment of that horrid necessity. At the very last moment, with the help of a certain amount of patronage, he had just managed to become a colonel. What more could he expect? The influential people whom he had wearied with his importunities had grown sick of him. He had had his chance. He would have all the rest of his life in which to dwell on the melancholy difference between what was and what, as a youth of twenty or twenty-five, he had thought of as a possibly magnificent future. Although he was still, as things went, in the flower of his age, the time was fast approaching when he would be an old gentleman. There would be nothing fictitious about the tears in his eyes as he bade farewell to his regiment. He would be an old gentleman, wearing his slightly old-fashioned clothes with an air, and sporting a decoration in his buttonhole. He would be entitled to a modest pension, and since the income of his wife, "Vicomtesse de Rumigny" though she might once have been, could not add much to the household budget, he would have to look forward to a straitened middle-class existence. Even the little extra that his Légion d'Honneur brought in was not to be sneezed at. His amusements would have to cost less than nothing. No going out. At best a few parties among intimate friends. Six months of the year he would have to spend on his little country estate, and it wasn't even certain that he would be able to afford a saddle-horse. (What would be the use, anyhow, since he would have to do without it in Paris during the winter?…Riding is so terribly expensive!) Even in the provinces no one would take much notice of him. A colonel on the active list is somebody. The authorities treat him with consideration. The local residents compete for his favours. But a colonel on half-pay is an old man no different from other old men. The ladies think of him as "so well preserved and with such nice manners," while the shopkeepers may sometimes take the trouble to close the door behind him with a "Oh, no trouble, sir, I assure you." And that's all. Life would

hold nothing more except the gradual increase of physical ailments, the slow worsening of his temper. That was what the
future would mean, inevitably. It needed no blackening of the
picture "for effect." The prospect was bad enough without any
touching up.

And then suddenly it was as though a dam had burst. The
future flowed in on him with a great surge of waters, caught
him up, floated him off the shoals. The world had become
suddenly new, transfigured. Everything was going to begin
again. Yes, that was the miracle. It was as though he were about
to play the whole game again from the word go, as though he
were back once more in his twentieth year. No, it was better
even than that, because he was starting with everything in his
favour (for a colonel has already got past the dangerous stage
where a man may be left marking time while fortune passes
him by). And this game was going to be incomparably better
worth playing than anything life had offered before; a game
in which everything moved at an accelerated pace, everything
was just a little bit bigger than life-size, everything was seen
at its highest power; opportunities, speed, stakes. He would
watch the advancement of his career with a heart as young as
when he was waiting for his second stripe. Best of all, the
excitement would not be just a recurrent thrill every three or
six years. No, every six weeks something might be expected
to happen. Destiny now was at full speed, and the brakes were
off! No sooner would he have donned the cap of a brigadier
(oh! that very word "general" which had so thrilled him in his
youth, which he had feared might never be his this side of the
grave! Here he was, now, a general! "General Duroure." Even
if he died tomorrow, they would put "General" on his tomb-
stone!) than he could look forward, with scarcely a moment's
delay, without indulging in any exaggerated hope, to mounting his third star, to becoming general of division, to attaining
the rank which, in theory at least, would open all doors, make
anything possible. "How soon?" And how soon would mean
for him, as for the youngest man, in how many *days*. He
would have the right, again without indulging in extravagant
hopes, to set no limits to his dreams. What, formerly, the

newly joined subaltern could hardly have whispered to himself as he fell asleep, without a sense of absurdity: "I shall command an army of five hundred thousand men. I shall win the great battle that will put an end to the war of revenge. It is I who will enter Strasbourg at the head of my troops," he could put into words now almost with the full approval of his reason. His once more was the most intense delight that a man can know, a delight to which he usually says farewell when youth is past—that of striding into the future with no check upon his forward march.

What wonderful luck too—this he confided only to the secret intimacies of his heart—that this great war, which might have broken out a little earlier or a little later, had coincided with his attainment of just the right age! All officers, naturally, dream of war and of the promotion it may bring them, but what rotten luck for the poor devils who happened to be thirty, thirty-five, or even forty when the 2nd of August dawned! It wasn't so much the physical danger that mattered; to have thought of that would have been unworthy. But what could a man of that age do to get himself out of the rut and send himself soaring like a rocket into the higher ranks? What chance would a wretched company commander have of showing his worth? Courage? Courage would be at a discount. All the courage in the world would do no more than get a man a mention or a Croix de Guerre. Of course, there were always staff appointments....Staff appointments were an excellent way of bringing oneself to the notice of the great and ensuring one's future—but only the sort of slow developing future that might bring its rewards when peace had come again. But what about the lightning promotion that only war could bring? A man of forty might be a colonel, and a favourite of Joffre, but even Joffre himself could not hoist such a one into an army command.

To take full advantage of this magnificent opportunity a man must be more than fifty and less than sixty-five. The margin was narrow. What luck to have been caught just at the right moment! When he thought of all the chances against it, he felt almost inclined to fall on his knees and thank somebody—God or destiny.

It was like one of those old legends in which, thanks to some magician, a man on whose shoulders the mantle of old age is about to fall, suddenly puts off the burden and walks away once more a youth.

And it really was youth, not a mere fantasy, youth in its every detail, and reflected in the eyes of all. Riding now on his horse down the streets near which he lived, escorted by the head of his staff—for he had a staff, he could refer to his staff without people laughing in his face—with what eyes would the women look at him? Their attitude would be rather different from what it would have been when he was just a half-pay officer coming out of the tobacconist's shop. Who would attract them more, he or that ass Cabillaud for all his elegance and his being almost twenty years younger? If he had been the kind of man who ran after women, couldn't he have very soon proved that he was still a man capable of inspiring genuine passion, a man with all the feminine world to choose from?

It was true, he had begun, when the war started, as colonel commanding the artillery of the *n*th division, forming part of the Vth Army, Lanrezac's. On the 23rd of August, after the check on the Sambre, the general in charge of the corps artillery had been superseded. His immediate superior had said of him that he had handled his guns "like a damned vegetable"! Duroure, obeying a sudden impulse, and without orders from anybody—whence could an order have come in that chaotic action?—had hurriedly concentrated his thirty-six guns on a single hill and had set them all firing "at top speed" on the same hundred yards of river-bank which the enemy were trying to force in mass formation. The resultant barrage—remarkably formidable at that period of the war—had had an immediate effect on the German morale—to say nothing of the casualties it had caused—had thrown the advancing troops into confusion, started a panic, and, in general, so much retarded their movements that the French retirement had been successfully covered over a considerable portion of its front. Duroure had replaced the ungummed general, but only as an "acting officer." He had not received promotion in rank.

On the 6th of September, in the opening phases of the Marne, he had been at Monceaux, under Franchet d'Espérey, with his forty-eight guns of corps artillery. But, unlike his predecessor, he had been careful to establish close contact with the two colonels of divisional artillery and had let it be seen that he regarded them as acting under his orders. In this matter he had been given carte blanche by the corps commander and the two divisional generals. Since his lucky stroke on the Sambre, his reputation as an artillery officer had been on the increase. One of the two divisional generals had said publicly: "That chap's daring reminded me of the Napoleon touch." When an officer has reminded his superior of Napoleon, if only for fifteen minutes, it is not likely that any plans he may have will be interfered with in the trivial interests of divisional seniority. Duroure, therefore, found himself in practical control of all the hundred and twenty guns of the corps artillery. His earlier stroke had left the germ of an idea, confused but capable of development, in his mind. It was not yet definite enough to be called a "system." It was little more than a desire to "try again." He was given the chance he wanted on this very day, the 6th. Receiving an order to support an infantry attack which was to be delivered on a front of less than a kilometre, he did not confine himself, as another officer in his position might have done, to utilizing four or five batteries only, on the ground that even so he would scarcely have enough reserve fire to meet future eventualities. Instead, he concentrated on the extremely narrow sector the fire of eighty-four guns which he had concentrated, by sheer good fortune, in the course of the previous night. Luck so had it that the point which he had chosen for his concentration happened to be close to the point, unknown to him at the time, from which he would have to support next day's attack. He was thus enabled to make the necessary moves in time. This lucky coincidence was in no way due to any previous exchange of views with the commanding officer. As a matter of fact, he had rather exceeded his right of initiative. But, in

view of the fact that the enemy's front was broken, Duroure's
dramatic intervention came to be regarded as the result of an
instinctive "nose" for a situation and of a rapidity of decision,
both of which were decidedly out of the common. On the
7th he was promoted brigadier and confirmed in his command. From that moment G.H.Q. never lost sight of him. He
became one of those officers who were ear-marked for
employment on tasks of exceptional difficulty. In October he
was attached to Foch's staff and given the special duty of co-
ordinating the various actions on the Flanders front. There he
learned to take his share of responsibility on a large scale. Two
months later he was sent to the Champagne and put in temporary command of one of the divisions selected to take part
in the offensive of the 20th of December, from which great
things were hoped. He was able to put to the credit side of his
reputation a small success in the neighbourhood of Perthes. It
looked as though he would be permanently employed on this
front, which during 1915 was regarded by G.H.Q. as the sector in which decisive actions were likely to take place. He
took part in the operations of February and March. On the
20th of February he was confirmed in his rank of divisional
general. In May he was detached from his division to collab-
orate in the long-distance scheme which was to result in the
great offensive of September. He suggested several improvements in the grouping of the artillery, the placing of
dumps, and the methods to be employed for bringing up the
reserves. At the end of August, the preliminary arrangements
being almost finished, he was given command of one of the
corps of the IVth Army (Langle de Cary). He took an important part in the attack of the 25th–26th of September between
the Mill of Souain and the Saint-Hilaire–Saint-Souplet road,
during which he penetrated deep into the enemy positions,
though at the cost of very heavy casualties. His corps, having
been very roughly handled, was sent back to rest preparatory
to being moved later to a quiet sector of the front. This
change gave G.H.Q. the opportunity of making one of those
careful readjustments of which it was so fond. Not only did
Duroure retain his corps, but he was given, in addition, a divi-

sion taken from another corps, two independent Territorial divisions, and the requisite number of technical troops. The whole, renamed the "Duroure Group" was sent to one of the quietest parts of the Lorraine front, on the left of the 1st Army.

This new move implied, in about equal doses, reward for past services, present disgrace, and promise for the future. The reward (of rather moderate dimensions) was for his activities in Champagne. He was given a larger command, though one considerably short of an army, composed of troops from which nothing much could be expected, and on a part of the front where very little was happening. This might look, at first, as though he had been shelved, or at least relegated to a position of secondary importance. But since the general belief still obtained that this sector to the left of the Armies of the East—that is to say, this part of the front where, at the moment, nothing of importance was to be expected—might form the starting-point for an offensive towards Briey and Metz which should take the enemy in flank and so force a decision, there was nothing to prevent Duroure (and others) from thinking that he had been sent to his present post in deliberate anticipation of such a forward move, in order that he might have time to make his plans, familiarize himself with the ground, and, generally, absorb the necessary "atmosphere." This hypothesis, which had the advantage of salving his self-pride, corresponded pretty accurately to his actual reputation in responsible quarters. Ever since the Champagne battle, it had been customary to speak of him, at Chantilly and else-where, in something like the following terms: "He's the kind of man one wants for hard hitting in some local offensive which will give him room for improvisation and free move-ment." There were those who added: "There's a dynamic quality about him, even as an artillery officer." By this it was meant to imply that the patient planning which he had brought to the massing of the artillery prior to the Cham-pagne offensive had not blotted out the memory of his more dashing exploits of '14. What it all came to was that he was not, perhaps, an ideal army commander for the kind of war-fare which was at present being forced upon the High Command, a type of operations which, though it might aim at breaking the enemy's front and leaving the way clear for open fighting, had first to cope with siege conditions; conditions, that is, which involved slow and detailed preparation, and, when once battle was joined, a power of control over a wide front, unhampered by too many preconceived theories about the points to be attacked or the objectives to be attained, and an ability to take immediate advantage of local conditions, no matter how limited the actual degree of penetration might be. Sooner or later, probably sooner, men like him would have their chance. For the time being, it was safer to rely on less brilliant officers, on officers not likely to embarrass the situation by their touches of genius.

This summing up of his character, the details of which he did not know, would in certain ways have flattered, in others shocked and surprised him. He had no objection, certainly, to being thought of as a man of inspired improvisations, but he regarded himself, too, as an organizer of quite exceptional powers, and as a model of the scientific soldier.

As a matter of fact, the growth of his reputation and his consequent success had been due to very different causes, of unequal importance, the nature of which he was not in a position to judge.

What had perhaps been of greatest service to him was his ability to forget the past, to think always, rapidly and nimbly, in terms of the present. Second only to this was the fact that his mental attitude was composed in almost equal parts of realism and fantasy.

It had needed only a fortnight of active service to banish completely from his mind the fact that he had once said hard things about heavy artillery and had regarded the 75 as too cumbersome. After the Marne he had thought no more about the "initial shock," the "uninterrupted advance," and other favourite phrases of military theory. He never allowed old ideas to hamper his present conduct. If circumstances spoke loud enough he was always on their side. He never said: "That's where I was wrong," but "Obviously this is the way to do things." That alone would not have been enough to establish his reputation, even assuming in others a power of forgetting, an unwillingness to remember, equal to his own; nor would his actual successes in the field. But what he had, in a remarkable degree, was the ability to use some immediate experience of his own or his colleagues' as the starting-point of a theory. He could "talk" war better than most, and talk it to an accompaniment of brilliant and vivid illustration. Now, caught as they were in the hurly-burly of events, and conscious that the convictions with which they had entered the war were being daily more and more shaken to bits, the senior officers in every branch of the service wanted, above all things, some anchorage for their mental processes, wanted, that is to say, to find somewhere among this constant bombardment of new impressions something that could be called a "general idea." Duroure was never shaken out of his serenity. At any given moment he was ready to say: "It's all perfectly simple. It comes to this, that modern war is so-and-so or so-and-so." With a deft twist of the hand he could furnish there and then a perfectly reasoned and convincing demonstration, just as though it were ten years after the declaration of peace and he were giving a series of lectures on the "late troubles." Since, furthermore, he had from time to time, by dint of adapting himself brilliantly to circumstances, actually held up the Germans, as on the Sambre, or driven them back, as at Montceaux, his hearers were more than ready to believe him. Thanks to an excusable confusion of focus, his latest theory always had an air of having anticipated events, even, in certain cases, of having controlled them, whereas in reality it was nothing more than a quick and instinctive comment upon what had actually occurred. His gift of convenient forgetfulness, too, acted as a filter, and chose from among past events just so much and no more of what it wanted. As soon as some lesson of experience presented certain analogies with one of his former "views," his memory reasserted itself. When the French troops at Charleroi learned by bitter experience the deadly effect of machine-gun fire, Duroure immediately recollected his previous insistence upon "maximum development of rifle power" as a *sine qua non* of successful infantry action—the machine-gun being, in fact, from that point of view no more than a concentration of rifles. Later, when the Germans initiated the use of very light field-guns—which the men in the line wrongly described as "quick-firers"—and small trench-mortars, he maintained triumphantly that what he had always said was being vindicated. What else were these weapons than the "pom-pom" or the equivalent of the pom-pom adapted to stationary warfare? He even spent some of his leisure time during the winter months of 1914–'15 in designing a trench-mortar which was subsequently tested and turned out in considerable quantities. Finally, since it threw too light a projectile, it was superseded by other models. The incident, however, was not without benefit to its author, who thereby consolidated his reputation as a man who "thought along modern lines," and as a technician who did not disdain "putting his shoulder to the wheel."

But he was not the kind of man who has always got to be "in the right." He took far less interest in the Duroure of the old days with his theories, than in the Duroure of today with his lucky strokes. If he wanted to bolster up his actions on some general theory, he could always find one conveniently to hand.

It all, of course, came back to mental agility. In the world of politics men of his sort are commonly called "trimmers." But in his case this agility was little more than a free use of common sense. He did not have to outrage any cherished convictions in order to see things as they were. But his common sense only functioned successfully when stimulated by the facts of a situation. It was a kind of reflex activity of the mind. Once remove the pressure of circumstances, and his power of response immediately suffered. It was fatal for him to be separated, for however short a time, from first-hand experience. Successful though he might have been in the world of "pure thought," the isolation of the thinker irked him. As soon as he started working things out in the privacy of his office, his mind lost its clarity. If in the days when he had been a lecturer on military tactics he had said and written a good deal of nonsense, it was because at that time he had had no contact with the experience of war. He lived in a world of books and talk. And if, today, in his office at L— the mistakes of his ratiocination were less glaring, the reason was that his conclusions were being constantly tested in the school, often the brutal school, of hard fact. The telephone calls, the telegrams on their flimsy paper, the sudden interventions of Radigué, the glimpses of trench life which he caught on his tours of duty, were always conveniently at hand to prevent him from becoming a Descartes brooding over his stove. His theory to the effect that the Commander must be able to rely upon a scholar's quiet detachment was born of his taste for theorizing on everything; it did not really express any profound need of his being. And, in any case, he was perfectly ready to shelve it in favour of some completely contradictory theory as soon as a war of movement should involve him once again in all the excitement of the battlefield.

The mere fact of his being able to open his eyes and see things as they were at the precise moment of their occurrence, of keeping his head when others were losing theirs, gave him an advantage over most of his colleagues, which became increasingly apparent as the chaos of action grew more marked. To judge by the amazement caused by his famous strokes on the Sambre and at Montceaux, this coolheadedness of his was, at times, not far removed from genius. For it seems that certain perfectly simple ideas which at times appear to be no more elaborate than those which dictate the behaviour of a policeman directing traffic at a crowded street intersection, or of a fireman distributing the water from his hose on the various centres of a conflagration, become extremely difficult to apply when they have to work with masses of armed men, in an atmosphere of tense collective emotion, and in an access of personal responsibility. How otherwise can one explain the immense acclamation which has been accorded to a few soldiers who figure in the history books, when the manœuvres which have led to their most resplendent victories have been childishly simple and have had little intrinsic merit other than being, in the circumstances, slightly preferable to a few no less simple alternatives?

The miracle seems to have been no more than that these men retained sufficient clearness of vision to see that, conditions being what they were, one set of decisions was better than another. A piece of good sense which would have passed unnoticed in other spheres where it might have been the common property of many individuals becomes suddenly— and perhaps genuinely—a mark of genius.

Duroure had shown this mark of genius, or had let it be seen by others, on two or three occasions. The consideration shown to him in a number of other matters owed its existence to that fact. He knew it. He knew, too, that the particular turn taken by the war since the Battle of the Marne was not favourable to genius as applied to purely military matters. The direction of trench warfare demands the qualities of a born administrator: conscientiousness and perseverance, slow thinking, and an open mind….Dashing inspiration is at a discount. Even to organize a break-through in such circumstances calls for abilities that are commonly met with in the peaceful civilian. The commander in a war of position has to take his time and balance risk against risk; a crowd of technical advisers are at his beck and call, ready to solve, in quiet detachment, the particular problems of any given situation. Any great industrialist, given six weeks in which to learn the ropes, could do the job as well as the most highly trained soldier.

Duroure knew himself well enough to say: "My particular genius is something quite different. It will never be free to develop until the front has been broken or crushed. All I need is to be warned in time, and to be sure of having an adequate instrument to hand when the moment comes."

But he was far from drawing the conclusion that he was therefore unsuited to holding high command in a period of stationary warfare. The greater includes the less. Had he not seen more clearly than most the needs of the moment? Had he not formulated a theory of trench-war organization? It would have seemed to him a perfectly natural thing that he should have been entrusted with a real army (ten or so divisions at the very least, and of first-rate fighting material; none of this Territorial trash), an army that should form part of the

normal, glorious nomenclature of the front, an army desig-
nated in roman numerals: Ist Army, IInd, IIIrd....And had he
even been offered the command of a group of armies (boasting still more glorious initials: G.A.N., G.A.C.—Group of
Armies of the North, Group of Armies of the Centre), he
would have felt himself equal to the task. To be able fully to
play his part when fighting once more became "open," was-
n't it essential that he should have been placed already in a
position of eminence? Otherwise what sort of job would fall
to his lot? Some small local operation, doubtless, the kind of
thing that the strategists call a "demonstration." At all costs he
must avoid being one of those officers held in reserve for
demonstrations or local operations.

There were moments when he felt really angry—though
with no deep sense of bitterness—to' think that the authorities
were taking so long to accord him his proper position. He had
no fondness for Joffre, though Joffre had been responsible for
much of his promotion. It was largely a matter of temperament. He disliked Joffre's paunch, his thin legs, his southern
accent, his air of being a superior gamekeeper. Joffre lacked fire
and quick sensibility. Good at organizing, he might be, but his
gifts were those that would have found their best chance of
employment in the job of recruiting officer or station-master.
He turned his back too deliberately on genius, was too much
the veteran stuffed with theory. He was terribly jealous, too, of
his authority, always ready to take offence, always afraid lest he
were not given full credit for his achievements. For that reason
he was careful to surround himself with mediocrities, with
officers of junior standing on whom public opinion would not
readily father the acts of the generalissimo, though, in fact, he
did little more than adopt their decisions and paraphrase their
views. He never took into his confidence the commanders on
whom eventually would fall the responsibility of putting his
schemes into action, nor consulted them except formally. He
was always exposing them to petty vexations, such as depriv-
ing them of their chiefs of staff without first asking their leave.
Hundreds of other grievances there were, of most of which
Duroure had had no experience at first hand, but which he

was only too ready to believe on hearsay.

Foch he adored, though there was a trace of jealousy in his adoration. He was very jealous, too, of Pétain, though he thought highly of him. As for the senior officers whose reputations had been made before the war, the Castelnaus, the Langle de Carys, the Franchet d'Espéreys, he affected to regard them, in varying degrees, as a lot of old fogies. Nothing would free them of their old-fashioned views. Though he was not the author of an epigram which had been current in staff circles, he took considerable pleasure in hearing it: "This is a war fought by the subalterns of '14, and directed by the subalterns of '70." The space between the two dates was somewhat excessive. To say that a man had learned his job as a soldier in the year 1870 was in itself an insult (not so much because of the implication of defeat as because it meant that he had been apprenticed to the trade of arms in an antediluvian world). That blot, unfortunately, attached even to Foch....Subalterns of '80 or of '85—that would have been nearer the mark so far as the High Command was concerned.

Since his installation at L— he had moved warily. He had not lost touch with Gurau, whose position in the present Ministry, though ill defined, was nevertheless influential. He was trying to circulate in high quarters, and through various channels, an idea, the latest fruit of his imagination, which had the advantage of being very much in his line and with which he thought his name might fairly easily be associated: the idea of specially selected "shock troops," and of a breach of the enemy front by means of a "shock army." He had developed it with spirit to Gurau, to some of the G.H.Q. people, and to others. He counted on it to do him a lot of good. "You've heard Duroure's scheme?" "Duroure's shock army...." New developments begin by talk; later they are translated into fact.

When it comes to seeking wide diffusion for an idea, even the smallest tributary channels are not to be ignored. He might find an opportunity, at luncheon, or in the car, to slip in a word about his "shock troops" to these two obscure members of the Army Commission. "That'll depend on whether their heads are screwed on the right way."

CHAPTER FOURTEEN

A Harmless Joke

The car had taken them as far as brigade headquarters, the most advanced point that could be conveniently reached by road.

This particular headquarters had been dug deep into the reverse slope of a hill. The walls were of concrete, lined on the inside with wood, and the natural roof had been reinforced with several layers of logs. The place offered safe protection against even heavy shells.

From there to the front line meant a walk of about two kilometres, through communication trenches which, for most of the way, skirted the left side of a very open valley consisting of meadow-land dotted with several clumps of shrubs.

Duroure glanced at his watch: 3.15. He almost regretted his school-boy inspiration. The two deputies were pleasant fellows, and not at all stupid. They had at once seen the point of the "shock troops" theory. Unfortunately the telephone message had been sent at ten o'clock that morning. It could not very well be countermanded now.

Duroure set off cheerfully at the head of the little procession. The two deputies followed. A captain, lent by the brigadier, brought up the rear, with a private to act as runner. Duroure had begged the brigadier not to come with them:

"I'd very much rather you stayed here. The Boche has been showing a good deal of activity these last few days. You'd better be within reach of the telephone."

The brigadier, though he had no great belief in the Boche's alleged activity, knew that Duroure liked to do the honours himself, and did not insist.

The trench was fairly clean. The earth, with its occasional

projecting roots, smelt good. Unfortunately, the walls had
been cut back at too oblique an angle and here and there
were too low to give adequate protection. On the other hand,
it was pleasant to be able to take a look round now and then,
to glance at ground level into the valley, which was not without a charm of its own. More than once the faces of the party
were brushed by encroaching undergrowth.

Duroure, who was feeling slightly worried by the whole
affair, remembered his telephone message in detail. "Even if
they haven't started by then," so his instructions had run,
"open at a moderate rate of fire about 3.30. They must be
shown that the initiative lies with us."

In any case, the results would not be very serious. His orders
could rouse no possible suspicions. The normal activity of the
sector could not be interrupted just because there happened
to be a few visitors about. The Boches would reply, of course.
But it would mean no more than a short artillery duel....

The walk gave rise to an exchange of courtesies and a certain amount of good-natured chaff.

"I'm afraid I'm giving you rather an uncomfortable journey, gentlemen. I hope you don't find the mud too bad?"

"Certainly not, general. Why, this is nothing."

Now and again one of the two visitors showed that he
knew how to use his eyes.

"Tell me, general, aren't there one or two places where men
using this trench are rather exposed?"

This was said in a tone that was meant to imply: "It's not
our own safety we're bothered about, you understand, but
that of the dear fellows in the line."

"You're quite right. The earth has a way of settling and collapsing....One can't always be on the spot to give an eye to
these things.... The men are so careless." He added: "I'll make
a note of it," which was as much as to say that he would flatter his visitors by taking their comments seriously.

Suddenly—tzanc! A splitting bark that seemed to take them
full between neck and cheek. Then a sharp whining sound
which obviously came from behind them, slightly to the
right, deepened to a more accentuated tone as it passed over-

head, still to the right, continued its angry grumble skywards, while there came to their ears an echoing "boom," as though a heavy door had been slammed in their rear.

"One of ours?" said M. Audincourt in a voice that he strove to keep as expressionless as possible.

"Yes, one of the 120-millimetre guns."

At that moment they heard another explosion, very far away, but quite different from the first, and coming this time from in front.

"They're replying, eh?" asked M. Audincourt.

"No. That was the explosion of our shell…. We're using mark-D ammunition."

They continued their walk in silence.

A second "tzanc!" a long-drawn whine, a "boom"! They stopped, waiting for the explosion of the "mark-D" shell.

Duroure, turning his head, thought it wise to give a word of explanation.

"We're trying to demolish"—the distant, faintly comforting, thunder-clap came again—"some enemy guns which have been giving us trouble." He addressed himself to the captain: "Has the Boche been firing this morning?"

"Yes, sir."

"Ah!" His next words were for the benefit of the visitors: "You see, we've got to go on at them."

Messieurs Audincourt and Mousson nodded their heads in polite agreement. It was as though they were saying to somebody who had begged their pardon for opening an urgent letter in their presence: "Please do!" However, they spoke no actual words. They were probably busy absorbing this genuine front-line atmosphere which had come their way so suddenly.

A third discharge; a fourth; always from the French side. They continued their walk. Messieurs Audincourt and Mousson began to get used to the various noises. The idea that it was their own guns firing comforted them. In tones a shade too detached they began to ask questions about the 120-millimetre gun.

The general did his best to answer, but his attention was

wandering. He was waiting for the first sign of a reply from the lines opposite.

A fifth, a sixth discharge from the French batteries.

The German answer was long in coming.

A fatigue party proceeding the other way saluted the general and gave a wondering look at the two civilians who politely flattened themselves against the trench wall to let them pass.

Tzinc!—there it was again, but this time from some point ahead of them, and not in the nape of the neck. A whine, no less angry than the others, but slightly different in quality, and, like the noise of the discharge, coming from in front. Yes, there could be no doubt of that. Just as it reached the top of its trajectory and swung over for the downward swoop, the whining sound paused a trifle too long, while at the same moment a gurgling undertone became audible, a sort of "oua-oua-oua!" Duroure, who had stopped dead, bit his lip and exchanged a glance with the captain. He had just time enough in which to think: "That's odd!" before shouting:

"Get down!"

Farther along the trench the men of the fatigue party had been on their stomachs already for some seconds.

Bang! Bararoom! Boom!...followed by reverberations of the echo. It was as though some enormous locomotive dragging a series of lighter and lighter cars, had crossed the trench on a metal bridge.

The general risked a peep. About three hundred yards away, at the bottom of the valley, just where the opposite hill began to rise from it, a great jet of smoke leaped into the air, a thick column of soot and chalk edged with yellow.

"Can they have been all that off the target?" he wondered.

Another distant bark, a short whine which, this time, kept to one shrill note, an explosion. A second shell from away in front. It fell roughly on the same line, but about two hundred yards farther forward, almost precisely at the spot where battalion H.Q. must be. This was no wild shooting. Instead of retaliating on the French batteries, the enemy guns were plastering the trenches, or rather the approaches to the trenches, as though they were searching for dumps, or headquarters, or the communication trench itself.

It took but a second or so for Duroure to explore alternative hypotheses: "Do they merely want to make a nuisance of themselves? Have they, by extraordinary luck, got wind of the fact that I'm making a tour of the line?…Quite possible; there's still a number of spies hanging about in the back areas."

A third German shell burst just as another French one passed overhead. It fell about the same distance as its predecessors behind the lines, but considerably more to the left, and much nearer the trench, to that part of it which the general and his guests would have to negotiate in another three minutes or so.

Duroure shot an anxious glance at the two civilians. The two civilians were behaving very well. They were doing their best to copy the precautions which they saw the others taking, but no more. They were like a party of well-dressed people who had been taken to visit the greasy engine-room of a ship. "We don't want to get our clothes dirty if it can be helped, but we mustn't look ill at ease."

Another German shell in almost exactly the same spot.

Duroure was clearly much put out. He had noticed scraps of earth and metal falling less than a hundred yards from where they were standing.

"Gentlemen," he said, "I suggest that we turn back."

"Do you really think that's necessary, general?"

Messieurs Audincourt and Mousson questioned one another silently in an exchange of looks. Neither seemed anxious to beat a retreat. No doubt their host thought they were frightened at a few miserable shells (nothing to what the chaps in the line had to put up with). Their self-respect as men and their honour as representatives of the people were at stake. They protested:

"So far as we're concerned, please go on. Don't you agree, Mousson?"

Two more shells came whistling towards them. Duroure, who was crouching in the bottom of the trench, glanced at the captain. The captain made a face. As soon as the burst was over—still in the same place—Duroure got up, pushed past the two deputies, and joined the captain.

"You really think we ought to turn back?" he whispered.

"Yes, sir."

Duroure nodded towards the spot where the shells were falling.

"Seems rather odd, doesn't it?"

"It does a bit, sir….They're probably annoyed that we started in again this afternoon. They may have been meaning to leave us alone."

"Possibly….Anyhow, you don't see what else we can do?"

"Than turn back? I certainly don't, sir….We might ring up the gunners and tell them to shut up, but that means getting to one of the H.Q.'s, and the nearest is just where they're putting all this stuff over….Besides, it would take time."

M. Audincourt had just caught the phrase about stopping the gunners. He moved towards the two officers.

"I beg your pardon, general, but we should hate to think you'd interrupted the shooting because of us….It's necessary, I imagine, and we mustn't stop the boys doing their job."

"Yes, gentlemen, yes….Allow me most sincerely to congratulate you on your courage. But in that case I'm afraid we shall have to get back—in double-quick time…there's no alternative….It would be sheer foolishness to go on now…. Follow me, if you please. And next time you hear the whistle of a shell, you'll be able to recognize the sound, eh?—even if it's one of our own….Look out! There's another!…Get down quickly, as low as you can. Copy us. Look at that man over there. He knows what shells are like…. Do just what he's doing….You've got to put your pride in your pocket." Broum! Doum! …Redoum!…"Over for the moment; now run! We can take a bit of a breather at brigade H.Q….I'll get them to make us a glass of punch. At any rate, gentlemen, you'll be able to say that you've seen things at first hand!"

CHAPTER FIFTEEN

A Letter From Jerphanion to Jallez.
How One Manages to Carry On

I can't tell you how pleased I was to get your long letter; not so much because of its news—you don't tell me much about yourself (more's the pity!) but because it serves as a link, a life-line, connecting me with what I still insist on regarding as the only reality.

I am tempted, instead of answering your questions, to ask a few of my own, such as: "Is it, then, really possible still to find something that resembles a genuine existence? Did the 2nd of December 1915 actually happen, or was it like something one finds fossilized in books? How can it possibly fit in with the rest of the picture?"

I suppose you'll say to yourself: "He's working himself into one of his states—it's all just words." There, alas, you're wrong....But, all the same, you won't be able to give an answer to my rather absurd and self-pitying question, because you can't know what it's like to suffer from the sort of intellectual atrophy, the pernicious mental scurvy, that comes of long privation of all the things that make life real; because even the analogy of thirst can't possibly give you an inkling of what it's like to be tortured by the absence of everything that makes life worth living.

I don't mean that the things you ask aren't difficult enough in all conscience to answer. Here we just don't let ourselves think of them, and I have a feeling that, just because you guessed as much, you put off raising these particular questions until now. It is natural, indeed inevitable, that you should be infinitely curious. Incidentally, let me say that you've missed something in not having had the experience for yourself. No letter, no amount of talk, and, still more, no literary descriptions in second-rate books—and books on the war cannot but be second-rate—could ever give you the faintest idea of the reality. You, perhaps, with your acute sensibility and your long training in coming to terms with the inexpressible, might succeed in bringing into consciousness what the average consciousness refuses to register. This I say sincerely and with no intention whatever of irony.

The most one can do is to throw one's line at a venture in the hope of hooking some fragment of experience that may serve as evidence, or, rather, as one scrap of evidence among others. I try to think forward to the day when some man will try to put together the thousand and one statements of those who were witnesses of these events which at present are beyond the power of thought to compass. What will he make of them? God knows!

You must take everything I say as no more than a purely personal version. I no sooner write down a phrase than I want to scratch it out again as false, conventional, intolerably one-sided, as a wholly distorted view of the facts.

What you want to know most of all is how a man, brought up as we have been brought up, can put up with this life, day in, day out, week after week, month after month. "What is his attitude of mind?" were your actual words. What attitude will give him least sense of pain? To put it more simply still, what is this life of mine like, you ask, and whence do I draw sufficient courage to endure it?

Need I remind you of the enthusiasm of the first days? I shared in it. I don't attempt to deny the fact. What produced it? Ignorance; love of the dramatic; an accumulated spiritual vitality which found no employment in the things of every day and so was ready for anything out of the ordinary; belief, too, that enthusiasm, given its head, could irresistibly mould events. What it comes to is this: on the 2nd of August I felt convinced that victory would be ours by the 1st of September, and that the only real problem would be how best to use it in the interests of humanity.

I admit that I was rather ashamed of my share in that enthusiasm, that I recognized it as something irrational, but you yourself felt something of the same sort, you told me, for about forty-eight hours, which proves that it must have been terribly contagious, a kind of acute form of influenza. With me it lasted longer. How long? Three weeks ? Six weeks? Let us say three weeks at its most violent stage, with a few weeks longer allowed for slow convalescence and occasional relapses. Looking back, I realize that enthusiasm of that kind could not stand up to the proof that enthusiasm alone is quite incapable of winning a war.

How much of it do I retain today? With my hand on my heart, and not at all wishing to pose, by reaction, as "hard-boiled," I can say: almost exactly nothing.

Sometimes I try to fan it once more into flame, because, in a way, it would be a help. But it's difficult. I cannot now begin to conceive how this war can possibly turn out "well," meaning by "well" something that our idealism could accept. Its main consequences, so far as I can see, will be something of this sort: Entry of the Tsar into Constantinople; or the unchallenged supremacy of Great Britain from Liverpool to Singapore. Nor does my egotism as a Frenchman see anything really comforting ahead. I know perfectly well that my country will be far too exhausted to impose its will on Europe, even assuming that will to be good. Meanwhile I see only too clearly what the positive results—I'm not speaking now of intangible things—have so far been: a rich harvest of profiteers; a baseness of soul in people at the rear which leads them to find it perfectly natural that we should continue to act as a bulwark behind which they can carry on their filthy little lives, their filthy little activities of buying and selling. Nor am I forgetting what may be a comparatively unimportant detail, though to me it means a lot—the utter stupidity of all those gentlemen of letters, those so-called intellectuals, whose words and attitudes are a constant insult to the spirit, to ordinary common sense, to any reasons we may have for continuing the struggle, to us who are continuing it. Never—and I can't stress this too strongly—never shall I forget the feeling of shame that these oafs induce in me.

Add to all this the bestiality, the gloomy bestiality, into

which this business has flung us so that it has become our daily food.

I've just thought of three sentences (I'm writing this by the light of a candle, in my dug-out, with a board across my knees) which sum up my present state of mind: (1) I no longer believe that a "crushing" victory would be an advantage. (2) If all we can hope for is an inconclusive peace, what is the use of going on? (3) Meanwhile, everything we see happening, whether at the front or in the rear, is horrible.

But, above all, these five words seem written in fire on the walls of my dug-out: *Nothing can be worth this*. Nothing = any conceivable argument. This = the kind of life we are leading (with a hideous death for ever hanging over our heads). That is the final word of wisdom so far as the war is concerned. Everything else is mere fine writing.

You will say: "If you feel like that you must be a very bad soldier."

No, I'm rather a good one. Or so I think, and my colleagues and superiors think so too. I have been given a company over the heads of a good many others, and in spite of the fact that I have been away from the line for several months. Since I'm certainly not "as brave as a lion," and have never captured an enemy battery and pinned the gunners to their guns with my bayonet (which is the least of the noble exploits with which M. Henri Lavedan regales the ladies and gentlemen at home), I can only assume that a sort of pig-headed mediocrity is all that I have to recommend me. Odd, isn't it?

What helps me to carry on (me, regarded as typical of all the others)?

Perhaps the thought that I might be worse off. You may laugh, but it's probably true. I might be in a worse part of the line, where hard fighting was going on all the time. I might have had both my legs blown off. I might be dead. I might be a private.

This last consideration has a slightly comic look; a week ago I quite likely shouldn't have included it. But it so happens that I've got in my company a rather extraordinary man. His name is Griollet, a Parisian from the 9th arrondissement. In civil life

he's a leather-worker (with his own little business). I couldn't
make him out at first, because he doesn't say much. He's one
of the very few among my men to whom I can talk freely
without any danger of his taking advantage of the fact. For
instance, he's the only man I've dared to question on what he
really thinks and feels. The day before yesterday we were having a chat. In the course of the conversation he suddenly said,
without the slightest trace of impertinence, like someone
who has been thinking out a problem and weighing the pros
and cons: "You officers do have certain advantages, but I'm
not sure that they amount to much compared with all the
worry and responsibility. Still, they're something. And your
work's more interesting." Another of his remarks was: "Even
though an officer runs the same risks as us, it's easier, in a way,
for him to be brave."

I've been thinking a good deal since about the truth of
what he said. It's certainly a fact that having to bother about
my men is a "diversion" in the Pascalian sense of the word.
You've no idea how much office work there is in the trenches. I have endless returns to render, some daily, others at short
and recurrent intervals: a report every forty-eight hours—
trench state, list of casualties (even in quiet times we have casualties, alas!), lists of this, that, and the other; suggestions for
decorations and promotion (*sic*). I have to go and take a look
as often as possible at the sort of second-hand dealer's, or
rather ironmonger's, shop which we've rigged up here in the
bowels of the earth, for which I'm responsible. It really is like
the sort of old-iron store one sees at Belleville or Vaugirard,
and I'm the proprietor who's for ever looking at his shelves
and nosing into the corners wondering: "Have I got enough
stove-pipes? Has Alfred, my clerk, forgotten to let me know
that we're short of wrenches or screw-drivers?" But my stock
is rather different. It consists of rifle ammunition, bombs,
grenades, tools, signal rockets, steel plates, anti-gas sprays, pails
of hyposulphite, boxes of biscuit, and all the hundred and one
gadgets we need for killing or to avoid being killed. At any
moment when there's a chance of my being left to myself,
free, that's to say, to take a plunge into the dark waters of the

river Kafar (the oued-el-Kafar, as one of my friends is fond of saying), I suddenly remember that I've got to find a working party, and twenty minutes later a fatigue, and that that's going to leave me short of sentries, because, of course, half the men are having their time off for sleep. All that, and numerous other details, divides my waking hours into small sections, each one of which is thus made easier to swallow and contains only a dose of poison so small that the organism can absorb it.

And what about your physical condition? you'll ask. Surely that bulks pretty large? How do you manage? For instance, what about cold? I don't mind telling you that all last winter it was a haunting obsession for everyone in the line, with its refinements of torment such as frost-bitten feet, or, rather, mortified feet, feet rotting to pieces with a sort of pallid corruption. A living man might at any moment discover that his feet were those of a corpse in an advanced stage of decomposition. Today we mind rather less about the cold. We have woollens and blankets, trench boots—a whole primitive technique of living which has turned us into the semblance of prehistoric man.

Food? So far as that's concerned, we obviously have less to complain of than the men. They're pretty badly off just now, worse off than they were during the first winter of the war. God alone knows why! They're issued a sort of prison gruel, and not enough of it to satisfy a hungry man. If they didn't get parcels from home....But a number of mine are from the occupied territories and consequently get nothing of that sort. It's terrible to see the poor devils weighed down with this load of purely animal misery in addition to everything else. We officers don't do so badly. The cook concocts some sort of stew for us while we're in the line. It tastes pretty funny, but at least there's enough of it. When we're in billets, things are better for everyone, the men included. After all, if the war had nothing worse than bad food to offer, it wouldn't be so terrible.

Dirt. I've got a few things to say about that. It's a subject worth a certain amount of thought. Here, for the moment, as a result of various causes which have to do with the nature of the place, the permanence of the line, the relative state of quiet, we are not experiencing degree of dirt No. 1; I have experienced it, though, and I shall experience it again: having to go, I mean, four or five days without washing so much as one's face. Under present conditions I manage to get my face clean every morning, and my hands about twice a day. Naturally, one goes to bed with one's clothes on, though one can usually unlace one's boots. (Sometimes, in an access of daring, I take mine right off.) The result is rather less foul than the evidence of your nose might lead you to guess. Out at rest we have a thorough clean-up. This open-air life solves a good many problems. We don't overeat and our skins act pretty freely. Many impurities, both internal and external, evaporate or undergo a sea-change. On the whole I probably stink rather less than did Louis XIV. I've noted one or two odd things. I don't deny that the men I meet in the trenches do smell pretty strong, but it's the kind of smell I've often come across, at home, among the peasants who work in the fields, a sort of animal smell (animals don't wash much, either); a smell that has about it something earthy and alive. Far from being repulsive, it gives one an idea of what men, mankind in general, would be if one had to rely for one's impressions on the sense of smell alone, a counterbalancing impression to the one that comes through the eyes. Since we do not, as a rule, mind the shape of a man, why should we object to his smell? I'll even whisper a private little theory of my own. Imagine a few young women living here in the same physical conditions as ourselves, and as healthy as most of us are. Not only should we find their open-air smell quite definitely not unpleasing, but I have an idea that it might be positively attractive, that it might set us dreaming, might wake our desires and exercise upon us a magic charm.

Lice…it's hard, I must confess, to find anything much to say for them. In my own little cubby-hole I'm fairly free of them, but they exist none the less. There are trenches no more than five hundred yards away to our right which are infested with them, and by a giant species too, which bear about the same resemblance to the ordinary decent louse as the gutter rat does to the field-mouse. Fortunately, the louse does not believe much in walking. He uses carriages (ourselves, to wit), and when the carriages move, he moves too. I've told my men to keep as far as possible from their pals in the trenches to our right, and when they do meet, to avoid "transfers."

All the same—since I'm being honest with you—I do have a few lice, not all the time I'm in the line, but almost. I don't attract them much, it seems (though I've always been a happy hunting ground for fleas. I've known dog-fleas to smell me out across a room and rush pell-mell from their master to make my acquaintance). Shall I pretend that one gets used to lice? Certainly not! But, provided there are not too many of them, one does find oneself regarding them as among the less important trials of the human state. When I was in La Rochelle one June, we had a plague of tiny mosquitoes. Especially between six and eleven at night, they used to come in at the windows, and when I was working at my table they worried me incessantly. They had a way of making a dead set at my elbows, my ankles, and round my knees. Well, I got into the habit of working through it all, of concentrating on what I was doing, of reading poetry without losing my sense of form or of content, while all the time scratching away at my ankles and my elbows, and smacking away at the little beasts—a game at which I developed considerable skill.

I've even come to believe that man is so made that the presence of a small superficial irritation, provided the sensation is acute without being symptomatic of any serious trouble, is a definite aid to his mental equilibrium and serves to keep occupied the restless margin of his consciousness. He regards it, too, as a sort of ring of Polycrates, for I suspect that there is in all of us, always, an obscure sense of fate, inherited from numberless ancestral misfortunes, which whispers: "We are not sent into this world to live peacefully. When there's nothing to worry us, it's not natural, it's a bad sign." A small irritation gives us the assurance that we are paying our "residence tax" so far as this world is concerned—not much, to be sure, but enough to ensure us against the jealousy and the thunderbolts of Heaven. (Do you think mankind will ever get over this hereditary mistrust of everything that looks at all like happiness? This war will have intensified the feeling of nervousness for at least a century to come.) Well then, I want you to understand that the presence of lice in the trenches has served to inoculate me sometimes against that vague uneasiness of which I am conscious when we have been left too long without being bombarded. (To cover the ground completely, I ought to mention the rats. But they're not really worth worrying about—merely one source of irritation the more.)

I have written about the smell of the living. Now I've got to send you a few words about the smell of the dead. I'm sorry, but you've got only yourself to thank: you asked me for a complete picture of my days, and I shall spare you nothing. Don't worry, though; I'm not going to start being romantic. We no more live in "the odour of death" than during the spring of 1914 in Paris we lived in "the odour of gasoline." But the smell of corpses is all part of our daily existence. We can never entirely forget it. Sometimes, and without warning, unfortunately, it takes the centre of the stage—and that means that we've got to be ready at all times to face the possibility with steadfastness and unconcern.

Generally speaking, our attitude to death and its trappings is symptomatic of a really remarkable change in outlook. It makes one realize, looking back, how much quiet efficiency went, in the old pre-war days, to keep the living from being obsessed by the idea of mortality, from finding themselves suddenly face to face with its material evidence. Sanitary precautions were admirably organized, so admirably that we never really gave the question a moment's thought. In the world of our present existence they are badly handicapped by circumstances—have, in fact, been literally overthrown. I don't mean that there's any deliberate attempt to force the dead on the attention of the living, but we can't help spending our days next door to them or constantly meeting the signs of their proximity.

The oddest aspect of the business is the way the men treat it. It's not at all simple. The constant reminder of death seems to nag at their consciousness, to provoke and awake in them sentiments of a very different kind, many of which are rather surprising. In the first place, and this is almost too obvious to mention, the living have become extremely familiar with the look of death. They are not easily moved to a display of emotion. When the wind brings to their nostrils the smell of corpses, they say almost jokingly: "God, what a stench!" rather as though they were in some workshop while the sanitary men were emptying a neighbouring cesspool. When, at some turn in the trench, they happen to see sticking from the earth two feet still in their boots (a very frequent sight), they're as likely as not to remark, if the feet in question are pretty large: "That chap took an out size, I'll warrant." The very sanity of their outlook gives it a sort of human quality. The fact that the feet are French no more moves them to pious reflection or sentimental silence than if they were Boche—though Maurice Barrès would like to have us believe it does. But side by side with that attitude there goes a tendency to be disgusted, and a very real superstitious dread. I've seen men stand up to a cursing and to the threat of punishment rather than use their shovels to move a few fragments of corpse that happened to turn up in a parapet or trench wall. But I've seen another knock out his pipe against the head of a tibia, fleshless of course, but quite obviously human, which was sticking out of the earth near where he was sitting. A friend of mine told me that when he was in the line near Soissons last winter, his men used regularly to hang their caps or sling their haversacks on a blackened and dried-up human hand that jutted out from the trench wall at a convenient height, close to the entrance to a listening-post, but that when, disgusted by the sight, he gave orders for the hand to be cut off and buried, he could find no one willing to do the job. This blackened hand, which they treated with complete unconcern so long as it was merely a question of using it in a friendly way, became suddenly an object of superstitious terror when the question arose of doing it a violence. You will tell me that the reason is obvious, that for the simple souls of common soldiers, unconcern has nothing in common with profanation,

while cruelty has. Maybe. It's important, though, to stress the
degree of malice or deliberate cruelty which might be held to
be sufficient excuse for the calling forth of a spirit of
vengeance from the dead; and, in other cases, to take into
account the far more obscure thought that it is bad luck to
touch a dead man, or bits of a dead man, and still more to
move them from their chosen resting-place. So far from the
idea of profanation, taken in its widest sense, always acting as
a deterrent, I'm pretty sure that it quite often is an actual
stimulus. I've noticed that the men are not content with having gained a familiarity with death which hardens them and
renders them less susceptible to being shocked, if, indeed,
shocked at all, at the idea of doing things that in the old days
would have sickened them. Such an attitude is an inevitable
result of the deadening effects of war on human sensibilities.
But their moral deterioration goes much further than that. In
many cases they seem actually relieved at being freed from the
particular attitude of respect for human life in which most of
them have been brought up. That is something quite different
from a mere deadening of sensibility. It is an active satisfaction
in loosening the bonds of sentiment, and it worries me very
considerably. It's hard to mark the subtle difference without
being guilty of exaggeration. Don't believe the people who
tell you that war has made the average man more ferocious.
They're either lying or letting mere words go to their head.
When my men, as occasionally happens, talk of "hating" the
enemy, it's really only so much talk (unless, perhaps, they are
from the occupied territories, or are suffering from a species
of shell-shock). If they never let a chance of retaliation slip,
that's because they feel their self-respect involved. I've never
known the joyous anticipation of jabbing his enemy's guts out
get a man over the top a moment sooner than he can help.
On the other hand, there's no doubt whatever that they are
delighted at the thought that they need no longer approach
life with kid gloves, and that they do derive a sort of gutter
satisfaction from treating life and its manifestation in the bits
and pieces of human beings like so much dirt. Nor can there
be any doubt that such an attitude can, superficially at least,

be confused with ferocity.

The whole business reminds me vividly of the Middle Ages. We are rapidly taking on again the mental outlook of the Middle Ages: lack of reverence for the human carcass and for mere flesh whether living or dead; the very large part, on the other hand, which we accord, in our preoccupations, to this same flesh; the mocking unconcern which we show for those aspects of the human body which are most degrading, such as excreta, carrion, skeletons; the whole side of mediæval consciousness which produced the *danse macabre* and found delight in setting charnel-house, gargoyles, obscene bas-reliefs, and latrines in the shadow of the great cathedrals. We of the fighting services seem to be saying: "We've been poisoned ever since we were children with a hundred and one sugary refinements, shamefaced prejudices, and lies. What nonsense it all is! We're nothing but a mass of guts after all, damned useless guts, which only stop rotting inside us the better to rot on the ground." *Quia pulvis es.* The real hymn of the trenches is the *Dies Iræ*, which, as you once pointed out to me, ought to be sung to a brisk and brutal rhythm with a touch of crude joviality and insolence, a sort of triumphal challenge to the whole beastly business of living from which at last we are to be set free.

The same attitude, I am convinced, accounts for the courage with which we go into action when we can no longer help ourselves. Courage is by no means incompatible with terror, with the general nervousness of the trenches. The irreverent laughter induced in us by the spectacle of life prevents us from taking our own individual lives too seriously. Men in the mass are seen to be like a shoal of fish or cloud of locusts swarming to destruction. The individual man is less than nothing—certainly not worth worrying about. The act of clinging to life is merely so much extra and useless trouble. We just let ourselves be swept along; the tide of danger picks us up and carries us with it. It will leave us high and dry precisely where it chooses and how it chooses: dead, mutilated, made prisoner, or even still living—not that that really settles anything.

This, it seems to me, is the one irreparable loss. It has taken civilization centuries of patient fumbling to teach men that life, their own and that of others, is something sacred. Well, it's been so much work thrown away. We shan't, you'll see, get back to that attitude in a hurry.

For people like us, this particular disaster is but one aspect of a far more extensive disaster, from the effects of which I, for one, shall never recover. How can I explain what I mean without making the sceptics smile? (But you're no sceptic.) Let me put it this way: Without subscribing to the cruder forms of the belief in progress, we did think—I hope you don't mind my saying "we"—that the last few centuries of Western civilization had given to human nature an orientation, a culture, that, no matter how one viewed it from the point of view of metaphysics, had had certain very important practical results. If we anticipated a continuance of the process, we could not, I think, be accused of undue stupidity. But that's a thing of the past. The anticipation, like everything else, has been swept away. My most haunting horror is not that I see men now willing to suffer and to act as they do, but that having so seen them, I shall never again be able to believe in their good intentions. Look at the thing how you will, it is now proved beyond power of contradiction that millions of men can tolerate, for an indefinite period and without spontaneously rising in revolt, an existence more terrible and more degraded than any that the numberless revolutions of history were held to have terminated for ever. They obey and they suffer as unquestioningly as the slaves and victims of the most bestial periods known to us. Don't let us blind ourselves to the truth by saying that at least they know why they are doing it, and that the fact of their free will saves their human dignity. We have no reason to affirm that the slaves and victims of past societies did not, between their rations of stripes, receive doses of moral drugs, injections of powerful suggestion, which created in them an attitude of consent. The slaves of the Pyramids may have been filled with admiration for the architectural ambitions of Pharaoh. The Hindu widows who were burned on the funeral pyres of their husbands were no doubt persuaded that those who hoisted them on to the piles of aromatic wood were only helping them to accomplish a painful duty. All our talk of man's dignity is but mockery unless and until a day comes when certain things will under no circumstances be required of him or accepted by him as inevitable. I can no longer believe that any such day will ever come. You have often laughed at my optimism, at my Rousseauism; well, I am now in a state of mind that forces me to a deep distrust of man, of everything he may enforce as master or consent either to do or to endure as slave.

We know now that men can be made to do exactly any-thing—after a hundred years of democracy and eighteen centuries of the Christian faith. It's all a question of finding the right means. If only we take enough trouble and go sufficiently slowly, we can make him kill his aged parents and eat them in a stew. I foresee appalling developments. We may live to witness the revival of human sacrifice. We may see thinkers sent to the stake or the electric chair for having preached heresy. We may see witch trials and persecution of the Jews as bad as any that took place in the Middle Ages. We may see crowds yelling themselves into a hysteria of adoration as the despot passes, and the sons of those who now vote Socialist rolling on the ground and crying: "Crush us, O living God!" But there is this grain of comfort: we may be dead by that time, or at least I may. Don't kid yourself that your old friend Jerphanion is playing the prophet. Everything he says is clear-ly visible by the cold light of common sense in what is going on before our eyes.

I can hear your comment: "It isn't as bad as that yet; the old boy is exaggerating as usual. He wants to punish himself for having believed too blindly in mankind and in the future, so he's just diving headlong into despair."

No, it isn't as bad as that yet, I agree. But we have crossed the Rubicon. However short a time ago the attack began, the fact remains that our defences have been shattered, and we are now in a world where all these things are natural, simple, and, I repeat, only too much a matter of practical politics. It was on the 2nd of August 1914 that the real front was broken, the front held by civilization against barbarism.

But I must be fair. The war has brought us one positive advantage. It could hardly do less. Its name is comradeship— a rough kindness of man to man; a touching confidence of the soldier in his junior officers (not always, and it stops before it has got very far in the hierarchy); unselfishness; an absence, or a diminution, of the tendency to look ahead, at least very far ahead; a carelessness, though it is bred of despair; a clinging, sometimes a blind clinging, to the minute and the possible happiness it may offer.

I was going to add, in my desire to hold the scales even, that from these temporary virtues—for they all spring from our present discontents—durable benefits might result: such, for instance, as physical hardness; a definite incapacity to make mountains out of molehills; a willingness to seize the passing moment and enjoy what it has to give; a refusal to spoil one's life by indulging in trivial anxieties; and, chief of all, a readiness to accept as an incomprehensible miracle the mere fact of breathing and living, of being able to drink a glass of wine under a tree, of being able to go to sleep in a bed, without the ever haunting fear of shells.

But let me tell you what happened on the occasion of my last leave, my second, as it happens (the one when I so much regretted missing you. The first, when I was convalescing, I spent, as you probably remember, in the Charente-Inférieure, so that the same situation didn't arise). Well, when I got home, when I saw my apartment and my wife just as they had always been, all the familiar things of my life, I was so deeply moved that I believe I actually cried. That is all perfectly natural; but now mark the sequel. Suddenly I found myself feeling that the apartment was small(!). My study, in particular, seemed airless, without light, melancholy. I was worried by some feeling for which I could not find words. Put crudely, it was like this: "Is it worth while going through all I'm going through if this is what I've got to come back to?"

I had been drunk with delight at seeing my wife again. But that didn't prevent me, the very next morning, from being pernickety, almost ill-humoured, like a man who has never had to do without the petty comforts of life. All my old habits, even the most trivial, closed down on me again. The only difference was that I was rather more impatient, more sensitive than I used to be. A spoiled cup of coffee sent me off into a rage. You understand what I mean? Nothing seemed to me to be good enough for a man who had to make up for so much lost time. The change from the life of the trenches wasn't complete, wasn't dramatic, enough. Do you know, I believe that if the war really does end one day, the men who have fought it, so far from feeling thankful that they have been able to get back to the humble conditions of their former homes, will see everything with a disillusioned and disgusted eye, They will say, as I almost said the other day: "Is this all?" Nothing short of the life of a prince, a cardinal, or perhaps a millionaire with a villa on the Riviera will convince them that they're not being fooled.

And at the same time there are moments when I am haunted by a vision of life as it used to be when it was real and lovely (for what we find, when we're lucky, on leave is not the real life; somehow it's all different). I see the Grands Boulevards on a June day; I see

> A busy harbour where my soul
> Can drink its fill…

remember the sauntering days of love, or one of our strolls about the outlying suburbs. At such times I pay, with a sense of delicious, overwhelming melancholy, my tribute to life as once it was. I don't really believe it can ever be like that again. I wear its picture on my heart as I might the portrait of some dear dead woman of the past.

CHAPTER SIXTEEN

Galliéni Is Anxious

At the conclusion of the Cabinet meeting Galliéni took Gurau apart.

"I have a favour to ask you."

"Anything I can do."

They withdrew into a corner of the great waiting-room.

"I want you, if it wouldn't be too great a bore, to go to Chantilly."

"To Chantilly? To G.H.Q.?"

"Yes."

"To see Joffre in person?"

"Yes, but that won't prevent you from having a word or two with members of his Staff. We'll settle on a plan of campaign before you go."

"My dear Galliéni, you know how anxious I always am to be of service to you, but I confess I find the suggestion a trifle unexpected."

Very politely Galliéni put forward a suggestion:

"If I'm not presuming too far on your good nature, I should like to walk with you as far as my Ministry. I will explain what I mean on the way."

"You must know that my relations with Joffre are extremely delicate....He's always been terribly touchy...and ever since the Battle of the Marne I've got on his nerves worse than anybody. It's quite natural. Public opinion has always regarded us as competitors. The last straw for him, of course, is having me now as Minister of War. His attitude makes any confidential relations between us impossible. Things have got so bad that I just can't go to Chantilly myself. If I did, I know that I should find just a row of wooden faces. Joffre would pretend to think that I'd come to spy on him out of pure malevolence....Naturally, I couldn't very well behave like a junior officer....On the other hand, I hesitate to summon him here, because I don't want him to think that I want to humiliate him. It's very awkward. There are things we could say face to face which would take on quite another aspect if made the subject of a written memorandum, of a letter....If only you could bring yourself to do what I ask, everything would be splendid...you can take my word for that. You are the only man who can do what I want. An army officer? Absolutely impossible! And I can't make such a suggestion to Briand. I did sound him one day, but I could see he was unwilling. I can understand his point of view perfectly. He wants to keep himself in reserve in case things get really bad....Joffre will be flattered by your visit. As a Minister of State you will approach him with all the necessary prestige. I needn't remind you that as a rule he is very anxious to keep on the right side of civilians, especially of politicians."

"But he can't help knowing that you and I are friends...and in particular"—Gurau hurried over the words so as not to seem to be reminding the other of a favour—"that I was no stranger to your appointment?"

"That doesn't matter. He'll listen to you."

"Even if he guesses that I'm acting more or less as your mouthpiece?"

"He won't have to distinguish between what comes from me...and what represents your own views, and those of the government in general."

"All right, then, if you really think it a matter of national importance."

"It could hardly be more so!"

Galliéni explained why he felt anxious. His concern was not of recent growth, but it had suddenly become intensified and confirmed. He spoke of the recent conference held at Chantilly between the allied High Commands.

"The first part of the minutes has just reached me. When I've had them all and been able to read them carefully, I'll consider whether it would be wise to communicate the matter to the Cabinet. Meanwhile it is obvious that the conference was kept well within the lines laid down by those who summoned it. Joffre, or the people behind him, led the whole lot by the nose."

"You think the program adopted is dangerous?"

"Dangerous—well, in the first place it's not for me to express an opinion. I have no more right than you have to meddle in operations. But it's not so much the program that I find dangerous....It does little more than lay down certain elementary truths such as: 'We must seek a decision in one of the main theatres, the Franco-British, the Russian, or the Italian.' Good God! Do they think we're going to win the war in the Cameroons?... 'Success can be assured only if we see that our attacks are sufficiently strong and adequately synchronized.' Why, I shouldn't wonder if La Palisse said something like that long ago.... 'We must act as soon as possible in order to forestall the enemy. But it would be imprudent to tie ourselves down to a date. The time of striking must depend on how soon the necessary preparations can be made, and also on the state of the weather; the blunder of last September must not be repeated....' All very nice! And now, if the enemy hasn't the decency to wait till we're ready, the one of the allies who is first attacked is to have the right of demanding that the others shall at once come to his assistance by staging a diversion as soon as possible and with all their available forces.... For three whole days the greatest brains of the allied forces have been in labour, and that's all they can produce! Isn't it, to say the least, a little disappointing ?"

"What's worrying you, in fact, is not what the Chantilly program contains, but what it doesn't?"

"Put it that way if you like. To be perfectly frank, it seems to me that the fools are sleeping where they stand. They got together round a table for no other purpose than to authorize one another to go on living in a world of meaningless talk. And now they'll start issuing orders to their patient flocks with the self-complacency of so many archbishops! The various High Commands will now start making their preparations in strict accordance with the books, and quite irrespective of how much time they've got to play with. It'll all be done as conscientiously and with as much careful foresight as though they were going to start digging another Suez Canal and had all their lives before them. And then, one fine day it'll be the Germans who attack, without warning, at some point which our fine gentlemen have ignored. Well, if they do, it'll be all over."

They entered the courtyard which faces the rue Saint-Dominique, saluted by the sentries and by various officers whom they met.

Galliéni took Gurau into his private room after giving orders that they were not to be disturbed unless he rang.

"Are you afraid for any particular point in the line?" asked Gurau.

Galliéni did not answer the question directly.

"I've drafted a letter to Joffre," he said, "after three or four false starts. I can't state the position clearly and firmly enough without taking up a line which might seem to him—well, critical." He sat thinking for a while in silence; then: "The immediate sector to be considered is Verdun. I've no definite reason for believing that the Germans mean to attack us there....The only reports that have come in might be furnished equally from almost any other part of the front. But then I look at the map, and I say to myself that if I were a German I should be sorely tempted to try it. An operation undertaken just there offers a chance of success in more ways than one. It could take Verdun and drive us from the right bank of the Meuse; it could reduce the whole of our salient between the Argonne and Saint-Mihiel, and it might achieve a big enough break-through to threaten all our lines of communication in Champagne. The consequences would be incalculable. The way to Paris lies open just as much from Sainte-Menehould and Châlons as from Compiègne. The mere capture of Verdun would have a terrific effect on morale. The defences down there are in an appalling state, whether you consider effectives, field-works, or guns. A number of people are responsible for this state of affairs. I don't, between ourselves, think very much of Dubail, who is nominally in charge of the area. But the first prerequisite to staving off disaster is to persuade G.H.Q. to give a little serious thought to Verdun."

Gurau had been listening to Galliéni with a sense of anxiety. Never since the beginning of the war had he known real peace of mind. The long succession of shocks, so far from making him callous, had but sharpened his sensibilities. Everyone with a worry to voice found in him a ready audience.

"You're counting on me, then," he said, "to make them see the danger of the situation?…Joffre will just show me the door…quite politely, of course, but quite firmly."

"I don't think so. He will realize that, rightly or wrongly, the government is alive to the Verdun possibilities. He will argue that if the place was attacked now, he would never be forgiven for having neglected to listen to the warning. He must look into the position; he can't help himself, even if only to set your fears at rest. And since he's neither a fool nor a criminal, what he discovers as a result of his inquiries may make him think a bit.…Don't hesitate to let him know that the official view is that the fall of Verdun would be far more than a mere episode…that it might be the beginning of the end."

"Won't he think that I'm meddling in what doesn't concern me? After all, it's not my job to play at strategy."

"Assuming certain premisses, your strategy is the only one worth considering. Neither Joffre, nor you, nor I have learned from the books what would happen to this war if Verdun fell.…You may set his mind working.…He's the kind of man you can work on by appealing to his sense of personal responsibility.…We must wait and see. My draft letter will remain in my drawer. If, when you come back from Chantilly, you tell me: 'Nothing doing, he's as obstinate as a mule,' then I'll send it."

A spasm passed across Galliéni's face, and for a moment or two he said nothing. Then, with apparent irrelevance, he muttered:

"If only my damned health was better!…"

CHAPTER SEVENTEEN

Gurau Lunches with Joffre. A Curious Charm

It was not until two days later that Gurau paid his visit to Chantilly. He had been anxious to get Briand's opinion on the matter.

"When it's a question of Joffre," Briand said to him, "Galliéni's views are not remarkable for their detachment. But in this case I believe him to be right. Nor, for that matter, do I see any good reason why we should not make all necessary preparations at Verdun. You are acute enough to wake the old man up without wounding his susceptibilities. In your place I should have a chat first with one of the younger members of his Staff, and put my cards on the table. You will be asked to lunch. If you've managed to have a few words with one of the youngsters, he will no doubt have put his chief wise and so made things easy for you. He may even have given you a hint or two about the way in which G.H.Q. view the question. You will be better equipped, in that case, to discuss matters with the generalissimo. You'll find my suggestion worth following."

Gurau did so. He put a call through to Lieutenant-Colonel G., who was personally known to him and whom he had occasionally helped in return for small services rendered. Lieutenant-Colonel G. was only too glad to take on himself the duty of warning the Commander-in-Chief of the impending visit.

"Please tell him," the Minister concluded, "that I want to discuss with him two or three things that are on my mind. But I'd like a word with you first. There are some routine matters I want to go over."

They made an appointment for eleven o'clock. A Staff car would call for Gurau an hour earlier.

Lieutenant-Colonel G., who was a man of exquisite breed-ing, began the interview by taking careful notes about Gurau's wishes, most of which referred to the military situation of certain electors from the Indre-et-Loire. He listened with patient attention, asked his visitor to repeat one or two details about which he was not quite clear, and inclined his head to signify that he had caught the other's drift. He appeared to attach as much importance to keeping M. Laubrault, the industrialist of Plessis-les-Tours, out of the line as he would have done to the sending of a division to Salonica. He smiled as much as to say that what he was being asked to do was the most natural thing in the world. Not once did he say "That's impossible," nor, on the other hand, did he make any definite promises. He merely let it be understood that if the hoped-for result did not eventuate, he, at least, would have done his best.

Gurau laid special stress on the granting of a Croix de Guerre to a certain officer of reserve, a M. Hector Trampagut, who was serving in an administrative capacity at Bar-le-Duc.

Lieutenant-Colonel G., pencil in hand, put a benevolent question:

"May I ask whether he has any active service to recom-mend him? What, precisely, is his war record?"

Gurau permitted himself a smile. "I rather think that the place where he is working has been shelled—at least once. Bar-le-Duc, you know, is quite close to the front."

"Certainly."

It was at this point that the question of Verdun was raised. It must have been difficult for the lieutenant-colonel to indi-cate by the tone of his voice or by his general attitude—so attentive was he already—that he considered the conversation, in its passage from M. Trampagut's Croix de Guerre to the defence of Verdun, to have entered on a more serious phase. He did, however, succeed in marking the difference. The out-ward signs of his change of attitude were the suppression of his smile and the introduction of a deeper tone into his speak-ing voice....Two or three times in the course of their con-versation he even passed the fingers of his right hand over his forehead in a gesture of concern.

"I am far from being disturbed, sir, at hearing that your attention has been drawn to this subject…I shall be only too glad if you will speak of it to the C.-in-C. You will be performing a very useful service. I have got to take in some orders for his signature before lunch, and I will seize the opportunity to say that I rather think you are going to raise the question….You can be of great help to us, sir. We're pretty clear-sighted here, a good deal more so than we are given credit for being in some quarters. But there are so many influences at work!…To be fair to the C.-in-C., if he listened to every suggestion he would dissipate all his available forces and so be unable to take any positive action. All decision involves choice, and choice involves risks." He hastened to add: "But I realize that the risks in this matter of Verdun are so great that they demand very special consideration."

Gurau felt encouraged to make a display of his military competence. "After all," he thought, "there's nothing particularly absurd about that. I might very easily be the head of the government. As it is, I'm second in command. If I was head of the government no one would dare to express surprise at my venturing to make suggestions about anything that vitally concerned the safety of the country." He sounded the lieutenant-colonel on his views in the matter of shock troops. Was the idea being favourably viewed at G.H.Q.? Was the generalissimo interested? (Gurau regarded himself as the godfather and mentor of the shock-troop school of thought. He no longer bothered about trying to recollect whether in fact, or how far, he had been converted to the idea by Duroure, or to what extent he had launched Duroure's active imagination along this particular road. He did not really think that the fate of the scheme would be determined by Lieutenant-Colonel G. more than by anybody else. It was far more important to win over Galliéni. Temperamentally, Galliéni was not opposed to the idea of shock troops, but he was not very fond of Duroure, whom he regarded as an "exhibitionist." Generally speaking, he was afraid that an army composed of shock troops, once in existence, might become an irresistible temptation and might lead to the commission of blunders. It was the kind of tool that might burn the hand that held it. And what would happen if it broke? What good would the other armies be if they had been shorn of their best elements? "I'm all for your shock troops," Galliéni had said to him one day, "but only on condition that I can keep them under lock and key.")

Lieutenant-Colonel G. was non-committal on the subject of shock troops. The old smile flickered once more about his lips, and he spoke about it in the tone which he had used in dealing with the business of M. Hector Trampagut, but with an additional subtlety of reserve which seemed to say: "You, sir, are deeply versed in this matter of shock troops. I, who have not studied the question so closely, find it difficult to give a definite opinion...." Quite possibly, too, he had no particular liking for Duroure. In the interests of the scheme, Gurau was careful not to let it seem that he regarded the shock-troop theory and Duroure as inseparably connected.

The Cabinet Minister was reintroduced to Lieutenant-Colonel G. at the C.-in-C.'s luncheon, which took place in a dining-room so perfectly ordinary that, after the first glance, he forgot all about it. Two other close colleagues of Joffre, both of them unknown to Gurau, sat down to the meal with them. Gurau did not know whether they were there because it was their habit to be so, or whether they had been asked specially to meet him.

The Commander-in-Chief was in a good temper and gave evidence of having an excellent appetite. "I don't wonder," thought the Minister, "that he's fat. I can well imagine him sleeping the sleep of the just in the middle of an attack, just as popular legend says that he does."

Set face to face with this man whose hands wielded such immense power, the least complex mind could not but have felt itself torn between conflicting conjectures, or rather could not have helped asking itself several definite and disturbing questions. "Is he simply an honest old fellow, quite unequal to the circumstances in which he finds himself, and merely kept by sheer weight from succumbing to panic? Is he, on the other hand, a man of genius in the tradition of unpolished greatness so much beloved of the history books, who cares nothing for appearances or of what other people think, but who has, for all that, a profound depth of vision? An intelligence, keen, well-balanced, and strong, for ever ready to carry out the dictates of a mighty spirit? A will so sure of itself that it can calmly ride the storm and dispense with all imaginative stimulus? One of those men for whom have been invented such superb sayings as: 'To undertake great enterprises it is not necessary to live in hope; nor is per-severance dependent on success'?" Was he one of those human miracles of whom we read, in whom our modern scepticism has ceased to believe—a great reservoir of intellectual power unaffected by nervous strain? Or was the explanation more subtle than that: was he one of those men, gifted above the ordinary with force of character, of first-rate quality, perhaps, but no greater than a thousand others in a single generation of a country's history; men capable of filling high posts in pol-itics or business, knowing how to advance themselves, clever at handling those who hold the reins; cursed with no theories to uphold, to the danger of their careers and at the risk of finding themselves in conflict with the powers that be; con-cealing much craftiness beneath a mask of joviality, as so often happens in the provinces?

His cheeks were full and rosy, his moustache white, his light-coloured eyes not without a suspicion of vivacity and mischief. His strong jaws chewed their food with obvious pleasure. His accent was strongly reminiscent of the Pyrenees, though softened by a middle-class intonation no more and no less accentuated than the day he left the Polytechnic.

It was for the observer to decide whether he had to do with a wise and kindly king, with a rustic and rather cunning old mayor, with a small-town shopman making the round of his customers, or even perhaps with an eminent but modest scholar anxious to put himself within the reach of all and sundry. The mind jumped from one hypothesis to another in response to a hundred tiny indications furnished by the model, or, more arbitrarily, in obedience to its own changing moods.

He said nothing silly, but nothing remarkable either. It was easy to assume that he distrusted the remarkable. He was not unconscious of the effect he produced on his listener, but seemed content to let it be one of sly good humour or assumed simplicity. It would have been more accurate, perhaps, to say that he made no effort to impress, but remained content to draw from the bottomless well of common sense which lay always ready to his hand.

Suddenly Gurau thought: "The most obvious thing about him is charm. He's a perfectly delightful creature. This great fat fellow has made his way entirely by charm. Its particular quality—which distinguishes it from what is generally understood by the word—is the feeling of tranquillity which it diffuses. One has only got to be with him to feel at peace. When I came here I was nervous and worried, as we all are these days. The lieutenant-colonel gave me a preliminary stroking-down with plenty of oil. Joffre is the great sedative bath. He dissolves the sense of tragedy. One feels that in his presence all problems fade to nothing. One is conscious of a certain sense of shame at having worried about this, that, and the other. The tranquillity that emanates from him can even overcome the promptings of common sense, which proves that his influence is not merely that of a contagious optimism, but is a real product of charm. If a shell burst at this moment a hundred yards off, it wouldn't, somehow, seem as dangerous as most; one would have the feeling that it was not an irremediable disaster even for the people among whom it fell. If someone at this table started talking of the war as being a terrible scourge for civilization, Joffre would certainly not protest, because he is obviously a sincere lover of peace, but we, bathing in his radiance, should find ourselves wondering whether the words 'terrible scourge' were not perhaps a trifle turgid, whether the speaker wasn't, after all, painting things rather blacker than they were. A few minutes ago I started the subject of Verdun. Joffre showed no sign of displeasure. He replied that he, too, was much concerned about the state of affairs at Verdun, and that before the winter was out he would have got the place into a proper state of defence. But his reply reached me on such a buoyant tide of confidence that it was as much as I could do not to say: 'Please forget anything I said about Verdun. I should hate to think that you were giving yourself a moment's uneasiness about it.' Obviously such an atmosphere might become very dangerous. But what a comfort it must have been at times like the great retreat after Charleroi, when even the calmest heads began to panic!"

Gurau thought of Mme Godorp. He found a vague analogy between the effect of her presence and Joffre's. "Nervous people like me have a terrible craving for those who can spread a sense of calm."

He had to admit—not without a certain feeling of guilt—that had he been the head of a government, or better still the king, of a country whose armies were commanded by Joffre, having once got the Joffre habit, he would have found it difficult to do without him. "I should keep him always at hand so as to be able to steal a little of his calm. I should want him always at my side when I had to brace myself to meet the impact of events. He would become my private vice. His shortcomings?…I should say:'Hell, what do they matter compared with his power of diffusing peace over everything he touches?…' If he lacks genius, I've got enough for two."

Galliéni listened to Gurau's account of his visit to Joffre. In spite of himself, Gurau slightly heightened the tone of the conversation he was setting himself to report. He made the general's comments on Verdun rather more definite than in fact they had been. Nevertheless, now that the charm of Joffre's presence was removed, the harvest did seem a bit thin.

Galliéni, nodding his bony head and narrowing his eyes behind their glasses, gave expression to a rather embarrassed smile.

"I think," he said, "that I shall send that letter all the same."

CHAPTER EIGHTEEN

A Visit to the War Lord

Maykosen stretched out his hand to raise the blind which obscured the right-hand window. But Captain von Stiegert checked him at once:

"Please!"

Slightly disconcerted, Maykosen apologized:

"Oh, I'm sorry."

He noticed that another blind, just at the back of the young lieutenant who occupied the folding seat, cut off any view forward. The only light in the constricted space came from a small lamp in the ceiling.

"You must excuse me," said the officer, "but we have strict orders. Naturally, we are quite easy in our minds about you. But you know that the only way of keeping a rule is to see that it is never infringed."

He added, in an agreeable and explanatory tone:

"We have to be a great deal more careful than we should be at home. There are a great number of spies about. They get information from the other side of the line extraordinarily quickly. Where we are going is quite close to the forward area. It could very easily be bombed from the air."

"In any case," said Maykosen with good-humoured resignation, "I don't suppose I could have seen much on such a dark night as this."

He made a mental calculation: "Quite close to the forward area? We've been going about three quarters of an hour. They told me the trip would take rather more than an hour….It must be at least eighteen miles from the front."

Out loud he said:

"These precautions of yours can only be applicable to visitors, surely? The inhabitants of the place can't help knowing, eh?"

The captain smiled. "No. They think that the house is occupied by some of the Staff, certainly, but why should they guess at anything else? When His Majesty or His Imperial Highness comes here, it's always after dark, and in a car just like this one. It's only visitors who, by quite innocently describing the place or its surroundings, might enable people to put two and two together."

"Oh, I don't mind," thought Maykosen; "and I've no doubt the dear chap finds it all more romantic like this."

Now and then the car slowed down or stopped. Sounds of heavy transport could be heard, and the voices of men talking in German, but in such a mixture of local patois that Maykosen could not understand what they were saying. It began to be very cold. The road took on the resonance of frost.

Occasionally, too, a sudden glare on the blinds showed that a car was coming towards them with lights full on.

Their arrival was over in a flash. Maykosen had scarcely time to notice the sound of gravel beneath the tyres. The car stopped. The right-hand door opened to display the lowest step of a short stone stairway, covered with an awning and very badly lit. Maykosen had the impression of being rushed up the steps with people to his right and left. He found himself, without quite knowing how he had got there, in a small, shabby room upholstered in faded blue, where he was asked to wait. The lieutenant remained with him.

The delay was very short. An officer appeared—a colonel.

"His Majesty requests that you come downstairs."

This was precisely what he discovered he had to do. The descent was made by a narrow, winding stairway, which must have been the cellar stairs of the villa, though now, carpeted and hung with Oriental stuffs, it had assumed a somewhat different appearance.

On reaching the basement Maykosen crossed an anteroom which seemed designed to accommodate an orderly officer, or perhaps two. His guide led him into a second apartment,

low-roofed like the other, but much larger. There he found
the Emperor. What, however, first caught his eye was a
Christmas tree standing in a corner, with its tiny candles lit
and its branches loaded with small objects wrapped in paper
of different colours. His second impression was that the place
had an air of being padded, wadded, and made perfectly
sound-proof. The ceiling and the walls were hidden by Oriental hangings, as on the staircase, but the colours here were
finer, the material thicker. These hangings were not stretched
taut, but hung in folds, and were draped, here and there, in
festoons, noticeably in the corners and in the middle of the
ceiling. Soft rugs covered the floor. There was a large work-
ing-desk, two small tables, as well as several chairs and odds
and ends of furniture. In one corner stood a camp-bed half
concealed by a curtain. On one of the walls hung a mediæval
panoply framed between two lances with their pennants. Facing this was a modern equivalent (dating perhaps from 1870).
The other two walls displayed large maps: one of the western,
the other of the eastern, front. The general effect was reminiscent partly of Napoleon, partly of Genghis Khan, with a
distinct leaning towards the latter. Modernity was represented
by a telephone on the desk, and several shell-cases of various
sizes standing about on the floor and tables.

There was no heating arrangement visible, but the temper-
ature, for all that the place was below the level of the ground,
was so dry that there must have been some installation.

Maykosen found the Emperor looking markedly older. His
hair was whiter, his face pale, and there was a haunted expression in his eyes. Since the beginning of the war he had seen
him only once, at Metz, during the preceding winter, and
then but for a few minutes. His last distinct memory of the
man dated from July 1914. What a world of difference
between the yachtsman in shining white, laughing and talking, and this sad, exhausted soldier!

At sight of Maykosen, however, the Emperor's face cleared.

He got up, extended his hand, and shook his visitor's warm-
ly and at length.

"How glad I am to see you! Your coming has given me real pleasure."

He seemed more affectionate than ever. He had the air of a man clinging to an old friendship. He tapped Maykosen on the shoulder.

"I hope I have not put Your Majesty to too great an inconvenience by asking for this audience?"

"Why, of course not! I've got all today free....Leave us," he said to the colonel, who immediately withdrew. "Now we can talk comfortably....I've got some work I must finish this evening, but from now till then we've more than enough time. I sleep so little." He took from the Christmas tree a crystallized fruit in a pink paper frill and offered it to his visitor. "Tell me, my dear fellow, what you've been doing with yourself since this terrible war began."

"Your Majesty probably does not remember," said Maykosen quietly, "that I had the good fortune to meet Him last winter at Metz."

"Why, of course! You told me a lot of things, but I confess that they've all gone out of my head."

"To make a long story short, then, Sire, I've been doing my job as well as circumstances would permit. I was in England when mobilization took place. After that, I went to France. When I had the honour of seeing Your Majesty last winter, I had just arrived in Germany. I had a look at both the fronts, after which I paid a visit to Scandinavia. Then I went to England again, and thence to Egypt. I tried to get to Asia Minor, as far as the Dardanelles, but I found considerable difficulties in my way. I came back via Italy. Then once more to France, where I found myself at the time of the great September offensive. And now here I am again."

The Emperor sighed and smiled. "You're having the best of the war. You're seeing it. We never see it at all."

A moment later he continued:

"Don't they put obstacles in your way of wandering like this from side to side?"

"They certainly do, Sire!—and more than one, as is only natural. They are, however, numerous rather than insurmountable. All I need is a little determination, and a few useful friends."

"You've never been suspected, you and your colleagues, of—carrying confidential information?"

"Put more crudely, Sire, of espionage?" said Maykosen with a laugh. "There have been rumours, of course…but it's really all a question of 'standing.' Most people realize that an international journalist enjoying a certain reputation is not likely to play that sort of game. I find, too, that my American citizenship comes in very useful. I am more than careful, I need hardly say, to behave with complete correctness."

"So much so, no doubt," suggested the Kaiser lightly, "that even if you were in possession of Allied secrets which might give the victory to your old friend, you would not betray them?"

"I doubt whether I have any such knowledge, Sire. But if, as a result of confidences made to me, I had, I should not consider myself at liberty to pass them on. Your Majesty knows me well enough.…"

"I was only joking."

The Emperor continued in a more serious tone:

"That does not, I hope, prevent you from wishing well to the good cause?"

Maykosen bowed politely.

"I should be deeply pained," insisted the Kaiser, "if I thought that you were not heart and soul with us."

Maykosen showed signs of embarrassment.

"Your Majesty," he said, "has clearly not had time to read my articles. Your Majesty would, in that case, have realized that I have done my best to maintain a strict objectivity of approach. That is essential for a man in my position, besides being a matter of professional honour. But Your Majesty can hardly doubt the affectionate solicitude with which, from afar, I have followed His movements in these terrible times."

The Kaiser pretended to he satisfied. He went on:

"You don't mind my asking you a few questions?"

'I am at your disposition, Sire, and will do my best to answer them."

William II appeared to hesitate before his next words. Then, looking the other straight in the eyes, and with a slightly ironic smile (in which there was disenchantment and a trace of defiance): "The question," he said, "which I am about to put to you may seem strange coming from me. But I should value your opinion. How much longer do you think the war will last?"

Maykosen was obviously taken by surprise. He made a face. "It is not," he said, "a mere problem in physics—that is to say, merely a question of calculating forces. If it were, I might venture to draw conclusions in the matter of duration....But even so, the force available on one side might be increased by the sudden appearance on the stage of a new ally, or might be diminished by the defection or defeat of one already there.... How is it possible to foresee such things? The general problem is, to a large extent, one of morale. The rise to power of a single man in some one country may well hasten or delay the end. This becomes all the more obvious if one looks at the warring nations as a whole. It is already extremely difficult to calculate how long any of them can carry on. But God alone can tell how long the *will* to carry on can last. 'To the bitter end,' they say in France. But that is just talk. The end may be victory, defeat, complete exhaustion, or simply refusal to continue."

"You have not answered my question," said the Emperor.

"Good heavens, Sire, I have spoken as honestly as I know how!"

The Emperor pressed his point. A vague note of pathos had crept into his voice:

"Do you really mean to tell me that you don't, at times, in the privacy of your own mind, hazard a guess about what is likely to happen? When, for instance, you have made one of these trips of yours through the countries concerned, and drawn your own conclusions?...You may be wrong, of course, in your deductions. It is human to err. But what is your impression?"

Maykosen hesitated. He seemed to be the prey of acute embarrassment.

"You don't exclude from your calculations," went on the Emperor, his voice perceptibly trembling, "the possibility that a sudden decision might be obtained as a result of some large-scale victory in the field?"

"No, Sire, I certainly do not exclude any such possibility." He chose his words with care: "But even there I can see that experience has considerably altered the views generally held in such matters. Perhaps Your Majesty has not entirely forgotten certain conversations that I held with Your Majesty, many years ago, on the subject of the Russo-Japanese War? I told Your Majesty that, in my opinion, that war might have lasted a great deal longer, might even have had a very different ending, if the Russians had not, at a certain moment, become convinced that they were beaten. The same thing is even truer of the war of '70. No one could wish less than I do to belittle in any way the glorious victory of the German armies, but the fact cannot be ignored that the Emperor of the French and his marshals came to the conclusion that they were beaten, and surrendered their colours and their best troops, after six weeks of fighting which today would seem mild enough, and while the resources of France were still intact; so much intact that the revolutionary government was able to carry on the struggle with improvised forces and in the worst possible conditions."

"You seem to forget that Napoleon III was captured at Sedan with all his troops. What liberty of decision remained to him?"

"I am not forgetting it, Sire. But without being a specialist in strategy, I think I can maintain that Napoleon III and his army never would have been captured had they not gone into action with the firm conviction that the day would prove decisive, that there must be, as in a game of cards, a winner and a loser, and that the loser would have no alternative but to submit to fate like a good sportsman. Let us suppose for a moment that the Emperor and his generals, when they made their dispositions for the Battle of Sedan, had said firmly to themselves: 'Whatever the outcome of today may be, let us make up our minds that France cannot be beaten so easily, and that if we lose it, the war will only just have begun.' In the first place, it is probable that they would have adopted quite different tactics. But the main point is this: that they would never have let themselves be captured, nor their armies and their colours with them. They would have fought a rear-guard action before it was too late. The man who refrains from fighting a rear-guard action is the man who argues: 'The rules of the game have decided; why [Maykosen finished his sentence in French] *chercher midi à quatorze heures?*' As for Bazaine's shameful capitulation, that would have been radically impossible, given a state of public opinion ready to regard Sedan as no more than an unfortunate start. The present war, Sire, proves beyond doubt the truth of what I have been saying. Throughout the centuries all wars, at least in Europe, have been decided according to a strict convention. One side admitted defeat because there was a general agreement to recognize the 'rules of the game,' or because it suddenly became too bored to go on playing and preferred paying a small forfeit to continuing the struggle. The convention had only to be changed for everything else to be changed too. Eighteen months of a terrible war have failed to decide anything. Once you realize that, you realize also that it is dangerous to prophesy. What now are the necessary prerequisites of a decisive victory?…"

Maykosen became aware that he had been talking for a long time and was thereby guilty of a breach of etiquette. But William II had let him talk—which was something still more out of the ordinary. William II had listened without taking the words out of his mouth in an attempt to say better what his visitor was in the course of saying. "The Kaiser has indeed changed!" Maykosen noticed, too, that, without intending to do so, he had been addressing his august friend with greater freedom, and with less apparent respect, than he had ever done in the past. What an extraordinary thing! And yet never had the Kaiser controlled a greater show of strength. This war had accentuated and hardened the spirit of hierarchy among men. There was already a noticeable gulf between the authority of a mere captain and the situation of a simple private.

What an abyss, therefore, must there be between the All-Highest War Lord and a journalist! That, at any rate, was the common-sense view. But instinct was aware that all was not as it seemed. Both Emperor and journalist moved in a world that had lost its stability, in conditions that were in a state of flux. At times of great disturbance, hierarchies might assert themselves with crude brutality, but that didn't alter the fact that their foundations were unsure. Only in times of peace is the attitude of respect endowed with permanence. Men saved from a shipwreck, whatever the social differences between them, treat one another as equals. The captain of a ship would not long command obedience once his passengers had become convinced that his incapacity was responsible for the disaster and that he was doing nothing to retrieve it. At the back of Maykosen's mind a little voice was making itself heard, quite irrespective of his will: "You, the Emperor, are just like the rest of us. Before you caused the storm to break, you knew very little more than anyone else. But naturally people didn't realize that, and there was still a lot you *could* have done. Today all the world realizes it. You, like the rest of us, are lost in the maelstrom of events, and you've no longer any real control. You must follow in the wake of circumstance like your companions in arms. You are reduced to asking a mere journalist anxious questions about the future, even to begging him for a little advice, a little comfort."

"You have been in France," said the Emperor a few minutes later; "do you think that the French can hold out much longer?"

Maykosen turned over the question in his mind.

"They are a very curious people," he replied. "Who would have thought that they could have put up such a magnificent resistance?....Their failure last September had a profound effect on them. But I don't, somehow, see them throwing in their hand yet."

"Mm...ah...are you personally acquainted with Falkenhayn?"

"Only just, Sire. But I have watched his career from a distance."

"What sort of man do you think him?"

"A brave man."

"Capable of seeing things clearly?"

"I don't know enough about him, Sire, to say."

"What I am going to tell you is absolutely confidential, not that I think it necessary to say that to you....I'm not quite certain what I ought to do. I have just received from Falkenhayn a report which opens up very large problems indeed. According to him, England is the directing spirit of the coalition, and it is England on whom we ought to concentrate."

"Yes, Sire."

"But we can't strike a decisive blow at England—not, at any rate, soon enough. The alternative before us is to smash the instruments of her supremacy, and primarily France. Falkenhayn is of the opinion that a victory on the Russian front would not bring England to her knees, and that an Italian defeat would hardly affect her at all. But if we can crush France, then England will be like a fighter who has lost his sword. She will listen to our peace overtures. Once France is out of it, what Russia may or may not do will cease to matter. The probability is that she will be no less anxious to come to terms."

"That certainly is one point of view."

The Kaiser lowered his voice:

"Unfortunately, my friend, I cannot support Falkenhayn without abandoning Hindenburg. I am faced with a terrible responsibility."

"Hindenburg does not agree with him?"

The Kaiser shook his head without taking his eyes from his companion's face.

"Hindenburg has a high idea of the quality of the French Army—and even of the English...." The Kaiser allowed a note of surprise to creep into his voice: "Of the Belgians too, so far, that is, as they are concerned. He holds the view that the western front cannot be forced by either side, not even by us, so long, at any rate, as we cannot move an appreciable number of troops from the eastern theatre. If we make fruitless efforts to break the western front, he argues, the only result will be that we shall expend vast resources of every kind and dangerously weaken ourselves. He thinks that at the cost of a very much smaller effort we could definitely put the Russians out of the war, and that once our rear was secure, we should have a much greater chance on the western front either of taking the offensive with all our forces or of forcing the Allies to negotiate. He is convinced that once the Russians have laid down their arms, the morale of the French will collapse, and that England will be unable to keep her in the field....In short, his plan is to win a victory in the east in order to dictate conditions in the west....Do you know Joffre?"

"Yes, Sire. He once gave me a long interview on the strength of a letter of introduction from the American Ambassador."

"What do you make of him?"

"I think he is extraordinarily cool-headed. I can't imagine him losing confidence in any circumstances whatever. Nor can I see him admitting defeat or thinking it useless to go on."

"Mm...is that attitude typical of the French?"

"Sire, the French are capable of any attitude."

William II gently shook his head with the air of a man deep in thought. He gazed a long time at the Christmas tree as though he were counting the candles.

"To go back for a moment to Hindenburg. He's a fine soldier, you know. But he's got a bee in his bonnet about the eastern front, and one's got to take his views on it with a grain of salt."

He turned once more towards Maykosen and put a direct question:

"If you had to choose between Falkenhayn and Hindenburg, which would it be?"

Maykosen at first attempted to avoid the issue. "Whatever I say, it won't have the slightest effect on him!" He remembered the conversation he had had in July 1914 with the Emperor in the saloon of the latter's yacht. He proceeded to stress the point that he had not sufficient evidence on which to base a decision. He didn't, he said, want to risk making a fool of himself by giving an opinion on so important a matter, and in the Emperor's presence.

"But since I ask you to?"

The Baron remarked that there might be reasons, unknown to him, for preferring one line of action to another, reasons, in particular, of military strategy.

"Let us assume for a moment that there are not."

Maykosen ended by pointing out that what most embarrassed him was the fact that the Emperor had presented the problem in rather different terms from those employed by the German commanders.

"Your Majesty's generals see the situation in a purely military light, as it is only natural that they should. It may be that they are right to do so. My own tendency is to subordinate military to political considerations."

"What precisely do you mean by that?"

"I may be wrong, Sire, but I rather think that the problem for the soldiers may be expressed like this: 'We must force the enemy to his knees by every means in our power. What'll happen then remains to be seen.'"

The Kaiser threw himself back in his chair, folded his arms, and made a great business of raising his eyebrows.

"Isn't that only common sense?"

"Perhaps," replied Maykosen; but his tone lacked conviction, though he accompanied his words with a gesture of acquiescent deference. But the Emperor insisted once more, with friendly warmth, on the other's saying clearly what was in his mind:

"I swear that you will not displease me. On the contrary." His sigh was obviously sincere. "You've no idea, my friend, what a privilege it is for me to discuss these matters with a man like you. I love free discussion…" (Maykosen could scarcely believe his ears. Or rather he wondered what deep-seated cause was responsible for this momentary outburst. "I suppose," he thought, "that there's something in me that stimulates him to these outpourings for which, now and then, he feels a sudden craving, when, as the French say, 'there's something biting him.' The mood soon passes, though.") "It's something I've never had," continued the Emperor. "Quite often my advisers are willing to contradict me, to oppose my

wishes, or to make me do things I don't want to do, by mis-
representing the situation to me. But their attitude is always
that of the subordinate,[1] of the disloyal or churlish foreman.
…My ideal, as you know, has always been that of the great
periods of the Middle Ages. There is nothing in me of the
Oriental despot, not even of Louis XIV. I have always dreamed
of being the supreme leader in a world of noble knights who
speak to their chief respectfully, affectionately, but with complete freedom.…Hindenburg is capable of approaching me
on such terms of free give and take. But his view of things is
restricted. He knows nothing of the great world.…"

"What I should like to say," Maykosen proceeded, after once
more excusing himself for the impertinence of which he was
to be guilty, "is this: that if I had charge, as, thank God, I never
shall have, of this war and had to bring it to a conclusion, I
should never lose sight of the fact that victory is never an end
in itself, but only the means to an end. The end is Europe as
we wish it to be when the war is over. Or rather—for in this
world we can never exactly realize our wishes—the prac-
ticable end to keep in view is the making of the best possible
plans for the future, so far as we can envisage them at the
moment."

He added, stressing his words with care:

"Let me modify that. When I say so far as we can envisage
them at the moment, however unsatisfactorily that may be, I
realize that in six months' time new circumstances may have
arisen which will necessitate a complete revision of our attitude, and that true wisdom consists in knowing how to content ourselves with the second-best that we may not have to
accept worse."

He continued:

"Acting on this principle, I should demand of my generals
not so much that they should gain a victory for me, no matter how and no matter where, as that they should put me in
a position to implement the schemes I had in view. In short,
it is I who should decide what I wanted of them, and the

[1] *Beamte.*

results I wished them to produce. I should not wait until they had finished their job before proceeding with my own—which would be in the field of politics."

"All very sensible, my friend, but too vague. Theories almost always look well. It is when one comes down to detail that the difficulties begin. What I want to know is the demands you would make on your generals, and the political moves you would initiate in the meantime."

"Well, then—but Your Majesty must not complain if I show myself a fool—I should tell my generals to beat the Russians to a standstill and to drive back their armies as far as possible. I should not wait for the Tsar to open negotiations before declaring the complete liberation of Poland, including Cracow and Posen, and of Finland and the Baltic States as well. I should also proclaim the independence of Hungary."

"You would, would you!"

"For the moment I should leave the Southern Slavs and the Balkan peoples to fight matters out between them. I should annex Austria as compensation for the sacrifices I should have to make elsewhere...."

"Ho, ho!"

"Sire, remember that you gave me leave to talk nonsense.... Whether one likes it or not, the fact remains that once this war is over, Austria–Hungary will no longer be a living entity. Speaking for myself, I am not too pleased at the prospect. But it is inevitable. Far better preside over its partition than let it be performed later by someone else.... That done, I should turn my attention to the west. I should be tactful with France. I should offer her an extremely advantageous peace. I should insist on the establishment of a European customs union. There remains England, and England, I admit, is a hard nut to crack. But she would not be in a position to carry on the struggle single-handed.... I should, for instance, propose a treaty of alliance and perpetual friendship."

The Emperor had been listening with attention, even with some show of excitement. But there was a smile of amused incredulity on his lips. He made his guest repeat certain points. Now and again he gave vent to a suppressed chuckle.

"All things considered, my friend, I must admit that your solution is no worse than many others. The only thing lacking is the possibility of putting it into effect....I'm afraid we must take a more limited view. The first duty of Germany is to win this war which has been forced upon her."

Maykosen agreed that if they were to limit themselves to matters of immediate importance, France was undoubtedly, from a purely military point of view, the chief adversary.

"It is true that once France is beaten to her knees, the war, militarily speaking, will be over."

"You see eye to eye with Falkenhayn, then?" the Emperor exclaimed loudly.

"On this particular point, yes."

The Emperor lowered his voice again. "You no doubt agree that certain positions, apart from their purely strategic value, have for the French an exceptional moral significance, a sort of legendary prestige...fortresses which the man in the street regards as the keys to his country. Chief of these are Verdun, Belfort, eh? Now imagine for a moment that as a result of striking hard enough we got possession of one of these key positions, of Belfort, for instance...or Verdun. Don't you think that such a blow, coming after a year and a half of useless efforts on their part to make a breach in our wall of steel, would be sufficiently severe to make them lose all hope of winning the war?"

"Perhaps....From that point of view Verdun would be better than Belfort."

"There are reasons, though, that might make Belfort the better proposition."

"Belfort is farther from the heart of the country. Symbolically it stands for less."

"You really think so?"

"From the purely symbolic point of view, I think that the entry of French troops into Strasbourg would stand for victory; similarly, the loss of Verdun would signify defeat."

"That's very interesting."

"Except, of course, to Joffre...but in that case, they probably wouldn't listen to him....Yes," agreed Maykosen after a few more minutes of consideration, "a great victory there, followed immediately by the offer of a generous peace, might be the end…."

"It is very interesting to find you so far in agreement with Falkenhayn."

"…always remembering," urged Maykosen, "that I have no qualifications whatever for saying whether such an operation stands any chance of succeeding."

"I have reason to suppose it has. It would not cost a great deal to take the place. The forts have been partly dismantled. The French line forms a very dangerous salient. The field works have been neglected. The general in command is inefficient."

Maykosen was on the point of saying: "What I don't understand is why—since you want to finish with France once and for all—you don't choose a point of attack nearer Paris and try to march straight on the capital." But his love for Paris, which was very strong and very deep, prevented him from uttering the words. He was not particularly fond of the French, but he was devoted to Paris. This dichotomy in his feelings did not much trouble him, for it exemplified one of his favourite maxims: "Men are like bees. They are worth a great deal less than their products."

CHAPTER NINETEEN

The General Wants to Be in the News

They were returning by the corduroy road. They felt as though they were walking on rollers that twisted beneath their feet. A light fall of snow two days earlier had thawed and then frozen, with the result that the balks of wood had a thin coating of ice which followed the natural corrugation of their surface.

"We shall break our necks. Let's get on solid earth."

But "solid earth" just here was a mass of wintry, waterlogged mud with a frozen top layer through which the grass poked like the bristles of a brush.

They exchanged occasional brief sentences. Now and again the leader stopped to mop his forehead. In spite of the cold, their acrobatic progress had made them sweat. The man who halted took advantage of the pause to tell the other three what was passing through his head at the moment.

Not that it ever varied. But it seemed to crave the vent of words. Clanricard, in particular, seemed a prey to nervous excitement. His voice sounded sharp and almost angry, indignant and imploring by turns. It gave the impression that he was calling his companions to witness, invoking the wrath of Heaven, or striving to rouse an apathetic crowd to action.

"I've seen a good deal, one way and another," he declared, "and it takes a lot to turn my stomach these days. But I don't think I've been quite so furious about anything since the 2nd of August. And that's saying something when one takes into account those crater scraps when we were in the Butte sector. All the same…"

"I always told you we should be in for it one of these days," put in Norestier. "Personally, I don't mind anything so long as old Troubedano doesn't start one of his speeches."

"Oh, him!"

"I can't help thinking of that poor devil Girard," said Brimont, making an effort to speak calmly and without prejudice. "He was going on leave tomorrow morning, on account of the birth of his granddaughter. He's been so bucked up about it. Only today he was discussing all his plans. 'In a way,' he said, 'I'm sorry I wasn't there when she was born; but as things are, there'll be a bit more of her to see now; and her mother will be over the worst; at least, I hope so.'"

"Yes, it's damned hard luck on Girard," Clanricard agreed; "and he's a decent chap too. But you've only lost seven of your little lot. Think of me, old man, with eleven killed and twenty-four wounded, of whom three at least won't recover, and about ten'll be maimed for life...." (This was the third time since they had left the little cemetery that Clanricard had announced these figures. Not that he minded whether the others thought him a bit hysterical; it suited his mood to wail. This constant evocation of the dead would bring peace to their spirits. Through him they should be avenged on the silence of the living, which, after all, was nothing but cowardice.)

"It's true we only had seven killed," Brimont retorted, "but there are two missing and eighteen wounded, half of them pretty badly. Imbard'll be as sick as hell when he gets back off leave."

"When's he due?"

"This evening. He's not expecting this little present! He'll find his company in a pretty bad way."

"He'll at least have the consolation," said Clanricard, "that he wasn't there. He's not like us. He hasn't got to bite his knuckles with indignation. He's spared the awful feeling that he can't do anything."

A moment later he went on:

"We've had our share of useless attacks and damn fool raids. I've almost got it in me to regret the bloody Butte de Vauquois—which is saying a good deal—but if the men who copped it there, to mention nowhere else, could come back from the grave and ask what they were killed for, there's not much one could say....And the same sort of thing's true everywhere....But as a rule there's at least some kind of reason or excuse. This last show was absolutely pointless. Don't you remember the expression on the men's faces when they were told to get ready? I could hardly meet their eyes. What I wanted to say was: 'My friends, we're cursed with a brigadier who's nothing but a rotten little go-getter, a dirty pusher without any feelings at all. It's occurred to him that there won't be much in the New Year's Day communiqué, and that it's a good opportunity to rivet attention on himself. That's the only possible reason for this raid we've been saddled with, for which otherwise there is no shadow of justification and no conceivable chance of success. I'm ashamed for the Staff, and I beg your pardon for what I've got to ask you to do.'"

They had left the corduroy road and had reached solid ground. The path, hard but no longer slippery, went uphill through a patch of woodland. A few distant detonations sounded from the direction of the north and north-east.

"I don't think he means to be a swine," said Brimont, in an attempt to be judicious. "It's just that he works things out superficially, by map, and without really going into conditions."

"The murderer! As though it wasn't his plain duty to come and make a personal study of the ground! Joffre can't do that, naturally; he's got to go by the map: but what else is there for a little runt of a brigadier to do, with a sector no bigger than a pocket-handkerchief? Take my word for it, the reason he's never been near us is that he doesn't want to have to realize that his damned scheme is just criminal lunacy, or to hear it from other people."

"Would he have heard it from you?" asked Norestier, not mockingly but as though conscious of their common humility in the military scheme of things.

"I should have observed all due forms of discipline," replied Clanricard with determination, "but I should have expressed my mind."

Norestier and Brimont nodded. They knew their Clanricard. In his mouth "I should have expressed my mind" was no mere rodomontade of words.

The young subaltern Mévon had not dared to take any part in the discussion. In silence, and not without perturbation of spirit, he drank in some of the hard truths of his new life.

"Anyhow," observed Norestier, "there was one man who could have spoken as soon as he knew what was in the wind—Troubedano."

"Do you mean that seriously? Can you really see Troubedano doing anything?…In the first place, as you know perfectly well, he's a coward to his fingertips. He's frightened of shells, frightened of the general, and we could make him frightened of us if we liked. But don't you realize that this'll give him just the chance he's always looking for? He'll be able to deliver a grand patriotic speech over the open graves!…'The laurels of victory are watered by the blood of sacrifice…' and so on, and so on. 'Forward, lads, with the dawn in your eyes!'…with an occasional dirty crack thrown in to show how well he understands the common soldier….Don't you remember, last month, when they put poor Lengrangé away, how he stood there proud as a damned peacock, and talked about him having been a 'regular fellow, with hair on his chest'? I happened to glance at Vidal at that moment, Vidal who's a rough-neck if ever there was one, and I could see that he was thinking: 'That's not how a battalion commander should talk of one of his men they're shovelling underground.' No, this Troubedano of yours has missed his vocation. He ought to have spent his life making speeches or writing books."

"A troubedanour—whence troubadour…."

"When he was doing garrison duty at Orléans, his addresses at regimental horse-shows, or on the 14th of July, or on Jeanne d'Arc's birthday must have been famous. Can't you just hear him ?—'Je-hanne, the fair maid of Lorraine….'"

"With hair on her chest, and a nice pair of…"

"Precisely…and the blue line of the Vosges…and the gleam of bayonets…."

"You'd better ask his old pal, Sergeant Cavette, about it."

"Talking of Cavette, do you know what the quartermaster told me?—that Cavette is still getting money from some girl he's got at Orléans. He's living on her. What fun Troubedano

and old Cavette must have had at Orléans in peace-time! Can't
you just see them exchanging notes about whore-houses?"

"Ubedano ought to have been put on to making confidential reports at the time of the Combes dust-up," put in Brimont, who, as a rule, didn't much like rash statements.

Clanricard was inclined to resent uncomplimentary refer-
ences to the "Combes dust-up." The system of confidential
reports couldn't, he thought, be quite so airily dismissed. No
doubt circumstances at the time had made them necessary.
The war, however, had brought him in contact with a good
many left-overs from the old professional army. It was his
considered opinion that if some of them had become instruments of reaction from pure stupidity, others had been only
too delighted to find employment for their natural baseness
of spirit in the carrying of tales. Nevertheless, he changed the
subject.

"Do you know what Ubedano had the cheek to whisper to
me just now at the cemetery? That rather too many officers
had turned up. That it was a risk for so many to be out of the
line when the Boche might take it into his head to retaliate."

"And what did you say?"

"That having had the misfortune to be compelled to lead
our men to slaughter, it was some comfort for us—to say
nothing of duty—to see them safely buried."

"How did he take that?"

"He gave me a nasty look. I added that the Boches were not
in the habit of attacking at that time of day; that anyhow there
were plenty of N.C.O.'s on the spot, and that our two companies had suffered so heavily that no doubt the neighbouring units would be standing by to give them a helping hand.
He must have seen in my face what I was feeling. Anyhow, he
realized that he'd better not press the point."

Norestier smiled quietly to himself at the idea of what the
other might have seen in Clanricard's face.

"I was just waiting for you, sir."

"Have you been here a long time?"

"No, I've only just come, sir. Orders from the brigade, sir."

"Give them to me."

Clanricard read the paper, gave vent to a deep "Ha!" and started moving his feet as though he were standing on hot bricks.

"The man's a lunatic!" he muttered between clenched teeth; "a dangerous lunatic." Then, to the runner, as he scribbled his initials with a hand trembling with suppressed fury: "Thank you, that'll do."

"Norestier!" he shouted.

"What's up?"

"Have a look at this!"

"Hm…from the brigade.…What! They want us to have another go? Tomorrow morning?…Us?"

"You didn't expect that?"

"I certainly did not!"

"We must find Brimont."

"I was with him a moment ago."

"And Imbard's not back yet!…I must say they're preparing a nice little welcome for him."

"You've noticed, I suppose, how charmingly considerate they are. The 75's and the heavies to the north and north-east of Neuvilly will stand by to support us. But since we are to make full use of the element of surprise, they won't open up until we ask them to, and not until we've got a footing in the enemy lines, when they will lay down a barrage against possible counter-attacks. They've become quite fatherly all of a sudden!"

They both started off to look for Brimont, whom they found at the entrance to his dug-out. He too had just got brigade orders. He read them once, twice, and seemed to be turning them over in his mind.

"It's God-awful," he said.

He looked at his companions and shrugged.

"What are we going to do about it?"

Clanricard was nervously shuffling his feet and pulling angrily at the thumb of his right hand. Brimont's reaction, when it came, was unexpected: he looked at his watch.

"Imbard's not here yet. I wonder what's keeping him."

"Imbard won't know any more than you," Clanricard snapped back at him; "in fact, on the contrary, you'll have to put him wise."

He paused, then added gloomily:

"Well, *I* think we ought to do something about it."

"But what, my dear fellow, what?"

Brimont appealed for support to Norestier, who shook his head in reply and silently pursed his lips.

Clanricard waited a moment before continuing.

"There's one perfectly simple thing we could do," he said at last; "go and see Ubedano."

"All of us together?"

"Yes."

"And what should we say to him?"

"That in our opinion such an order cannot be executed, and that he ought to ask the brigade to reconsider it."

"If we go in a bunch and talk like that, he'll think there's a mutiny afoot. He'll feel obliged to ride the high horse."

"All right....Perhaps Norestier would be one too many...." He saw a flicker of relief in Norestier's eyes, and the sight hurt him. "You and I will go alone.

Brimont looked as though he were feeling very uncomfortable.

"I swear I'm not trying to get out of anything," he said, "but I don't think I've any right to do a thing like that just before Imbard gets back. Think what it means. He'll be in command tomorrow morning. What'll I feel like if he says: 'You're a nice sort of fellow, aren't you, taking advantage of my absence to compromise the honour of the company?'"

"No big words, Brimont. Leave that sort of thing to Ubedano."

"It's not a question of big words."

"Imbard would never say a thing like that if you explained the circumstances to him."

"I'll explain all right, and you can do the talking. I swear I'll back you up."

"Meanwhile, time's passing. Ubedano'll be only too delighted if he can tell us it's too late....Imbard may not be back until ten o'clock, or even midnight....He may still be in Paris, he may be ill, anything may have happened...You've got to make up your mind now. If you won't come I shall go alone."

Brimont overtook him before he had gone more than a few paces along the trench.

"Look here, old man, I should hate you to think me a whited sepulchre. I call God to witness that it's not fear that's holding me back. It's just that I've got a conscience."

"Do you authorize me to say that privately you agree with me, that if it wasn't for your conscience you'd join me in making a protest?"

Brimont thought for a moment, then:

"Yes," he said.

But his tone was rather less firm than his companion could have wished.

Clanricard found Ubedano in his extremely comfortable dug-out, absorbed in the making of some punch. His adjutant was with him.

The commanding officer assumed a jovial air:

"Well, well, what good wind brings you? You'll take a glass of punch with us?"

He was a stoutish man with a short neck. His eyes, though heavy, were restless and nervous. A smile of sham good nature played about his moustache, and there was a note of assumed truculence in his voice.

Clanricard refused the punch politely and came straight to the point. The effect of his words on the senior officer was comic. The latter repeated them more than once and started to sputter for want of anything better to say. At last:

"What's that?...Wh-wh–what's that?...Say that again. ...What?...God bless my soul, what are you talking about?"

Clanricard repeated quite calmly that he relied upon his commanding officer to notify the brigade at once, through the colonel of the regiment if necessary, that both morally and materially the orders just received were quite impossible to carry out.

By this time Ubedano had recovered his presence of mind.

"You're stark, staring mad. You're frightened, that's what's the matter with you."

The lieutenant explained that he was far from being mad, that hitherto he had never dreamed of questioning an order, but that it was his duty to draw his commander's attention to the fact that he had been misinformed. Brimont entirely agreed with him.

Ubedano tried a more fatherly approach.

"You think your two companies have been through it too recently? You think I ought to have detailed another lot for the job?…The trouble is, you see, that you're in position already, and you can't be relieved until tomorrow morning.…You know where the other companies are. I can't let them take over from you, because there's no one to put in their place. But they'll be in close support. The other two battalions are unfortunately out at rest, beyond Vraincourt. No good talking of a last-minute change. The most I can do is to put in a request for reinforcements…and to insist on your being relieved by tomorrow night at latest.…"

Clanricard protested that it wasn't a question of sending one lot of men to be killed rather than another. It was the whole operation that was "absurd."

Ubedano took advantage of the word to gather his brows in a frown. Clanricard felt that he had put his point clumsily. But it was too late to alter the sentence now. The other flew into a rage—or pretended to:

"I don't know what the devil we're coming to when a lieutenant takes it on himself to say whether the orders of senior formations are or are not absurd! The next thing'll be, I suppose, that I shall start writing letters to General Joffre and giving him the advantage of my advice!—and when you give orders to alter the position of a machine-gun the company cook'll tell you you're a fool! Up to now I've always regarded you as a good officer; I've made that clear, I trust, by the way I've treated you. But be careful! I'm beginning to have doubts about your soundness.…" A moment later he added, as though he were voicing a profound observation of his own: "That's just what makes the difference between reserve officers and professionals. I suppose it's only to be expected!"

Clanricard had ceased to listen. He was trying to think out some devastating rejoinder. This time he wanted to make sure of his effect. But he was frightened, in spite of himself, at the audacity of what he was about to say. He had to get himself to the sticking-point. "If the attack takes place," he told himself, "you probably won't come back. But that possibility won't stop your going over with your men tomorrow morning. Why, then, are you afraid of irritating this ridiculous old dotard? Troubedano can't do anything worse than what's coming to you in any case."

"Sir," he said at last, with a not very successful effort at solemnity, "I have not done what I have done frivolously, or without being fully conscious of its serious nature. I am worried about the men's state of mind. My companions and I will do everything we can, have no fear of that. But when things are difficult, our modest example is hardly enough to turn the scales. For one thing, they're too used to it. But I am convinced that if this evening when we tell the company what's expected of them, we can say: 'Our commanding officer is going to do us the honour of being with us in person…[Clanricard spoke sternly and looked the other straight in the face] when we go over …' [his voice trembled] the result will be excellent…really excellent."

Ubedano rolled his eyes. He looked half frightened, half furious. It was obvious that he was thinking: "The fellow's making a fool of me!" But the thought was one that could not easily be put into words. Clanricard was standing at attention, and this attitude took from his words all suspicion of impertinence.

Ubedano contented himself with growling:

"I am not obliged to explain my intentions to you.…I shall be…where I feel it my duty to be…and where I can most usefully control the operation.…That's all.…I have nothing more to say."

"Still not come?" asked Clanricard of Brimont, whom he found alone in his dug-out.

"No. It's beginning to be a bit odd."

Clanricard gave vent to an ironic sigh:

"What did I tell you?"

"And what sort of a reception did you get?"

Clanricard described the interview as shortly as possible. When he had finished, Brimont looked at him as much as to say: "You've done everything you could. Your conscience is clear. From now on it's in the hands of the gods!"

But Clanricard was obstinate.

"The question's precisely where it was."

Silently he asked himself: "What would Sampeyre do in my place? What advice would he give me if he were here?" He conjured up the vision of Sampeyre's house, of the courtyard, the walls with their ancient roughcast, the scattered greenery of the garden. Sampeyre's house on the slopes of Montmartre, with Sampeyre himself at the window, among his books, became, at this tragic moment, an anchorage for his spirit, a landmark on which words of wisdom were inscribed. Perhaps if he could only think himself vividly enough back in Sampeyre's house, he would be able to find the solution to his problem. A moment later he evoked the memory of one of the meetings of his lodge. He tried to imagine the scruple which obsessed him figuring on the agenda of his lodge, being made the subject of general discussion. In what sense would the brethren have expressed themselves? Alas! such debates are easy when one is sitting comfortably in one's seat, in one's "column," when one's conscience is bathed in the light diffused by free thought in a company of men at peace. But in an Argonne dug-out, on the eve of a dawn attack, the case of conscience becomes something bristling with terrifying points, like a cheval-de-frise fallen into one of the trenches at Vauquois. Suddenly an idea flashed into his mind: Wasn't Ubedano a Mason? He had heard people say so. Clanricard had never bothered to verify the point, perhaps because he was afraid it might be true....Should he go back and find out? Give the secret countersign...then the sign that meant he was in distress? The world is apt to laugh at such things. But there are circumstances in which they might take on a tragic grandeur.

Brimont's voice broke into his meditations:

"I'm just as worried as you are, old man. I was thinking hard all the time you were away. I even prayed. You didn't know, did you, that deep down I was a Christian? Well, I know perfectly well that Christ is not on the side of those who order men to certain death just to satisfy their personal ambitions. But I know, too, that we are here to carry out our duty as soldiers. I don't think it's any part of a soldier's duty to question his orders—whatever those orders may be. We have, perhaps, a right to judge them in the secrecy of our hearts, but that's all. If we go further than that, we cease to be soldiers, we break loose from our moorings, and I don't see any way of getting back to them. Once you start this game of questioning, there's no reason why it should ever end....In the last resort it is Christ who will judge us all. He will not blame me for having obeyed, since to obey is what I am here for."

At sight of his friend's sad smile, he added with a show of affection:

"I approved of what you did. In doing it you showed great courage. It went far beyond mere duty."

"Thanks, old man....But look here, you say that my argument might lead one to any lengths....But what about your own?...Just suppose that one day we were in enemy territory as part of an army of occupation, and suppose some brute ordered you to put a lot of women and children against a wall and shoot them...for some pretext or other, reprisals, or the need of terrorizing the population, or something of that sort....Would you obey, without first moving heaven and earth to get the order rescinded?...Would you just leave it to Christ to pass the final judgment? Is your conscience really clear because one of your friends had fifteen minutes' quite useless conversation with the battalion commander?...Mine certainly isn't."

Clanricard got up.

"I do see your point of view, really I do," repeated Brimont with a note of genuine anguish in his voice, "and I'd do anything to help you find a solution. If your conscience really won't let you contribute to the execution of an order which

appears to you abominable…you could—Oh, I don't know
—yes, I suppose you could let Norestier take over the company tomorrow morning…"

"And stay in my dug-out making punch, like Troubedano?"

"Your men know you. They wouldn't think it was because
you were afraid. They'd guess the true reason."

"Exactly! And they'd think it quite natural that rather than
injure my sensitive conscience I should let them go alone to
the slaughterhouse like men and heroes.…No, Brimont, you
don't understand. It's not my conscience that's worrying me;
it's"—he spoke slowly, separating the syllables in his earnest-
ness—"it's how to pre-vent a crime from being com-mit-ted!"

He found himself staggering down the trench in the gathering dusk. His distress of spirit had made his legs feel weak
and destroyed his sense of balance. His mind had ceased to be
rational.

"I'll manage somehow to get killed at once, after telling the
men that I didn't want to give them an example of disobedi-
ence, but that I wouldn't survive those who were going to be
massacred as a result of my orders."

Then, a moment later:

"I'll send a message to Ubedano that I refuse to take command of the company tomorrow morning, and that I resign
my commission.…Could he force me to carry on until after
the show?…A moment comes when one must suffer for what
one considers one's duty. I've suffered enough for what others consider my duty. I shall be court-martialled…but unfortunately the proceedings will never be made public. No one
outside will ever learn my reasons for acting as I did.…Prob-
ably my men will be told that I let them down through cowardice. My gesture will not save a single life."

Suddenly he made up his mind.

"There's one last chance. I'll telephone to the general. What
is there to stop me?—rules?—custom? But if I insist hard
enough? He may punish me later, but he'll have to hear what
I've got to say. It may make him think twice, who knows?"

"Who's that speaking?"

Clanricard gave his name and rank.

"Whom do you want to talk to?"

"To the general in person."

"Do you mean that seriously? What about?"

"Who are you?"

"An officer of the brigade staff, Captain…" (Clanricard could not catch the name.)

"It's about something of the greatest importance and urgency. I can explain it to nobody but the general himself."

"You realize that it is most unusual?"

"I must speak to him."

"The general isn't here…he's up the line."

"Isn't there somewhere I can get him?"

"I can give you no idea where he is."

"What time will he be back?"

"I can't say. Perhaps in an hour. Won't you leave a message with me?"

"No, sir, thank you. That's quite impossible."

Clanricard's voice was so despairing that it must have produced an effect at the other end of the line. His distant interlocutor added, on a note of greater kindness:

"Try again in an hour's time; perhaps…"

"I will, sir; thank you."

Clanricard had been sitting for about two minutes on a packing-case, his head buried in his hands, when Norestier came in.

"Imbard's just arrived."

Clanricard leaped to his feet.

"Ah! Well?"

"Brimont's started to tell him what's up.…I've come to fetch you."

"Let's go! I only hope Brimont's told him the whole story!"

They found a sentry at the door of the dug-out.

"Ah, it's you, sir, and you…Lieutenant Imbard and Lieutenant Brimont are in conference. They told me to let you in, but no one else."

Imbard, half lying on his bed, and still in his leave uniform, had just heard Brimont's explanation. Mévon, the subaltern, was making himself scarce in a corner. Imbard seemed very thoughtful. His eyes were fixed on the ground. He was picking his nose.

"Hell! Oh hell!" he said more than once.

The others were awaiting his decision.

"One thing's certain," he said at last, without raising his head; "it just can't be done."

His companions seemed unable to trust their ears. Clanricard was afraid of rejoicing too soon.

"You mean?" asked Brimont.

"I mean it can't *be* done, but it must have *been* done. That's plain enough, isn't it?"

"Not what I should call plain."

"What's the use of talking French to a lot of cabbages! Listen to me. In the course of tomorrow, the brigade will receive an irreproachable report of the operation. But that won't prevent our staying snug in our trenches when zero hour sounds. Do you understand now, gentlemen? All that remains is to polish up the details."

The others heard him with expressions of amazement and incredulity.

"Really!" he exclaimed. "Anyone would think you were a lot of rookies. Have you never kept your eyes open? Do you think this is the first time men have decided just how much of a stupid order they are prepared to obey?"

"But…" said Brimont, "it strikes me that you're proposing to obey just nothing at all."

"Simply a case of taking the thing on its merits. The stupider an order is, the less of it one carries out. That's a matter of elementary logic.…It's what the regulations call—I can quote you the exact paragraph—'the intelligent use of initiative by all ranks.' I gather, my dear Clanricard, that our respected chief, the father of his men, accused you of lacking in soldierly spirit. And he's perfectly right. No one with the least touch of military virtue in his veins would dream of making anything approaching a protest, of even hinting at a refusal, of so much as breathing the word 'no.' The soldier never says no. The soldier is supposed to refrain from anything that might remotely resemble criticism of orders. But, damn it all, carrying the orders out is quite a different question. That's where intelligent initiative comes in."

"But," objected Norestier, "how are you going to manage about your intelligent initiative when it comes to rendering a report?"

Imbard shrugged his shoulders.

"You don't seem to me to know the first thing about reports. You must have been badly brought up in civil life. What happened when your boss told you to let him see the day's orders—and any complaints there might be? Obviously you never had the advantage of being educated in a great business organization. If you had, you'd know, as I do, that there's no relation whatever between facts as they are and facts as they are represented as being. A report has nothing to do with the facts, and everything to do with the boss. It should hold up a mirror in which he can see his own thoughts. What the boss wants to find there is the reflection of what he intended to do. The closer the resemblance, the greater his happiness."

Brimont, though obviously scandalized, could not refrain from laughing. Norestier gave vent to a frank guffaw. Clanricard was so sincerely relieved to see a way out of the moral maze in which he had lost himself, no matter how tortuous and dishonest it might be, that he was only too glad to echo the laughter. He felt as though the tension of his nerves had been suddenly released. As to the subaltern Mévon, he chuckled in delighted amazement at sight of the treasures of experience thus displayed before his eyes.

"Still," said Norestier, "I imagine this report of yours won't go so far as to describe our getting a footing in the German trenches, with the number of prisoners taken?"

"That, my young friend, is all a matter of tact. There's nothing I mightn't say, at least in theory. I can, if I like, arrange a triumphal entry into the Boche line for eight a. m. and capture quite a respectable number of prisoners, including one *Feldwebel*, or even two. I'm at perfect liberty to announce a furious counter-attack as having been launched at eight thirty by the equivalent of a battalion (for we have our pride), the said counter-attack succeeding in retaking the captured trench and all the prisoners, including, unfortunately, the two *Feidwebel*, after a heroic fight with grenades and cold steel— all officers of brigade rank and over have a weakness for cold steel. Thanks to prodigies of valour, we succeed in cutting our way out with a minimum of casualties, and without leaving a single man in the hands of the enemy. What do you think of that? It is perfectly obvious that by ten o'clock the general sit- uation will be precisely what it was three hours earlier. In the interval there will have been an attack. The brigade will have had exactly what it set out to have. The advantage, this time, will be that the business will have injured nobody."

"Ah, but here's the rub; we must have *some* casualties. What are you going to do about them?"

Imbard was cudgelling his brains to an accompaniment of unintelligible noises.

"No one been killed today?" he asked Brimont.

"No."

"Pity.…No, I don't mean that exactly, only—well, I only mean that since there has to be a daily average, I should rather it hadn't gone back on us just today."

"I can manage a couple of wounded—three at a pinch; but the third's hardly worth talking about."

"Put him on ice! That's just the sort of casualty I want for my *pièce de résistance*…only I shall need three or four more. There oughtn't to be much difficulty about that. How about you, Clanricard?"

"I had three men hit early this afternoon—trench-mortar splinters."

"Evacuated yet?"

"No. They're slight cases; probably'll remain on duty."

"Good. Not a word about them in your situation-report tonight, understand? We'd better carry them forward to tomorrow's account.…And then, of course, we shall have to kick up a bit of a row, just to give an air of verisimilitude, you know—grenades, some rifle-fire, machine-guns…we shall

have to fix the details of all that later, but the Boche'll be
bound to send a certain amount of stuff back, and that, unfortunately, is bound to mean one or two chaps getting knocked
out. Oh, yes, we shall be all right; don't bother. Besides, it's
quite a common thing when an operation report is drafted in
the heat of the moment or just afterwards for the casualty figures given to be purely nominal. It's always understood that
proper details will follow later—and when they do follow, no
one bothers about comparing the two totals.…It makes me
blush to have to teach you the elements of your job like this!
With Mévon it's excusable, but you! The sentence of the
court is that you each stand your uncle Imbard a bottle of
wine, and none of your ration stuff either—proper wine!"

Under Imbard's inspiration, the business became a kind of
joke and rapidly took shape. Each of the officers had to produce some suggestion of a difficulty (whether he really
believed it or not), and put forward a possible solution. Brimont alone seemed disinclined to play.

"Don't be a fool," Imbard said to him. "Would you really
rather have the death of twenty-five or thirty poor devils on
your conscience? Try to believe you're working for the eternal salvation of your general's soul. The soul of a brigadier
general's not to be sneezed at! Help us to give him a clean
sheet on the Day of Judgment. Besides, I'm the man who'll
have to take any kicks that may be coming—Clanricard and
I. You can wash your hands of the whole thing."

The next problem was when to take the men into their
confidence, what to tell them, and how.

"They know nothing yet about the show? Good.…We'd
better go carefully. Spread it about first among the N.C.O.'s.
Just a few hints, and in the strictest confidence. I guarantee
they'll catch on all right."

Norestier agreed, but he had doubts about Cavette.

"He's old Troubedano's familiar. He'll split, as sure as fate."

"That's true. I'm not worrying about Troubedano himself—
he'll be lying low, as usual."

"Unless Clanricard's protest has put him on his mettle."

"Not likely! But I agree Cavette's a snag. The only thing'll be to get him out of the way. When he knows what's in the wind for tomorrow—and the odds are he knows already—he'll be only too damned glad of the excuse. But we must think up some plausible story....I'll manage him all right....Now you fellows just clear out. I'll send word that I want to see him in here."

"Come in, Sergeant Cavette. Sit down. Have a look at these orders that have just come in."

Cavette took the paper which Lieutenant Imbard held out to him. His little brown eyes flickered once or twice, and there was a slight tremor in his thin, colourless cheeks with their deep, symmetrical folds running downwards to the pointed chin. It was difficult to make out whether the order came as something new to him. However that might be, there was certainly no enthusiasm in his response.

He handed back the paper with a grimace.

"Not much fun, eh?" observed the lieutenant, "especially after what happened the other day...at least, to judge by what I've been told. Pretty thick, wasn't it?"

"It was terrible, sir."

"Well, orders are orders. My idea is to divide the operation into two phases. Here's a rough plan. I shall begin by sending a section or a section and a half over to the left of the stream, and I shall concentrate our fire on the same spot, so as to make the Boche think our objective is his trench here, at W, and the strong-point they've been working at just in the rear of it. As soon as I think their attention's fully occupied, I shall send the 6th company with the remainder of our own fellows to attack just here where the trench follows the contour line, before the Boche has time to realize what's happening. That's the trench I'm really interested in....The first lot, over to the left, will have to manage as best they can. Their part of the business will be to draw as much rifle and artillery fire as possible. Naturally, they'll feel they're being sacrificed. It'll need guts to do the job properly, especially after what happened the other day, and somebody with his head screwed on the right way to take charge. I was thinking of you."

Cavette looked at Imbard as though the latter had suddenly inserted the point of a knife into his left side, between the sixth and seventh rib.

Imbard took his time, turning away his eyes like a man following out some line of thought of his own. Then:

"Unfortunately," he said, "I need you for something else. What a pity it is you can't be in two places at once!"

Cavette managed to produce the ghost of a smile.

"Yes," continued the lieutenant, "before we knew anything about this show, we'd had orders to fetch some ammunition from Buzemont some time tomorrow. I could wait, of course, but I don't want to run the risk of finding myself short. I'd rather send a party down there early. Since it's important to get the stuff up, and since there may be difficulties on the last part of the journey owing to our engagement at dawn, I can't send just anybody.... You'd be doing me a service if you'd take it on. You won't gain so much glory, perhaps, but you'll be doing something just as useful. You'll start at five a. m. Can I count on your being back at ten precisely?"

Cavette, with the colour once more in his cheeks, and an almost affectionate look in his eyes, promised that he'd report at ten to the dot.

His place in the dug-out was soon taken by Sergeant Xavier. Imbard and Clanricard had agreed that he would be the best man to take into their confidence first. They would explain the whole scheme to him and get him to pass the word along to the men with all necessary precautions. Xavier, a former hall-porter from one of the big hotels of the rue de Rivoli, could take a hint better than most, and had had extensive experience in the handling of delicate missions. In the old days, when executing confidential errands, he had always been careful to keep himself as much as possible in the background, and even his whispered messages had had the quality of airy nothings. No one, two days later, could have sworn to his identity. Moreover, he was absolutely reliable. For all his cleverness in making himself useful, there was nothing about him of the sneak or blackmailer. His particular genius was due entirely to his possession of a quick intelligence and to the fact that, in civil life, he had taken pride in carrying out efficiently duties that were frequently amusing.

He was all the more willing to take his share in the plot, since it needed no prompting to make him see the crass stupidity of the orders it was designed to elude. The way in which Cavette had been got rid of gave him particular satisfaction.

"The only thing is," he said, "the men'll have to be careful not to start pulling his leg about it, either before or after. They'll want to, you see, because they all hate him like poison. And some of them aren't any too bright, either; besides, they might forget."

He suggested that he should put the whole business plainly to Vidal.

"He's a tough customer all right, but I think I can manage him, especially as it's a question of saving a dozen or so of his pals. I'll undertake he'll keep his mouth shut. He wouldn't trust Cavette farther than he could see him, but they're pretty much alike at bottom, and I reckon he can make him see sense all right. He'll tell him a thing or two on the q.t."

"What sort of things?"

"Well, that if any of the chaps or the officers get into trouble over tomorrow's doings, he'll know who's done the talking. That ought to settle matters all right. Cavette knows that Vidal wouldn't hesitate to knock him over like a rabbit, once he'd made up his mind to it."

"But won't it make him suspicious?"

"Perhaps it will, but no matter.…That sort of chap knows by this time that it's not healthy to find out too much about some things."

On the evening of the following day, the brigade received a fully detailed report drawn up in a thoroughly workmanlike fashion. In matters of style, concision and an absence of "fine writing" are military virtues. The key sentence ran as follows:

"At 7.00 o'clock precisely, No. 1 Platoon of No. 7 Company attacked with fixed bayonets on the left flank of the area shown.…"

CHAPTER TWENTY

Armchair Strategy

Mme Godorp's salon had ceased to function only for a short period during the opening months of the war. About the time that the front became "stabilized," it began, rather timidly, to revive.

At first it was confined to a few intimate friends who, now that the confusion of the early days was over and it seemed clear that life was to go on after all, were only too glad of somewhere to meet. Sunday remained the chosen occasion. There was no reason to alter that; in fact, rather the contrary. Conversation kept closely to public affairs and to the fortunes of those absent members of the circle whom the winds and eddies of various duties had scattered. Chief of such absentees were those who had been mobilized, or those, at least, among them who were not serving in the Paris area. Next to them in importance came the wives and mothers of mobilized soldiers who, since there was nothing to keep them in the capital, had gone to live in the provinces for the sake of cheapness and in order to be near their relatives. Next, those who had fled on the approach of the Germans and had never returned, and a few who, having been caught by the outbreak of hostilities while they were on holiday, had stayed away either because they thought Paris would be gloomy or because the war had upset their businesses. Finally, there were the foreign friends, almost all of whom had returned to their own countries, many of them not without having to face difficulties which Mme Godorp had been instrumental in helping them to overcome.

Those who still met showed a craving to discuss public events which had never marked them in times of peace. The

events in question were terribly exciting and quite without
parallel. The way they forced themselves on the attention, and
hung, as it were, in the very atmosphere, made them apt subjects for gossip and small talk. The papers contained little
information. What news they did give was heavily censored,
and the editorial comments were boring beyond words.
Curiosity had to look, for nourishment, to older methods of
communication. Confidential remarks made by those in high
places, indiscretions, by no means anonymous, rumours of
unknown parentage, enjoyed a circulation of which the modern press had long ago deprived them. A place like Mme
Godorp's salon, where such confidences, such indiscretions,
such rumours, came as regularly as vegetables to market, was
no longer, for its habitués, merely somewhere to pass the time
or pick up some occasional piece of particularly entertaining
scandal; it had become a wholly necessary institution.

Tea was served, because at that hour the various visitors
would, in any case, have had it in their own homes. But there
was no display, and the general tone was one of relative aus-
terity. Toast took the place of cakes. At the end of the winter
of '14 and during the early months of '15 some of the ladies
who came made a point of bringing with them their knitting-
needles and wool—with which they were popularly supposed
to be busy from morning to night—and, seated in Mme
Godorp's armchairs, worked away, rather too obviously, at
things for the dear soldiers. But the mistress of the house was
inclined to regard this display as being in rather bad taste and
did her best to discourage it.

As some compensation, however, she lent herself readily to
work of a more serious kind. The Sunday meetings were
often made the occasion of discussing in detail enterprises of
public utility in which women could employ themselves
without any vain display of patriotism. Nor was the activity
of the salon always confined to such matters. Occasionally the
visitors increased in numbers and variety and included members of Parliament, journalists, soldiers on leave, foreigners of
importance from one or other of the allied or neutral countries. All of them either were suffering from long weeks of

isolation, from enforced silence, or from ignorance of what was happening outside their own limited little world, or were taking advantage, with a sort of frenzy, of an atmosphere of freedom which was far from common at that time, added to which was a feeling that this particular circle had a distinction of its own where nothing that was overheard could be ignored, and nothing that was said need be lost. As a result, conversation was abundant. No subject was forbidden. Criticism could be safely aired of the government, the High Command, the Staff. Little knots of talkers got together in corners and wove a hundred petty intrigues, ranging from questions affecting the composition of a ladies' committee to that of the next Ministry, or the identity of the new commander-in-chief.

The salon had very early declared itself in favour of Galliéni. At first its partisanship had been moderate and retrospective, consisting in little more than claiming the merit of the Marne for the thin general in pince-nez, and tending to agree that Joffre was probably the right man for the work of co-ordination and final decision which fell to his lot as generalissimo. Little by little, however, the habitués had grown tired of Joffre. They complained of his slowness, of the repeated failure of his offensives, and chiefly of the kind of flabbiness which, in the long run, was held to mark his conduct of affairs. Didn't it come to this: that the great Temporizer was really the great Incapable? The Godorp salon had worked hard for the appointment of Galliéni as Minister of War, and it was an open secret that this appointment was but an initial stage in the campaign that was to lead to the application to Joffre himself of that policy of "superseding" of which he had been the inventor. Unfortunately, Galliéni's health was giving rise to a good deal of uneasiness. Should he, at last, have to resign as a result of doctors' orders, the whole cherished scheme would become infinitely harder of realization. It might not be difficult to find a successor to Joffre, but it would be, to discover a minister enjoying sufficient personal prestige to take responsibility before the bar of public opinion for such a shelving of the man in charge.

Similarly, the Godorp salon had been no stranger to the

rapid rise of Duroure. None of its members, to be sure, knew anything about the ex-professor's tactical theories, which could not, therefore, diminish his reputation in their eyes. But even the women knew that he had given evidence of "brilliant initiative" in the presence of the enemy. Now, what everybody frequenting the salon held for self-evident was that the conduct of the war was suffering precisely from a lack of "brilliant initiative." The taxis of the Marne, the "eighty-four" guns of Montceaux, were matters to thrill the imagination. When the Godorp salon sighed, precisely in the same way as the frequenters of every provincial café sighed at precisely the same hour each Sunday: "Ah! What we need is a Napoleon!" —when its members sought high and low for the name of the genius who should get the wheels of the nation out of the rut in which they were stuck, it was Duroure's that came most readily to every lip, even though the tone in which it was pronounced might be interrogative.

For some time now the "army of shock troops" had found numerous recruits—theoretical of course—among the habitués of the Godorp salon. Shock troops made an admirable subject of conversation. They belonged to the same level of the sublime—yet within the comprehension of the profane—as the taxis of the Marne and the guns of Montceaux. Like them they thrilled the imagination. And why should not the great truths of military strategy, like the great truths in other walks of life, thrill the imagination?

On the occasion of the second meeting in January, when the visitors had left, Gurau began to reproach his beloved:

"You talked a great deal. You were very indiscreet."

"Do you really think so?"

Her conscience was not altogether easy. She had, as he said, talked a great deal, and in a self-confident tone, or rather in a mood of foolish excitement, which before the war would have seemed entirely out of tune with her nature. She had no difficulty in remembering the main heads of her indiscretion, but she wanted to hear them from his lips.

"What did I say that you particularly disliked?"

"Disliked!—it's not a question of disliking. Much of what you said I'm inclined to agree with, but you ought to keep these things to yourself….You said, for instance—oh, I know it was in a corner and only to intimate friends, but everything gets repeated—that Joffre had become quite impossible …You'll say, of course, that you were only expressing your personal opinion, and to a certain extent that's true…but then you said that Joffre had at last been goaded into sending Castelnau to report on the defences of Verdun, and that, if he didn't keep his eyes shut, he'd find that things there were in a pretty bad state….That's much more serious, because the public is not supposed to know things like that….You said that the decisive battle of the war would take place on the French front during the first half of the year, that the real danger lay in the possibility of the Germans getting in first, and that, unfortunately, owing to Joffre's habit of always taking his time, the danger was a very real one. All that's terribly foolish in view of our relations, which are known to everybody. People will believe that I've been talking to you about the secret intentions and fears of the government. If only one of the agents whom the Germans keep in Paris got wind of what you said, he could make a report which would be of the highest possible value to his employers."

The more Gurau talked, the more his irritation increased, until finally he made no bones about alluding to the evil rumours that were going about in connexion with her and him: how, for instance, a good many people had been scandalized by the fact that a member of a National Government should have a "foreigner" as his mistress.

"You make me feel so terribly guilty!" cried Mme Godorp as he proceeded, and she made no attempt to restrain her tears. "I see now that I was wrong. But it's all because I'm so passionately anxious for the welfare of this country. I can't help myself. I have a feeling that the great crisis is coming. And I am quite sure that the Germans are not losing a moment. When I see the fate of France in the hands of that old grandpapa Joffre, who never gets excited about anything and moves about as quickly as a superannuated gardener watching his vegetables grow…oh, I am sorry, truly I am. I promise I'll be more careful in future; it shan't occur again. …I'll discontinue my Sundays if you like.…"

CHAPTER TWENTY-ONE

Behind the Scenes at Chantilly

The company was numerous and animated, at least so far as the amount of conversation went. For the most part, however, the tone of the exchanges was confidential, and whoever happened to be speaking at the moment was careful to lean forward so as to be heard without having to raise his voice. Now and then there was a pause in order that one of the two orderlies on duty should leave the room before certain things were mentioned. "You needn't bother about the other," the general had said; "he doesn't understand anything."

Duroure's guests included, in addition to all the usual members of his mess—Radigué, Clédinger, Cabillaud, and the officers in charge of the first, second, and third bureaux—two of his divisional generals, Despois and Marie, as well as a certain young Captain de Vaussorgues, who, for all the modesty of his rank, seemed to be everybody's spoilt child.

"Try a drop of this local wine. Not bad, I think."

Captain de Vaussorgues was attached to G.H.Q.—Adjutant General's department, personal staff. His special duty was to keep up to date the record of general officers awaiting promotion. Not a "rise," not a change of command, but he knew of well in advance and could speak of with confidential knowledge. He had at his fingertips which member of Parliament it was, or which Minister, who had insisted that so-and-so should not be given a rap over the knuckles. He knew precisely who had been thought of for an army command, what opposition had developed at the last moment, what changes were in contemplation, the names of possible candidates for this or that post—sometimes before they knew it themselves. He was privy to the rivalries among the great, to the hatreds, the intrigues, the coteries, of the military world. Since he moved about a great deal, he had opportunities of picking up from his friends a good many of the inner secrets of G.H.Q. His presence at a "provincial" dinner-table—Chantilly was the "capital," the various armies were the provinces—was bound to arouse a good deal of eager curiosity. Generals of division, fresh from their backwoods, hung upon his lips. He was fully aware of the fact, and was careful to stage his effects for their benefit.

His devotion to Duroure was known to all. It was understood that he had done his best to further his interests at each stage of his career, even if it had been no more than to keep him informed of what was going on behind the scenes. Radigué had even said on one occasion: "If de Vaussorgues had been attached to the Organization department instead of to Appointments, if, for instance, he'd got the job of that little swine Halletin-Fauchères, the shock-troops idea would have been a reality by this time." That was probably an exaggeration of the captain's influence.

He had come straight from Chantilly. The official pretext for his visit was to study with Duroure, on the ground, certain questions of no very great importance. They had been quickly settled in the course of a morning's talk, and conversation was now free to play about the delicious intimacies of court life.

"The thing everybody's talking of at the moment," said de Vaussorgues, lowering his voice (he was seated on the right of General Marie, almost directly opposite Duroure, towards whom he turned for the most part each time he opened his lips), "is Castelnau's report."

"Was it bad?"

"Terrible. And what he said was even worse than what he wrote. Apparently there's practically no organization at all. There are one or two rear positions here and there marked in blue on the map, but in fact they can't be seen at all on the ground, not even with a magnifying glass. No support positions. Front line's in an appalling state. Most of the trenches are not deep enough, and a bombardment would flatten 'em out completely. The less said about guns the better. Herr, of course, can always say that he's been given none, that he's even had some withdrawn. But he'll find it difficult to prove that he's ever made the slightest effort to get G.H.Q. to move in the matter. He might have said, for instance—but he didn't—'I ask to be relieved of my command if I'm not given the means of defence which I consider indispensable.' Same thing's true of the men, both front-line troops and sappers. He says, I gather: 'How could I possibly carry out the work laid down? I should have needed an additional fifteen thousand men, at least a whole territorial division.' That's as may be. If they'd started on the job six months ago…you can do a lot in six months with three or four thousand men if you really keep them at it.…But did he tell the world that he needed these extra fifteen thou-sand—that it was absolutely essential he should have them?…Do you know, gentlemen, when it was he first put in his demand for reinforcements? The 16th of January."

"Last January?"

"Yes, general; a few weeks ago."

"Incredible!" cried Duroure.

"All I can say is we were damned lucky the Boches didn't try anything at Verdun last autumn. They'd have just walked through."

"And now?"

"Not much better. Luckily they're not planning anything."

"Do you really think they're not?"

"I rather agree," put in General Marie; "all the same, one shouldn't trust to luck to that extent."

"The upshot of it is," went on Captain de Vaussorgues, "that the C.-in-C. is furious.'

"With Herr?"

"Chiefly with Herr."

Duroure observed, without mincing his words, that the C.-in-C., as soon as any situation for which he was ultimately responsible, turned out badly, was quick enough to shift the burden on to the shoulders of one of his subordinates.

"In other words, he's past master at the game of spotting a scapegoat.…"

But according to the captain, if General Herr, in command of the Fortified Region of Verdun, was being made to bear the blame, because nobody much cared what happened to him, official disapproval was directed at a much more important individual, no less a person, in fact, than the officer in command of the Army Group of the East within whose area Verdun lay, General Dubail.

"But one has to go carefully with him—you know why."

"He is," said General Despois, "the symbol of the g-r-r-eat r-r-epublican army!"

Duroure declared that it was simply sickening to think that after a year and a half of war one still had to take account of political considerations.

To mark the importance of the occasion, coffee and liqueurs were served in the drawing-room. The captain drew General Duroure aside. Their conversation was carried on in a confidential whisper.

"I want to explain to you, sir, that this Verdun business isn't by any means ended."

"What do you mean?"

"They want to treat Dubail as tactfully as possible, but there is a limit. Castelnau, in particular, can't bear him. They're looking for a way out of the difficulty. Anyone else would have been sacked. But they'll try to save his face for him. He can't do much harm on the Vosges front....If it came to the point, sir, would you take Verdun?"

"In addition to my present command?" asked Duroure sharply.

"That I can't say....It might not be very convenient....Your sector is not exactly next door to Verdun. But they're bound to reinforce the troops of the Fortified Region, which would mean, no doubt, that you could take a certain number of your present troops with you....Perhaps, too, they might let you extend your front a bit to the right."

"To beyond the Saint-Mihiel salient? In that case it would join up with my present sector....Why take it away from me, then? I'm just beginning to know it really well. There'd be no difficulty whatever in looking after both at the same time...."

The captain smiled with an air of rather amused sympathy, as though, of the two, he were the older, the wiser, the senior officer.

"I ought to warn you, sir…it won't do to be too greedy. You see, there's another solution under consideration. In certain quarters they're playing with the idea of just altering the dividing line between the Groups of the Centre and the East. In that case, Langle de Cary's front would be extended as far as Paroches. The Fortified Region would be detached from Dubail without any fuss and come under Langle de Cary's command."

"What! That old fool? It's only a month ago that he was shoved into the command of the Army Group of the Centre. What more does he want? At any rate, no one could say that he was over-scrupulous in his r–r–epublican sympathies! You remember what happened about the emblems of the Sacred Heart?"

"But I assure you it's not he that's asking for the change. Just the contrary, as a matter of fact."

"Then what's all the fuss about? I don't understand."

"I'll tell you, sir, what I think's at the bottom of it.… You'll keep what I'm going to say to yourself, of course?"

"Naturally."

"Well then—in certain—circles—there's an idea, quite wrong to my mind, that things are going to happen before long at Verdun. If that comes true, it's not going to be much fun for the man whom public opinion holds responsible for the sector. They want to shift that responsibility from Dubail while there's still time, or at least to saddle his successor with most of it. It would not, therefore, altogether displease them if the successor in question belonged to the opposite political camp. It's all a nice little exhibition in acrobatics, you see. But from the C.-in-C.'s point of view, the change would have other advantages, too. When the worst had happened he could say: 'You accuse me of not having kept my eyes open, of not being wise before the event. And yet, in spite of the fact that I had every reason to avoid offending Dubail, I didn't hesitate for a moment to take Verdun away from him and give it to a sound soldier, Langle de Cary, who had already proved his worth in the Champagne battle. What more, humanly speaking, could I have done?'"

"And you want me to pull the chestnuts out of the fire?"

"What I want, sir, or even what I advise, has nothing whatever to do with the matter....I repeat that in my view nothing's going to happen at Verdun. I'm pretty sure there's no immediate danger, and my colleagues of Intelligence agree with me. On the 15th they received a report from Intelligence, Fortified Zone, which they studied closely. It bore out our view that any attack in the near future is extremely improbable. All the rumours going about really took their rise from certain remarks made by deserters in connexion with these *Stollen*."

"*Stollen*? What's that?"

"A system of very deep and elaborate dug-outs, complete with electric light, kitchens, w.c.'s, and all modern comforts, which the Boches have been busy constructing for the last few weeks on the right bank of the Meuse, especially in the forest of Spincourt. I gather that it was the description of these famous *Stollen* which so shook General Herr's normally placid mind that he realized all of a sudden that the Verdun defences could hardly be said to exist at all, and decided to write that letter of his dated the 16th. As a matter of fact, the evidence of the *Stollen* goes just the opposite way. When an army settles down into such luxurious quarters, it's, as a rule, with the intention of staying there and not of starting a big offensive. These *Stollen*, as they've been described to us, are more in the nature of siege works intended for long occupation than preliminary positions for an attack....But there's even a more decisive argument: the Germans have not shown the slightest sign of constructing assault trenches. We know that from air photographs which reached us at G.H.Q. yesterday. The distance between the lines in the sector which is said to be so clearly threatened is more than normally large...two hundred, five hundred, six hundred, even at places a thousand yards....Well, can you see the Boches launching an attack over a piece of no man's land a thousand yards wide?

Especially in these days when the tendency is to reduce as far as possible the amount of open ground to be covered by attacking troops. There, of all places on the front, assault trenches would be absolutely essential. When you're dealing with distances as great as that, you can't dig assault trenches, with all the necessary approaches, in a night....We should know what was in the wind long before anything happened....As I see it, sir, the man who takes on this job will acquire considerable merit and run less risk than is generally thought to be likely. If he takes the trouble to improve the defence system and nothing serious happens, he will get the reputation of having saved the country."

Duroure made a face.

"I'm not a great one for digging," he said. "If it were merely a question of field-works, I should soon get bored....I don't much cotton to the idea of having to take a hard knock...with conditions as they are...with my freedom of action hampered by the mistakes of my predecessors. ...Besides, I should never hit it off with Langle de Cary. We've had one or two collisions already....I'd much prefer Dubail, who at least would let me get on with the job in my own way. ...If the IInd Army was to be re-formed to include the Verdun zone, I might feel very differently...."

"But that's out of the question, sir. The IInd Army's being kept for Pétain, as you know!..."

"Pétain—"

Duroure left the sentence unfinished.

CHAPTER TWENTY-TWO

Jerphanion Writes to His Wife.
Who Will Give Us Back the Days That Are Gone?

I love you, Odette darling, I love you, my precious wife. You are always in my mind. It is sheer agony for me to be separated from you. I am writing now as though we were talking face to face. I am writing in order to give myself the illusion of your presence.

Even here, in mid-winter, we could be so happy, dear child, you and I together. Through my attic window I can see the spread of sky above the plain. In spite of the season it is very blue, incredibly blue, like the sky in some southern land. Here and there its brightness is framed in bunches of white cloud such as one sees in summer. And the distant view has nothing in it of January. There seems as much green in it as brown and grey. I can see lovely long roofs, great simple masses, and roads, and the grassy verges where they twist and turn. To make it into a background of quiet happiness against which we two could spend long hours loving and sauntering, all that is necessary is to wipe out of the landscape the figures of all these poor fellows in faded blue who move about like so many great heavy ants.

The plain in which this village lies hidden is completely pastoral, with nothing military about it at all. An hour after the last man in blue has vanished, it will look once more exactly like one of Millet's pictures. Even the village has a curious beauty of its own. It is the one I told you of in my previous letters. To think that we've been here a month already! It's all so good that it's really rather frightening. I keep on wondering what horrible thing is going to happen next. But I do my best to enjoy the moment. The great thing is just to go on living.

The village rather reminds me of the places in the Beauce that we used to visit in the car. (Dear car! I often think of it. Do you remember how we used to bump along those village streets?) A group of large, squat farms, neither too crowded nor too far apart. Huge walls with only a few windows. Plenty of big square buildings. Great roofs with their slopes set at right angles. In the middle of the village is a large open space with a pond surrounded by a wall—there's even a balustrade on one side—which serves as a drinking-place for animals. They reach it by a gentle slope which leads straight down into the greenish-grey water.

Oh, I can tell you the name of the village. Until now I've always concealed it because instructions on that subject have again been renewed. But what possible harm can it do? We are so far from the front! Besides, no one but you is going to read this letter.

It is called Grandes-Loges. Perhaps you can find it on a road-map (about twelve kilometres south of Mourmelon-le-Grand). I like the name. It is as old and solid as a farmer's clothes-press. I can imagine us staying here, you and I, with some rich peasant uncle and his stableful of animals. He would put us up for a month during the winter. We should have good solid meals, washed down with the local wine (which is no more nor less than Champagne!), and we would go for long walks in the plain. When night fell we would make love for hours together in our room—it would be a bit cold (but there would be a feather bed with plenty of thick blankets and a huge eiderdown).

There are two battalions of the 151st regiment here. The second battalion is at Bouy—a few kilometres away—with the regimental details. That makes it all the quieter for us.

I have got for my company an enormous loft, which is over a stable, and so quite dry. My own quarters are in a real room belonging to a building near by. It must formerly have belonged to one of the farm-hands. It's got a great rough floor, a beamed roof, and a tiny window through which I can see the plain and the blue sky I have told you of.

For once, Cotin—the fellow who obsesses and terrifies my

mind like a problem that is at once insoluble and quite uninteresting—has had what might be called a good idea. He has
made the men gather, from the neighbouring wood, logs and
branches of pine and fir, even ivy and mistletoe, and has
shown them how to build little cabins, rustic huts, dotted
about anyhow, in the huge, healthy loft, which is about as hos-
pitable as a desert and as cold as a railway station. This has
given the men no end of fun. Some of them have been extraordinarily ingenious in building and adorning their little
hide-outs. One of them has even built a miniature house,
with two floors, an outside staircase, and a balcony. It looks
charming. Each of these small constructions is inhabited by a
squad, a half-squad, or sometimes by still smaller groups, just
as the men want to arrange. They pay one another visits.
Quite apart from occupying their minds, they keep warmer
this way and get a sense of greater intimacy. The whole thing
looks rather like a model of a charcoal-burners' camp in a
booth at the Lyons fair. It is all very cheerful.

But the most marvellous thing of all, the thing that really
makes this place seem like paradise, is that we don't hear a single gun—or not what you would call hearing—not one. I
wonder whether you can understand, can realize exactly what
that means. Not only does a stray shell never come our way,
but even by straining our ears we can hear nothing that even
remotely resembles the sound of a gun firing or the burst of
a shell. For instance, since I started this letter I've heard the
sound of voices, the clatter of mess-tins, the noise of wheels
on the road—even, though you'll hardly believe it, the cluck-
ing of a hen that's just laid an egg—but not the remotest suspicion of boom-boo-oo-oom, boom!…

It makes one want to cry, to tremble, with the sheer wonder of it. Oh, my dear darling! For all your sensitive understanding, I don't suppose you can begin to realize what it
means for all us poor wretches to live beneath a blue winter
sky, with white clouds, unsmirched by even the faintest whisper of gunfire.

There is very little for us to do. We are spared the awful drill
in the bare fields with which they used to poison our periods

of rest. For the last few days they have been sending us to a point rather farther to the north to dig trenches, machine-gun emplacements, communications, and to set up a lot of wire. The only trouble about that is the distance we have to cover, and the uncomfortable thought: "They must be worried, to organize positions so far to the rear." But, as I said before, it's no good meeting trouble half-way. We'll do as much digging as they want if only we can stay a bit longer at Grandes-Loges.

Odette darling! When next you write tell me something of the quays of the Seine near where we live, between the Halle-aux-Vins and the Pont National. How I'd love to be walking with you by the river and watching the Métro viaduct, graceful as a leaping goat, and the Bercy reservoirs beyond! I'd like to plunge with you into the narrow lanes of Picpus. The days are already lengthening. When it's clear and not too cold, the evening light seems to hang suspended just a second or so longer than one expects, and for the two or three minutes before darkness falls, there is a feeling of spring in the air.

Here, where we are, the thought of spring is not wholly a mockery. The heart soars, and then suddenly awakes to all the horror of what it is missing, what it has lost. Who will give me back this day as it might have been if only I could have spent it with you, our evening together, the walk we might have taken, the silent laughter with which you would have turned to me when I took you in my arms as we climbed the slope of one of those Picpus alleys? Who will give me back the happiest years of my life—even if I live to know others just as happy? Who will compensate me for these long months of exile? Poor us, dear, darling wife, who have not even had the consolation of finding life empty, who would have been contented with modest treasures which we could have enjoyed without harming anybody. Sometimes I think I have discovered the secret of this monstrous tragedy in which we have been caught. There are not enough people in the world who value living for its own sake, not enough who can find in the peace of every day the most wondrous miracle of all. Most men and women are tormented by miserable little worries and demand the dramatic as a dog devoured by fleas demands a violent counter-irritant and jumps into the fire to find it. I would go even so far as to say that many human beings ought never to have been born at all and spend most of their lives trying to correct that elementary mistake. The pity is that they should have to involve us in their attempt to get back to the primordial chaos.

CHAPTER TWENTY-THREE

The Country Grows Inquisitive

"Shall we take the car, gentlemen? I'm not really sure that it's worth it. We've such a short distance to go, and we shall get along a lot faster on foot."

Messieurs Audincourt and Blanchart protested that they would very much rather walk. By this time each member of the party was anxious to show that he was as alert as the others. Among the older men the emulation was particularly keen.

"Then I'll tell the chauffeur to wait for us in front of the Citadel." The old colonel went off to give the necessary orders. In his faded cap and red trousers he looked distinctly antique. He wore rough leather gaiters and heavy boots which gave him somewhat the look of a private. He limped slightly.

The car was one of the rickety old bone-shakers dating from the early requisitions. Hundreds of them could be seen parked in the back areas, with nothing military about them but the grey artillery paint with which they had been daubed.

Colonel Fargeau came back to his charges. M. Blanchart—who was addressed as Colonel Blanchart, since he had held a regular commission in the old days before he had entered Parliament—had prepared one or two questions which he was anxious to put. But he did not wish to look a fool in the eyes of the officer, his equal in rank and almost in years, who had been given them as a guide, and who had the advantage over him of having returned to active service and being now in uniform. On the other hand, he wanted to take every opportunity of showing how much more competent he was than his civilian colleague on the Army Commission. He did his best, therefore, to put his questions in the most technical language he could muster. This needed time. No sooner had he opened his lips than the colonel in uniform was off on one of his explanations:

"Here we are very slightly above the level of the Meuse—that is to say, somewhere about the 650-foot mark. The Citadel, at which we are going to take a look in a moment or two, is quarried out of a rocky eminence standing about 130 feet higher—giving us a total altitude of roughly 780....Over there, in the direction of the enemy, north-east from where we are standing, our front line runs along a crest with an average height of somewhere between 980 and 1,200. It takes in the forts of Belleville, Saint-Michel, and, farther off, Souville and Vaux, all of them now dismantled and without any military value. In the same sector we hold a second crest which starts quite close to the Meuse in the vicinity of the field-work known as Froide-Terre, standing at a little more than the 1,100-foot level, and ends at the fort of Douaumont, at some 1,250 feet. Finally, there is a third crest, beginning at the Côte du Poivre, just before the river swings out in a big bend, at a level of 1,000, and running along the high ground by Louvémont, Hill 378, and the heights of Bezonvaux....On the left bank the contours run quite differently....First of all, over here, you have an easy rise which finishes, at about 980 feet, just where the forts of Sartelle and Chaume stand.... Next comes a short, sharp escarpment, with a maximum height of still something like 980, which includes the woods of Bourru, Marre, and Vacherauville; and very much farther off are Hill 304, the Mort-Homme, and the Côte de l'Oie...."

Messieurs Audincourt and Blanchart, who could see nothing of all this, gave but half an ear to the explanations. But the topographical digression had succeeded in making Deputy-Colonel Blanchart lose the thread of his thoughts.

At this moment they turned into a little street which seemed scarcely more deserted than many streets in provincial towns situated well behind the lines. Two or three shops were open. There were several pedestrians about. A few of the houses had their shutters closed and appeared to have been abandoned. But the rest looked ordinary enough.

"Life seems to be going on much as usual," said M. Audincourt.

"Oh, there's a great deal less than there used to be," Colonel Fargeau corrected him. "We've got, I should say, about five thousand inhabitants compared with the pre-war figure of eighteen or twenty thousand. And every week sees new departures."

But M. Audincourt, who had expected to find streets completely destroyed, such as he had seen elsewhere in the forward areas, and could discover nothing worse than a dead-alive market-town, insisted on expressing surprise:

"It all appears to be very quiet....The place has suffered very little."

"I beg your pardon, sir, but I must correct that impression!" The old colonel was now well mounted on his hobby-horse. He probably thought that his visitors were trying to make light of his little corner of the war. "We were bombarded eight times in the course of 1914. No less than forty shells fell on the town."

"In all?"

"Yes, sir, in all," said Colonel Fargeau, with a show of irritation, "and twelve times in 1915, with a hundred shells."

"They seem to have had plenty of time to count them," thought M. Audincourt. "I only hope things go on like that."

"The worst bombardment of all," continued Colonel Fargeau fiercely, "was the one on the 4th of June '15. The enemy had got a 380-millimetre gun—380, mark you—on the edge of Muzeray Wood, to the north-east of Spincourt, firing at a range of seventeen miles. It sent over twenty-five shells—shells as big as this."

"Really!" said M. Audincourt politely.

"They were trying to get the Citadel. But they never hit it, though they put down two groups five hundred metres apart, and there was scarcely more than a thousand metres in depth between the shell bursts. Not bad shooting, that. They destroyed three houses in the Upper Town, and part of the College Buvignier, where we had a hospital."

"Really!" repeated M. Audincourt.

"I'll take you there so that you can see for yourselves....On the 1st of October last we had another bombardment of the same calibre. This time they were firing from Warphemont Wood, rather farther north than Muzeray. They destroyed five houses, and one of the buildings of the Anthouard Barracks which we passed just now. I ought to have made you go inside."

He took them to the foot of the Citadel by the Porte Neuve road. In front of the entrance to No.1 listening-post he asked them to wait a moment.

"I must warn them that we're going to pay them a visit. I don't think they'll raise any difficulty."

The two members of the Army Commission remained alone on the damp platform, across which the mass of the Citadel cast a melancholy shadow.

"He's making fools of us," said M. Audincourt.

"Do you really think so?" replied Deputy-Colonel Blanchart, more than half inclined to agree with his companion, but rendered cautious by what remained to him of the military spirit.

"Good heavens! This is my fifth mission to the front," said M. Audincourt on a note of pride; "I'm beginning to know these soldiers; I can smell 'em a mile off. Not that I'm accusing this jolly old fellow of any personal malice. He's had his orders, that's all."

"What sort of orders, do you think?"

"To keep us amused with a lot of nonsense. The old fool probably doesn't know it's nonsense. But that's not the point....They've sworn not to let us see anything. They played exactly the same trick on me the other day at Nancy— you weren't there....I'm beginning to have enough of this sort of thing....The only time I ever managed to see anything was when Mousson and I went to visit General Duroure....He at least had the decency to treat us seriously....But the others!" He shook his head. "Oh, word's come from higher up. G.H.Q. hates the sight of us!" He turned his head to take a look at the dank grass of the Citadel. "What's he going to show us here?"

"The casemates....They may be very interesting."

M. Audincourt shrugged his shoulders. "We haven't come all this way to see a lot of casemates dating from Heaven knows when—probably from the days of Vauban.... We're not a lot of tourists. The Army Commission's no joking matter. It's not only us they're making fools of, but Parliament, the country itself. I think we ought to refuse to go in, and tell him exactly why."

The deputy-colonel seemed to be upset.

"But, my dear fellow, I assure you we shall probably see something that will really be of interest to us in our official capacity."

"What? In God's name what? What's our job? To find out whether the defences of Verdun are as deplorable, as non-existent, as some people make out. We're to get Driant, in particular, to put us wise. He knows what he's talking about, because he's on the spot, because he's a fighting soldier who's seen service in the line at Verdun and not just at an office table at Chantilly. I'm concerned only with what we've been sent here to do. What we want to see is not here, but over there"—he pointed towards the north-east—"or there, if you prefer, round those forts and crests he was talking about. That's what I'm after; the rest can go hang. Is it, perhaps, that they're frightened for our safety? When we were with Duroure we saw shells falling no more than fifty paces from where we were standing. I flatter myself that we behaved pretty well....No, it's not *for* us that they're feeling nervous, but rather *of* us."

As a result of several weeks spent in visiting the front and the areas just behind it, M. Audincourt, usually so gentle, had acquired great firmness of language. But his colleague, Blanchart, continued the discussion in a quieter tone:

"But you must admit that the Citadel forms part of the defence system...and an important part. They may have turned it into a very strong artillery position, secretly organized, of course....Modern battles have a character quite of their own. Some of the Boche guns have a range of eighteen miles, as you heard just now. But so have ours. It may be from this very spot, from beneath this invulnerable cupola, that our fellows plan to open a devastating fire in the event of a Boche attack....They may be going to show us hundreds of guns of all calibres, marvellously protected and camouflaged...."

M. Audincourt showed signs of being slightly shaken:

"But," said he, "they've told us that the forts up there are dismantled or stripped of their guns....Why should they have dismantled them in order to stuff all the artillery into this hole?"

"In the first place, it isn't a hole," retorted the deputy-colonel in the tone of a man who knows what he is talking about. "It's a hill-top in the middle of a plain, with a wide field of view....And then, don't forget the effect of plunging fire....That's why they probably thought that the forts were too far forward, too visible, too much exposed, as they say: regular shell-traps. Up here, on the contrary, it seems to me that the position is particularly favourable, always considering the conditions of the modern battle."

"All right. I don't mind—provided they do show us a hundred guns of all calibres....But I warn you that I shall insist on going over there. That's what I've come for."

They had traversed a number of vaulted galleries, set at right angles to one another, and rather like the cellars of some big grower of Vouvray or Champagne, except that there were no bottles. The air was damp, at times almost freezing, at others warm and rather stale.

"We have central heating, and it is turned on in all this part of the fort," explained Colonel Fargeau.

Two of the galleries were occupied by soldiers who had transformed it into a sort of barrack-room, with mattresses on the floor and packs lying about. The two visitors asked to what formation they belonged.

"They've come up as reliefs, or possibly as reinforcements. We can't fit them all into the barracks in the town, since certain buildings have been destroyed."

A little farther on they came to a gallery filled with civilians. It had the appearance of a civilian dormitory. That is to say, it was marked by that little extra look of poverty which is the particular contribution of women, children, and general disorder. It might have been a night shelter, into which had been shoved just anyhow a number of peasant families, with their bundles and their cooking-utensils. There was no doubt about these people being peasants. They gave off a mingled smell of tobacco, barn, and stable.

"Refugees?" queried M. Audincourt. "Where do they come from? There's been no enemy advance recently."

Colonel Fargeau assumed a mysterious look and lowered his voice.

"No… but the military authorities took the precaution, early this month, of evacuating a certain number of villages or hamlets which might be particularly exposed in the event of a…but since we can't get rid of them at once, we've turned this place into a sort of depot."

"Odd," murmured M. Audincourt to his colleague. "You notice that they are taking 'certain precautions.' That means, presumably, that they expect something. And yet, at the same time…it's certainly odd."

When they had gone still farther, in spite of feeling convinced that the humidity of these vaulted caverns would undoubtedly give him an attack of lumbago, he whispered in his companion's ear:

"What about those guns of yours? I don't see many of them about."

The deputy-colonel touched the arm of the colonel in uniform.

"Tell me, please—where are the guns?…What arrangements have been made for the artillery? We should be interested to know.…No doubt you have a good deal in the Citadel?"

"Oh, certainly we have—in the gun vaults.…"

"Ah!" said the deputy-colonel, his eyes sparkling, and with a triumphant glance at his colleague.

"We have—let me see—yes, we have, if I'm not mistaken, two 75's and two 95's."

M. Audincourt started.

"What!"

"In all?" asked M. Blanchart with a show of nervousness.

"Yes…" said Colonel Fargeau, and added, with a knowing wag of the head: "and the 95, let me tell you, is a good old gun.…It can fire at eight thousand.…"

The car had been bumping them up and down for the last half-hour over a road that was full of holes and frequently obstructed by convoys.

"But aren't we going south?" The question was suddenly snapped out by M. Audincourt, who had been keeping an eye on the sun.

"South? Well—yes—if you like to put it that way," answered Colonel Fargeau cautiously.

"Where are you taking us?"

"To Dugny."

"What's Dugny—a fort?"

"There is a fort there, but it's not to the fort that we're going. I'm taking you to headquarters—the headquarters of the Fortified Zone, which is at Dugny."

"That's the first I've heard of it. Why weren't we taken to Dugny at once, as soon as we arrived?"

"I don't know.…I telephoned there just now to say that you wanted to visit the forward system. Major Plée, one of General Herr's senior staff officers, is waiting to receive you."

"What did he say about our request?"

"He wants to talk to you himself."

"More time lost! Wouldn't it have been simpler, when he had you on the telephone, to have given the necessary instructions direct?"

Deputy-Colonel Blanchart nudged his colleague's elbow.

"Come in, gentlemen."

They found themselves in a small room which had once, presumably, to judge from the flowered wall-paper, been a bedroom, though it had been emptied of furniture and turned into a makeshift office. There was one large table, and two small ones. At the former was seated Major Plée. One of the other two was occupied by an officer who rose, bowed, resumed his seat, and started once more to write. The owner of the third table was absent.

After an exchange of courtesies Major Plée, who seemed an honest sort of fellow, came straight to the point:

"You wanted to see the front line...." (M. Audincourt noticed his use of the past tense.) "...I see no particular reason why you should not. But the ground at this time of year is in a frightful state. You would wear yourselves out to no purpose. Communication trenches, fire-bays, wire entanglements—you know the sort of thing. After all, they don't vary much whatever part of the line you're in. If it was merely a question of amusing you I could easily organize a conducted tour to a carefully selected point. You would return enchanted with what you had seen, but actually you'd have learned nothing.... That sort of thing's just eyewash. To get any sort of valuable impression of a sector as extended, as complicated, as difficult to get round, as this is, you'd need four or five whole days on the ground...and even then...I can offer you something better than that.... First of all, naturally, I give you full permission to study the plan of all the field-works in course of construction or already finished.... Since the visit of General Langle de Cary, under whose orders, as you know, we now come, having been attached to the Centre Group of Armies, we've been getting a lot of extra labour, to say nothing of first-line reinforcements, and that has meant that the work could be pushed forward more rapidly...."

The major enumerated the various facts of the situation with unruffled good humour. Whether, in his heart of hearts, he really approved of Langle de Cary's appointment and of the merging of the Fortified Zone in the C.G.A., whether he was resentful of the period just past when there had been no reinforcements and the work had gone at a snail's pace, it was quite impossible to judge from his expression.

"But it is not that," he went on, "to which I am alluding."

He took up a folder and proceeded rather solemnly:

"I am about to confide to you gentlemen the contents of a document which was laid on my table only a few hours ago.... You will notice the date" (he turned the front page towards them), "the 13th of February. There could be nothing, I think, more topical, given the nature of your preoccupations—nothing that could supply you with more up-to-date information. You, I assume, gentlemen, like ourselves are very properly concerned with the possibility of a German attack on Verdun.…Well, and what is the nature of this document? It is, gentlemen, a survey of all work undertaken by the Germans on the Verdun front between September 1915 and the end of January 1916.…You will agree, I think, that it is extremely apposite. It is the result of many months of work by our Intelligence staff…and must be regarded, I need hardly remind you, as strictly confidential. As it is long, and enters into details which you would only find tedious, I do not propose to read it in full. I will give you its gist. What, then, are its general conclusions? From September until the middle of January the enemy has been continuously at work altering the nature of his advanced positions. A number of villages have been turned into places of assembly served by narrow-gauge railways, and connected by a fan-shaped system of communication trenches with the front line. From the middle of January a considerable amount of labour has been expended on the provision, well forward, of extremely elaborate and extremely comfortable dug-outs at a depth of anything from twenty-five to thirty feet below ground level. The existence of these dug-outs was already known to us, and deserters have referred to them under the name of *Stollen*.…Here is a plan, drawn to a scale of 1/200,000 millimetres attached to the report. Take your time, gentlemen, and have a good look at it."

His visitors bent over the 1/200,000 plan and gazed at a number of kidney-shaped marks the limits of which were shown by lines and cross-hatching. Major Plée left them for a minute or two to take in what they saw; then:

"Those are the facts, gentlemen. In what sense are they to be interpreted? The title of this report, which I have not read you in detail, contains one extremely significant word—an epithet placed there by the pen of those who drew it up when, having finished their task, they wanted to express shortly its essential character. Read it for yourselves: 'Survey of German'—

what?—'of German *defensive* works.' Not, you will notice, *offensive*....Defensive. The word is deliberately employed.... Yes, these works are clearly of a defensive nature. To the professional eye there can be no doubt whatever on that score....I feel sure," he added, with a gesture towards Blanchart, who was leaning over the plan, "that the colonel agrees with me."

"They certainly look so to me," said the deputy-colonel.

"But there's something else....For the last two months, and earlier still, but for the last two months in particular, ever since, rightly or wrongly, Verdun has been in the public eye, our Intelligence people, with that meticulous concern for detail which marks all their work, have been waiting, I might almost say magnifying-glass in hand, for the appearance of the one piece of evidence which could clinch the matter: the digging of assault trenches. Last month, when General de Castelnau paid us his visit, we said to him: 'General, so far no assault trenches have been dug.' Today, the 14th of February, I can but repeat that statement: no assault trenches have yet been dug. It is one point among many, but it is conclusive. You, no doubt, colonel, will share my curiosity as to how the Germans, whose lines here are at an average distance of six hundred yards from our own, can possibly launch an attack without first preparing the necessary assault trenches."

"I entirely agree!" said the deputy-colonel.

"But in that case," put in M. Audincourt, "what does all this work mean?"

"Mean?" Major Plée gave vent to a laugh. "Simply this— that the Germans are afraid of being attacked. They too, with an eye on what we are doing, might be tempted to say: 'What the devil are the French up to?' It's the old story. Each side is frightened of the other."

"But can they be seriously afraid of our attacking them just here?"

"Why not, sir? There's nothing essentially absurd about the idea. Verdun, I admit, forms a salient in our front, and the enemy might therefore be tempted to cut it off. But it is also a magnificent base, a jumping-off place for an offensive of our own—which leads me to the final, incontrovertible argument which I am sure you will grasp at once. Look here, gentlemen."

They straightened themselves, and he took them across to the wall on which was pinned a map of the Verdun area drawn to a scale of 1/50,000.

"Here we have the front line. If the Germans were planning an attack with the object of cutting off our salient, where would they most naturally make their preparations? Here...and here...that is to say, at the two points which would enable them to apply the necessary pressure, to pinch off the neck of the pocket, to amputate, so to speak, the rupture...to the left, in the neighbourhood of Varennes, and to the right, near Saint-Mihiel. But where, in fact, have they been concentrating their field-works? Here, between Consenvoye and Spincourt, or, rather, Étain—that is to say, immediately opposite the point where the rupture attains its greatest swelling, just where our salient is most pronounced. When a commander elaborates a system of field-works opposite the nose of a salient, what does it mean?—that he is preparing to attack, to dash his head against the strong projection opposite? Not, I assure you, unless he is mad. No, it can mean only one thing: that he wants to establish adequate defences against an attack coming from that projection, to break up an offensive which he is afraid may be launched along the axis of the salient. You will ask me, gentlemen, what practical steps ought to be taken, given the situation as I have described it. Well, there can be no harm in perfecting our defence measures to a reasonable extent. But we ought not to let ourselves be hypnotized by an eventuality which is very unlikely to occur, and so ignore other dangers which are more pressing, and undertakings of a more positive nature. I have reason to know that G.H.Q. does actually fear that an offensive will be made by the Germans, but the likelihood is that the chosen point will be in Champagne. What luck it would be for the enemy if we were fools enough to strip our Champagne front of men in order to mass them behind Verdun!...Ah, you will say, why not use Verdun as a base for an attack of our own towards Briey or Metz—which is precisely what the Germans are afraid of? That would demand quite a different organization of our forces, and one, I admit, which would give me personally much greater satisfaction."

In the car which took them back that evening to Verdun, Blanchart whispered to Audincourt, low enough not to be overheard by Colonel Fargeau:

"Are you happier now?"

"Certainly not about the part I played. I was a fool not to have thought of saying to him: 'We didn't come here, sir, to listen to you explaining your views as to whether the Germans do or do not intend to attack. We came to see what steps you were taking to meet him if he does.' But it's too late now."

A moment after, he started grumbling again:

"I was told that General Herr believed a German attack on Verdun to be imminent…that he was very much afraid of it, in fact….If that is so, I simply don't understand what everybody's up to."

CHAPTER TWENTY-FOUR

A Distant Rumbling

On the 14th of February, Clanricard—who had returned with his company to Vauquois-East, where he had found his old stinking dug-out with all its unpleasant memories—spent a day calculated to depress anyone's spirits. The rain drummed down almost continuously. The mass of decomposing rubbish which formed the Butte seemed to be turning into liquid and was oozing like a dung-heap. From time to time a stray shell, directed by sheer malice, succeeded in demolishing a section of parapet which had been repaired only the evening before. But he was comforted by a piece of news which had just reached him. He was only too ready to rejoice, to let the promised possibility go to his head, but he was afraid to give the rumour too much credence, having been too often disappointed in the past. The information had come from two or three different sources, though no one seemed sure of its real origin.

The 7th corps had just arrived, with guns, transport, and staff complete. It had been seen at Clermont-en-Argonne and at Récicourt. Some of the men belonging to it had said they were going to relieve the 5th. The miracle was going to happen at last! The 5th corps, which for over a year had been attached, as it were, to the hateful Butte, circling round it even when they were out at rest, like a watch-dog on the end of a chain, was to leave it, was to be sent to some other sector, was to escape. Where would they go? That was a matter of secondary importance. To a man who had spent a whole year at the Butte, the rest of the world, front line included, could not but seem a delicious rest-cure. Three cheers for the 7th corps!

With such a happiness looming in the near future, it

became increasingly important not to get in the way of one of those projectiles which the Boche sent over from time to time just to give a bit of edge to the rain. To get oneself killed the last day at Vauquois would be an unpardonable stupidity. Well, it was all a matter of luck and a reasonable amount of care. But there was something a good deal more tiresome than the possibility of becoming a last-minute casualty: a noise of gunfire, very far away, to the north-west of the Argonne slopes, somewhere in the neighbourhood of the great bend in the river Aire. It might be coming from somewhere round the woods of Chatel or of Cornay, or from still farther to the left. If only the Boche didn't have the ridiculous idea of attacking!—didn't launch that monster offensive which everyone had been talking about for weeks, some saying that it would be in the Champagne, others at Verdun, or at some point between the two, or somewhere quite different. The threat could be heard snuffling up and down the front like a beast of prey nosing round a house door. It would be just like the luck of the poor Vauquois devils to have an offensive started next door the very day before they were to be relieved. If that happened, good-bye to all hope of leaving the line! The 7th were on the spot all right, ready to be dished up, but in that case they'd be used to reinforce the threatened sector and not to take over the Butte.

On the morning of the same day Jerphanion had left Grandes-Loges with his unit. The wonderful interim of peace and quiet was over at last. For some time past there had been evil omens of an impending move. Drafts had been turning up with too great a regularity. The regimental staff had been moving a bit too frequently between Grandes-Loges and Bouy. What was to be their destination? No one knew exactly, but presumably the south-east, to judge from the route they were taking. South-east was not the direction of the front, unless they were to be sent far away, to Lorraine or to some point beyond Saint-Mihiel.

On the 15th the rain was still falling at Vauquois, and the men were still hoping to be relieved. The presence of the 7th corps to their rear was now known to be a fact. There were witnesses beyond counting. Like the rain and the hope, the distant gunfire also continued, but it had changed direction, had made an odd twist through a whole right angle. It was not very heavy. It came now from the north-east, and, so far as one could tell, most of it was of French origin.

That same day Jerphanion arrived at Pagny, south-east of Châlons-sur-Marne, after having broken the march the night before at Saint-Martin-le-Pré. The rumour spread that they were going to stay at Pagny. Was the move over so soon, then? Why Pagny? What was happening?

Orders soon came to confirm the rumour. The regiment was to remain at Pagny, at least for the time being.

It was worth while, then, seeing what sort of place Pagny was. It was a small village. At one time it must have had a good deal of charm. At any rate, it was a long way from the front, and even more peaceful, if such a thing were possible, than Grandes-Loges. But it had suffered in September 1914, first from the retreat, then from the advance. Many of the roofs had fallen in, and this fact, in view of the state of the weather, gave a melancholy aspect to the landscape and complicated the billeting problem. On the other hand, the inhabitants were unusually friendly, offered, indeed, a warmth of welcome which, taken in conjunction with the battered houses, was reminiscent of the early weeks of the war. Jerphanion, Fabre, Cotin, and another officer had to share a room with two beds which a charming old woman, who might have stepped straight out of the pages of Déroulède, put at their service.

That evening, before dinner, Fabre said to Jerphanion:

"Come over here a minute."

He led him to a corner of the garden, just by the wall.

"Do you hear anything—over there?" and he pointed towards the north-east.

"Yes…sounds to me like gunfire…very spasmodic gunfire…and a long way off. It's probably somewhere in the Argonne, or round Verdun. Wherever it is, it doesn't sound very bad."

On the 16th the rain at Vauquois became at times torrential. The Butte exuded its innards in a sort of thick slime. A few men still talked of relief, but others were spreading a new and sickening rumour. The 7th, the precious 7th, were moving back towards Sainte-Menehould. What on earth were they going to do there? Not relieve Vauquois, so much was certain.

There was another rumour too, calculated to give anyone the blues. Reliable witnesses from the rear reported that they had met large convoys of heavy guns all moving eastwards. Those who thought they knew declared that they had identified 105's, 120's on tractors, 155's on caterpillars, all between Clermont and Parois; and Rimailho howitzers on the road from Clermont to Auzéville. Even the heavies mounted on railway trucks were moving. Someone had even seen a train of 155-millimetre guns and one of naval 24's arriving at the station of Récicourt. The noise of firing continued, though no heavier than before, still coming from the same direction.

At Pagny, no sooner had the officers settled their men than they received a program of training and field exercises quite different from the sort usually laid down for troops out at rest. These were accompanied by special instructions the gist of which was that troops must be brought to a high state of discipline and efficiency. The officers said among themselves: "Look out for squalls!" Jerphanion became a prey to his obsessions of the previous autumn: "The war is not going to end. Here it is, starting all over again. It'll go on for the whole of this year, and right through next winter, with intervals of delusive rest (for those who don't come by that last, long rest about which there can be no delusion); and periods for recuperation and 'reconditioning'—for ever and ever, until further notice. . . . He concentrated all the forces of his mind on that Meygal day-dream which he had never wholly abandoned, though during the happy interlude at Grandes-Loges he had cherished it in a more absent-minded fashion. Meygal. The warrior band safe within its forts and embattled lines. The outposts stationed at the principal points of entry to the forest, six of them in all, consisting of four men each so as not to draw overmuch on the available effectives....And always, in the background, that problem of ammunition. They would have to economize what they brought with them from the front, but some means would have to be found, too, of getting new supplies. It was all very complicated.

The 17th at Vauquois passed much like the 16th. At Pagny, field exercises began in open country. The senior officers were nervous.

"What the hell good do you think you are!" cried the lieutenant-colonel, who as a rule was so moderate in his language. "You've been out at rest too long; you've gone soft! I suppose you all think you're on holiday? Well, I'm going to put some life into you. Jump to it now!"

When he had run up and down the flank of his company and could find time to get his breath, Jerphanion took another hurried look at his fantasy, much as he might have taken a hurried puff at a pipe which he had thrust lit into his pocket: "My own headquarters will be in some rocky cavern. It will have three rooms. Somewhere in the Testoire foothills, facing south towards Boussoulet. About a morning's ride from Boussoulet."

On the 18th, when Duroure got back from his morning's outing, he was surprised to see Clédinger waiting for him in the courtyard.

"Anything serious?"

"Not for us, sir….But a telephone message has just come through from de Vaussorgues about what happened yesterday."

"Yes?" said Duroure eagerly, throwing the reins to his orderly.

"Nothing doing, sir….Everything's fixed up. But he took the opportunity to give me the latest dope. You remember when he was here three days ago he said that G.H.Q. had sent a special emissary to Langle de Cary's headquarters, and to Verdun, to make a fresh survey?"

"Well, what happened?"

"This morning Chantilly got the first report in from the officer in question. It seems that from what he has seen, and in particular after examining the air photos taken yesterday, he's pretty sure that the Germans are going to attack at Verdun after a bombardment on the grand scale. . . . We shall get official notification like all other formations, but de Vaussorgues wanted to let us know at once. Pretty decent of him. A hard knock at Verdun won't affect us directly, but if the thing spreads, it's quite possible that it may affect everybody before we've done."

"Obviously, obviously!" said Duroure, deep in his thoughts. A crowd of ideas thronged his brain.

At Vauquois there was no longer any question of a relief. The men listened to the distant bombardment, an odd feeling in their stomachs, their ears turned towards the north-east. The noise had increased slightly; though as yet it could hardly be called intense. It was obvious that the French heavies were at work, though at intervals that sometimes amounted to several minutes. Some of the firing sounded farther off still, perhaps in the neighbourhood of Récicourt or Blercourt. The target must be well to the north of Verdun, in the enemy's second line. It was difficult to distinguish in the discontinuous rumble of the nearer gunfire how much was due to the French batteries round Verdun, and how much was German retaliation. But it seemed, at any rate, as though most of it was due to their own people. Did it mean that the French were laying down a preliminary barrage—that it was the French who were going to attack?

At Pagny field exercises were in full swing. The men had no heart for joking. They even avoided any exchange of views. Fabre said to Jerphanion:

"Looks to me as though we were being put through a special course for some big show. You and your shock-troops theory!—Well, now you've pretty nearly got what you wanted."

The 19th resembled the 18th, with this difference: that, so far as could be heard from Vauquois, the general axis of the bombardment seemed to have shifted slightly, so as to be directly—so far, anyhow, as one part of it was concerned—opposite the Butte. There was still a general impression that the initiative lay with the French guns, though their fire had not yet reached what might be called maximum intensity. The enemy seemed half-hearted in his reply.

On the 20th attention at Vauquois was turned nearer home. There was a heavy trench-mortar demonstration on the hollow road to the east of the Butte. Clanricard's company alone had two men killed and about a dozen wounded. Could it be that the Germans, aware now that an attack was preparing at Verdun, had made up their minds to make a diversion and had chosen, damn their eyes, to have a smack at the miserable Argonne and this poor, bloody Vauquois?

The men of the 151st regiment at Pagny, although a sharp wind had set in from the north, were sweating blood. Some of the inhabitants had come out to watch them. In the rare pauses of work they chatted with the soldiers and gave them wine to drink. Everybody was thoughtful.

At Vauquois it seemed that the activity of the morning was not going to be followed up. For the rest of the day nothing happened beyond a few shells from the Cheppy gun, which plastered the poor old Butte. Towards evening the weather grew colder. The mud hardened. The dung flowing down the slope began to congeal. Farther off, the ground had become more resonant. The sound of the distant gunfire could be heard more clearly. But its meaning was just as difficult to interpret. Some held the opinion that the activity of the French batteries had weakened, and that the enemy were opening up with greater intensity. Had the idea of a French attack been abandoned? Perhaps the explanation was simpler. Perhaps the spasmodic bombardment of the last few days had been a feint only, an attempt to feel out the enemy's weak spots and make him unmask his batteries. Now that the French command had got the information they wanted, it might be that they were going to slacken off gradually. When rations were dished out that evening, somebody spread the rumour that Joffre had been seen at Parois in the course of the day. When dark fell, the clear, frosty air made it possible to see gun-flashes far away on the heights of the Meuse, though the magnificent moonlight to some extent dimmed them. Clanricard, Norestier, and Imbard spent a whole hour smoking and watching them. Brimont was in the front line.

On the 21st, at seven fifteen in the morning, when it was already quite light, the men at Vauquois, shivering in the keen cold of the dawn air, heard the whole eastern horizon torn suddenly asunder, as though somebody had taken a knife and ripped up a canvas suspended brim-full of water. At that moment there started a vast rumble, which grew in intensity from moment to moment and never stopped.

VERDUN

PART TWO

THE BATTLE

CHAPTER ONE

February 21st: Morning

At seven a. m. of Monday, February 21st, Major Gastaldi, accompanied by Second Lieutenant Mazel, emerged from his headquarters on his way to visit the front line to see what progress had been made with the night's work. Since their arrival in the sector, this morning tour of his had become a regular habit, and when the weather was fine, he almost enjoyed it. During the last three days the weather had improved, and the day promised to be very fine. There had been just enough frost to give a firm surface to the layer of snow that covered the ground. There was snow, too, on the branches of the trees, and it was beginning to sparkle now in the level rays of the sun, which had been up for a quarter of an hour. The wind was still from the east, and had a nip in it, though without being too cold. It brought certain sounds from the direction of the forest of Spincourt—that is to say, from the German side of the line—sounds not in themselves remarkable, and no more disquieting than those of a distant market-town waking to the day's work.

One of the major's small pleasures was to note each morning the earlier coming of daylight.

"In another week," he said to Mazel, "if we're still here, we shall have to start half an hour sooner."

They skirted the eastern edge of the Bois de Champneuville and then, following the contour line which marked the limits of the Bois de Ville, known rather oddly as the Bois Vendu (or "Sold Wood"), took their way towards that part of the north-east edge which was called "Les Rappes," and which represented, on this side, the limits of the forward zone allotted to the battalion.

The major would gladly have abandoned himself to the cheerfulness inspired by the brisk morning air, and it needed no effort on his part to respond to the "Good mornings" of the men whom he passed at their breakfast in the various holes and shelters which marked his progress. But, without sharing the pessimism of certain of his colleagues, he found it difficult not to be ever so slightly perturbed by the gloomy rumours which had been making the rounds in the course of the last few days. "The Boches will attack, you see if they don't. Now that the fine weather's set in, we shan't have to wait long." Such had been the burden of the constant refrain. No longer ago than last evening a sergeant just up from Herbebois had painted things very black. "There's a great deal of movement behind the Boche lines on the approaches to Azannes....A lot of fires were reported the day before yesterday, and smoke can be seen quite clearly over the village. No one seems to know what it means, but obviously they're up to some dirty game or other....When the wind's from the east, our fellows can hear the sound of trains all day long from the forest of Spincourt. But what's worrying the staff most of all, it seems, is the almost complete silence of the enemy guns. Our batteries have been plumping shells into them at various times all these last days, but nothing seems to get a rise out of them." True, if one was always going to look for trouble, life, especially at the front, would become intolerable.

As they passed Guard Post No. I, he shouted:

"You there, Raoul? Come along with us!"

Lieutenant Raoul came out of his hole, fastening the holster of his Browning.

The three men continued their way towards Les Rappes, chatting gaily.

"What a morning to go shooting!" said Gastaldi.

They discussed shooting. They argued the advantages and disadvantages of snow—just a nice light fall, not a storm, naturally—for a day's sport. The answer varied according to the nature of the game. Each of the three was anxious to impress his companions with his detailed knowledge of the business.

They had just crossed the space separating strong-points 8

and 10 and were making their way through the undergrowth in the direction of 8a and 9 when: "Boom!" came the sound of a gun from the east. All three stopped as at a word of command. The sound had been deep and full-throated. It must have come from a gun of medium calibre, probably a 150. It broke with more than usual solemnity on their ears by reason of the bright February stillness which it so markedly disturbed. How long the three men stood there it would have been difficult to say. They said nothing.

Suddenly, "Boom, ban, ban, ran, ran, ranranran…" followed by an enormous sequence of explosions, as though thousands of mines had suddenly gone up, strung out along a half-circle of the horizon stretching from north to north-east. Almost immediately came the crash of shells near at hand, in the air, in the branches, in the ground. Fragments of steel and wood, lumps of soil, stones of every description, flew over their heads. Great columns of smoke jetted upwards from twenty different spots all around. The whole earth seemed to tremble. The air was filled with the smell of hot gun-breeches suddenly thrown open.

"Quick! Get down!" shouted Major Gastaldi.

All three threw themselves flat in a newly dug shelter, while the heavens continued to be rent above their heads. They found there two other men who greeted them with faces already haggard with fear.

The shelter was deep and led down beneath a natural hummock. At the bottom and to the left was an unfinished sap designed to open in the hillside, about the nine-hundred-foot level, whence it would command a fine view in the direction of Ville. But it had not yet been cut through. They had to content themselves, therefore, with crouching in this murky excavation, unable to see anything of what was happening outside, except—by dint of creeping towards the exit which faced away from the parapet—a circular glimpse of sky and brushwood, obscured every minute by the debris of shell-bursts, spouts of earth and smoke and scraps of broken branches, as far as the eye could reach, all mixed with a powdering of dry snow, which sparkled attractively in the

morning sun and gave to the whole the appearance of a trans-
formation scene in some children's pantomime.

"This means business, or I'm a Dutchman," said Gastaldi to
his companions.

They were his first words since they had tumbled into the
shelter. The uproar was so great in the narrow space that it was
only with difficulty that the human voice could be heard. Not
that there was anything very encouraging to say. Each of them
there could draw his own conclusions without having to be
told.

"Here we are, stuck in this hole," thought Gastaldi. "This
may go on for ages. It only needs a couple of well-aimed
heavies in the entry to bury us like rats....Let's hope we shan't
be so unlucky. Short of that, we're pretty well protected
...What infuriates me is being caught like this while the battalion's getting all this stuff...."

To Mazel he said:

"This is a damned nuisance....They'll be looking for me
everywhere...you too....Probably brigade'll be telephoning
like mad to know what's happening."

"As soon as things get a bit quieter," replied Mazel, taking a
squint through the door, "I'll make a shot to get as far as
Leriche's company H.Q...but not just now!"

"Of course not, it would be sheer madness!"

They waited a quarter of an hour, half an hour, scarcely
exchanging a word. Occasionally, when a detonation more
violent than the rest, or nearer at hand, set the walls of their
shelter rocking or brought down a spatter of earth from the
roof, they gave vent to a low oath: "Hell!" "God!" "Christ!"
They waited with sinking stomachs for the 210 or the 280
which would put an end to their little adventure. But this particular fear, which they made no effort to keep at bay, did not
prevent them from feeling the same sort of irritation as might
have been felt by a workman caught by a shower on his way
to the factory, who, sheltered beneath a neighbouring door-
way, keeps on murmuring to himself: "Damn it all! This'll
make me bloody late. Just my luck to find that the boss has
chosen this morning to send for me. It's probably raining

harder here than it is there, and they'll say I was afraid of getting wet."

"What time do you make it?" shouted Gastaldi.

"Five to nine, sir, I think," answered Mazel.

"I make it two minutes to," put in Lieutenant Raoul.

"You're probably right! I thought my watch was wrong. What time did this begin?"

"I don't know, sir....Somewhere between seven fifteen and seven thirty...."

"Nearer fifteen than thirty," said Raoul.

"It's been going on for more than an hour and a half, then. I may not be hearing properly, but it seems to me that it's as heavy as ever. What about you?"

"It certainly is, sir," said Mazel.

"If it's preparatory to an attack," observed Raoul, "there's no reason why it should leave off yet. . . . I heard from somebody that brigade got it from a deserter that the bombardment was going to last a hundred hours."

"A hundred hours! You're a cheerful sort of devil, I must say!" grumbled Gastaldi, shrugging his shoulders. "Well, any-how, here we are."

Reserve Captain Pierre Lafeuille, attached to the staff of the 30th corps, had left Souville at five forty that morning. He had been detailed to spend his day making a reconnaissance of the front of the 72nd Division, paying special attention to the ground lying between the Bois d'Haumont and the Bois des Caures. In case of urgency, he had been told to send back a telephone report in the course of his tour.

He had got a lift in a car as far as Louvemont from a friend who was going to visit 51st corps headquarters. From there he had set off alone, on foot, his nose buried in his map, which he could just read in the early light of dawn. He intended to join the road from Vacherauville to Ville and then climb the hill as far as Mormont Farm, where were situated the headquarters of the Sub-Sector Reserve. He meant to have breakfast at Mormont Farm (having started out after no

more than a cup of black coffee). After that he would proceed
to the south-west corner of the Bois des Caures and make his
way thence to the Bois d'Haumont by way of the ravine, taking in Haumont village on the way back, or vice versa
according as time and circumstance dictated. If it were not
too late he would even push on as far as Brabant, failing
which, he would return direct to Samogneux. At Samogneux
he would have no sort of difficulty in finding a vehicle bound
for Verdun, and thence another as far as Souville. The distance
he would have to cover on foot was quite long enough, but
even that might be shortened if he could beg a lift for part of
the way on some lorry or regimental transport.

As things turned out, he had barely left Louvemont, where
his friend had dropped him a little after six, when he was
overtaken by a light Ford truck on its way, like himself, to
Mormont Farm. Consequently the journey took him no
more than fifteen minutes.

He hurriedly ate something at one of the messes at Mormont, collecting a certain amount of information meanwhile,
and by six forty—that is to say, just as the sun was rising—was
on his way again to the Bois des Caures.

Some vague idea, not unmixed, perhaps, with concern for
his personal safety, warned him not to take the most direct
route, which lay along the crest, or, strictly speaking, which
led to Anglemont Farm, and sent him downhill to where,
three hundred feet lower, lay the valley road leading upwards
to the north-west corner of the Bois des Caures.

The detour was a long one. Lafeuille, realizing how much
time he was losing, began to reproach himself for having
made it.

He had reached the bottom of the ravine, and was just identifying the road before him with the route marked on his map
when the first sound of gunfire reached his ears.

He raised his head and, checking an inclination to start, listened. The whole horizon to the north-east had crashed into
uproar. The effect was less immediately overpowering than it
had seemed to Gastaldi and his companions, but it was easier
for him to realize the full extent of the bombardment. He

could see it come down like a tornado on the great arena of
hills and woods under their light covering of snow. The catastrophe was setting its mark on an area which, both in width
and in depth, extended to many kilometres. It had involved all
the country that lay before him and to his right, between the
bottom of the valley in which he stood and the front lines,
the whole area comprised by the Bois d'Haumont, the Bois
des Caures, the Bois de Ville, Wavrille, and Herbebois. For all
he knew, its effect might be being felt even farther eastwards,
where the continuous rumble seemed to have reached its
fullest intensity. Hundreds of field-guns must have opened at
one and the same moment. But on the slopes behind him and
on the wooded knolls that closed the horizon to the south,
heavy shells were bursting. Lafeuille could see the smoke of
the explosions jet into the air one after another, since no
sooner had one begun to dissipate than another took its place.
The ragged circle of woods soon gave the impression of being
set with milk-white puffs, as of lit torches, at ever lessening
intervals. The heavier shells streaked the sky with a trundling
and metallic sound that was scarcely audible above the general pandemonium. It was easy to guess that they were on their
way above the visible hill-tops to fall farther off among the
slopes and ravines of the back areas, on Louvemont, on the
Côte du Poivre, and farther still, on the twists and turns of the
Meuse, on the villages of the river valley, on Verdun itself.

Pierre Lafeuille felt, at one and the same moment, completely lucid and utterly idiotic. His lucidity consisted in losing nothing of what was happening, of realizing everything
perfectly clearly and not as the effect of some nightmarish
vision; his idiocy, in a complete inability to take the smallest
decision about his personal safety, in a failure to register even
the first stage of any rational reaction. It took the form, too,
of words going over and over in his mind, words which he
knew to be foolish, but which he could no more control than
if he had heard them spoken by some particularly stupid
companion at his side: "You're trembling like a leaf....Your
name is Lafeuille and you're trembling like a leaf...." As a
matter of fact, he was not trembling at all. But all the warmth

had gone out of his body and he felt paralysed.

He became aware, finally, that some thirty yards from him, on a reverse slope, was a hollow, covered with brushwood and several feet of earth, in which a man could crouch. He reached it in two or three rushes, stopping to fling himself on the ground when a shell threatened to burst near him, and finding that each time he was badly out in his reckoning.

Once comfortably installed in his hollow, he began to consider the position more at his leisure and to calculate his chances. He took account of the fact that within his own field of vision, which was not very extensive, a large number of shells was falling, but that since these shells were intended to search a certain area, were aimed at no particular target, and, coming from different batteries, kept to no one line, their explosions were scattered almost completely at random. Even though the bombardment should last, therefore, for several hours with undiminished intensity, the odds against any given point being hit were heavy. It was not, in consequence, altogether absurd to plan a series of changes in his position—a sort of itinerary—within the limits of this very good imitation of hell. The ordinary precautions, such as throwing himself flat, making use of holes in the ground, hillocks, etc., would probably not be of much use. For the noise was so deafening that it would be impossible to distinguish the approach of any one shell among so many. They were of such a size, too, that one was not safe from them even at a fair distance. Crouching in a hollow, one could easily be hit by a descending splinter, so wide was the area of explosion. Shrapnel, detonating high in the air, would make hay of any temporary cover he might find. The only thing was to face the risks squarely. The only reasonable precaution was to keep away from the apparent heart of the uproar, which was indicated in the general noise by a kernel of even greater concentration round the woods to the north and north-east, and to take as much advantage as possible of dead ground.

He came to the conclusion that he had better move on towards Haumont, skirting the south side of the hill on which it stood. He anticipated in imagination his arrival at Haumont, heard himself saying: "Yes, I've just come from Mormont Farm." "What, all alone?" "Good God, yes!…I can't say I met many people on the way!" "And you came right through the barrage?" "Damn it, of course I did.…No one seems to have thought of digging a tunnel for me!…" And, in the most natural way in the world, he would ask to be allowed to use the telephone in order to report to Corps H.Q. the preliminary results of his tour.

He started off, profiting by what seemed a local slackening in the violence of the bombardment, and keeping as near as he could to the bottom of the ravine. He saw some suspicious-looking explosions at the bottom of the opposite slope. The smoke, instead of rising, seemed to cling to the ground, and he thought he felt a pricking in his throat and nostrils. "Gas? That would be the last straw!" He climbed the hill obliquely, making his way through the undergrowth. Suddenly he came on a small group of men. A detachment of the 165th was occupying a rudimentary trench system that had been dug among the trees. Everyone was lying flat on the ground. Not without some difficulty Lafeuille discovered the shelter which served as headquarters of the officer in charge—a captain.

"Where have you sprung from?" asked the latter.

Lafeuille described his adventure as briefly as possible. He was amazed at his own calmness.

He asked for information. The other told him, what he already knew only too well, the hour at which the bombardment had begun, and the degree of intensity which it had immediately attained. But he added certain details which were not without interest. Between seven twenty-five and eight o'clock communication with the Bois d'Haumont had remained good. Battalion H.Q. had told him to hold himself in readiness for the moment when the enemy would attack. He had learned that the bombardment of the wood, after beginning with high explosives and shrapnel, had latterly been confined to the former. He had given shelter to a runner who, after leaving the Bois des Caures in the direction of Mormont Farm, had been bewildered by the rain of shells and had lost his way. According to this man, the bombardment of the Bois des Caures had begun with an intense concentration of trench-mortars on the front line. This had been followed by a mixed barrage of 77's, 150's, and 210's. But what had been especially noticeable, both in the Bois d'Haumont and in the Bois des Caures, apart from the violence of the gunfire, was the fact that the enemy artillery, instead of giving its main attention to the fire-trenches, had obviously been trying to "box" and isolate certain definite objectives. While it pounded away at the northern edges of these two woods, seeking to destroy the defence works and bury their garrisons beneath the ruins of their shelters, it searched with equal intensity the southern approaches—that is to say, the roads by which the French High Command would send up reinforcements. The woods, consequently, could be neither held nor relieved. It was impossible even to evacuate them, had they wished to do so. It looked as though the forward units would just have to submit to being completely annihilated. The poor devils would have to show no particular courage in order to stay where they were. To retreat through woods riddled by shell-fire would have been more terrifying, would have demanded a higher degree of despairing energy, than to remain waiting for death crouched in their trenches.

"We might still have got back," shouted the captain in Lafeuille's ear, "if orders had come. But I don't mind betting that a mile ahead—that is, just over the ridge, they've all been done in." They had to make their voices heard above the deafening roar, but both of them were beginning to get used to it. "Not much chance now of my getting any orders," went on the captain. "I'm cut off like everybody else."

It was the Bois d'Haumont that had gone silent first. A few minutes later the captain had received urgent inquiries from the brigade. "Are you in touch with Bois d'Haumont? We can get no reply from them. What's happening? Do everything possible to get information. As soon as you know anything, send it through."

Everything possible!…What was there he could do? *He* couldn't repair the line to the Bois d'Haumont; it was probably cut in twenty places by this time. He had told one of his runners, a particularly brave chap, to try to reach the southeast corner of the wood. The man had come back a quarter of an hour later, covered with dirt, his face filthy, his eyes, ears, and nostrils full of mud, and with blood flowing from a number of flesh wounds. "I'd only got a hundred yards up the slope, sir, when I was knocked clean over by an explosion. I could see there were shells falling all over the place between here and the wood. It was hopeless to try and get on. Not a bit of use sending anyone else, sir. No one could get through." Meanwhile brigade had been on the telephone again: "Still no news? For God's sake, get a move on!" He had replied that one of his runners was trying to get forward in spite of the terrible barrage, and that he was waiting for him to come back, if the poor devil didn't stay there for good and all. On his return he had tried to get brigade on the wire, but there had been no reply.

"From that moment I have been completely cut off. You could have knocked me down with a feather when I saw you arrive. You must have had a sort of negative effect on the shells."

Lafeuille felt no little pride at the thought that in his person the officers of the staff, so often the target for much cheap fun, had received homage from a front-line captain.

"It might have been the Boches instead of you, and I couldn't possibly have known that they were coming over. They could have picked us out of our holes as easily as you pick snails out with a pin. . . . Though, as a matter of fact, I suppose they'll lengthen the range before attacking. . . . But with all this row going on, what chance shall we have of noticing it?"

"Tell me one thing," said Lafeuille, who had been busy thinking; "does brigade know what you say you've found out about the Bois d'Haumont, the Bois des Caures, and the rest? . . . Was the line already down when that information came in?"

"That's the most annoying part of the whole thing," said the captain in a tone of distressed embarrassment. "While I was still in touch with the Bois d'Haumont, it never occurred to me that it was part of my job to pass on their information to the brigade. Brigade must know more than I do, I said to myself. After all, I've only got the facts at second hand. And then when brigade rang up and said: 'We can't get any answer from the wood. What's going on there?' I understood them to mean: 'So far we've been kept posted.…What we want is later news.' But I hadn't got that any more than they had. Besides, you see, they seemed so wrought up, so panicky, that I thought they'd tick me off: 'Yes, yes, that's ancient history. You're merely wasting our time. That's not what we wanted to know.'"

"Did you pass on what the runner reported, the man from Bois des Caures?"

"Hell, no…It wasn't my business, you see.…It wasn't brigade's either, if it comes to that."

"You belong to the 144th brigade?"

"Yes."

Lafeuille seemed not to understand.

"The chaps in Bois des Caures are light infantry," went on the captain. "Driant's in command there."

"True enough. But where's the other regiment of your brigade?"

"The 164th? . . . I think they're still in the line between Bois de Ville and Ornes.…They must be getting it in the neck too, to judge by the row.…They were attached to the 51st Division when they took over the sector. I don't suppose it's my place to criticize, but I should like to say, all the same, that this shifting about of units seems perfectly idiotic to me."

His words were cut short by an explosion quite close at hand which brought down a little cataract of earth in one corner of the shelter.

"Another one like that and the roof'll fall in.…I only hope to God that didn't lay out a dozen of my fellows in some dugout. Hardly healthy to go and have a look, eh? What was I saying?…Oh, yes, here's this brigade of ours, cut up into two halves and attached to different divisions holding different parts of the line. The 164th has been taken away bodily, though it's still under brigade orders, with the result that the brigade as a whole is left with one of its regiments taking instructions from the 51st division, and the other from the 72nd!... No one seems to know what orders to obey....It's pretty rotten, you know."

"Maybe....But if I've understood you correctly, you're not absolutely certain that the brigade has ever received the information that has reached you about the position in Bois d'Haumont?"

"That's so...."

"And you've no reason to believe that what the runner told you about Bois des Caures has been passed on to any-body?...Where's the man now?"

"When he was a bit rested, I put him on his road for Mormont Farm. You might have met him."

"Precious little likelihood of that. I didn't come the short-est way. If the poor devil was fool enough to go straight ahead, the odds are he's dead by this time...."

Lafeuille began to pace nervously up and down.

"What it all comes to," he said, "is that in all probability your brigade is still in ignorance of what's happening in the front line....Division, too, perhaps....If the same sort of thing's been going on on the flanks, there's no reason to believe that now"—he looked at his watch, and went on— "at nine fifteen, the corps or even Fortified Zone H.Q. are any better informed."

The captain was sufficiently cheerful to make a joke of it:

"I shouldn't be surprised if they'd guessed something was up." With a jerk of his thumb he indicated zone No. 1 of the catastrophe.

"All I know," said Lafeuille, "is that I've got to find a tele-phone somewhere."

CHAPTER TWO

How a Front Is Breached

In the Bois de Ville, Captain Delpeuch, commanding the reserve of the Centre Forward Zone troops, whose dug-out was close to Gastaldi's headquarters, had felt worried about the latter ever since the bombardment started. He had done his best to trace his whereabouts and, now that he had not returned, was inclined to think that he had been killed along with his two companions, Mazel and Raoul. He decided, therefore, to take over the battalion. Under present conditions there could be no question of issuing orders. All he was concerned about was to discover what precisely was the situation in his immediate neighbourhood and to transmit the information to higher quarters.

One of the first things he learned was that a dug-out five hundred yards forward had collapsed and buried a platoon. A little while later a half section, still farther forward and to his left, suffered the same fate. The news served to confirm his suspicion that the battalion commander and his two lieutenants must have perished. He wanted to send word back, but the telephone line was cut. He dispatched a couple of runners.

Meanwhile Gastaldi had ordered one of the two men he had found in the shelter to try to get to the rear edge of the wood.

"Let them know what's happened to us. You needn't come back....And tell Captain Delpeuch to take over the battalion in my absence. He must ask for immediate artillery retaliation—and plenty of it. So far as I can make out, our fellows aren't sending anything over. What the devil are they up to at Chambrettes and the other positions? If they don't lay down

a barrage hot and strong three hundred yards in front of
where we are now—remember that: three hundred yards—
the Boches'll be able to stroll across just as they like. A barrage
ought not to be beyond their capabilities. Here are written
instructions, in case you forget. Off with you, and don't get
killed if you can help it!"

"Poor bastard," muttered Lieutenant Mazel, watching the
man vanish.

The undergrowth looked like a desert caught by a sand-
storm, a forest fire, and a powder magazine in the act of
exploding. The air was thick with dust, flying earth, and
smoke, mixed with broken branches, scraps of bark, pine needles, stones, splinters of metal, flying in all directions like the
odds and ends of refuse thrown up by a storm-lashed piece of
muddy water. There may have been snow too, but it was
unrecognizable in the dense clouds of dust, which was like
nothing so much as atomized plaster, whirled about with the
rest of the debris in the general turmoil. It was impossible to
see more than fifty yards ahead. The visible horizon was as
though engulfed in a roaring furnace.

"No use doing nothing," said the major. "We've got tools.
We'd better take turns at cutting through the rest of the sap
until we reach the open air. I'm sure there's not much more
than a couple of yards of earth left. We shall be able to see into
the ravine and across to the Boche lines, as was originally
planned. I'd rather turn to at something than stick about idle
here. If we get the job done in time we shall have the pleasure
of being able to take pot shots at them from our loop-hole
when they come over."

Over the whole of the front, from the Bois d'Haumont to
Herbebois, taking in the Bois des Caures and the Bois de
Ville, to a depth of several kilometres, the same dance of dust,
smoke, and debris went on, to a thunderous accompaniment
of noise. Thousands of men, in groups of two, of three, of ten,
sometimes of twenty, bent their backs to the storm, clinging
together at the bottom of holes, most of which were no better
than scratches in the ground, while many scarcely deserved

the name of shelter at all. To their ears came the sound of solid earth rent and disembowelled by bursting shells. Through cracks in the walls that protected them they could breathe in the smell of a tormented world, a smell like that of a planet in the process of being reduced to ashes. Most of them had given up all hope of surviving, though a few still clung to a belief in their lucky star. These were the men who, as like as not, would be killed just as they thought it was all over. The rest were content to wonder whether the next shell, or, rather, one of the next dozen or so, since no one could count them individually, would send their number up and release them from this agony. Sooner or later, certainly before nightfall, they must be in for it.

As for the gunners, even when they did receive orders—and for many reasons those they did receive were few and far between—they had no idea at what to fire. Before them lay a tornado-swept zone through which it was impossible to see. Of what lay within it they knew next to nothing. For all they could tell, the Germans might have attacked already, might at this very moment have gained a footing in the woods. How could they be sure? The most they could do was to fire blindly through the red and white eddies of a blazing forest.

Shortly before half past ten Lafeuille, nerve-racked and lost, who had been moving along a zigzag course like a hunted animal, avoiding the zones where the shells seemed heaviest, losing his way more than once and afraid even to look at his map, who had on three separate occasions made a detour through the undergrowth to reach some formation which he thought might have a telephone (one of the three had none, and the line from both the others was cut), came out unexpectedly on the road from Ville to Vacherauville, a little lower than the Louvemont road, and stumbled by sheer good luck on a telephone that was still functioning.

On his way thither he had collected a certain amount of additional information which he was anxious to send back to headquarters before it should be entirely out of date.

So surprised was he to find a line intact and to hear a voice at the other end that he twice repeated his question:

"Is that really the 30th corps?"

"Yes, yes. Get a move on! What is it you want to say?"

"Captain Lafeuille speaking."

"Good. We'd been wondering what had happened to you. What's the news?"

"I was almost in the front line when it started. There was a lot I could have told you, but I couldn't find a telephone working....That's why I'm too late."

"But you're not! Tell us everything you know....We've hardly heard a thing. It's frightful."

In reporting what he knew of the earlier phase—it must, he thought, by this time be stale news to corps headquarters— Lafeuille had adopted the rapid tone of a gentleman who realizes that he is repeating something already familiar. But he heard the voice at the other end of the line say: "Wait a moment while I get a pencil....Now say that again, slowly."

At Dugny, Major Plée was deep in discussion with two of his colleagues of the same rank as himself on the staff of the Fortified Zone. He refused to admit that the bombardment of the northern front was the preliminary to an attack.

"You're the most extraordinary fellow!" exclaimed his companions. "What more do you want?"

"In the first place, it's not sufficiently violent."

"Oh, isn't it! Ask the poor fellows out there!"

"Of course the enemy's sending over a lot of stuff because he wants to deceive us. I don't like contradicting you, but in view of what modern artillery is capable of, I don't consider this a real smothering barrage."

"How on earth can you know? We've had no reliable information yet."

"Then you've no more right to your conclusions than I have to mine."

"How about the heavies that have been falling on Verdun?"

"They're not the first. Remember the 4th of June and the 1st of October."

"Those weren't to be compared with this."

An orderly came in to say that 30th corps H.Q. was on the telephone and wanted to speak to one of them at once. Plée, with just perceptible hesitation, replied:

"Ask Captain Geoffroy to take the call."

For the benefit of his two colleagues he added:

"The 30th corps's getting panicky, too....Probably asking us for at least a hundred heavy guns!"

Despite his air of assurance, this call from the 30th corps had worried him a bit. If the message were not serious, Geoffroy, who had good judgment, would not trouble him. If it were...

None of the three men spoke. A moment or two later Geoffroy appeared.

"Excuse me, sir. The 30th corps has just sent through a report from Captain Lafeuille. I've taken it down. It's the first authoritative piece of news we've had....Lafeuille can be relied on...."

"Go on, read it!"

"Here it is." Geoffroy adjusted his monocle with the gesture that, in old days, had made Manifassier smile more than once. "At seven thirty, violent trench-mortar bombardment on the Bois des Caures (front line). Searching fire on Bois des Caures with 77's, 150's, and 210's. Barrage on southern edges of Bois d'Haumont and Bois des Caures. In Bois d'Haumont shrapnel and high explosives at first, later H.E. only. Gas from Haumont wood to Vacherauville. Reserves brought up under favourable conditions. A few shells reported on Vacherauville and Bras. Shells on Vacherauville fort, and probably on Marre fort as well."

"There!" exclaimed Plée in a tone almost of triumph. "Do *you* think it's so serious, Geoffroy?" He glanced at the two others.

"I know Lafeuille," replied Geoffroy calmly, "and I think it sounds quite serious enough."

"Bah!...Give me the paper."

"It's very badly written, sir."

"That doesn't matter. 'Searching fire on Bois des Caures....' No one's saying there wasn't. 'Barrage...'"

"He doesn't say, sir, '*partial* searching fire,' or '*intermittent* searching fire'…he doesn't say: '*indications* of barrage.'…"

"What are your conclusions, then?"

Geoffroy put the position in a few words:

"I conclude, sir, that they're hitting just about as hard as they know how."

CHAPTER THREE

A Minor Battle at Headquarters. General Order No. 15

During the minutes that followed, there took place at headquarters in Dugny a sort of mental crystallization, progressive but rapid, from which emerged a general idea of what had been happening which bore considerable resemblance to the fact.

This idea did not establish itself without first having to overcome a certain amount of resistance. It had to eat its way into the dense mass made up of previous beliefs, individual prejudices, and self-pride. It was aided, however, by the arrival of a number of fresh reports from front-line units, which, however incomplete they might be, and however falsified by error, did manage to combine to form a more or less continuous and coherent narrative of what had occurred.

It was now difficult to deny that the enemy had concentrated an exceptional weight of artillery fire on the front north of Verdun, on the right bank of the Meuse, extending over an arc of a circle measuring something like seven or eight miles. The specialists set themselves to make an approximate reckoning:

"There must be at least six hundred field-guns in action," they said, "and almost as many heavies."

This last figure appeared excessive to one or two of those present who suspected that the reports had been coloured by momentary excitement.

The enemy's activity was not confined to the arc of the circle above mentioned. His guns had been active as well on the left bank, in the region of Vauquois, and in the forest of the Argonne. But for the moment, at least, it was wiser to regard these secondary bombardments as diversions only, which must not be allowed to draw off attention from the main action, though that too, it could be argued, might in itself be nothing but a diversion on a grand scale undertaken to mask an offensive elsewhere, the precise locality of which would only be made clear in the days that were to follow. This point of view was strongly urged by Major Plée and by the officers most in his confidence. But with every half-hour that passed, the theory became less tenable. It was ridiculed, in particular, by the gunners.

"Has Plée thought for a moment," one of them asked, "how much of his reserve ammunition the Boche has already used on us since this morning? If he really thinks they've gone to all that trouble merely to pull wool over our eyes, he doesn't know what he's talking about!"

By the end of the morning conflicting opinions had so far combined as to agree on a working plan:

"Even if the Boches don't really mean to attack here, the threat cannot be ignored. If it becomes intensified, we are in no position to reply, in spite of our recent efforts to improve the position. We are short of material, especially of heavy guns and of shells of all calibres. We have enough men neither to fill the gaps nor to hurry on the defensive works. The men and material now on their way to the menaced sector are insufficient for the purpose. We must ask for as much more as they can let us have. We can't have too much."

General Herr, who was personally convinced that an infantry attack was imminent, but who was not yet sure what precise point of assault would be chosen, or whether the impending action would be a "full-dress affair," tended to support those of his staff who anticipated the worst, while doing his best to counter the arguments of the opposition.

"After all," he said to Plée, "it is for G.H.Q. to decide whether we are being faced by the opening phases of a first-class show or whether what we've got to deal with is only a demonstration, however violent it may be. . . . G.H.Q. have information and means of comparison which we have not. The ultimate responsibility is theirs. They will send us pre-cisely the reinforcements they think necessary, and no more.

But that is no reason for us to restrict our demands or to avoid doing what we can to prevent them from making a mistake. Here, at Verdun, the responsibility is ours. What we have got to do is to save Verdun."

Prolonged examination of the position made perfectly clear one thing which, in a sense, had been known already, but which was now seen for the first time in its full gravity and felt to warrant a justifiable anxiety:

Verdun was difficult to defend, and perhaps—if the enemy really laid himself out to capture it—difficult to save, mainly because there were severe obstacles in the way of its adequate reinforcement. It was all very well asking for men and material. But how were they to get there at a speed sufficient to cope with the demands made on both by a major action? How could all these extra troops be fed and supplied? "You say 'Let them send us at once a hundred thousand, two hundred thousand, men. . . .' But when you've got them, are you going to let them die of hunger? When they've exhausted the cartridges in their pouches and the shells in their caissons, are they to fight with slings? You'll have to reckon on having a thousand or so wounded a day; how on earth are you going to evacuate them? With all these troops coming up, you're already faced with the enormous difficulty of sending back all the civilians who've got to be cleared out of the town and its environs. Just look at the map!"

The map showed, in fact, that as the front then stood, the salient of Verdun was a wretched bulge condemned to slow death and anæmia owing to lack of communications.

There was only one ordinary railway line still functioning, coming from Sainte-Menehould. The other, from Saint-Mihiel, had already been cut for some time by an enemy salient and was of little use save as a siding for heavy artillery. And who could tell how long the line from Sainte-Menehould would remain open—how many days, how many hours even, it would be before it became impossible to use it?

"Have you seen the latest report? The Boche is sending heavy stuff on to the big bend it makes at Aubréville. It is quite possible that by tonight no train will be able to pass."

The Aubréville bend had been under consideration for months. Certain gloomy persons had pointed out, as long ago as the middle of 1915, that the German batteries to the north-east of Vauquois could demolish it whenever they had the mind to try, but that meanwhile they were careful to fire over it, even when registering, so as not to give warning of their intention. The danger could be parried—so argued these subtle advisers—by constructing a by-pass of several kilometres in length. "That would involve an enormous amount of labour," the pundits had replied, "and we haven't the men available."

The only other railway communication was a joke: a narrow-gauge local line, known as the "Meusien," coming from Bar-le-Duc, and capable, even in peace time, of supplying only a minor garrison town. In addition to this there were odds and ends of other local enterprises, still more microscopic, and used only for short-distance traffic, such as the two-foot line from Clermont to Dombales, or the similar small-scale system running through Verdun itself.

There was but one miserable traffic artery, hardly to be taken seriously at all, along which food and supplies could be circulated to the wretched salient: the road from Bar-le-Duc to Verdun by way of Rumont and Souilly, and that was narrow and in bad repair.

"So far as I can see," murmured an officer present, one of Plée's intimates who voiced their chief's views more openly than he did himself, "the best reason for not asking G.H.Q. to swamp us with men and material is that, once we get a concentration here, it'll be the end of everything. See what I mean?"

Whatever the personal doubts of those concerned, something, obviously, would have to be done about the single road linking Verdun with the rest of France. To improve and widen it would take time and an enormous amount of labour. The engineers declared that it was no good even thinking of it. The only thing was to make the most of the modest resources it offered, to see that when it was needed for urgent traffic it was not encumbered by farm animals, by refugees from the villages, or even by slow-moving regimental carts; that it was not used piecemeal by odds and ends of formations; that legitimate users should not loiter. It oughtn't to be impossible to ensure this minimum of discipline.

Those clamouring for "energetic action" managed to get steps taken for the policing of this road, and succeeded, at the cost of surrendering certain clauses which were held to be "too draconian and vexatious," in getting the following regulations committed to paper and immediately distributed, through the machinery of the 3rd Bureau, to all formations of the Fortified Zone. The memorandum bore the registered number 4093, and was issued under the title: "General Order No. 15":

I

The use of the road from Bar-le-Duc to Verdun through Rumont and Erize is strictly forbidden to horse convoys and to single horse-drawn vehicles.

II

All motor vehicles using the above-mentioned road must comply with the regulations laid down for them by the traffic-control authorities.

III

All troops or transport columns actually using the road when this order comes into effect must clear it without further delay (maximum time allowed: 3 hours).

[Signed:]
Herr
Divisional General commanding the Fortified
Zone of Verdun

At the last moment Major Plée's supporters, who professed to regard "energetic action" as nothing but "premature panic," delivered a counter-attack. This was not entirely unsuccessful, since its promoters managed to get the following words added:

The above order will be put into effect only upon receipt of telephone instructions worded as follows: "General Order No.15 to be put into operation forthwith."

"That," said one of the officers in question, on his way out of the room where the conference had been held, "will give time for us to look round and for the hotheads to cool down. But"—and he mopped his brow— "Whew! We had our work cut out!"

CHAPTER FOUR

From Bois d'Haumont to Herbebois.
"What's the Artillery Waiting For?"

Gastaldi, bending over Lieutenant Raoul, said in a low voice to Mazel (in as low a voice as he could make audible above the continuous thunder of the bombardment):

"It's really very odd. I can't make out what's wrong with him. I can't see a sign of any wound; can you?"

"No, sir....What's that little mark behind his ear?...No, just dirt."

"I was just going to shout: 'Come in! What are you doing out there?'"

"The shell burst very close, we know, but he's not bleeding."

"Must have been the blast of the explosion, or perhaps some splinter got him where we can't see it....Better undress him."

"Most unlikely. These shells break up in huge chunks."

"I know. And gas is out of the question. We should have smelt it....I've had eighteen months of the line and seen any number of men killed....One's always coming up against odd cases. I suppose there's always something to learn about this sort of life....By God, though! If—"

"What were you going to say, sir?"

"Oh, nothing. It merely occurred to me that we shouldn't have to go on learning much longer. It's a miracle that there's been no more than one direct hit on the roof so far, and that only a 77. You may have noticed that miracles in warfare don't recur indefinitely. I don't think he's dead, do you?"

"I'm pretty sure he isn't, sir."

"His pulse is weak, but it's still beating....What's to be done? We've shaken him, pinched him, pricked him....One's got to go carefully. I might slap his face, but somehow I don't like to....Hullo! did you hear that? Must have been in Herbe-bois....They're getting it worse than we are, for the moment, I think."

Gastaldi lifted Lieutenant Raoul's head slightly and rested it on a low protuberance in the earth floor.

"The fire's slackening here," he went on, "and becoming more intense on the southern part of the wood. I blame myself for sending the second of those poor fellows out. He's almost bound to have got it in the neck. It was a damn fool thing to do, but one's nerves get so on edge. Well, here we are now, just we two—that's to say—"

He glanced at the prostrate form of Raoul, then turned once more towards the end of the sap still blocked with earth.

"Perhaps we ought to have a squint at what they're doing. They're perfectly capable of launching an attack before the barrage's lifted. Anything's possible. God knows we were told often enough that they hadn't got any assembly trenches dug! In this sort of war no one really knows anything."

He crawled to the end of the sap and put his eye to the loop-hole.

"Can't see a thing. Needs somebody to go outside and cut back the undergrowth. Besides, there's so much smoke and dust."

At Herbebois the 2nd battalion of the 164th regiment had been subjected since morning to the same annihilating bom-bardment as the troops in the Bois d'Haumont, the Bois des Caures, and the Bois de Ville.

The 6th company was in the worst position of all. It occu-pied the extreme north-easterly point of the natural bastion formed by Herbebois, looking down on Soumazannes, where for the last few days so much Boche activity had been noted, and which would undoubtedly be one of the chief points of departure for the coming assault. The enemy artillery was busy pounding away at the whole of Herbebois, as was obvi-ous at a glance, though it seemed to be concentrating with particular violence on the defences which the attacking waves would have to deal with first: namely, the line of trenches

marked 17 to 25. There was nothing unreasonable about the
Boche point of view. The only people who were unreasonable were the men of the 6th company, who were holding
those same trenches—as they would have been the first to
admit if anybody had asked them. But nobody did. Nor was
that the worst trick that fortune had played on them. They
had been already twelve days in the line—more than enough
in such a sector—and were to have been relieved that very
morning. At seven o'clock a lot of the men had been strap-
ping their packs and festooning themselves with parcels and
bundles, whistling for sheer joy, when suddenly—Boom! Put
that in your pack! Boom! Shove that in your haversack! And
then roum-boom-boom…endlessly like drums beating at
reveille. And great clouds of smoke as though the whole hill
had been transformed into a cup of boiling chocolate, with
dead men falling into it like flies. "What chance of relief now!
God in heaven, who could have guessed we'd have been in for
it like this! And to think of the lucky devils of Ménétrier's
company slouching along down there with all their stuff on
their backs." Boom! Roum-boom-boom! "'Not too healthy
up there,' they must be thinking. 'If that's the sort of welcome
waiting for us, better stay where we are.'" They were probably
lying snug in the bottom of the valley at this very moment,
laughing like hell. "The dirty swine!—only hope the Boche'll
send some heavy stuff on to them. It can't all come our way."

  Beneath its rain of shells, the 6th company brooded on its
bad luck. It was in process of being smashed to bits; at least
one man was being killed every five minutes; but that didn't
prevent the survivors from feeling that the worst thing about
the avalanche of death was having to face it when it was, by
rights, no longer their turn. The men didn't have to be
reminded of that fact by their neighbours. It was the one
thought in everybody's mind: "What damned awful luck!"
Not that it found no audible expression. Again and again the
phrase was repeated, muttered between clenched teeth,
shouted aloud. Men flattened against the earth, shaken by the
repeated explosions, would repeat the plaint: "Damned awful,
I should say so!" But such interchanges were superfluous. The

fellow in the next shell-hole, quite unaware whether his pals were alive or dead, would be muttering: "Talk of luck!" when the next burst sent the earth jetting into his face. Those in trench 25 might have no idea what the Boche shells and aerial torpedoes were doing to trench 18, which lay in the other angle of the salient (and the angles were about the unhealthiest places of all), but they could bet their lives that if a single man was still alive in trench 18, he was grousing to himself: "And just when we were going to be relieved too! It's about the limit!"

It was precisely this trench 18 that was forming the subject of discussion between Second Lieutenant Delmas, who was in charge of the front line, and the company commander of the 6th, whose head-quarters lay a short distance to the rear inside the wood. The remarkable thing was that the discussion was carried on by telephone. All the other lines were down. But this particular one, though it was in the thick of things, had remained intact. The captain asked the second lieutenant for news of T. 18. Since that morning, nobody, including the second lieutenant, had known anything about T. 18. The captain asked the second lieutenant to do "his damnedest" to get into touch with T. 18, where he would almost certainly find Sergeant Major Vigaud. The second lieutenant replied that he had already done his damnedest, but would have another shot.

"You send somebody," said the captain, "and I'll send somebody. Let's hope that one of them will get through and come back."

Second Lieutenant Delmas had a half-platoon sheltering near him. He asked for a volunteer. The men took three seconds to turn the matter over in their minds. Then one of them said:

"All right, I don't mind, sir…" as though what he really meant was: "When one's been unlucky enough to come in for a Boche attack on the day set for relief, nothing much worse can happen."

Half an hour later the man returned. He said that he had managed to crawl as far as T. 22, but that it was quite impossible to get farther:

"It's not that I was afraid, sir, but the stuff's coming over so thick I should have been blown to bits in a second. It would be like trying to put your hand in a gear-box while the engine was running."

"All right…thanks."

At that moment a call came through from company head-quarters. By some miracle the line was still functioning.

"Lieutenant Chabrier and one man started out for T. 18. They managed to get there on all fours.…They report that ruins don't describe what they found. The whole place is completely smashed to pieces. Not one man left alive. Just a few odds and ends of bodies and equipment mixed up with the wreckage."

A completely exhausted runner reached Chambrettes. He was swaying on his legs. His eyes were the eyes of a madman. At last he managed to stammer out that he had come from Herbebois, that he had been sent by Major Jamond, and must see the colonel in person at once. He said that he had been running for about two miles, flinging himself flat every few moments, and that no less than ten shells had fallen close to him. He had forgotten the name of the colonel.

"Riverain?"

"I don't know."

"Have you got a written message? The name must be on it."

"No, sir. Major Jamond forgot it. He was in too much of a hurry."

"Do you think it was the colonel commanding the artillery?"

"Yes, sir, that's it."

He was taken to Colonel Riverain, to whom he handed a message scribbled in pencil. But while the officer was trying to read it, the runner panted out the contents, which he had committed to memory in case he lost the paper. He had repeated it to himself at least twenty times while he lay flat on the ground with the shells bursting all about him. He recited it now with some crude additions of his own, and occasional explanations. He was far from being a mere machine. He knew perfectly well what the message was about, and realized as clearly as did the officers how urgent the situation was.

The gist of the message was that Major Jamond implored the artillery to open fire. They had been waiting for it for hours, and nothing had happened. The French batteries had not done a thing, or so little that the men in the front line had not noticed it. Nobody expected that it could silence the Boche guns but it could at least bring fire to bear on their front lines. The Boches might attack any minute now. They mustn't be allowed to come over without being even inconvenienced. The men were already demoralized by the effect of the bombardment. It would put new heart into them to know that their own guns were doing their best.

Very sadly the colonel replied:

"You're a brave fellow to have come through all that....You must know I'd help you if I could!...Sit down here and rest a bit."

He rang up the brigade on the telephone. Luckily the line was still working; it had to run for only a short distance and had not yet been cut.

"I've just had a new request, sir, by runner, from Herbebois this time....It's awful, sir, just sitting about doing nothing. I'm just about fed up."

He was doing no more than continue a conversation, equally despairing, which he had broken off a quarter of an hour earlier.

"But what can you do?" said the general.

"I'm out of touch with more than half of my field batteries....Those I can get at tell me they've had to put their men under cover. A lot of their guns have been smashed and most of their dumps have gone up. Impossible to keep up any reasonable rate of fire. I tried a little blind counter-battery work with the heavies. I told the people at La Coupure to send some stuff over on to Warphemont....I've got hopes that the 305 will be in position very soon now near your headquarters....It may manage to put a dozen or so shells over at a range of ten or twelve miles, but a lot of good that's going to do the infantry!...Poor devils, that's not what they want.

What they want is a blanket barrage on the Boche front lines....I know only too well how they're feeling!"

"Well?"

"The worst of all, sir, is this fog of dust and smoke that's blotting out everything."

"But you've got your barrage lines laid down?"

"I know, sir; but that's not the same thing, especially with the 75's. The men feel paralysed when they can't see a thing, when they've no idea what effect they're producing, when they're shooting blind into a sort of wall of cotton wool. And there's another thing, sir: I haven't got shells to throw away—and a hell of a lot of dumps have been hit! If I begin wasting ammunition now, what's going to happen when the Boche infantry comes over? I can't count on any more coming up. They're sure to have put down a barrage between us and Verdun...."

"All I ask is, do something!" The general's voice was taut with anxiety. His words were less like an order than a supplication addressed to a doctor on behalf of a dearly loved friend who is at death's door. "The men are in a perfectly frightful situation."

"You don't have to tell me that, sir!"

"We can't let them feel that they've been left in the lurch, that we're sacrificing them in cold blood without so much as stirring a finger."

"That's true, sir. I'll do everything I possibly can. You have my word for that, sir: everything I possibly can!"

Towards one o'clock the men at Herbebois noticed that the enemy fire was lessening. They took advantage of the lull to stick their noses out of their holes and exchange news between shelters. The shells were falling at greater and greater intervals. It really looked as though the bombardment were dying down, in their sector at least, for away on the left it seemed as heavy as ever.

They hesitated about rejoicing too soon. This relative calm might merely herald an infantry attack. Perhaps at this very moment the Boche observers, before sending back word that the advance might begin, were taking advantage of the subsiding dust to take a look through their glasses and see what effect their artillery had had upon the French defences.

But in war the rule is to take what the moment offers without looking too far ahead. Many men who had not had heart enough to swallow a morsel since morning, began to take their rations from their haversacks and try to munch a little food, pushing away the corpses that lay about them, sharing out the dead men's wine, saying as they did so:

"Better than letting the Boche have it!"

Suddenly: "Tsinc…tong…tsinc-tsinc-tsinc-tsinc…tong-tong-tong…."

There could be no mistake about it: the 75's! And mingled with them, other sounds, coming also from behind the French lines: 90's, perhaps even 155's giving a burst of rapid fire.

The men looked at one another, a dawning radiance in their eyes, though not unmixed with anxiety. They almost joked, but so highly strung were their nerves that the words hovered between laughter and tears.

At last! Well, it was better than nothing; it wasn't much, but it was a bit cheering. The French guns hadn't gone to sleep after all; they were firing at the Boches. Not so heavily as they might, perhaps, and probably their sudden activity would goad the enemy into starting up again on their side. Well, let 'em! Anyhow they'd see that the French could reply. If they meant to attack, they'd soon realize that two could play at that game!

CHAPTER FIVE

The Event and Its Image

It was only after considerable delay that headquarters of the Fortified Zone at Dugny had come to realize the full extent and intensity of the bombardment unloosed since morning, and to get an adequate impression of its effects. The circumstances produced by it explained and, to a certain extent, excused the extreme slowness with which a clear image of what had happened had formed itself in the minds of those whose duty it was, four miles away, to register the events of the front line. What was less easy to explain was the rapidity with which the news of the lull, partial and ambiguous though it might be, reported from the Herbebois sector, had travelled the same distance. It arrived at the very moment that the 3rd Bureau had just settled the text of a message to be telephoned to Avize, where the staff of the Centre Army Group was stationed. The object of this message was to furnish the senior formation with a preliminary report on what had been happening since morning. It had taken much time and trouble to concoct, and a regular conference had been assembled for the purpose. Everyone knew that the substance of the report would at once be embodied in a further message which would be dispatched by telephone from Avize to G.H.Q., Chantilly. A single misplaced stress might influence the decisions taken by the Commander-in-Chief and so determine the future course of events.

"You see!" exclaimed Major Plée. "You were painting things too black. Don't let us make fools of ourselves by talking of 'crushing barrages' and 'formidable preparation' all leading up to a 'full-dress offensive,' when in two hours we shall probably have to ring them up again and say that we have been misinformed and that the position is not as we had described it."

Someone remarked that if it was thought excessive to trouble the Staff about a bombardment which had gone on for several hours, it might be lacking in prudence to reassure them by reporting a lull which might last only a few minutes.

"Better add that it is purely local," remarked another officer in support of the last speaker. He opened the window. "Listen."

The horizon formed by the Heights of the Meuse was rumbling. Was the sound less intense, less widely spread, than it had been that morning? No one dared to venture an opinion. There is no fact so definite that an obstinate man cannot twist it to support his own argument.

As a result of the discussion, Plée managed to get the text of the message considerably modified. He was curiously insistent, too, that instead of the chief honour of the day being given, as it had been in the original draft, to the woods of the northern front—Haumont, Les Caures, Ville, and Herbebois —an honour with which the poor devils would have gladly dispensed, as they would have gladly dispensed with the eight hundred and eighty-two field-pieces and the seven hundred heavy guns which had been concentrated on them—full mention should be made of the several places on the vast semi-circular front of Verdun from which shelling had been reported since the previous evening, such as Hautes-Charrières, Pintheville, Champlon, the Bois du Chevalier, and Forges… "in order," he said, "that the C.-in-C. may be able to get an objective view of the situation as a whole." So far as objectivity went, the only effect of this addition was to blur the contours of the main event and keep it from standing out in proper relief.

One of the officers present was courageous enough to remark to his neighbour in a perfectly audible undertone:

"Les Hautes-Charrières! Champlon! Bois du Chevalier!… Fancy mentioning them in the same breath as Herbebois, Haumont, and the Bois des Caures! Why, there's no sense in it!"

Plée seemed not to have heard.

On the northern front the French guns, from a desire not to deplete the reserve of shells, were slackening and spacing their fire—much to the disgust of the men in the front line. Nor was this disgust far from turning to despair when the lull in the enemy's activity ceased as dramatically as it had begun.

"The swine! They just broke off for a cup of coffee; and now they're at it again!"

Once more the Bois d'Haumont, the Bois des Caures, the Bois de Ville, and Herbebois had to endure the continuous thunder of explosions, the tornado of dust and smoke, the rending of earth, and the crushing of men beneath the smashed ruins of their shelters. It was two o'clock.

CHAPTER SIX

First Communiqué from Verdun

A few minutes later Lieutenant-Colonel G— presented himself before General Joffre, holding a paper in his hand. In his soft, refined voice he said:

"I confess I am rather surprised....A message has just come in from Avize. In general, it confirms what we already knew, but I find myself in considerable disagreement with its interpretation of the position. You remember, sir, the telephone reports we received from the various headquarters, and the language in which they were couched?"

"Yes...what of it?"

"Only this—d'Olonne took the message....I'm pretty sure his transcription is correct...."

Lieutenant-Colonel G—started to read from the paper in his hand, breaking off now and then to make certain comments of his own.

"'Avize, February 21st, 2 p.m. By telephone.

"'Enemy artillery still active between the Meuse and Ornes...'—it *was* the right bank, then. 'Chief targets seem to be Bois des Caures and Bois de Ville. Fire heavy, but might be heavier....' That's important; it may turn out to be very important....It's puzzling, though. Collas has just told me that he had had a private conversation over the wire with his friend Geoffroy—you know whom I mean, sir?—Caillaux's former principal private secretary, who's on the staff at Verdun. He said that Geoffroy had it from friends of his who had just got back from the front line that the bombardment was terrific...much more intense and much more destructive than our artillery preparation last September in Champagne. ...Geoffroy is not, I gather, a panic-monger. And yet here's

Langle de Cary saying: 'Heavy, but might be heavier,' or words to that effect....I say Langle de Cary because I can't suppose he would let such a message be sent without going over it pretty carefully first. He goes on: 'Up to the present, damage appears to be slight...' "

Joffre shook with happy laughter.

"If he says so, you can take it that it is so. Up to the present, in his opinion, the damage has been slight....We can accept that as a fact....Go on."

" 'Gunfire reported also from Hautes-Charrières...' "

"Where's that?" asked Joffre.

"There are two places, sir, with similar names, Charrières and Hautes-Charrières, both of them well behind the front north of Verdun....Charrières must be well within the Fortified Region, where the defences are strongest....He can't mean that place. Hautes-Charrières, if I'm not wrong, is—oh, well down towards the base of the Saint-Mihiel salient...that's to say, about twenty-five miles as the crow flies from the Bois des Caures and Herbebois. Would you like to look at the map, sir?"

"No, don't bother."

"The report goes on: 'I have given orders for our batteries to keep up a lively fire on all enemy salients....' "

Joffre interrupted, a twinkle in his eye:

"What are you laughing at?"

"I wasn't laughing, sir; only smiling...."

"But why?"

"Nothing...I was just imagining Langle de Cary firing on the enemy salients....The idea, too, of firing on 'all' of them impartially at such a time is slightly comic."

Joffre's body was just noticeably shaken by silent mirth.

" '...And in the neighbourhood of Pintheville, Champlon, and Bois du Chevalier...' "

"Where are all these hole and corner places?" In the phrase "hole and corner" Joffre's provincial accent was pleasantly apparent.

"I don't remember precisely, sir...I have an idea that Pintheville and Champlon are somewhere in the Woëvre plain. The Bois du Chevalier…"

"I know," said Joffre, "it's near Éparges, only lower down…. There was some hard fighting there last winter…."

"That's right."

"But I thought it was called Bois des Chevaliers."

"I believe it is."

"That is, if it's the place I'm thinking of. There are a number of Bois Juré's and Bois du Chauffour's round Verdun. It's the devil of a job recognizing them all. They ought to put the exact map reference in brackets after each name….Still, it doesn't matter."

"Shall I continue?'… But it was probably retaliation for our activity yesterday. According to a deserter, the Germans expected us to attack in that sector.

"'On the left bank of the Meuse, enemy guns seem to have confined themselves to registering. Near Forges a number of shells are reported as giving off a very thick white smoke, which does not appear, however, to be gas.' That's all, sir."

Joffre was no longer laughing. He was sunk in thought and seemed to be worried. A minute passed.

"What are your personal impressions?" he said at last.

"I can only repeat, sir, I'm puzzled."

"There's certainly plenty to bite on. It reminds me of the sort of telegrams that circulate among members of a family—'Uncle Oscar ill. No need to worry.' And by the time you have made up your mind to make the journey, Uncle Oscar is dead."

"The feeling I get," replied Lieutenant-Colonel G— "is that Langle de Cary is not interested in Verdun, and can't persuade himself that the enemy is, either. All that matters to him is the Champagne front. The odd thing is that there are quite a number of people at Verdun who agree with him."

"We shall have to get that clear in the course of the next few days. Meanwhile it doesn't make things any easier for us. If the present attack on Verdun is only a blind, we must admit, I think, that, from the enemy's point of view, the place has been well chosen. The Germans know that for us Verdun is a bottle-neck; that having, with considerable difficulty, massed

troops there, we can withdraw them only with greater difficulty still. Given the configuration of the front and the communications available, they are much better off than we are,
no matter what their intentions. Once they have pinned us
down to Verdun, they will be far better placed than we to
move their divisions to Soissons or Artois and start their serious offensive there, leaving us cooped up without proper
roads or railways. That's what's always frightening me....Of
course, until their infantry is engaged, we can't really tell what
they mean to do. I'd like to see all these clever critics in my
place. If in three or four days' time the Germans open their
main attack elsewhere and I've been unfortunate enough to
get my effectives pinned down at Verdun, they won't find
words bad enough to condemn my foolish simplicity. On the
other hand, if I didn't take this business seriously enough and
lost Verdun as a result, the same gentlemen would describe me
as a slow-witted old fool....Well, the 7th corps, I gather, has
arrived, and the 20th is on the way, eh? Good. We must see
whether we can't do a little something along the whole
front."

At three p.m. G.H.Q. saw fit to release the following communiqué, which the people of Paris read a little later in their
evening papers, and thus learned of what had been happening since the morning:

COMMUNIQUÉ FOR FEBRUARY 21ST, 3 P.M.

*Slight artillery activity on both sides along the whole front, except to
the north of Verdun, where fire developed considerable intensity.*

CHAPTER SEVEN

The Infantry Attacks. "Those Damned Gunners!"

" I'm wondering whether we oughtn't to have taken advantage of that apparent lull just now to try to get back to our men."

"So am I," said Mazel.

"They'll think we've been killed."

"They certainly will."

"On the other hand, we couldn't know how long it would last, nor what it meant. Their infantry might have started coming over at any minute."

The major went to the end of the sap, glanced through the loophole, and came back.

"There's obviously nothing we can do here....What it needs is a sergeant and a section of men. It would make a first-rate observation post from which to watch the attack develop; probably the best we've got. To get the full advantage of it we ought to have a second loop-hole and a machine-gun."

"And a telephone."

"A telephone of course! What use would it be for the fellows in here to be able to see the Boches coming over if they couldn't send us back word...and call for a barrage? It wouldn't be far off the mark to say we'd mismanaged things badly. ...We could have had a well-placed line of defences here. Just think how things might have gone if the work had been properly carried through....An N.C.O. on the look-out. As soon as the Boche shows his nose: 'Hullo! Hullo! Barrage on the line of the ravine—give it to 'em like hell!' Instead of which...!"

"But even if there had been a telephone," said Mazel, "the line wouldn't have lasted long with the kind of bombardment we've been having."

"Do you think so?" asked Gastaldi, as much as to say: "You're probably right; I ought to have thought of that." He continued, in a thoughtful tone: "Even farther back you think the line would have been cut?"

"I'm afraid so."

"That the whole wood must have been isolated?—all this sector of the Forward Zone?"

"One line might have held. The fire may have been less heavy on the southern edge, though to judge by the noise…"

"The linesmen are a lot of rotters," exclaimed the major. "They always bungle their job. The truth is they don't bother about it. It's frightful to think that the Boches may attack any time now and that Delpeuch can't even ask for a barrage!…When a position's been held as long as this, the lines ought to have been buried deep, the main ones at least, and protected with concrete.…Listen! Was that Raoul groaning?"

"I don't think so."

Mazel went over to Raoul, bent down, and touched him. The light was so dim that Mazel, though his eyes were accustomed to it, could scarcely see his friend's features. So far as he could make out, the wounded man's face was pale but peaceful. His eyes were shut, there was no visible pulse, and his skin was neither cold nor hot to the touch.

"I don't know what to think. He seems to be in a sort of coma or lethargy. I don't think he can be suffering much. If a shell came now, he would die without noticing it. It's all very odd.…One can't help wondering whether a man in that condition has still, even deep down, any consciousness of existence, whether, so far as he's concerned, he isn't as good as dead already. I've been reading a lot of books about death lately."

"Coals to Newcastle, eh?"

"I read a great deal. I've never read so much in my life. I find it the best cure for boredom."

"Perhaps. But why books about death?—as though the subject wasn't being sufficiently forced on our attention as it is.…Things slackening a bit, don't you think? We can hear ourselves speak."

"I rather think they've lengthened the range a bit. They're putting stuff over on Champneuville and Wavrille, round your H.Q."

"Talking about books, in your place I think I should have chosen love-stories."

"They pall, sir. I began by reading a lot of detective stories, but I soon got sick of them. The only point about them is that they're cheap. I like something that makes you think. The other day my sister-in-law sent me Maeterlinck's *Death*. It's a very deep book, full of ideas."

For the next few minutes neither of them spoke. The bombardment did really seem to have shifted more to the south.

"To go back to this question of linesmen," said the battalion commander, "they're always a lot of shirkers. I remember something that happened when I was a lieutenant, serving under Lyautey in southern Oran. In those days the field-telephone was, so to speak, in its very early stages, and for that kind of campaigning it may not have been absolutely necessary. Still, Lyautey—he hadn't made his mark then—loved to have all his equipment up to date. He was very jealous about the reputation of the colonial troops. He often used to say: 'Do you think you're a lot of Second Empire wrecks?...' Well, one day—"

Gastaldi broke off suddenly, his eyes on Mazel, who was standing with his mouth open.

"What's the matter?"

"I—"

"Sh!..."

They listened, as a few hours earlier they had listened to the fading beat of Raoul's heart.

There was no further doubt possible. Not a sound could be heard. This time it was more than a comparative or local lull. To the farthest point of the horizon all was silent. The bombardment had quite suddenly stopped dead, as a storm will sometimes do.

"Bad sign," muttered Mazel. He looked at his watch: 4 p.m. After the stillness had lasted for a minute he crept, still moving cautiously, to the dug-out entrance. He saw the underbrush still thick with dust and smoke. Broken twigs were falling from the branches. The smell of recent destruction was over everything. It was all rather like the hush that follows the collapse of a house. Silence had fallen on the scene like a sheet laid upon the face of a dead man.

Meanwhile Gastaldi had crawled to the hole at the farther end of the sap. He looked attentively at the portion of the ravine and the narrow segment of the enemy lines which fell within his line of sight. As yet there was no sign of movement in the failing light.

The two men joined each other in the middle of the dugout.

"Are they coming over?"

"Didn't see any sign of them."

"What are we going to do?"

The major shrugged.

"If I thought we should have time to get back…"

He returned to the far end of the sap.

"Come here, quick!" he cried. "There they are!… Give me a rifle! There are some of the poor buggers' rifles over there in the corner opposite. Give me one of them. When I've emptied the magazine, give me another. Can you see clearly enough to reload?"

"Don't you think," said Mazel, handing up the first rifle, "that we should be more useful with the others?"

But Gastaldi was in a state of nervous exaltation.

"You go if you want to. I'm going to shoot. There's nobody to do a thing. Everyone's dead. They're not just going to walk up here if I can help it."

Here and there in the front line, at Bois d'Haumont, at Bois des Caures, Bois de Ville, Bois de Montagne, and Herbebois, were a few men who by chance had escaped death. They lay huddled together in groups of twos and threes, in trenches and dugouts. Occasionally a single man found himself the sole living survivor in a world of torn earth and corpses. In every mind was the same thought as in Gastaldi's—that everyone to right and left had been killed.

Like him too, these isolated survivors saw the tiny figures of men, coloured grasshopper grey, emerge from the enemy trenches, not in a solid mass and all at once, but gradually and almost one by one. There was nothing hurried about their movements. They looked like men working on a railway line who, after a day's work, see the train of flatcars arrive to take them home, and walk towards it dragging their boots along the gravel of the permanent way.

The figures were bent. Their right arms hung down, the hands grasping short implements, which were rifles. Their heads drooped forward beneath the weight of their helmets, till they looked like inflamed pimples or swollen glands.

They moved slowly up the slope, not in a straight line, but as though they were picking their way. Nothing could have looked less like an assault. An uninformed onlooker might have fancied that they were out hunting for something that had been dropped, might have thought they were gathering mushrooms in the grass or snails in the bushes.

Each of the survivors imagined that he was the sole living spectator—save, perhaps, for a few comrades in a like situation—of these visitors moving so slowly forward in their grasshopper grey. What could one man do? What even two or three in the ruins of their trench? Nevertheless, they started firing, pushing aside the dead comrade who prevented them from leaning against the parapet, as, a few hours earlier, they had freed themselves from other corpses in order to get a bite of food. Here and there, where a machine-gun had escaped the bombardment, one man would train the barrel while another fed in the belt.

They were amazed to hear, at intervals all along the front line, other rifles firing, other machine-guns giving out their tac-tac-tac.…"They're not all dead, then!" they thought; and, a moment later: "What's happening in the rear? Why don't they send up reinforcements? Why don't they get the artillery to do something?"

The grasshopper-grey figures came slowly on, walking with their noses to the earth as though they had been told to move very carefully. Now and then one of them would fall, roll on the ground, or plunge headlong into the undergrowth. But as

more were continually emerging from the trench, the total
number grew. The slope before the French lines began to
swarm uncomfortably thick with men. But there was still an
air of nonchalance about the scene. The moving mass was less
like a crowd intent on reaching some definite goal than a
sauntering concourse with plenty of time before it; like, for
instance, an outing of East End Parisian holiday-makers who
had been to watch a firework display on the Buttes-
Chaumont and were now wending happily homeward
through the grassy undulations of the park.

"What are the guns waiting for?"

For all the slowness with which the grasshopper-grey figures moved, they were gradually drawing nearer. The distance
to be covered was not so very great. Occasionally, when a
machine-gun had knocked over seven or eight fairly close to
one another, the rest seemed to hesitate, to be in two minds
whether or not to retrace their steps. It looked as though
these few rifle-shots and machine-gun belts were a good deal
more than they had bargained for. No doubt their officers had
said: "You'll be able to stroll over with your hands in your
pockets." If only a few hundred shells could have fallen into
the valley, it was pretty obvious that the grasshopper-grey
men would not have been at all happy.

Behind the front-line trenches the few company commanders left alive, warned by the sudden cessation of the bombardment that something was afoot, and confirmed in their
suspicion that the infantry were attacking by the sound of
sporadic rifle-fire, prolonged shouting, and the occasional
sight of a man running, rushed down into their dug-outs for
the few remaining signal rockets which they had put aside for
use only in the last emergency. These, while issuing fighting
orders to the few men who remained to them, they sent up
in the hope of getting the gunners to lay down an immediate
barrage. Immediate, or as near immediate as might be. There
were not thirty seconds to lose. The Boches were steadily
making their way up the slope, advancing along the paths,
pushing their way through the bushes and clumps of trees. In
thirty seconds a man can, without hurrying, dragging his feet

heavily, cover at least fifty paces. The guns must not lose a moment before setting their close-set barrier of shells between the approaching Boches and the edge of the position on which they are moving, that torn and shattered edge with scarcely a man to defend it among the dismembered corpses.

The rockets rise into the sky. Not all of them, however. Some of them are damp and fail to go off. Others get caught foolishly in the high branches which the bombardment has left unbroken, and, thus deflected, spill their light uselessly in the undergrowth. Still others soar upwards unimpeded, to fall again without bursting, like burning brands extinguished in water. Even those which duly spread their rosy glow are not wholly reassuring. The atmosphere above the lines is murky and thick with smoke. There is still some time to go before nightfall, and in the failing daylight the floating fog of fumes and dirt takes on the appearance of a whitish cloud such as spreads behind a forest fire, so that it remains doubtful whether the little smudges of red light will be visible at any great distance.

The thirty seconds passed, then a whole minute. A second minute. No sign yet of the barrier of shells which would have put such heart into the defenders if only they could have heard them rushing through the sky to burst with massive detonations two hundred yards ahead; not even a few sporadic shots to herald the coming help. Instead, a renewed burst of enemy fire, directed this time, no doubt about it, behind the forward zone, a mile or two to the rear of the front line. For the moment it was the German field-guns that seemed to bear the brunt of the action (they must have been moved forward) and were concentrating their fire—apart from a few heavier shells destined for more distant targets—on the French batteries with the intention of choking off any design they might have—little enough sign of it though they might so far have given—of taking part in the battle. This bombardment of the southern edge of the wood became every moment more intense, until it took on the character of drum-fire. Someone was laying down a fine barrage; but, unfortunately, it was the enemy, and well between the French front line and the rear.

There was nothing particularly mysterious about the intentions of the Boche artillery, which had as its aim no more than
to prevent the arrival of reinforcements; to isolate completely the various sections of the advanced positions which the
enemy had decided to take in his first advance; to set a box
round each of them—Bois d'Haumont, Bois des Caures, Herbebois, and the rest—so that the infantry would merely have
to mop up the remains; to give the assaulting troops plenty of
time in which to occupy the captured ground and organize it
at their leisure to be the jumping-off place for a new attack—
in the same way as men at work repairing the floor of a dock
are protected from the possible inrush of water. No doubt the
Germans had assumed that after their smashing preparatory
bombardment not a man would be left alive in the first
French line, and that their infantry would find no worse
obstacle before them than the tangle of the ruined trenches.
In fact, however, a number of men had survived, but only to
find themselves hemmed in between the barrage at their
backs and the assault on their front, between the fixed wall of
fire behind them and the moving wall of grasshopper-grey
infantry sweeping upwards to the trench.

Still that hoped-for barrage of 75's failed to materialize! It
was enough to make men scream with fury, enough to make
them want to kick the sacks of hand-grenades and send
everything up in one last great crash of destruction. Those
damned gunners. Without wishing to be unfair, the wretched
men in the line couldn't help wondering whether they
weren't doing it on purpose. Or maybe they were lying in a
funk at the bottom of their dug-outs waiting for the bombardment to finish. It was quite possible, of course, that they
hadn't seen all the rockets, but they must have seen some. The
fellows over on the left, and those on the right, too, had sent
up red flares. Why, they had found some extra ones and were
at it again. The same thing must be going on all along the
front covered by the woods. Who was going to believe that if
the gunners were really on the look-out, had really got their
eyes fixed—as it was their duty to have—on the strip of sky
over the woods, they couldn't see at least one in ten, even one

in twenty, of the throbbing red blurs, despite the floating cloud of smoke and dust? Sailors can see a lighthouse beam through fog and storm. Why, a little thing like a car light, a lamp lit in a farm window, even the reflection of the setting sun in a pane of glass, can be seen sometimes miles away across a distant plain! Besides, they ought not to need signals. If it was a question of firing on positions which their own men were evacuating, some degree of doubt might be legitimate. In such a case they might wonder, might say: "Are they clear? On whom are our shells going to fall?" But as things were, what was the risk? They knew it was not the French who were attacking! They'd only got to put their barrage down a hundred yards in front of the trenches. Nothing particularly difficult about that. They'd had enough lines of fire given them. They'd had enough time in which to check their ranges, make allowance for wind, and all the rest of it.... True, if they aimed now a hundred yards in front of the trenches it would be too late to do much good. The *Feldgrauen* by this time had reached the advanced positions and were settling things with the few poor devils who had been left alive by the bombardment. Still, the barrage would stop those behind from coming on. Even if it didn't do much damage to the enemy, it would serve to hearten their own men to make a stand on the smashed defences and throw their grenades in the faces of the first *Feldgrauen* who emerged from between the trees. Never let it be said that they hadn't done everything that was humanly possible. Nothing left for it but to send runners back. "Two men! Two smart fellows!... You've got to start off, each in a different direction, as hard as you can go. You've got to get to some unit that's still got a line working to the gun positions, and have a message telephoned back at once. If you don't find one, you've got to go on legging it until you get to the artillery, and when you have, tell them to start shooting, and go on shooting, for the love of God! Tell them to send every bloody shell they've got on to the hundred yards immediately in front of the line and the first hundred yards along the edge of the wood. If some of our chaps are still there, so much the worse for them! Off with you!"

Four thirty p.m. It was enough to send men mad! The
Boches were still coming on. They must be in the wood by
this time. They could be heard quite distinctly. What were
those flames low down between the branches? Must be those
things they tried out at Azannes the other day. The Boches
were attacking with flame-throwers! Mopping up the
defences with flame-throwers! Oh, those damned gunners!
The swine, the bloody swine!

CHAPTER EIGHT

Prisoners.
T. 18 to T. 22

They had a feeling that the *Feldgrauen* had worked round the dug-out, and instinctively they rushed for the entrance. They would probably be welcomed by a dozen bullets or so, but anything was better than being blown to pieces at the bottom of their hole by grenades tossed down from outside like balls at a cockshy, or burnt up, perhaps, with flame-throwers.

On the threshold they recoiled. A number of *Feldgrauen* were waiting for them, drawn up in a half-circle, two or three of them with their rifles levelled. They had left their own rifles down below; they did not even try to get their Brownings out of their holsters, so hopeless did it seem. They moved their arms in a gesture of helpless despair.

"Prisoners!" cried one of the *Feldgrauen* in French, a sergeant, while with his hand he pushed down the barrels of the rifles which some of his men had got to their shoulders.

Gastaldi and Mazel let their arms fall to their sides and remained where they were. The wooded ground in front of them was still rumbling and smoking in the failing light.

The sergeant, who had just recognized their rank, gave them a sketchy salute.

"Are you alone?" he asked.

They were just going to say yes when they remembered Raoul, whom, in the excitement of the last half-hour, they had forgotten.

"There's a comrade of ours down there—almost dead—*fast todt.*"

"Officer also?"

"Yes."

He made a sign to his men to watch them, moved off a few paces through the trees, and returned almost immediately with a young *Feldwebel*.

The *Feldwebel* saluted. He looked at the two French officers for a moment, then, feeling for his words:

"You are—major, yes? And you—lieutenant?"

"Correct," said Mazel. Gastaldi turned his head slightly, pursed his lips, but said nothing.

"You are prisoners, yes?"

Both of them bowed their heads in assent and once again made their former movement of the arms away from the body.

"It was you who were firing at us from the other side?" went on the *Feldwebel*. "I congratulate you. You fought bravely, and right in the front line. Your men, killed, I suppose? They tell me you have an officer comrade inside, wounded?"

"Almost dead," repeated Gastaldi.

"All right. We will look after him. Have no fear for him. Be so kind as to give me your revolvers, and follow these men, please."

He saluted again, stood a moment or two watching the two prisoners moving off with their escort, and then turned back in the twilight to where the fighting was still going on.

At Herbebois, Sergeant Major Vigaud, regular N.C.O., was not lying dead in trench 18, as had been supposed that morning. After the collapse of part of the earthwork which had buried him with a number of his men, and the explosion of a heavy shell which had blown several more to pieces and wounded him in the face, Vigaud had succeeded in extricating himself from the wreckage and, covered with mud and blood, in taking refuge with the three remaining men in a dug-out slightly to the rear of T. 18.

When, at four o'clock, the bombardment suddenly stopped, he knew precisely what was happening.

"Just now," he said to his three men, "when they stopped firing, it was all my eye. This time it's the real thing. They've only got about an hour of daylight left, so they must attack.

Just you wait and see. We were all right here so long as it was only a question of getting cover from as many shells as possible, but it's not so good when it comes to fighting off an attack. We shan't see them coming. We shall be badly placed for shooting. They'll either kill us or corner us like rats. There's only one thing for us to do—get back to trench 18."

"But don't you remember what an awful state it's in?"

"What the hell's that got to do with it? There'll be enough of it left for the four of us. I bet there's some grub left too. Come on, boys, let's make it!"

To make sure of mopping up all the grub there was, he routed out from neighbouring shell-holes first two more men, then a further three, and finally four others, including a sergeant, all that remained of a platoon and a half-section. This gave him twelve men in all.

"Into T. 18, the lot of you!" he shouted. "The Boches are coming up. T. 18 will be the best place to put up a fight."

With his twelve men he held on for three quarters of an hour in T. 18. So busy was he shouting orders and running behind first one and then another correcting their aim—"Those two down there to the left of the bush, see? ...Good, at 'em. ...That lot over there just crossing the path....The fat fellow who's getting down on all fours...."—that it never occurred to him to notice the absence of any artillery barrage. He watched the lines of skirmishers rise from the ground, one after another, creep zigzagging up the slope, and cover the ground as though they didn't quite know where they were going, like a lot of ants invading a blanket, and the sight occupied his attention to the exclusion of all else and kept his eyes starting from his head.

At four forty-five he realized that T. 18 was about to be attacked. With no more hesitation than he had shown before, he ordered a general retirement.

"Out of this! You three over on the left, you go last. Fire like the devil to the left."

He had his plan ready, which was to rally his men in T. 21, which he knew well and regarded as the best spot available in the circumstances, after T. 18.

On his way back he collected a few more stragglers from neighbouring points where they were threatened by the enemy's advance, and even one or two sailors from an observation post which had been established there in connexion with a naval gun hidden in the Coupure valley. The telephone line had been cut, and it was no longer serving any purpose.

Unfortunately, they found T. 21 smashed to pieces. Vigaud, with his little force, withdrew to T. 22, where in normal times there had been a machine-gun section. The machine-gun was still there with a handful of men. Vigaud took command of T. 22 and did so well, that at half past five, by which time darkness had fallen, the enemy had been brought to a standstill at this particular point, and showed signs of uncertainty and even of a desire to retreat.

Furthermore, he had managed to get into touch, by runner, with his captain and with Second Lieutenant Delmas. To them he submitted a detailed report of the position and asked for reinforcements. The only result of his efforts, unfortunately, was that one of his machine-guns was taken from him to stop a gap which had developed on the left of the battle line. Nevertheless, the second lieutenant and the captain sent back runners in their turn to inform Major Jamond of the successful fight put up in T. 22.

Major Jamond, after reading the four-line report sent in by Delmas, started shouting aloud in his dug-out:

"By God, I've got a splendid lot of men and N.C.O.s! If they'd had any support at all, the Boches would have got it in the neck! But not a single man have they sent me from Wavrille, and as for the artillery—just a damned lot of skunks! I've done everything I could—used up all my red flares, one after the other, every one of 'em! Couldn't send up any more, haven't got any more. I had the bugle sounded, sent it to the highest point of the Bois des Bouleaux, so they'd hear it better. I've sent runner after runner. It's more than an hour and a half since the Boches started coming over. They came out of their trenches in absolute peace and quiet, wave after wave of 'em. And not so much as a sniff of a barrage. Nothing, nothing, nothing!"

He clenched his fists. His voice broke.

A runner entered. "There's some of our shells, sir, falling about two hundred yards in front of the wood."

"A barrage?"

"'Not a real barrage, just a few shells....They're not doing much good, because the Boches have been in the wood a long time now....It would be better to ask the guns to fire shorter....That's what I was told to tell you, sir. The officer was sorry he hadn't put it in writing."

"I'm to ask the guns to fire shorter, am I! And how the devil am I to do that? All my lines are down, I haven't got a flare left, nothing. The guns don't care a damn what happens to us. They're putting shells just where they like, for fun....Not too done-in, my man? Good. You shall have four days' extra leave if you can get this to Colonel Duval at Wavrille. It's not very far."

He wrote:

"I've done what I could, but I shall be wiped out.

"I must have reinforcements; at least two companies.

"I must have an artillery barrage on the northern edges of the wood, between T. 16 and T. 18."

CHAPTER NINE

A Battle of Ghosts

Night had now fallen. But it was not pitch dark, for the moon had risen. Its beams, however, falling at an angle athwart the scene, had little effect upon the smoky, dusty atmosphere of the undergrowth.

From Haumont to Ornes there now developed, over a half-dozen miles of front and to a depth of several hundred yards, an extraordinary battle of ghosts. No one could see more than a few paces ahead, and what he saw was but a concourse of moving shadows, the occasional glint of light on metal, the flashes of guns, and, now and again, the red vomitings of flame-throwers, which, set at a distance against the background of tree-trunks and shattered branches, had a curiously theatrical effect. In the early stages there had been the light of flares as well, but both sides had soon given up using them—the French, most probably, because they had none left; the Germans because they found it better tactics to make their short sharp dashes, their slow infiltration into the area of wooded country, under cover of darkness.

No one knew exactly what was happening to his right and left. Men recognized their nearest neighbours as friends by the sound of their voices, the outline of their figures, the heavy breathing, the grumblings and exclamations bristling with familiar vocables, which surged and eddied with the moving mass of bodies. They identified the enemy by reason of some difference in outline, by some strangeness in the noises he emitted, and chiefly in response to an obscure feeling, which the mere material situation of the two sides was insufficient to explain, that he was on the opposite side, that he was *against* them. They were conscious of his pressure, and aware that it was they who formed the obstacle, the principle of resistance, which must neutralize, counterbalance, and overcome his effort.

Along the line of these nocturnal woods were thus strung out hundreds of tiny independent battles and night-blanketed struggles, the participants in each one of which scarce knew of the existence of the others. Advances and retirements were measured in yards. The darkness was full of forms stumbling over stones and mounds of earth and steel plates. Feet were caught in wire. Men found themselves treading on yielding surfaces which could be nothing but corpses, or flung themselves head-foremost into something long and dark which turned out to be all that remained of a trench, to rest their rifles for a moment on the parapet and fire a few cartridges without aiming at a few shadows which they had reason to suppose were "on the opposite side," were "enemies." Everyone was hungry, since, needless to say, no rations had come up, and most of the men had finished what they carried on them, or refrained from touching the little that remained, for fear of having nothing with which to keep up their strength when dawn should come. Their insides were hollow, as though they had, indeed, been ghosts.

The extraordinary thing was that through the chaos of this darkness orders still kept on arriving, some of them from far back and having reference to the movement of considerable masses of men:

"Battalion orders: Spread out on the left towards strongpoint H. Pass it along."

From moment to moment this "Pass it along," "Pass it along," sent a tremulous whisper through the world of scattered ghosts.

No reinforcements arrived, or, if they did, only in twos and threes. Still less was there any sign of that artillery barrage on which, for three hours now, the hopes of so many had been dwelling. But orders flowed in an unbroken stream. How did they manage it? Orders, too, that seemed but little embarrassed by the difficulties of the situation:

"Company orders: The line now reached by the retiring

troops must be held at all costs."

"Battalion orders: A counter-attack, strength one section, must be launched at once against strong-point E."

"Battalion orders: Flank to move outwards along edge of wood with object of turning strong-point H."

Darkness covered everything. The various movements were carried out in comparative silence and almost furtively. Now and then might be heard a burst of rifle-fire, explosions of grenades, the tac-tac-tac of machine-guns. Scarcely a cry was audible. Many a manœuvre was carried out in complete silence. A dozen or so men would creep forward through the trees, making use of the cover provided by heaps of rubbish or what remained of parapets, whispering among themselves. They would succeed in just edging round to the left of some field-work in which the enemy had managed to get a foot-ing, and as though to mark the successful accomplishment of the movement, the two or three men forming the spearhead of the tiny thrust would start firing at the objective without aiming, almost without seeing. The occupants of the point attacked would run out, bent double, from the shell-holes where they had been crouching, and withdraw through the darkness and the trees, firing as they went. A little farther on, to right or left, a similar operation would develop in the opposite sense. Now and then a man would fall. The official reports would speak of "bitter fighting." That it was obstinate there could be no doubt. Not a blunder, not a sign of weak-ening on the part of either adversary, but was noted at once and exploited as far as the darkness would permit. But there was no fury of hand-to-hand fighting. Those who had not been there would reconstruct the scene in imagination as a struggle to the death of man with man, a madness of frenzied warriors, feeling for one another in the darkness and battling with fists and knives. In reality, this confused scramble which no one could see as a whole, know anything about, or, in any actual sense, control, was like some muddled sort of game. It was as though, vaguely visible in the darkness, confused teams, drawn from two opposing sides, were attempting to bring off a series of strokes against each other, scoring points, for the time being at least, in accordance with a system of unspoken conventions. "Strictly speaking, you've worked round my flank. I'm in danger of being surrounded. All right, I shan't contest it. Let's go back and start again twenty yards to the rear." The mortal blows, beneath which from moment to moment some man would fall, were evidence that this was no bloodless sport. But their real value was that they served as "marks." In spite of them, and quite apart from what those engaged intended, the fight managed to retain a certain purely theoretical character. Its various phases were determined less by the actual clash of contending forces, by the effective destruction of one by the other, than by a balancing of possibilities and chances between the two.

Suddenly, a hail of shells from the 75's. The French gunners had at last understood that something was going on out there in front which might be considered to have a personal interest for them.

The men's hearts rose, not so much because the assistance was effective, but because it was, at least, support. But their joy was shortlived. It is not wholly beneficial to take part in an action at quite so late a stage, to start doing something at eight o'clock which ought to have been done at four. The shells were falling not in front of the lines but on the wood itself. The gunners, who had set themselves to find out quite a lot of things, had discovered, among others, that the enemy had got a footing in the woods and could best be hit there. The trouble was that he was no longer the only person there, that the action now in full swing had become so confused that God Himself, had He been in charge of the artillery, could not have distinguished between French and German.

'That's enough! Tell 'em to stop! Send up flares! Send back runners…"

Those who had survived the German bombardment were now to be blown to pieces by their own guns!

CHAPTER TEN

A Minor Victory at Headquarters

All evening at Dugny headquarters the members of the staff who were not called away on other business remained in conference, even those officers who should, by rights, have been off duty. Everyone was anxious to be at hand should their seniors have need of them. They sat waiting for news from the front, whiling away the time by exchanging views and forecasting the trend of events. Those who had been up in the battle zone during the course of the day contributed their personal impressions.

One large room in particular, well known to all because the presence in it of a large round metal stove made it considerably more cosy than the rest of the house, became the scene, until well after midnight, of a continuous debate which was as lively as custom and the differences in rank of those present permitted. No sooner had an officer come in from making a tour of the lines and made his report in due form to senior authority than he was seized hold of, dragged into the circle, and questioned just as though he had been a prisoner.

"It rather reminds me," said Geoffroy to a friend, "allowing for the altered conditions, of an election committee waiting for the results to be declared."

Every quarter of an hour or so the general atmosphere of the room would undergo subtle modifications. The most fleeting indications of a change in the situation one way or the other were canvassed and discussed with as much excitement and exaggeration as though the party had been composed of laymen. The optimists, in particular, tried their utmost to make what facts they had go far beyond what was justifiable in support of their views.

"What did I bet you? Admit now that it's no good exaggerating."

"An attack launched after no more than nine hours' bombardment, interrupted by a longish interval, may be a serious matter; but it's hardly a full-dress offensive."

"How far have they been able to get up to now?...The thing's to all intents and purposes a frost."

Or even:

"They're held up, I tell you."

When the speaker sported four stripes, his listeners, who might have no more than three or even two, found it easier to agree or to say nothing than to contradict. The most they allowed themselves were doubtful glances. Those who quoted unpalatable facts did so as though they wished for nothing so much as to be contradicted.

From ten o'clock onwards, several of the principal wiseacres, who were moving constantly from office to office, began to look more than usually anxious. The party round the big stove heard a rumour that Major Plée was "changing his tack." He still maintained that "originally" the Germans had had no intention of opening a major offensive against Verdun, that they had aimed only at testing the line and pinning down as many French formations as possible to the sector. But if in the course of the operation they had come to the conclusion that it might be worth pressing for its own sake, they were perfectly capable of concentrating their efforts on it and of extending the movement farther than they had planned to do. Such behaviour would be perfectly consistent with the basic principles of strategy, and the proximity of their main reserves would make it particularly easy for them.

What it came to was that Plée was inclined to admit that certain steps, demanded since that morning by the 3rd Bureau and so far relegated to a possible future, such, for instance, as General Order No. 15 relating to the Bar-le-Duc road, had now become matters of "comparative urgency." But he could not resist registering one last small victory before finally capitulating. When the chief of the 3rd Bureau insisted that the order should be put into operation as early as possible on the day following, and finally, at the end of his patience, exclaimed: "Good God, I'm not asking you to blow up the bridges, destroy the Verdun forts, or call on the country to make a last stand! I'm merely anxious that the road shall be kept clear!" Major Plée, round-faced and smiling as ever, pointed out that undue hurry would be bound to produce a "jam" and succeeded in getting the order postponed until the following midday.

The result was that at eleven p.m. Captain Cosmet was sent for by the chief of the 3rd Bureau, who gave him a paper and remarked, with something very much like a sigh:

"This is the complete text of the order. Please take all necessary steps to have it circulated by telephone before midnight, to all formations of the Fortified Region, and to all the chief formations to right and left…I've jotted them down here in case you don't remember them all.…Check them off so as to be sure none of them are omitted. If there are any you can't get in touch with, report to me. I shall be here until one a.m."

Captain Cosmet withdrew, reading the paper in his hand:

F.R.V.   *Headquarters, 21st February, 1916*
From G.S.O.1, 3rd Bureau

No.4568

By telephone

To—Staff 2nd Corps, 7th Corps, 30th Corps, 8th Corps, 1st Army, Duroure Group, III Army, Centre Group, Officer Commanding Details, F.R.V. Artillery, F.R.V. Air Services, O.C. Communications F.R.V., O.C. F.R.V. Motor Columns, O.C. F.R.V. Hospital Services, O.C. F.R.V. Veterinary Services, O.C. F.R.V. Supplies, Town Major, Verdun.

General Order No. 15 will be in force as from noon February 22nd.

P.O.

G.S.O.1

Cosmet made a face.

"It'll take me till three o'clock to get that through."

As a matter of fact it was only twelve fifteen when he went back to his chief and reported:

"All formations informed, sir."

"Excellent....Let me have the paper back."

The senior officer glanced at the black wood clock hanging on the wall. "Quarter after midnight...."

He added in pencil the marginal note:

"Transmitted to formations between 11 p.m. and 12.10 midnight, 21st."

CHAPTER ELEVEN

Listening at La Neuville corner.
Duroure Prepares for Squalls

"You're coming with me, Radigué, aren't you?"

"Yes, sir. They should have brought my horse round by now."

For the last three days Duroure had got Radigué to join him in the morning ride which followed his examination of the previous night's reports. For the last three days—that is to say, ever since the 19th, two days before the German bombardment of Verdun had begun. By a sort of sixth sense, comparable to the instinct which animals have for an impending storm, he had felt it coming. Reasoned argument had played a very small part in forming this conviction. Dispatches from G.H.Q., reports from neighbouring formations, all sorts of vague rumours, had, of course, given him some indication of what was in store. But such things could lead to a lot of nonsense being talked, as was only too obvious from what was going on elsewhere. Duroure, too, could have talked nonsense, and more brilliantly than most, but there was always the evidence of his nerves to be taken into account. Little by little they had begun to tingle. He could not keep still. He wanted to put what was going on in his mind into words, but the words were dictated by his instinct, and their chief value lay in their power of relieving his nervousness, since, unfortunately, he was precluded from finding relief in action.

Ever since the 17th he had found that the silence forced on him by the sole companionship of Cabillaud was intolerable. The man was such a fool that no conversation was possible with him. Even thinking aloud in such company was an outrage. Quite apart from the fact that there were matters to which he could not be made privy, his never ceasing "Yes, sir, certainly, sir," was enough to put a damper on the most intrepid of monologues.

On the 18th Duroure said to Radigué:

"I'd like you to come riding with me tomorrow morning. It'll do you good, and we can chat."

"As a matter of fact—Never mind, sir. I'll manage it. But what are you going to do about Cabillaud?"

"Cabillaud can keep thirty yards in the rear….I'll tell young Beauvaison to keep him company, just to be sure he won't cling to our heels."

On the morning of the 22nd of February, therefore, Duroure and his Chief of Staff set off side by side as they had done for the last few days. Cabillaud followed them at a respectful distance. He had dropped easily into the new habit. The presence of Beauvaison was no longer necessary.

Duroure had no desire to talk continuously. On the contrary, he liked giving free rein to his thoughts and carrying on a silent soliloquy. But from time to time a thought would become insistent, and then he would have to put it into words. At such times he liked the feeling that he had someone beside him who could be counted on to understand and to react to what he might have to say.

Among the previous night's reports had been several communications from Verdun, among them the message relative to Order No.15. None of these documents provided even a rough sketch of the general situation which had developed on the 21st of February, or gave any definite indication of its gravity. The impression produced was simply that everyone was, as it were, "standing to."

As they rode along, the general brooded over the information that had come to hand.

"They're beginning to worry their heads about the Bar-le-Duc road," he said out loud. "It's the only line of communication they've got besides the Sainte-Menehould railway…." (He knew nothing about the Aubréville bend being cut, and the narrow-gauge Meuse line never even entered his thoughts.) "It's not very wide….If they were unlucky enough to have to deal with a heavy influx of men and material, I don't know what they'd do."

"Nor do I," admitted Radigué after a moment's thought.

A hundred yards farther on:

"Damned wise of me not to accept, eh?"

"I should think it was."

After a pause Radigué continued in a tone something less detached than was usual with him:

"Your general impression, then, is, sir—that it's serious?"

"Yes. And yours?"

"The same."

"Well, anyhow, we shall soon know."

Duroure put his horse into a trot. He was in a hurry to reach one particular point on his route, situated on the north-westerly edge of the Bois de la Neuville, just where the road swept round the hill before entering the wood for some little distance. On its right was a rounded slope dotted with rocks and small trees, which rose in a bold eminence towards the skyline of the neighbouring ridge, across which led a sec-ondary road branching off from the main highway just beyond the wood.

The day before, riding there with Radigué, he had been suddenly struck by a very unusual noise which had seemed to come from far down on the horizon.

"Psst! Stop a moment....Keep your horse quiet....Guns!... But what a devil of a row! Do you hear it? Just like an avalanche that's never going to stop....There's the hell of a fight going on somewhere—perhaps on the Heights of the Meuse, or in the Argonne, or maybe farther off still. There's no means of telling! You hear what I mean?"

"Quite distinctly, sir."

"When we were lower down, I didn't notice it. Did you?"

"No, sir."

"Wait a moment. Here's the north, there's the west. Yes, it must be coming from Verdun. When we left L— there was nothing to be heard at all. Do you agree?"

They had chatted on the curious habits of sound heard over long distances. With reference to the point of origin of the

noise in question, the Bois de la Neuville must lie in a conducting, L— in a non-conducting, area. In the afternoon,
when the first reports from Verdun came in, they had both
exclaimed together: "It *was* coming from there, then," but the
moderate tone of the dispatches had surprised, had almost
disappointed, them.

"I can trust my own ears, I suppose," Duroure had said that
evening when they were all sitting in the big drawing-room.
"All I can say is that if what I heard wasn't the preparatory
bombardment for a first-class show, I'm a Dutchman."

He was very anxious, therefore, this morning to reach the
Bois de la Neuville. At eight fifteen they drew near the edge.
Ever since they had been at the bottom of the slope they had
been listening attentively.

"Stop!" said Duroure.

They drew in their horses and tried to keep them quiet. But
the wretched Cabillaud was trotting up from behind. With an
imperious gesture of the arm, Duroure signed to him to stop.
There was nothing to be heard but the champing of bits.

"Do you get anything, Radigué?"

"Nothing, sir."

A little farther on they tried again.

They rode in among the first trees. To their right they could
see the beginnings of the rocky hill.

"Listen! I rather think—Yes, there it is!"

They sat in an ecstasy of concentration.

"Let's ride on a bit, if you don't mind. Just over there, where
the road makes a bend, would be the best place….Cabillaud,
stay here."

At the bend they found that the level of the road was continued by several yards of solid earth forming a clearing in the
wood. It was there that Duroure stationed himself, his horse's
nose turned towards the north-west. Radigué had remained
on the other side of the road.

The sun, already high above the horizon, struck along the
slopes to their right and shone warm in this sheltered spot.
On the highway of the road the snow had melted, leaving the
sandy soil soft and pleasantly pink. Even the turf and the

ground of the underbrush had retained only a fine powdering of white, which glittered in the sun and was too thin to hide the grass and the pine needles. The branches were covered on their upper sides with a sort of long caterpillar of glittering snow; their under sides were brown and damp-looking. The sun had warmed this rustic nook to such a degree that it gave off a sappy smell of spring and filled the air with a heady sweetness, despite the early season.

Duroure, upright on his horse, listened, intent on interpreting the meaning of what he heard. Beneath the brown-flecked, greenish eyes, with their hint of the dreamer, beneath the skull which had given shelter to, and still retained, many ideas that had been lacking in stability, the lower half of his face seemed, for the moment at least, eagerly tense, strained to catch the distant signs and to read a meaning into them. It had the appearance, this half, of being concentrated on the exercise of his "flair," alive to the promptings of an instinct that had about it something of an animal's scent and was apparently centred in his twitching nostrils. A stranger would have said that Duroure was listening, not with his ears, which were no more than meaningless ornaments below the rim of his cap, but with the tip of his nose and with the lips which the clipped moustache did nothing to hide.

"It's certainly no less intense than it was yesterday," he said. "Who could be fool enough to doubt what was going on?"

They remained where they were for ten minutes or so, after which Duroure made a sign that they should move. As long as they kept to the secondary road, the noise accompanied them, though with variations of intensity. But no sooner had they turned into another, which led off to the left towards the bottom of the valley, then they lost contact with it, and it seemed to move away above their heads like an awning twitched upwards by a rope.

"I suppose, as a matter of fact, that some of it can be accounted for by our own guns," said Radigué.

"Certainly…but that was one of the reasons, you know, why I wasn't particularly keen to take the job on. I don't know what artillery we've got at Verdun, but I do know it's too little. They've not even left them the obsolete guns that were in the forts." He started to laugh. "I ought to know, because I put them in line on the Champagne front!"

"Yes, but for the last month they've been sending them a lot of heavy batteries...."

"A lot?..."

"Well, as many as they could, sir....I've not shown you all the notes that have come in....Including a number of really big naval pieces."

"Just a lot of eyewash!"

"What, the naval ones, sir?...I happened to see a few of them, quite close too....Some are really splendid weapons."

"You're not a gunner, my dear chap....Not that I'm blaming you....In the first place, they've got a very low rate of fire. That's true, you'll say, of some of the others too....Then, their trajectory is much too flat, especially for use in a region as undulating as that round Verdun. At Verdun, a large naval gun has to fire at a range of twelve or fifteen miles, even when the target is only five miles from the front line. But that's not the worst part of the business, which is that their shells are quite useless...."

"Oh come, sir!..."

"...and much too expensive. Just think for a moment. What are they designed to do? To score direct hits on very thick, vertical, steel walls, and to penetrate deeply. They're not expected to make a hole much bigger than themselves. If they can do that, it's all that's asked of them. Consequently they are built with very strong steel cases and given a small explosive charge. When you fire a thing like that in open country, what happens? At ten or twelve miles your precious shell will strike the ground at an excessively acute angle—rather less so if it happens to strike the side of a hill—and will make a deep, narrow hole like a fox's. And that's the sum total. All you'll have done is to bury at the bottom of your fox's hole five or six thousand francs. Nothing else will happen at all. A trench lying as near as ten yards from the point of impact will not even be shaken, nor its occupants so much as wounded by splinters....A weapon designed for the sinking of ships can hardly

be expected to do much in completely different conditions.
… The only reasonably sensible use to which naval shells can
be put on land is in the bombardment of forts with concrete
emplacements. And even then a naval shell will never strike a
cupola at the correct angle, as a howitzer shell will. The most it
can do is to punch a hole in the thing without destroying it."

"Still, the garrison won't be any too comfortable.…"

"Maybe. Two or three men who are unlucky enough to get
in its way will get smashed to pulp, but that's about all. The
game's not worth the candle."

"But in that case, sir, why go to all the trouble of taking
them down there? God knows they're hard enough to move!
And in many cases special beds have to be made for
them.…All those girders, all that concrete!"

"I might answer that by saying that those who make these
decisions know nothing whatever about artillery.…But that's
not the real reason. The real reason is that they want to create
a moral effect."

"On whom? On the Boches? If they see that the damage is
so slight, the moral effect won't last long."

"On everybody—on the men in the line, on the civilians
behind the front…on public opinion, which derives its information from newspapers…on the Boches too, if it comes to
that, because of the noise the things make.…"

The general once more took refuge in his thoughts. A little
farther on, he said:

"One thing's worrying me."

"What's that, sir?"

"Despois's division."

"Why, sir?"

"I don't think they'll touch the two I've had all along. But
Despois's was given me as an extra reinforcement…Do you
see the danger?…Suppose this Verdun business gets worse,
which is more than probable. They'll start hunting everywhere for available troops. Besides, Despois is ambitious. He's
a busybody and he's bored with this sector. He's perfectly
capable of pulling strings.…Yes, it's a serious danger and we
must be prepared."

While Clédinger hurried off to fetch the heads of the three bureaux, Duroure, seated at his table, read the text of the message which Radigué had just handed to him.

When everyone was assembled:

"Be seated, gentlemen. I have just received an important dispatch from G.H.Q. It is dated today and is headed: 'Note for Army Group Commanders.' But, as you will see," he added with feigned modesty, "the contents also concerns very much humbler persons, which accounts for its having been sent direct to me....I will read it, gentlemen."

He intended, in accordance with his usual habit, to insert his own commentaries in the body of the communication. When he was presiding, as today, at a full meeting of his "council," he liked to hear himself talk. It reminded him of the days when he was a professor at the Staff College.

"'The enemy has launched a violent effort on the front held by the Army Group of the Centre'— Ah, so they do admit that there's something in the wind...No mention of Verdun— curious case of modesty...though, to be sure, Verdun is no more than an accident among many so far as the front of the Armies of the Centre is concerned. Well, let's see how it goes on. 'It is possible that this effort will not remain isolated, and that more or less powerful attacks will be delivered on other parts of the front.' Hm, keeping on the safe side, are they?...'Generals commanding Army Groups and Armies'" (Duroure was, as a matter of fact, extremely flattered at being treated as an army commander) "'should make all necessary dispositions to deal calmly with any eventualities.' Not very clear—unless it's just saying: do your job. Still, let's go on. 'If the enemy, in an attempt to force a decision, throws important reserves into the action'—They seem rather vague on that point—what's Intelligence doing?—'the Commander-in-Chief will concentrate against him'" (from this point Duroure seemed to be weighing each word) "'all troops available in the rear of the Army Groups and Armies'—in the rear! 'and any that can be spared'—Ah, now we're coming to it!—'from the line itself. The greatest possible number of large units'—

large units, eh? Not merely battalions or regiments— 'heavy artillery, air squadrons, etc., will be required…' Look out, gentlemen! '…and the utmost will be demanded of all men involved….' Presumably they're talking now of the troops that remain behind….'Generals commanding Army Groups and Armies will take all necessary steps in the event of such a demand being made on them. Signed: Joffre.' "

He put the paper back on the table.

"What did I tell you this morning, Radigué?…Well, gentlemen, we've got to be ready. I wanted to have your views without any unnecessary delay…because I have an idea that these urgent measures will be on us before we know where we are….We shall be asked to sacrifice a considerable number of our effectives. Personally, I don't see how I can hold my front with less men than I have already; but I may be wrong."

The heads of his 1st and 3rd bureaux assured him that he was not.

"Still, we must be in a position to offer them something, and must give the impression that we have studied the whole problem carefully. Otherwise G.H.Q. will just help itself.You know it can be pretty ruthless when it likes. If we are thought to have been lacking in the spirit of co-operation, we shall be treated pretty cavalierly."

Before calling on his colleagues for their opinion, Duroure made it sufficiently clear what line of argument he thought should be adopted: absolute impossibility of sparing a whole division, for reasons of internal administration and due alternation of troops in and out of the line. It would be the business of the 1st and 3rd bureaux to support this argument with an array of facts as convincing as possible. In case of urgent necessity it might be arranged for two or even three regiments to be spared, one from each of the first-line divisions. Unfortunately it would be no good offering territorial.

"Excuse me, sir, but may I suggest something?" said Radigué, and proceeded to elaborate his views. He agreed with his chief that they must show willingness to co-operate. But they must do everything in their power to avoid sacrificing any first-line units, whether large or small.

"What's the use of talking like that? How are you going to manage, then?"

Radigué replied that he had good reason to assume, from having studied the interchange of views that had been going on between Verdun and G.H.Q., copies of which had been passed to neighbouring Armies, that one of the most urgent requirements at Verdun was for manual labour.

"They have found it impossible to carry out their program of work owing to lack of available men. More than once they have said that they needed ten or twelve thousand more than they had. If my memory serves me, they have even mentioned a 'territorial division.' Well, we've got just what they want. Let us make them a graceful present of one of ours."

The general objected that he didn't think the present was very reasonable. What the Army of Verdun needed was combatant troops.

"Excuse me, sir. If the German offensive is not checked within forty-eight hours, it will become a matter of extreme urgency to organize the second and third positions, which, at the moment, exist only on paper. It will be necessary, too, to do a lot of work on communications in order to fit them to carry very heavy traffic, and to build new roads. You pointed that out yourself, sir, this morning. I am sure that our offer of a territorial division will be a godsend."

"Well, if you think so. But for Heaven's sake see to it that G.H.Q. doesn't start grumbling," said Duroure with a sigh.

Any reduction of his effectives, lessening, as it must do, his importance, was painful to him. The sending of even a detachment of clerks or workmen would have plunged him in melancholy and would have set him brooding on the insecurity of his position. But he certainly did not consider his two territorial divisions as the brightest jewels in his crown. He was even a little ashamed of them. He had got wind of a particularly nasty joke which had been going the rounds of the various staffs. It took the form of the following dialogue supposed to form part of an examination for intending officers.

"Give the battle order of the French front," asks the examiner.

"The battle order of the French front," replies the candidate, "consists of the G.A.N., the G.A.C., and the G.A.E." (the Group of Armies of the North, the Group of Armies of the Centre, and the Group of Armies of the East).

"Right, but haven't you forgotten the highest formation of all?"

"Highest of all is G.H.Q." (General Headquarters).

"And lowest?"

"Lowest of all is the G.W.O.C."

"And what do those initials stand for?"

"For the Group of Worn-Out Crocks."

"Right. But hasn't this Group another name?"

"Yes, it is known as Duroure's Group."

When a man feels between heel and ankle the irritation of that kind of joke—as persistent as an old mosquito bite—he is only too willing to hand over one or even two unattached territorial divisions to the second-hand dealer. But only in exchange for first-hand goods.

While Radigué, Clédinger, and the head of the 1st Bureau discussed together the most tempting way of presenting their offer in readiness for the day—soon now—when they should receive from G.H.Q. a peremptory note the tenor of which it was only too easy to guess—"Reference G.H.Q. mem. No. 15063, dated February 22nd, render at once statement of nature and value of troops which you can supply within two days on receipt of necessary orders"—Duroure was busy with his own thoughts.

"When this particular squall is over, I shall ask for my fifteen thousand men back. But I shall try to get them replaced by an active division."

CHAPTER TWELVE

Marching to Verdun.
Villages of the Argonne

During the night of the 24th of February, Jerphanion, who, worn out by the day's exercises, was fast asleep, found himself suddenly awakened by a prod from Fabre.

"What's the matter? Time to get up?"

Not a glimmer of daylight came through the window, and the room would have been pitch dark had not Fabre been holding the lantern which they were in the habit of leaving lighted behind the entrance door of their billet.

"Orders," said Fabre. "Didn't you hear the chap come in? He kicked up enough row."

"What orders?"

"Moving—morning—six o'clock. So much for Pagny!… What it means of course is that we shall start about eight or nine, but we'll be routed out at five."

"Where are we going?"

"They've neglected to inform us—but it's not difficult to guess."

"Suppose not. Well, we're in for a jolly time!"

"Go to sleep. I'll wake you."

But before he could drop off again, Jerphanion had to prove to his own satisfaction that there would be at least six, perhaps eight, stages between Pagny and Verdun. He compromised on seven. It was more or less certain, therefore, that he had a full week still to live. Things being as they were, a guaranteed week of existence was not to be sneezed at. At that very moment there were thousands of poor devils who would have given a good deal to be able to say as much.

They started at half past seven—Jerphanion's battalion, at least, together with another half-battalion, the three machine-gun companies, and the headquarters details. The rest of the regiment, which was billeted at Versigneul, would follow the next day.

The men were less depressed than might have been expected, but then, they had no idea where they were going. Apart from a vague mutter of artillery fire—not enough in itself to be disturbing—news of the battle of Verdun had reached them only through the medium of rumours, most of them contradictory and considerably distorted, according to some of which a French offensive had been launched and had already progressed several kilometres "in the direction of Spincourt." Such information as came through, however, was enough to make them realize that something big was afoot. But the last ten days, coming on top of so many others during which they had been "put through it" and made to "sweat their guts out," had had the result of disgusting them with anything in the nature of drill or field exercises or battalion work in open country. Their mental processes were now little better than those of children, and in their present state the life of the trenches, already softened in retrospect, seemed to them far preferable to what they had been recently experiencing.

The inhabitants of Pagny had gathered to watch them set out.

"So long, boys! So long! And good luck!"

Nothing more definite was said. They may have been thinking a lot, but it was better not to put their thoughts into words.

The villagers had brought numerous small gifts: bottles of wine, sausages, chocolate, cigarettes.

The band led off at the head of the column, playing the *Marche Lorraine*. The intention was cheerful, but the effect was just the contrary. The muffled blaring of the joyful brass, caught between the grey-black clouds and the flat plain across which the men began to move off, brought a lump into the throats of those who, five minutes earlier, had been trying to appear gay and careless.

That day they covered about eighteen miles. The weather

was comparatively fine, and the road neither too rough nor too muddy. Towards evening the men began to drag their feet. But it was difficult to guess whether their minds were occupied with thoughts more serious than those that come inevitably after a heavy day's marching. Perhaps they were not altogether sorry to have sore feet and aching shoulders. Such physical discomfort had at least the advantage of keeping them from brooding on other things.

Jerphanion and Fabre were billeted with their men in a hamlet consisting of three farms.

Next morning they moved off at seven o'clock. The route they took was in the direction of the southern Argonne. They covered about the same distance as the day before. From time to time they passed through a village the houses of which, depressing enough under any circumstances, bore numerous traces of the 1914 fighting. As soon as they saw the soldiers in the distance, or heard the tramping of their feet, the inhabitants came out of their houses, even ran up from their gardens or from some neighbouring field, to line the edge of the roadway. The women and young girls, who formed the majority of these onlookers, waved their handkerchiefs. The old men took off their caps. The very old, who were bent almost double and wore large and filthy hats, confined their activity to raising their arms in a series of spasmodic movements, while they mumbled odds and ends of phrases in a strong eastern dialect which it was almost impossible to understand

It was all rather unusual. Since the end of 1914 the men had grown unaccustomed to this kind of reception. In the course of their various treks through regions that still bore traces of human habitation—infrequent occurrences at best—they noted little curiosity and were received with nothing approaching affection or tenderness. Not that the villagers of the front-line zones and those a few miles farther back treated them with any particular evidence of ill will, but that they had grown used to regarding them as a species of public workers, very numerous and rather troublesome, whose labours looked as though they would go on for ever, and the only excuse for whose invasion was that they were willing to pay high prices for the wine and provisions that were offered for sale.

And now here were these Argonne folk standing by the roadside and welcoming them as those of the Ardennes had done hard by the frontier in the days of the fighting on the Sambre and at Charleroi. There was something solemn about this recrudescence of public emotion. The marching men felt little thrills running up their cheeks and round the roots of their hair. And with those thrills went various thoughts that it was better not to look at too closely.

Even more unusual was the ceremony observed by the regiment. On approaching the larger villages—Lisse, for instance—an order ran down the column:

"March at attention!"

The band struck up, sometimes in full force. The men more or less picked up the step and hoisted their rifles to their shoulders with the careless ease of old campaigners who have long got past bothering about appearances. The young officers who had got together in couples to while away the march with chat hurried back to the flank of their companies. Here and there some N.C.O. bringing up the rear could be heard setting the time for the men in his parade-ground voice: "Left, right, left, right!"

Occasionally there was a sound of subdued laughter. The first time all this business had occurred Jerphanion and Fabre had exchanged glances. Griollet, the tanner from the 9th arrondissement, had looked at Jerphanion with a sort of conspiratorial grin. But the ironical comment had got no farther than his lips, where it had remained, an unspoken commentary for all to understand who would. The inhabitants of the village, awkwardly ranged along the route, the children standing on stones, stared and stared. There was in their faces a look of exaltation, not so much expressive of confidence or joy as of an intense longing to be reassured and to recover a hope long lost. Some of the women, making an effort to smile, could not repress their sobs and had to bury their faces in their handkerchiefs.

Jerphanion, who had rejoined Fabre as soon as they had left
Lisse, said simply:

"What a responsibility!"

They arrived at Possesse completely worn out. There once
more the population turned out to welcome them. There
were even a few cheers. But there was another sound waiting
to greet the marching men—the sound of the Verdun guns,
rumbling away, quite distinctly now, on the far horizon to
north and east.

On asking what orders there were for the start next morning, which was a Sunday, they were told that there were none,
but that they would be warned in good time.

On Sunday morning they learned that they would be
spending another night there, and that the day would be
devoted to cleaning up and resting.

There were other units billeted in the outskirts. The place
was a regular junction. They saw field artillery on the move,
supply trains, and ambulances.

That evening, at the inn where they had gathered to drink
a bottle of "decent wine," Jerphanion, Fabre, and a few other
lieutenants, second-lieutenants, and cadets of the 151st, met
several young officers whose men were camped in the neighbourhood and who had come into the place on duty. One of
them, a lieutenant, was even attached to the staff of the Fortified Region. He had condescended to sit at the same table
as his companions of the fighting services, moved to do so
perhaps by that wave of emotion which now, as on the 2nd
of August '14, united all ranks and conditions.

Several of these officers had been concerned, in one way
or another, with the events on the Verdun front, or had spoken with eyewitnesses or with people in the know. In this
way Jerphanion and his friends got their first circumstantial
and reliable reports of the battle.

They learned in the first place that the French offensive had
never been anything but a legend. They discovered next that
the Germans had preceded their attack by a bombardment of
"unexampled intensity." This artillery preparation had been
marked by several curious features. The targets had been dis-

tributed over a wide extent of country, both longitudinally and in depth, and had been isolated, the intention obviously being to divide the battlefield into watertight compartments which the assaulting troops hoped to mop up one by one. Heavy and medium-heavy guns had been used for destroying the defences and for establishing a barrage. Tear gas rather than poison gas had been sent over into the valleys and into the low ground immediately behind the line in the hope of cutting the approaches which would normally have been used by reinforcements.

But the battle had had other marked features worthy of close study by professional soldiers. (Had not all those present become professional soldiers by this time?) The Germans had achieved an element of surprise by refraining from digging assault trenches. They had assembled their attacking troops in huge subterranean shelters—thanks to which they had been able to get them all well forward. All those who had taken part in the action were agreed that they had never seen so violent an artillery preparation followed by so cautious, so wary an infantry advance. The Paris newspapers were already describing it as an "onslaught." Nothing less like an onslaught could be imagined.

"A friend of mine who has an estate in the Gard," said one of the lieutenants, "said that he was reminded more than anything of a lot of labourers going to spray the vines….Some of the Boches had flame-thrower containers strapped to their backs, which increased the illusion."

For all that, the situation of the French troops had been a terrible one, and was so still.

The speakers were far from agreeing in their estimates of the depth to which the enemy had advanced. The gloomier maintained that the whole forest line from Brabant-sur-Meuse and Samogneux as far as Ornes had been overrun on the 21st, the 22nd, and the 23rd (those present who had maps of the Verdun area used them now to follow what was being said). Colonel Driant had been killed in the Bois des Caures at the head of his chasseurs, after achieving prodigies of valour. On the 24th and 25th, after moving up an enormous number of reserves, the enemy had made another forward jump which had brought them to the last but one of the ridges covering Verdun, the most strongly held and most important of all, that of the Côte du Poivre and Douaumont. The fort of Douaumont had been taken on the morning of the 25th as the result of an unforgivable mistake. In itself it might not be of any very great military value, but its position was unique. As soon as news of the fall of Douaumont had reached the troops defending Verdun, it had had a deplorable effect. It was known that the Boches were exultant. Leaflets had been thrown into the French lines as far afield as Vauquois, bearing the words: "Douaumont has fallen. Everything will soon be over now. Don't let yourselves be killed for nothing." Prisoners brought in on the 26th said that the taking of Douaumont had been announced to the German troops as a victory of the first importance which would bring the end of the war markedly nearer.

The staff officer, while admitting certain of these facts, contested others. He questioned their accuracy and disagreed with the inferences drawn from them. He argued, for instance, that unfortunate though the loss of Douaumont might be, it had not been trebled in value since falling into the enemy's hands. He pounced on the mistake—trivial enough in itself—made by one of those present in assigning the Côte du Poivre and Douaumont to the same ridge. The Côte du Poivre was part of a more northerly geological system which was continued by the Louvement massif and Hill 378. The line of heights on which Douaumont was situated was still intact almost up to Douaumont itself. He maintained, further, that the Germans had suffered a severe set-back the day before when they had tried to debouch from the bottleneck formed by the Meuse and the Côte du Poivre.

But all were agreed that one piece of news took precedence of all others. And since the party was composed of young men who were not naturally disposed to look on the dark side, they clung to it with peculiar tenacity:

Pétain had taken over the command. On his shoulders had been placed the burden of saving Verdun. To meet his requirements and the general nature of the situation, the IInd Army had been reformed, so that the whole of the Verdun front should now come under its commander, who would take orders from no one but G.H.Q.

It was not just a matter of rumour or gossip. It was certain, absolutely certain; as official as anything could be. The staff lieutenant could swear that he had seen at least a dozen orders with his own eyes headed "IInd Army" and signed "Pétain."

The change had been made with dramatic suddenness. Joffre, frightened out of his usual calm by the results of the first two days of the battle, had sent Castelnau to Verdun armed with full powers. Castelnau had seen that the position was extremely serious, had come to the conclusion that everything was in a mess, and had realized that Pétain was the only man capable of putting things straight. He had at once rung up Joffre, who had replied: "Pétain? Right. I agree." Pétain, summoned then and there, had gone straight to Chantilly, where Joffre had given him his instructions in two words: "Save Verdun. Ask for what you want and we'll do our best to see that you get it." Without wasting a moment Pétain had started for the Verdun region, which he had reached, via Bar-le-Duc, that same evening. Since everything he heard on the way made him take an increasingly grave view of the situation, he had not waited to reach Verdun before putting his plans into action. Halting at Souilly, halfway between Bar-le-Duc and Verdun, where he set up temporary headquarters in the mayor's house, he had examined the map, studied the order of battle, elicited what information he needed, confirmed what he already knew, put through a number of telephone calls, and in the course of that one night had modified the whole defensive organization. He had divided the Verdun front into four clearly defined groups, each under the orders of a general who was made entirely responsible for his own particular sector. He had marked on the map four successive positions in depth, which were to be put at once into a state of defence and held at all costs. He had seen that he was informed about the actual conditions of the supply services, roads, motor transport, sanitary measures, water, wood,

camping grounds, and the rest, and with a stroke of the pen
had put order into confusion, efficiency into chaos, and had
set about increasing existing facilities to meet the needs of the
situation. He had decided to transform the road from Bar-le-
Duc to Verdun, which was the only available means of access,
into a great traffic artery capable of carrying two thousand
trucks a day, and to give the Verdun forts their proper place in
the general defensive scheme (why should forts alone be useless in a war that attaches such value to any kind of fortified
position?). Finally, that this program should not remain a dead
letter, he reminded G.H.Q. of its promises and put in a
demand for a large supply of artillery and aeroplanes, for several divisions of reinforcements, all the heavy motor vehicles
that could be made available, and ten thousand territorials to
be used in the repair and upkeep of the road which would be
the defence's one and only life-line.

Seated in the inn parlour with their "decent wine" on the
table in front of them, they listened with admiration while
these facts were retailed to them partly by one of their friends
of the fighting services, partly by the staff lieutenant. The fact
that these two authorities were in complete agreement on all
essential points removed any doubts they might have had. The
only real difference between their informants was that the
lieutenant was at pains to acquit the staff of the Fortified
Region (to which he was still attached) of negligence. Not
that he failed to show great enthusiasm for Pétain. He even
went so far as to say that he hoped he would be "kicked off"
the staff at Dugny and sent instead to Souilly—a change
which doubtless could be engineered without any great difficulty, since IInd Army H.Q. was badly in need of officers,
and there was no particular reason why it should not make
use of the personnel on the spot.

His attitude was typical of that of many of his colleagues.
Even General Herr's younger officers who quite sincerely
backed up their chief were not immune to the wave of enthusiasm which Pétain's arrival had set in motion not only
among the front-line troops, but among the members of the
administrative services as well, and particularly among the

men of their age. In the case of those holding staff appointments, for whom the idea of work and the due ordering of
ranks in that work is strongly conditioned by the sense that
they are in living proximity to the responsible chief, that they
form part of an organization founded upon a hierarchy of
functions involving a variety of privileges within the sacred
precincts, this enthusiasm took the form of wanting to work
in positions as close as possible to the new commander, of
wanting to dedicate themselves to duties that seemed really
worth while, the performing of which carried with it a certain sense of exaltation—in other words, to be employed in
some way that would bring them in close contact with him.

While this conversation had been going on in the inn at
Possesse, Geoffroy, who had arrived from Dugny with certain
documents relating to the forts, which Pétain needed in a
hurry, and had had an interview—of exactly one minute's
duration—with the general in person, suddenly burst out, as
he was leaving the room, into a spate of rapid words:

"I could get a personal introduction to you, sir, but I don't
want to. I'd like to say this, though: I have a great admiration
for you, and a strong desire to be useful. I should be awfully
grateful if you'd ask for me to be transferred. I don't mind
what I do."

The general, who knew perfectly well who this particular
officer was, looked him up and down with eyes which, for all
their air of preoccupation, held a covert smile.

"Write down your qualifications and the details of your service on a piece of paper," he said, "and leave it downstairs. I'll
have a look at it later."

This part of their interview had lasted, like the former, a
bare minute. In that lay its excuse.

On leaving the inn, Jerphanion said to Fabre:

"We're just a lot of kids. Here we are, all set up again, just
because we've been told that Pétain is in command."

"That's natural enough."

"Oh, I didn't exactly mean that."

Next morning the rumour was confirmed that, unless
something unexpected happened, they would remain several

days at Possesse (another part of the regiment, including the three machine-gun companies, was at Saint-Jean). A number of drafts had arrived, and training would go on as before. Particular attention would be given to the "specialists."

"What it comes to," said Jerphanion to Fabre, "is that we're to wait here in second-line reserve. If the battle goes on, or turns out badly, we shall be thrown in."

"Yes…it reminds me of a song I learned at school:

> A job in life'll come our way
> When the old folk turn their toes up…."

"May I add," continued Jerphanion, who was in a mood for mischief, "that then, if ever, will be the moment to try a famous recipe of which I have heard tell."

"What may that be, old man?" asked Fabre with a sudden affectation of profound curiosity.

"I'm told it's stunning when a battle's going badly, as even the best-behaved battle will do at times, or is hanging fire a bit, and the authorities want to bring about a decision."

"This sounds interesting!"

"I'm glad you think so."

"And you know this recipe?"

"Yes; this is it—follow me closely.…You hurl yourself into the enemy ranks…"

"Yes."

"You're following me?"

"Closely, closely."

"And you let—" Jerphanion paused with carefully calculated effect—"cold steel decide."

"Cold steel! Why, of course!" exclaimed Fabre with the ecstatic air of one who has seen the light. "Of course!"

They decided forthwith that the moment was ripe for "a thirty seconds' burst of continuous laughter." This was one of the more recently invented parts of the ritual.

On the 2nd of March, just as they were sitting down to their evening meal, the order came to pack up. The battalion was moving off on the 3rd for Givry.

"Why Givry?" said Jerphanion.

"Why not Givry?" replied Fabre.

It was only two hours earlier that "Jerphat" had been developing for Fabre's benefit an argument aimed at allaying their fears. "The experience of this war proves, beyond all doubt, that the fate of any given major offensive is very quickly determined. In the first three or four days it either succeeds or fails. (As a matter of fact, up to now, they've all failed.) The present one has lasted since the 21st—well over a week. That's to say, it has outlived its natural term. What we are seeing now is the backwash. The end came actually during the forty-eight hours immediately following Pétain's taking over…. The reserves not yet called on stand very little chance now of being involved. Their only risk is having to relieve the formations which bore the brunt of the attack, and perhaps to come in for some last-minute show of bad temper on the part of the Boche."

The move to Givry did not entirely invalidate this reasoning, but "Jerphat" was nervous. It was always annoying, of course, to retrace one's footsteps, but, for all that, he would have far preferred to hear the men saying "We're going back to Grandes-Loges." One could have always exclaimed, in that case, with pretended disappointment: "What a hell of a nuisance for nothing!"

Reports of the battle had continued to arrive at Possesse, but they were so confused that a considerable margin was left for individual interpretation. According to some, the force of the German attack was broken. Douaumont had been its limit. The front would be stabilized again on its present line. Pétain would do no more than retake a few positions of special importance—Douaumont, for example.

There were those, however, who held that the situation was still grave, so grave, in fact, that Pétain intended to abandon the whole of the right bank of the Meuse, which could no longer be defended, and to establish new positions behind it. Such a withdrawal would have the added advantage of reducing the salient by fifty per cent. The movement had already begun. The French troops were already retiring from the plain of the

Woëvre and digging in provisionally on the lower slopes of the Heights of the Meuse. The only reason that the movement was not being carried out more quickly, that Pétain was still holding some of his forward positions and was even counter-attacking on the crests to the north, was that an enormous amount of material had to be evacuated from Verdun.

Although this latter version was put forward by seemingly responsible people, Jerphanion had decided, rather arbitrarily, that it was merely a "product of humbug." There was nothing about the move to Givry to make him alter his mind on this particular point. Even if the regiment had been sent for to reinforce, the fact that they had been sent for at all, even if it didn't quite bear out the theory that the force of the German offensive was spent, bore out still less the other theory that the French were abandoning the right bank of the river. If Pétain were really withdrawing to a considerably narrower front, he had already too many troops to move back. He was not the man to add to his difficulties.

At Givry the column divided into two. One part of the regiment set off towards Sainte-Menehould. The battalion to which Jerphanion and Fabre belonged took the Triaucourt road. The men seemed depressed by the separation though they had been through the same sort of thing before without apparently minding. What fates would attend the two groups? Which of them would be the lucky ones, which the unlucky? When things got hot it was nicer to be all together. But the battalion commander assured them that the separation was to be temporary, that the two halves would soon join up again.

"Which only bears out what I thought," said Fabre.

They marched through a country of forest and lakes. The map, at which Jerphanion glanced from time to time, was sprinkled with odd names, some of them charming, some merely comic: Les Belles Aulnes (Fair Alders), la Fontaine Bleue (Blue Spring), la Grande Bouillie (Big Pudding)—there was a Petite as well—le Bâtard (Bastard), les Braque-mères (Cracked Dames), les Culs de Loup (Wolf's Rump).... What a pity that so much whimsical imagination should be wasted at such a time; it was like offering a dish of cherries to a man in high fever, or throwing confetti at a funeral.

On leaving the forest land, they skirted the head waters of the Aisne. Suddenly the sound of the guns became more plainly audible. A rumour ran down the column that a long halt would be made at Triaucourt.

Triaucourt was a large place. It was impossible to march in with the band playing, the band having gone with the other detachment. But Triaucourt was treated to a fanfare of bugles and a spectacle of marching in step, with arms shouldered. The boom-boo-oo-oom, dong, boom, dong, dong, sounding from the distant horizon played its part in the general composition, but never quite synchronized with the bugles and the croac, croac, croac, of the marching feet.

The inhabitants had come out on the front steps of their houses. There were plenty of broken roofs and ruined walls to be seen, but these scars already had a look of long standing.

When the leading files reached the first houses, the onlookers began to cheer and clap their hands. At first they jabbered a lot of incomprehensible words, but after a while they could be heard crying out very distinctly "Hurrah for the 151st!" A few children and young girls offered the soldiers little bouquets of wild flowers.

The halt was prolonged. The people of the place brought small offerings of food and drink, wine and rum. They said:

"We haven't much to offer. Some lot or other marches through every day."

They refused to accept money. An old curé asked the major for permission to bless the battalion, adding: "Only don't bother them." He accomplished the little ceremony with great discretion, standing on a slight rise, while many of the men went on eating and chatting. Jerphanion reflected: "If my mother were here, she would be so deeply moved that I believe she would forgive the war....Alas!" He himself was feeling particularly sick at heart. Very certainly, though not very clearly, he saw that there was every reason to fear that in the years to come the world would be a place of many trials for men like himself.

A rumour began going round that the remainder of the 151st were coming in by the north-easterly road from Passavant and Sainte-Menehould. There was a sound of music. In their faded uniforms the men marched into the town in close column, no spring in their steps, their backs a little bent, their faces serious, with a look in their eyes as though they had been through an experience not of this world, something that had hardened and petrified their spirit to such an extent that it would never again recover its former elasticity. The general effect that they made was almost frightening. The regimental colours were there, furled and cased, like some secret fetish, but neither the colonel and his staff nor the machine-gun companies.

The sound of cheers once again filled the air. To the onlookers it seemed that the men paid astonishingly little attention to them. When some group was noisier than the rest they gave it a quick sideways glance, but most of them did not even take the trouble to smile. In so far as their faces were capable of showing any emotion at all, it was one of defiance, as though they were silently asking: "What do they want? What do they expect us to do?"

"I suppose we looked like that too," thought Jerphanion, "and yet we were touched. Some of us even felt a desire to swagger and bluster....What odd creatures we've all become!"

The only real smiles, the only softening of the strained looks, were reserved for their newly found comrades.

"Been here long?"

"More than three hours....Where've you been?"

"Villers-en-Argonne."

"What for?"

"Don't ask me....We weren't all there. Some went off with the colonel in the direction of Sainte-Menehould....I heard a quartermaster say they were going to camp near Valmy.... We've had a damned awful time on the road."

"Why?"

"All these damned refugees."

"Refugees? Where from?"

"Oh, Verdun and all round. I gather that no one's being left in the place....And we kept on having to get over to the side of the road to let guns and trucks by...."

The old curé turned up again with the intention of blessing this new lot which good fortune had thrown in his way. But the commander of the 3rd battalion, hearing some men close to him who had been present at the first little ceremony exclaim irritably: "Hell, why can't he wait till we're dead?" dissuaded the priest from proceeding with his design.

"It was all right once, sir; but I'm afraid it loses its effect in the long run."

The good man seemed very disappointed.

"But so many of them have only just come in," he said.

"I know...but the blessing you gave a little while back included the whole of the regiment, didn't it, and not my battalion only? I'm sure it will be effective....Thanks all the same, sir, for your good intention....There's nothing to prevent you from sending up a silent prayer on our behalf."

As a result of orders received during the course of the afternoon, the halt became a bivouac. Word came through later that the whole of the next morning would be spent at Triaucourt, doubtless to let the men rest, but also to let the detachment which had gone off with the colonel rejoin the main column.

The 5th was, in fact, given up to rest, though only in a purely physical sense. There was no easiness of mind. All morning there was an almost uninterrupted flow of civilians who were being evacuated to the interior, and their passage was marked by all the huddle and muddle inseparable from such heartbreaking spectacles—hand-carts with old women perched on top of mattresses, and odds and ends of clothes hanging over the sides; a couple of cows with mud-caked flanks; three goats in single file; chickens tied together by the feet in a wheelbarrow pushed by an old man.

In the opposite direction, moving, that is, towards the battle, came a stream of artillery and transport of every description, but consisting for the most part of motor trucks. Several of these were empty. Jerphanion pointed this out to his friend Fabre and took advantage of the fact to air some of his ill humour.

"What a shame to let all those trucks go empty when so many wretched devils have got to go shambling along the road and everyone's short of supplies and the poor bastards in the line are being forced back at this very moment for lack of ammunition. To think that such blunders should be possible after eighteen months of war!"

But when, a few minutes later, he heard Griollet and some other men of his company say the same thing and draw the same gloomy conclusions, he had no difficulty in finding an explanation and in imparting it in a tone of quiet reasonableness:

"I know it seems absurd. But Pétain needs an enormous supply of trucks in order to keep regular traffic going between Verdun and Bar-le-Duc. A staff officer was telling us all about it the other day at Possesse. It's essential to get the machine functioning at once. If they'd had to wait for a load before sending the trucks out it would have been a week before things got going…and Pétain can't wait a week."

The men asked nothing better than to be given a reason. Pétain was the reason, and it never occurred to them that Pétain could be guilty of a mistake which was obvious to the simplest private. As to Jerphanion, the business of explaining matters to his men cleared his own mind of its grievances.

They started off again early on the morning of the 6th, by the Evres road, which was the shortest route to Verdun. No news had come in of the detachment which had been camping at Sainte-Menehould.

Word was passed down to the officers of the company, and communicated by them to the sergeants:

"We've got to keep going as hard as we can. No more rest till we reach Verdun."

One extra piece of information was vouchsafed:

"We ought to get there by tomorrow evening."

CHAPTER THIRTEEN

The Bivouac among the Ruins.
"March to the Sound of the Guns"

From the moment the march started, the men were conscious of a feeling similar to that which they had experienced on leaving Pagny, and again when they had set out from Possesse, but this time raised to a higher power: the feeling that they were being drawn into the orbit of a whirlpool.

Over there, beyond the rolling landscape, brown, light green, dark green, dotted with great patches and stripes of shining white which was the snow; beyond the billowing grasslands and winter woods, twenty or twenty-five miles off, lay a great flaming object, still invisible, but roaring away in the distance, a furnace set in the hollow of the hills and sucking into its blazing heart everything within range. They felt themselves being dragged to the centre of attraction, shovelled into the vast and hungry maw. The thoughts that went on in the secret heart of any single man had very little importance when set against the cosmic activity in which he was called upon to play his part.

But since thousands of human lives, endless machines, great masses of material, were being drawn to the centre at one and the same moment, there was bound to be a certain amount of congestion and delay. And some of these lives there were with which the fire would have no truck, but ejected unconsumed like clinkers raked out among the ashes.

So long as the road remained clear, the column marched to a rather quicker rhythm than on the previous days. But there was hardly a mile without some check. Suddenly it would be overtaken by a line of trucks.

"To your right…to your right…."

The warning was passed up from tail to head of the column.

The men grumbled: "To hell with the damned trucks!…" and obeyed as slowly as possible, elbowing their right-hand neighbours, making their pals stumble, weighed down as they were with their equipment and indifferent to trivial considerations of balance.

Or it might be the head of the column which edged aside without a word of warning to make room for a crowd of refugees. The two bodies of human beings passed one another as a rule in silence. There were no cheers from these civilians, and the soldiers had no heart for joking. Many of them, who had come from the occupied districts of the north, even avoided looking to their left. The two crowds passed like pedestrians in the street of some great city, each intent upon his business.

Sometimes these meetings became complicated. It was necessary to make room simultaneously for a convoy of artillery moving up to the front and a batch of civilians straggling back to the rear. When this happened a whole company was forced to yield all the roadway and take to the grassy edge, or even to the ditch, in Indian file, sometimes actually to halt in the open fields. The rear of the column had to slow down, with much checking and banging as of buffers between one section and the next, to an accompaniment of angry exclamations: "Christ!" "Keep your eyes open, you damn fools!" "Enough to break a man's legs, all this sudden stopping."

In spite of these irritations, about which there was nothing new save the frequency of their occurrence, the morale of the men—in the language of the service—seemed higher rather than lower than it had been during the past days. It was hardly to be expected that they should show any particular enthusiasm, but they were distinctly excited. They seemed not at all anxious to delay their march towards the furnace. None of the many delays were caused by them. When the whistle cut short the three minutes of their hourly halt, they got to their feet again as much as to say: "All right, no point in trying to hold back."

Second Lieutenant Cotin looked like a fish just thrown into a running stream, or a freshly watered flower. He smiled at everyone, joked with the men, could be heard shouting: "Who's going to join me in *Auprès de ma blonde?...*" and then starting the song in that voice of his, which, as Fabre said, was more like a bicycle horn than anything else.

In his high spirits he romped round like a sheep-dog, covering more ground than anybody else. He would run up to Jerphanion with a "Lieutenant" so eloquently respectful that it sounded like "Captain," and spoken with such cordiality that he almost seemed to be making allowances for something the other had done or said. He was like a young seminarist oozing grace to such a degree that even the errors of Freemasons seemed to him no more than pebbles in the rushing stream of divine truth.

At the village of Evres, where, in spite of the congested road, they arrived fairly early, marching in with the band playing and welcomed by the sort of cheers to which they had by now grown accustomed, they learned, to their great surprise, that one half of the column would be billeted there, while the other went on as far as Beauzée. This second lot included both Jerphanion's company and Fabre's.

Beauzée was at least five miles away, but on a road that led towards the south-east, and therefore well off the direct line to Verdun. Were they not, after all, to be sent to the battle by the shortest route? Were they going into reserve somewhere in the valley of the Meuse?

They found the name Beauzée given to a huddle of ruined farm buildings. A few beams eaten and blackened by fire showed where a barn had been, or still stood supporting a fragment of roof which bore along its edge the traces of flame. Odds and ends of broken furniture filled what once had been the yard. The battles of September 1914 must have been particularly severe in this neighbourhood, and the shelling had obviously caused many conflagrations in addition to the more direct destruction which they had wrought.

There were scarcely any inhabitants left, and hardly a building was habitable. It was a problem to find billets in this scene of desolation. To make matters worse, it started snowing just as darkness fell. At last, when the men had more or less been fitted into the various corners, cellars, rooms open to all four winds of heaven, but with a scrap of roof intact—in short, anywhere that looked like offering protection from the cold and the snow without threatening too imminent a collapse— they were suddenly disturbed—it must have been nine o'clock at the very least, and most of them were already asleep—by the noise of fresh arrivals, shouts in the darkness, and oaths of every description. It was the remains of the regiment which had been marched round by Sainte-Menehould, from which they had just come.

"We've done twenty-five miles since this morning," they cried. "We're damn well done up.... We've not had a bite to eat.... What a game, sending a lot of poor bastards here who've done twenty-five miles, when there's nowhere to put 'em!"

Nor was that the end of their complainings:

"They wouldn't have us at Evres.... They sent us on because they said there wasn't room. 'You'll find plenty at Beauzée,' they said. What a hope! The dirty swine! There was a damn sight more room there, and not just heaps of stones either! And five miles less foot slogging.... Well, now we're here, here we stay!"

In this way passed two hours of recriminations and argument and blackguarding between the men and between the N.C.O.'s, in the darkness and the snow, before it was found possible to give them all the little corners of ruined shelter to which they thought themselves entitled.

Contrary to expectation, the 7th was a day of rest. On the 8th they were on the move again early. But this time they found themselves more or less retracing their steps. Instead of continuing towards the south-east or east, as the previous day's march had led them to expect, they marched off once more down the valley of the Aire, which here made a bend in a north-westerly direction preparatory to skirting the Argonne forest some miles farther on. The only explanation was that they were to join up at some cross-roads with the rest of the regiment moving from Evres in a straight line, which had avoided the detour by Beauzée. For Beauzée-the-Ruin had been just that—a detour. Beauzée-of-the-Black-Beams

was not on the route laid down. The staff must have planned
that Beauzée detour as a holiday excursion for certain specially selected companies, since the pretext of billeting men
there on a winter's night was nothing but a bad joke.

The anticipated concentration was effected, as things
turned out, near Nubécourt. The regiment, now at full
strength, marched down the Aire as far as Fleury, where it
turned right, crossed the river, and, making a wide curve,
climbed laboriously to the line of heights separating the Aire
from the Couzances not many miles from the head waters of
the latter.

If they were really on their way to Verdun, it looked as
though they would cross the Couzances at Ippécourt, continue straight ahead by the same road to Vadelaincourt, whence,
possibly by the direct route but more probably after several
detours, they would join the main highway from Bar-le-Duc
to Verdun. That at least was what Jerphanion and Fabre supposed after studying the map. They knew nothing about General Order No. 15, and, in their ignorance, it never occurred
to them to imagine the degree of chaos to which this sole
artery feeding the battle front could be reduced without having to absorb as well the sluggish stream of a slow-moving
column of infantry. They found it easier to blame the ineffi-
ciency or heartlessness of the staff, which, having to move
troops "to the sound of the guns," amused itself with sending
them zigzagging over the countryside like balls in a game of
croquet.

The sky, heavy with snow, looked threatening. The earth,
mixed with snow and trodden by thousands of feet, had the
texture of icy mud.

They halted for the night at the two adjacent villages of
Ville-sur-Couzances and Jubécourt. The accommodation was
far from grand. But there were a certain number of houses
still standing with their roofs almost intact, as well as a few
entries to stables and barns. That evening, at an inn table at
Ville-sur-Couzances, where they were billeted, reading their
map by the light of an oil lamp, Jerphanion and Fabre spent
a good half-hour convincing themselves that since leaving

Triaucourt they had covered just about twice the distance
necessary.

Again and again they repeated:

"And that, ladies and gentlemen, is what is known as
marching to the sound of the guns."

Whereupon Fabre, using the floor of the inn parlour as a
stage, improvised what he called a "strategic ballet" to be
called "Marching to the Sound of the Guns." The dancer, his
head and body strained forward, listening intently with his
hand curled about his ear, at first hesitating, then giving signs
that he was at last convinced—in short, making use of various appropriate gestures—indicated to the audience the precise direction from which the sound of the guns was coming.
Sure on that point, he straightened up, thrust out his chest,
frowned, assumed a bullying air, and set off resolutely in a
totally different direction. Then he halted, listened once more,
and started the same manœuvre all over again. "Jerphat,"
drumming with his knuckles on the table, provided the sound
of the guns as called for.

Second Lieutenant Cotin, who was present at this display—
though nobody seemed particularly anxious to have him there
—and whose mental ingenuity seemed quite equal to dealing
with such minor matters, declared, between two figures of the
ballet, that though it wasn't easy to understand the apparent
irresponsibilities of their route, there quite obviously must
have been some reason for them, but that the men, unable to
guess what that reason was, would be only too likely to see in
what had happened the evidence of "counterorders and confusion," with the result that their morale would suffer.

"Though of course," he added almost in the same breath, as
though to check his downward course towards "an infringement of discipline," "the men haven't got any maps, and are
less in a position than we are to know the truth."

Chapter Fourteen

The Jostling Confusion of the Road.
The March Down to Verdun in Flames

At dawn on the 9th the officers of the company were informed, through the regular official channels, that orders had been received "to make Verdun."

Jerphanion and Fabre burst into a spontaneous guffaw and then, after due consideration, decided that such a statement called for "a thirty seconds' burst of continuous laughter."

Well, well, they'd been told they were going to Verdun. What a piece of news! Who would ever have suspected it?...And we thought we were off partridge-shooting! A bit hard though, springing a thing like that on a chap!...Why, to be sure, to be sure, of course, and oh yes...but surely there must be something more in all this than met the eye....

The thirty seconds of continuous laughter was followed by at least thirty minutes of facetious comment, in the course of which they acted the part of various listeners—the country bumpkin who knew nothing about anything, the cunning peasant who wasn't at all taken in, the distinguished gentleman of patent good faith who was really surprised, bless my soul, yes, at such goings on.

They heard a little later that the colonel, the senior officers, and the commanders of the machine-gun companies had gone on ahead "to reconnoitre the sector."

"Ah, things are warming up," they agreed, "warming up with a vengeance. There are indications that the orchestra is getting ready for the finale of the strategic ballet."

It was well that they laughed when they did. The rest of the day put them out of the joking mood. In the experience of both, it was one of those days, rarely seen in such perfection, when war seemed intent, before flinging them into its ulti-

mate horrors, on displaying for their benefit its lesser, its secondary, abominations; on showing them that in addition to its
power of destruction on the grand scale, which could at least
produce a sort of intoxication of terror, it had in its gallery of
"effects" a power of squalidly degrading everything that the
civilization of mankind had created, a power that the human
spirit seems capable of noting with a sort of calm and scorn-
ful reaction. War, in such circumstances, seemed bent on taking the spectator into the sordid wings, the back-stage of the
show; bare of any and all illusion. This side of war was like the
squalid suburbs of some great city, which are never shown to
visitors; a world of filthy alleys, of shoddy plaster workshops,
of rag-pickers' huts, and swarming children with dirty legs
and unwashed faces. War's sordid slum.

The snow fell unceasingly: medium-sized flakes, half frozen,
which the north-east wind, bitter enough in itself, sent flur-
rying into one's eyes, down one's throat, and into the collar
and sleeves of one's coat. The back road on which they set
out, leading from Ville-sur-Couzances to Rampont, was
soggy and broken. The one from Rampont to the main highway was not much better. With considerable difficulty it was
just possible to move about as fast as a village funeral party.

The highway from Sainte-Menehould, to which they would
have to keep from now on until Verdun was reached, presented itself to the view from the very first moment as a struggling
mass of vehicles and pedestrians, and the idea of fitting into all
this chaos the kilometre-long column of a regiment with all
its transport was the kind of thing that had its place in a nightmare. Closer examination showed that the general confusion
was divisible into two streams, each being drawn in a different
direction. But these two crawling agglomerations were continually becoming engaged, so that they got in one another's
way and held up all movement. The vehicles were of all
descriptions; a motor trying to pass a horse-carriage would
find itself face to face with another motor coming the opposite way. No sooner were there signs of a gap than it would be
hurriedly filled by a hand-cart and its escort of sheep. There
were blocks every twenty yards. In spite of the slow rate of

movement, there was a sense of panic in all this jostling crowd, of helplessness, and even of absurdity. It was impossible to believe that any of these people or any of these vehicles knew where they were going. There was a general impression abroad that had some divine intervention suddenly endowed them with fluidity and complete freedom of movement, they would just have gone straight ahead and then after a while turned and retraced their steps at precisely the same speed, and so on for ever, just like those ridiculous armies of ants that can be seen coming and going eternally over the same strip of ground, feverishly collecting heavy grains of sand and then leaving them an inch or two farther on, giving every sign, in short, of a purposeless fussiness without any other result than to pro- voke the admiration of some second-rate savant with an ingenious mind and a brain that never rises above the unim- portant. Perhaps if some long-sighted God with a hopeful out- look had actually been leaning forward that day to contemplate National Road No.3, he would have been touched by the sight of so much marvellous activity.

Those more nearly involved felt themselves less prone to admiration. The mile-long column took a whole hour to force its way into this choked drain, and having done so, its component parts realized that they had merely succeeded in slowing down still further the general rate of progress, and that the whole crawling conglomeration resembled nothing so much as a centipede caught on a sticky surface.

The details of the scene were far from cheering. The road was filled higgledy-piggledy by those engaged in carrying on the war and those intent on fleeing it. All soldiers look alike, and the fugitives here had precisely the same appearance as those that the troops had passed at any time during these last days on the back roads of the southern Argonne. There was very little observable difference between the hand-carts and the wheelbarrows and the old folk with their anguished faces, the tumble of rags and bedding with which they were sur- rounded, the disorderly crowd of animals that they drove before them. (How was it that these cows and goats and sheep had not strayed? In the midst of so much calamity and confusion what nerve-racked sense of home was it, what identifiable smell of their own people even on the move, that kept them attached to one stream of struggling humanity rather than another?)

Certain inexplicable features heightened the absurd resemblance to ants on the march. Most of the fugitives were coming from the direction of Verdun and seemed to be trying to make their way towards Sainte-Menehould, which appeared reasonable enough, even though their future might be wrapped in mystery. But there were others who stood aside in the right-hand ditch to let the troops go by, and these seemed to be coming from Sainte-Menehould and to be making for safety in the neighbourhood of Verdun. The sight of them was so extraordinary that the soldiers, fully occupied though they might be with their own miseries, could not refrain from shouting questions at them:

"Where are you from?"

Some replied:

"Dombasle."

Others:

"Récicourt."

"Jouy."

It needed but a moment's thought to realize that Dombasle, Récicourt, Jouy, and the places round must have come within range of the German guns since the battle began. The truth of this was brought home to the questioners by the occasional burst of heavy shelling from time to time in their rear and over towards the left. But why, then, hadn't they made for the west? If there was some reason why they shouldn't, why was it that the other stream was doing precisely that?

The progress of the column was checked so frequently that Jerphanion had time to have quite a long conversation with these groups of fugitives. He gathered that their object was to reach Nixéville by a side road which left the highway some way farther on, to the right; that they were expected there, and would be given one or two nights' shelter, but that they had no idea what would happen to them afterwards.

"If it comes to that," he reflected, "we're all in much the

same boat. They may be fleeing from the sound of the guns instead of marching to it, but the rate of movement is about the same."

A little later, he managed to walk for a bit alongside Griollet, who was the outside man of a file. Ever since they had left Beauzée, Griollet had seemed gloomy and bitter, an unusual state of affairs with him. "Has he got any particular complaint?" wondered Jerphanion, "or is it just that the general atmosphere has got him down?" He attached considerable importance to the man's reactions. He thought him a sensible, solid sort of fellow. Griollet was not subject to moods. He never assumed a jollity that he did not feel, nor, on the other hand, did he suffer from the blues. His view of life was sane and tolerant. He had few illusions and was not often caught off his guard. A demoralized Griollet, therefore, was an indication that all was not well. Jerphanion took a serious view of the case. Besides, he felt a deep sympathy for this man with the keen, honest eyes. "He really is a fine chap," he used to reflect. "With a little luck and a bit more education he would make one of what is usually called the élite. He would do honour to any profession." He felt that this liking of his was returned. Consequently he would have been by no means unaffected by even a personal sorrow of Griollet's. "If I was in trouble, he'd notice it, and show me that he noticed it with the good manners that are natural to him. Humanly speaking, he's a more reliable and solid friend than a 'good sort' like Fabre." The idea that the man might be suffering from some private trouble, some overwhelming sorrow, was not altogether to be scouted. The morning of their departure from Beauzée there had been a distribution of letters. The part of the regiment which had come by Sainte-Menehould had brought several sacks of mail with them. "He's too reserved, too conscious of what is and is not done, to speak first, especially in the present circumstances. On the other hand, I don't altogether see myself saying, as some might do: 'What's up, Griollet?' The best thing'll be to start chatting just casually about the weather, or something like that."

"A bit rotten to see all that going on after so many months

of war." Jerphanion pointed to one of the groups of fugitives. "One had hoped that that sort of thing at least was over and done with."

"Yes…" replied Griollet in a dull voice.

"You don't seem much affected by it."

"Oh well, sir, these civilians, you know…"

Jerphanion managed to raise a laugh.

"What on earth do you mean? I didn't know you had it in for civilians as badly as all that! Especially for these poor devils."

"They're all the same, sir."

"Why, you're talking like any old veteran who's spent most of his life on foreign service. It can't be so long since you were a civilian yourself, and I hope you'll be one again soon."

"Oh, I don't mean to say I'm not sorry to see them going through it, but don't forget, sir, the way they did us in in the villages behind the line—not these, perhaps, but others just like 'em. Think of how they cheated us over wine and food."

Jerphanion was surprised, not so much that such grievances should exist—there never was a time when soldiers didn't have a grievance of some sort—but that a man like Griollet should give expression to them, and in a tone of such bitterness.

"But you can't deny," he said, "that they made us pretty welcome these last few days."

"I'm not denying it, sir. They'd been told that the Boches were coming again to loot and burn their villages, they knew they couldn't do much to stop them, and they suddenly remembered that we might be of more value to them as soldiers than as a lot of fools from whom they could get a couple of francs for a bottle of wine that was worth eight sous. I've no use for all their cheering and waving, sir. I suppose you'll say the circumstances are unusual…but to me it's just as though they were saying: 'Run along, boys, and get killed good and quick; the quicker the better. Can't you see that all these offensives spoil our night's rest? Life's not worth living like this. Hurry up and do something about it!' There's a sort of implication in it all that gets me on the raw, a sort of

'What's it matter if you do get killed? It's your job, after all. That's what you're there for, and it's pretty decent of us to thank you in advance like this.'"

"A day or two ago, in one of those villages—I forget the name—when they all turned out to give us a welcome, I saw you grinning all over your face. You certainly didn't look as though you were taking it all so tragically."

Griollet said nothing for a moment or two, but looked at his feet. Then:

"One thinks about that sort of thing afterwards," he said.

The column had just started moving forward again after a short halt caused by some blockage. Jerphanion still kept beside Griollet, though he left him to his thoughts.

It was Griollet who reopened the conversation:

"I don't want you to think I'm the sort of chap who gets all worked up, sir. I've thought about this a good deal, but it's not the kind of thing one likes dwelling on, is it, sir? I mean, there's quite enough to depress one as it is. No good looking for trouble....Soldiers are there to be sacrificed, and when I say soldiers, sir, I mean you just as much as us....I'm not a fool. You're a soldier just like the rest of us; so you're a sacrifice too."

The quiet melancholy of his voice, the absence of all cheap emotionalism, was more moving, more unusual even, than the actual words he used. Jerphanion listened without interrupting, nodding his head in sympathetic understanding, intent only on finding out what lay behind the man's bitterness.

Griollet continued:

"And there's another thing. Most of the people behind the lines, women and men alike, don't want the war to finish. They pretend to be sorry for us, to admire us. The papers treat us like pocket heroes. But they don't want to see us come back....We should be too much of a damned nuisance."

Jerphanion thought of his wife, venturing to ask himself: "How far, even though she may not realize it, does her mind work like that?" Obviously she had been quite genuinely delighted to see him, but he remembered thinking then that she was getting a little too used to living alone, a little too comfortably installed in her grass-widowhood, a little too much caught up again by old family ties.

Griollet said:

"Don't tell me that if everyone in the world really wanted to stop the business, they couldn't do it. It's the same with the Boches as with us; I expect their people at home make just as much fuss about the poor lads at the front, and groan about the horrible war, and the rest of it…but I don't expect the Boche women eat any the less heartily for all that, or try to keep the shirkers from pinching their backsides.…What gets my goat worst of all is reading in the papers of all these fellows who spout a lot of nonsense about how brave the women are! It's enough to make you sick. Brave little women! God in heaven! Some of them may be, I don't know, but the general run of 'em! Look here, sir, what's all this bravery amount to? Just to letting their men go, and saying to themselves 'It'll be good for his health, and his character too…and I shall be rid of him for a while, thank the Lord! It'll be all the nicer to see him when he does come back.…' I'm not referring to the bitches who think: 'Fine—if only my lover doesn't have to go too.…It's bad enough to lose one.…' You'll never make me understand, sir, why it was, when they mobilized us, that none of these women lay down on the railway tracks and cried: 'If you take our sons and husbands it'll be only over our dead bodies!' I know I can talk to you like this, sir; you take it the right way. It's not that I'm an anti-militarist…what I think about all that's quite another question.…I'm not arguing that the men ought to have refused to go…that's entirely different. I don't even mind admitting that the men ought to have said to their women: 'Shut up, it's our duty,' and explained the whole business to them. But you can't make me believe that these women are bursting with patriotism, or that they can't sleep for thinking about foreign affairs. If it comes to that, they just don't know what it's all about.…Brave little women, my eye!"

"Wouldn't you make an exception in the case of mothers?" said Jerphanion, not without a secret blush for the conventional flatness of his words.

"There may be some, sir; I don't say there aren't. But I could tell you cases of countrywomen—and I'm pretty sure it's not just talk either—who'd no sooner been told, with all the usual tact of course, that their son had been killed than they were off to some friend of theirs who'd been in the same fix, to find out all about the pension and whether they'd have to go through a lot of formalities before getting it....Same thing with all the nurses....Two or three out of every ten may be doing the job from a sense of devotion or because they're religious. All right, I respect them. But the rest! You've been in hospital, sir, and you know what I say is right....Most of 'em are there because they like flirting with the officers, or because they think they may pick up a husband, even if he is a limb short. That doesn't matter so long as he's got his pension, and it's no bad thing, come to that, to have a husband with a limb short—it's not so easy for him to keep an eye on what his wife's doing....Or perhaps it's just that they want the publicity: 'Miss So-and-so, who is devoting herself night and day to our dear wounded boys....' "

"But look here, Griollet: if one goes prying into motives one's almost bound to come on that sort of thing; but that's no reason for being unfair. When we're wounded we're glad enough to have nurses looking after us. They're a good deal less rough than those damned military orderlies who always look as though they're saying: 'You ought to think yourself lucky to be here.' When I was in hospital it was often a treat just to see a smiling nurse come into the ward. I didn't bother my head about whether she got mauled by convalescent officers in odd corners. She did things for me which were always difficult, and which she must often have found disgusting, and she smiled, even though I didn't maul her in a corner....You're feeling bitter about women in general, isn't that the trouble?"

Griollet showed signs of embarrassment.

"Oh, not specially," he said, "not specially. It's just that I'm getting fed up with all these people behind the lines...and, when all's said and done, there happen to be more women than men....But don't run away with the idea that I've got

any very kind feelings for the men who've been drafted for
work in the factories. I know too many of 'em personally...I
met a lot on my last leave, the fat, shining swine! Some of 'em
get as much as fifty francs a day....They take their apéritif and
they read their papers—that's about the only way they have
of knowing what's going on at the front....And they sit down
to roast chicken on Sundays. They go to the movies with the
girls who are working with them in the factories, or with
others who are conductors on the street-cars...."

"Well, but we've got to have them, haven't we?...We make
enough fuss about being short of shells and material..."

"Yes...but what I'd like to know, sir, is why they aren't mobilized like us, and getting five sous a day instead of high
wages and bonuses and God knows what besides. Aren't they
lucky enough as it is to be turning out shells and not having
'em plumped on their heads?..."

"Oh, I'm with you there, all right. But it's the big employers who are responsible. The big employers know perfectly
well that high wages mean big profits....The day that the
workers are made to do their job for nothing...for the good
of the country... it may occur to the government to force the
employers to do the same...."

Griollet smiled for the first time that day. For a minute or
so he contemplated with delight the vision of pure justice
which his lieutenant's words had conjured up. His eyes, as he
glanced at Jerphanion, expressed a warm friendship. "In a
world as beastly as this is," he seemed to be saying, "it's something to have as one's officer a man to whom one can talk and
who can discuss justice instead of merely jollying one."

He went on, dropping his voice slightly, but without the
slightest hesitation:

"All that I've been saying, sir, isn't really my chief grievance
against these fellows in the factories...no....You see, they've
betrayed us..."

"Betrayed?..."

"Yes. I was never what you'd call a militant, but I always
took an interest in politics, and went to meetings. I've heard
everything there is to be heard against war, and about what

the working class would or would not do if war came....Well, and what has the working class done? Just demanded not to be called up and put in a claim for high wages. Their chums in the trenches can take it in the neck till the cows come home for all they care....I'm through with them, sir, I can tell you...and their damned Socialist ministers...."

"And with women, eh?" put in Jerphanion, in an attempt to make Griollet smile again.

But all he got for his pains was a grimace that might have meant anything.

Jerphanion shot a covert glance at the thin face that he could see only in profile. There was little beneath the helmet to recall the leather-worker, or the Parisian of thirty or thirty-five. All that remained was just a depressed soldier of indeterminate age—the military age—no sturdier than he had been before, but with a sort of acquired gift of resistance, as though both morally and physically he had been tanned to the colour of a red Indian. The impression he got was of a legionnaire, in two senses of the word: a legionnaire of the Roman Army, and a legionnaire of the African desert. A man fined down to the essentials. (Jerphanion recalled something that Fabre had told him one evening in Champagne, about the men from the occupied areas.)

Griollet had a two days' growth of beard (he must have had his last shave at Beauzée); his moustache was clipped short in the fashion that was becoming popular at the front. He shuffled his feet through the snow with a sort of lithe grace and a calculated economy of effort that increased his resemblance to a soldier of some army of the ancient world. "A wonderful fellow," thought Jerphanion; "just the kind I should like to have in my Meygal band....Two or three more years, a few more roots torn up—I'm pretty sure there's been a good deal of tearing up already, within him and without—I've never seen him like this, and there'll be more to come—and he'll be just one of my band, just a good companion."

The column was making slower and slower progress. The halts now lasted for as much as a quarter of an hour, during which the men had to stand with their feet freezing in a churned mixture of mud and snow. No actual snow had been falling for some time, but the sky was still heavy with it, and it lay thick on the tops, the hoods, and the bumpers of the trucks. Patches of it still remained on the shoulders and packs of the men, and in the creases of their haversacks. It was getting dark, though according to clock time the sun could scarcely be below the horizon. In this snow-packed twilight the sound of the motors turning over in the motionless trucks gave to the landscape a quality of stuttering anger, like that of a very old man mumbling the words he cannot utter. But from time to time one of the two lines of traffic would suddenly move on for a dozen yards or so. The air would be filled with the sudden grinding of clutches let in, the sound passing from truck to truck above the heads of the men and the wagons, or actually through them as through some transparent medium. The rapidity of these jerky movements was in dramatic contrast to the general crawl. It was the only thing in all that countryside in the least resembling agility. But the oddest feature about it was the noise, which seemed to split the scene of snow and dusk like some endless cackle of laughter. At such times the bursting of the distant shells became inaudible.

It struck to the roots of the human spirit like the shuddering of a menaced world; in the walking misery of human bodies it became identified with the icy weight of feet in heavy boots soaked with muddy snow, with the perpetual shivering of necks in contact with wet coat collars, with the chilly twitching of wrists at the touch of sodden cuffs, with the gloomy thoughts that came in fits and starts to torment the mind.

Just before it reached the big cross-roads, the head of the column came up against a cordon of police with outstretched arms.

"Turn left!" they cried. "Turn left! Take the narrow road. Get a move on, there! Get a move on!"

The narrow road was a morass. After a few steps the men felt as though the weight of their boots had been doubled. But it was such a relief not to have their legs jarred every few minutes by sudden halts that their first feeling was one of delight at having left the highway.

After three quarters of an hour of splashing and slithering, they turned up a lane to the right which led between the fort of Sartelles and the wood of the same name. It was now pitch dark. They could plainly see the burst of the big shells falling on the high ground which closed the view to the north and north-east.

And now a new ordeal began. The lane traversed a number of valleys and ravines, going straight across the intervening ridges, climbing, falling, climbing again. The leading company, which should have acted as guide as far as Verdun, marched, without thinking about anybody else, at a pace determined by the rise and fall of the ground, very slowly uphill because the men were dropping with fatigue, very fast downhill, because they found it easy to let themselves slide and make up for lost time. The company next behind, fearful of losing the way in the darkness, did all it could to keep touch, but more often than not it was going up while the one in front was going down. This meant that the men had to take the hill more or less at racing speed, loaded down though they were with equipment; on the other hand, just when they ought to have been taking advantage of the descent to have a bit of a rest, they had to check their pace, and even occasionally to halt altogether, because the leading files were bumping into the rear of the company ahead, which was taking its time about negotiating the next rise.

The jerkiness of the rhythm could not but become accentuated as it was transmitted from company to company, until finally it became so fantastic as to be quite incomprehensible. The wretched men of the 3rd battalion—to which Jerphanion belonged—got the impression that they had been compelled to join a party of lunatics in a game which consisted in running full tilt uphill and down dale, in an attempt to keep up with a lot of fellows who were always on the point of vanishing in the darkness, and then coming up against them all of a sudden and being brought to a standstill, while their own men piled up on them from behind. Even the officers gave vent to angry oaths. Cotin's "bicycle horn" voice could be heard more than once saying:

"It's shameful. The officer in charge of the leading company's just playing the fool!"

After climbing for a long time the flank of a hill on the top of which there seemed to be some sort of fort, and just before reaching the crest, they could see the men of the company ahead silhouetted against the sky, and now and then these human outlines became very distinct. The sky itself, which had been getting redder and redder the closer they approached to Verdun, seemed now to be pulsating with an irregular rhythm, the glare alternating between pink and a vivid scarlet, as though gusts of light were continually coming and going just beyond the horizon.

On arriving at the crest they were presented with a sight such as many of them, for all their eighteen months of war, had never seen.

The whole city was in flames. It was not burning as a uniform mass, but in patches, ten, twenty, thirty different conflagrations each contributing to the whole effect. Some of them were small, round, and concentrated like an eye. Others flung into the sky banners of flame and smoke which eddied in the wind. Others again, spluttering and crackling, filled the air all round with flakes of fire and blazing sparks which described dissolving figures of suns and crowns. All were bound into a unity by a thick, reddish, greasy smoke that continually turned back on itself with a snake-like movement and now and again was dispersed by explosions. Sometimes this pall showed a sudden local swelling, opening like a flower to reveal yet another nucleus of flame. It was difficult not to think of the huge Bengal lights seen in old days on gala nights, diversified with rockets and bursting fireworks. But this Bengal light had a curious feature all its own: the rockets, instead of shooting upwards from its smoky maw, seemed to come from the sky above, nosing their way down into the thick glow to burst in its midst.

The men, even in the act of letting themselves begin to slide down the long slope, bracing their muscles against the weight of their packs, which pulled them backwards, trying hard to get a purchase for their feet on the solid earth beneath its covering of muddy snow, kept their eyes fixed upon Verdun in flames. They thought of many things—some common to them all, or almost so, some private to the thinker, and not a few marked by a certain strangeness.

But one thought there was that was silently present in every mind:

"And now what? Are we going down into that? Do they want to make us march through that? Perhaps even spend the night there? For it's after nine now and they can't mean to keep us going till past midnight. Spend the night there? Damned pleasant, that!

"Of course soldiers are used to dossing down in impossible places, like trenches under a barrage of 150's or 210's—and when it comes to real discomfort, the 210 has it every time! But if one's in the line, well, one's in the line. If we're going into Verdun tonight, we're going there to be billeted, and to be billeted in the middle of burning houses, at the risk of being suffocated with the smoke, and with a pretty good chance of being burned alive if one does get to sleep—that's just a bit more than a joke! Shelling's awful, but it's all in the day's work. Flames, to be done to death by flames, is more frightening than anything, more frightening even than being buried. The Boches know that perfectly well. That's why they invented flame-throwers."

There was another thought, too, almost as general:

"It's rather fun to look at, pretty, too, in its way. One doesn't often have a chance of seeing a thing like that—all these reflections on the snow, and the hills turned pink as far as one can see. Not a particularly depressing sight—rather fairy-like, really. The Boches are lucky to be able to stage a show like that at somebody else's expense. Wonder whether they can see it from their side."

The men from the occupied regions of the north—there had been a good many of them for some time now in the 151st—though they could not altogether refrain from admiring the sight, took it more seriously than the others. They thought of their own cities and villages and of what they'd been told had happened to them. They knew that not all of them had gone up in flames like this Verdun glowing down there in its circle of pink-stained hills; but they knew too that hardly any of them had been wholly spared. Their hearts were torn at the sight of all these houses burning away with everything they contained of furniture and of the savings of a lifetime. They were less inclined than their comrades to think resignedly: "Oh well, it's just the war." Instead, they clenched their fists and muttered to themselves: "This is the Boches' work!" They'd have liked to have a few Boches at their mercy now, a few of those Boches who, perhaps at this very moment, were making love to their wives and sisters in some billeting area away behind the lines, taking the pails which the women had just filled at the pump, with a "Don't you do that, madame, don't you do that, kid; let me." They'd have liked to be standing on a hill like this, on just such an evening, watching a Boche city blazing away in the darkness.

As for the men from Reims and the district round (there were a great many of them too, and they felt more at home than anybody in this particular regiment), they wanted to say to their pals: "Nothing to get excited about in this. Suppose you'd arrived at Reims after dark when the Boche shells had set fire to the cathedral and throughout the town, you'd have seen something to surprise you then, I warrant!"

But there was another feeling which none of these men could have found words to express, of which few even were conscious in the secret fastness of their hearts. But if some poet, marching with them in the ranks, pack on back and feet slithering in the snow, had given utterance to the fact of their miserable lives, had cried aloud: "Don't worry, lads, let the place burn, and everything with it. The whole world's got to go up like that. We're in for it, all right, we know that; *our* number's up, tomorrow or later, it's merely a question of when. But their blasted world's in for it too. Never let it be said that we're going to give the earth a bigger feast of rotting corpses than it's ever had before, and that when the business is all over, things'll go on just as though nothing had happened. To the bitter end, as they say! Just so. While there's a wall and a roof standing there'll be work for the shells to do. If the *Feldgrauen* were decent fellows, real comrades in misfortune, and not merely, as they are, receptacles for sausage meat and kicks in the pants, they'd retire into Bocheland and give us a chance of cleaning things up while they looked on for a change," the men might have said, half scandalized, half laughing: "The old chap's exaggerating, he's going it a bit strong!…" but deep down in their hearts they would have felt that they had been avenged.

However, they continued on their way down towards the patchy furnace of Verdun, and as the time wore on—moving considerably faster than their feet—they became more and more convinced that they were to be put to spend the night somewhere within its boundaries. They did, therefore, what they had long learned to do: forced themselves to believe that they were going to remain alive in a place where remaining alive was a sheer impossibility. Just as they did in the fury of a bombardment or in the terror of an assault, they tried to find a foothold for life where no life could be. Slithering down the snow-clad slope, buffeted from side to side by fatigue and the weight of their equipment, they said to themselves as they watched the red smoke above Verdun: "No good painting things blacker than they are. Up there on the hill one didn't see things straight. It's not all burning, not by a long shot. One's only got to look to see that. There are a lot of fires fairly close to each other, but there are whole blocks of buildings, solid chunks of houses, looking quite dark and peaceful. Same with the shells. They're big, of course, and they do a lot of damage, but they aren't falling as thick as all that. Parts of the town are quite peaceful. There are plenty of snug little corners still."

They were quartered in a wing of the Sainte-Catherine Hospital that had remained almost intact, between the Meuse and the Saint-Airy Canal. The neighbouring buildings had been hit by two or three shells since the battle started, but they were still standing and were not in flames. It was hardly what could have been called a "snug little corner," but it might have been a great deal worse.

Nevertheless, the human brain remained active. Even extreme fatigue failed to bring longed-for sleep. Quite a lot of shells could be heard. Through the shattered windows was blown a smell of burning, and even a quantity of fine ash. The mind lacked vitality to put aside the perfectly obvious thought that the Hospital of Sainte-Catherine might at any moment be hit by a shell as other near-by buildings had been, and burst into flame. The possibility was the easier to imagine, and sleep thereby kept hatefully at bay, because on their way there the men had passed through more than one street where the imagined catastrophe had in fact occurred: house fronts torn away; blackened debris of chairs, tables, wardrobes, and kitchen furniture vomited but a short time back into the roadway; here and there, a single smoking beam looking like a perch in an abandoned cage.

Jerphanion tried several of his "dreams of security," but not one of them succeeded in fulfilling its task. The worst feature of all was the complete absence of quiet. With the best will in the world it was difficult to argue that the sound of bursting shells all around was negligible. At last—it might have been about two o'clock in the morning—there was a short pause in the bombardment. Jerphanion took advantage of it to achieve a piece of mental acrobatics which was more difficult than might appear, but extremely cunning. With every ounce of concentration that he could muster, he imagined himself to be in Verdun (which gave verisimilitude to his fantasy), but inside the Citadel, in one of those deep casemates, to which no shell could penetrate, in which no fire need be feared— places which he had never seen, but of which he had heard tell. He took the precaution of admitting that the silence of the casemate where he lay asleep so snugly ensconced was not incompatible with certain heavy detonations from somewhere near by, but these he knew to be caused not by the burst of enemy shells, but by the discharge of the heavy artillery with which the Citadel was armed.

CHAPTER FIFTEEN

The Way up to Haudromont.
War Nocturne

The last stage—going up the line and entering the very heart of the battle—did not take place until the following evening. The detachment to which both Jerphanion's company and Fabre's belonged started after nightfall. Each company, luckily, had been provided with a guide, so that it was spared the necessity of keeping touch with the formation next ahead.

Jerphanion and Fabre had been told in the course of the day:

'You're going to Haudromont ravine. Both companies will be in support south of the road."

Their informant added that they would even be given a sketch plan (to share between them). Before moving off they took a look at the map—not a very careful look. Haudromont or elsewhere, what did it matter? They thanked their stars that they hadn't had to go up during the morning to reconnoitre the sector, which would have been a poor way of resting after the hell of a time they had been through the day before.

They could find nothing marked as Haudromont ravine on their map. But between Douaumont on the east and the Côte du Poivre on the west they did succeed in finding a certain Haudromont Farm, situated on rising ground close to Hill 325, with, on either side of it, two ravines forming a fork, with a track shown as running up each of them. The phrase: "You will be south of the road," led them to suppose that the right-hand track was the one that was meant, leading towards the Ravin de la Dame and Douaumont. The left-hand one led in a slightly more northerly direction and consequently had no southern flank.

They were given a scrap of paper with the promised sketch plan. This looked like a picture of a three or four-pronged root with its offshoots very vaguely indicated. The two most heavily marked lines indicated the two tracks. Their company numbers were pencilled in to the south of the right-hand one, which appeared as the Bras à Douaumont.

That, then, was where the front was, for the moment at least, the point in this particular sector to which the attack on Verdun had been pressed. It was more or less in accordance with what they had learned already. Rumour had not lied.

As soon as they had left the suburbs of Verdun behind them and taken the track which climbed to the front, they got a distinct feeling of being within the area of attraction of that battle, already famous, towards which they had been marching for the last fortnight. Verdun with its shells and its burning houses had been no more than an uncomfortable stage in their journey. Here, at last, they were in the zone of fire.

The moon, drowned in a mass of cloud, shed a watery light. But what there was was reflected from the surrounding snow. The light of flares, sometimes from very far off, slipped across the snow with a quick, silky touch.

They could see well enough, perhaps too well. The neighbourhood of the path, at times the path itself, was littered with debris: battered helmets, broken rifles, rags of clothing, mess-tins, wrecked limbers lying on their side with their wheels missing, ammunition wagons, their noses stuck in the earth, looking as though they had been hacked to pieces with axes.

An enveloping, nauseating smell which they had begun to notice all around them and had at first sniffed almost absent-mindedly could now be traced to its point of origin. Carcasses of horses, scattered at irregular intervals, lay along the track at some little distance from it. One was full in their path. They had to make their way round it. The stink was frightful. It was as though they had been forced to swim in a liquid mass of corruption.

They passed files of stretcher-bearers coming down from

the line with dead and wounded. Some of the latter were as silent as though they too had been dead. Others uttered faint groans at each jolt, the sound seeming to come from the springs of some contraption rather than from human beings. Shells were falling. These, apparently, were aimed at registered targets, or were at least being fired on predetermined lines. One of these seemed to be set at an acute angle with the general direction of the track, so that at one point it actually cut it, and only diverged from it very gradually.

The men of the company marched two abreast, with very little distance between files, and scarcely any at all between sections, with the result that the moving body was very vulnerable. In addition to this, the snow and moonlight would have made it very easy for an enemy aviator to spot them. Jerphanion said as much to his guide. The man answered that they still had a long way to go, and that moving in separated groups would check their pace as well as the pace of the formations in the rear. As to aeroplanes, there weren't often many about at night. Besides, marching in fours wouldn't make them any less visible.

"This track," he added with a laugh, "is pretty well spotted; and the Boches know it's used continually. If they want to get it, they don't have to bother about aeroplanes."

The farther they went, the more frequent became the shell-holes in their path. Other shell-holes dotted the plain to right and left; some of them, quite fresh, had not yet been sprinkled with snow. A few were as large as mine craters.

The journey seemed interminable, climbing and descending all the time. Most of it lay along the sides of valleys, at the far end of which gun-flashes were visible or the slow blossoming of flares, sometimes of the red lights sent up by the enemy to mask the discharge of their guns. Then the path would twist and turn about brush-covered hills and bare uplands, coming out eventually on some ridge of high ground from which suddenly they would get a wide-spreading view westwards of the whole valley of the Meuse with its burning villages. Everywhere the onward march was impeded by the difficulties of the ground, but even so, knowing the relative

position of all these places on the map, it was difficult to
understand how it could be that after four hours' going, after
five, the end of the journey had not yet been reached.

"Are you sure we've not gone wrong?" asked Jerphanion of
the guide.

"Oh no, sir, trust me for that. I know the way like the back
of my hand. It's not dark enough even to make one have any
doubts. The ravine we're in now leads down from Hill 321.
On the other side's the Ravin de la Dame, which you've
probably heard of. We've got to get on the far side of the ridge
you see in front, and then we're there."

"How long do you reckon it'll take?"

"About an hour more."

"God!"

"It's a long trek at any time, and it's often made a sight
longer by fresh shell-holes and the extra amount of stuff one's
liable to find lying about."

Since leaving the track they had originally taken for one
subsidiary path after another, they had come across considerably less traffic. How odd it had been—when one could shake
off one's weariness enough to think over what had passed
before one's eyes—that movement of ghosts, many of them so
much blood-stained baggage, across the snow, through the
woods and valleys, under a diffused and ghostlike radiance: a
veiled and waning moon, flickering will-o'-the-wisps, falling
stars, and signs and portents in the heavens. A true setting this
for processions in the darkness and crimes at dead of night,
for secret plottings of a massacre, for the coming and going of
wizards and witches on their way to some great meeting in
the forest; a little, too, for the vigil and the orgy in the dawn
of the Last Day. This war was a thing of glooms and shadows,
own brother to Walpurgis Night and the witches' Sabbath.

"We must go in single file here," said the guide: "This is
where the communication trench begins."

"I don't see it."

"There—just ahead."

Jerphanion said over his shoulder: "Single file. Pass it along."

"Single file; pass it along," the word went back beneath the trees, until it was nothing but a whisper hard to distinguish, an "*Ora pro nobis…ora pro nobis…*" dying away in the distance of a crypt.

Jerphanion caught up with the guide again, trying as he went to get an idea of the lie of the ground.

"Good heavens! Is this what you call a communication trench?"

"Well, it's what we have to make do for one, sir."

Their way, in fact, lay along what was no more than a slight depression in the snowy earth. It was more like the kind of drainage ditch one sometimes finds in woods than anything else. At its deepest, it brought the ground level about knee-high, or even less.

Jerphanion pressed his question:

"What possible use can the wretched thing be? It's just a bad joke."

"It helps to mark the track, sir, especially in snowy weather. Small detachments and working parties don't have guides, you see.…Besides, in case of shelling it gives a little shelter if one lies flat—keeps some of the stuff off."

The problem, luckily, was not, at the moment, of particular urgency. Round about midnight the bombardment had more or less ceased. Flares no longer soared into the sky. The most that happened was that now and then a few spent bullets came over, ricocheting from the upper branches of the trees and bringing down a fine powdering of snow.

The presence of these bullets was the chief indication that they were penetrating into the very stuff of the battle. They seemed almost like audible threads of many colours woven into the material. By virtue of them this war took on a certain resemblance to the wars of former days. It was the privilege of these bullets to give to one tiny area of space a marked characteristic of battle.

"Vui…i-i-i-i-…" there went another. "Zu-u-u-u…im…" and another. Who could possibly be bothering to shoot at this time of night when all movement, even local movement, had almost certainly stopped? Some bored look-out perhaps, whiling away the time by taking pot-shots at harmless shad-

ows? Two or three of his fellows who had spotted simultaneously the stirring of a patrol in no man's land? A sniper spending the night in some snug corner and deliberately choosing
a difficult target, such as the distant angle of a trench away to
his left or right, where he might catch now and then some
glimpse of a shape against the night sky, those who used this
trench having no idea that at certain points they could be
enfiladed at long range? Such a sniper would have made a
temporary rest for his rifle with a piece of white thread fastened to his back-sight to give him the line in the darkness.
He would aim at his ease, neither too long nor too quickly.
The only drawback from his point of view would be that he
could never be sure whether or not he had scored a hit. Without his knowing it, his bullet would sometimes wing its way
along the fixed line of enfilade, whizz over a rise in the
ground, and strike the hillside before spending itself harm-
lessly on the ground....Or—and this would be the most frequent case of all—a few scattered men, caught by a moment's
terror at the sound of some movement in the branches—or,
more strictly speaking, feeling a sudden accentuation in the
general sense of terror that had become their normal state—
and having rifles in their hands, would have fired aimlessly
into the air much in the way that a frightened woman cries
aloud.

In this way, even during the hours of rest, the battle never
managed wholly to sink into unconsciousness. It was like an
overtired traveller whose muscles twitch while he sleeps.

While they climbed the last crest, Jerphanion pondered the
meaning that lay in the whine of these wandering bullets. But
deep within himself he was astonished, even a little disappointed, to find that this battle of Verdun, which in the course
of a few days had assumed such unusual proportions in the
imagination of the men involved, should be willing to slack-
en and die down like any other.

"For when all's said and done," he thought, "here I am. . . .
For the last three weeks the idea has never left me that something would happen to prevent me, to prevent us, from getting here…and yet here I am. Right in the thick of it. In less

than half an hour now I shall be at my post in the battle of Verdun, taking my part in the present phase of the battle of Verdun, occupying a position a bare forty yards from the front line—forty yards which at any moment might be reduced to ten, or to nothing at all. I shall know then, as well as anybody, just exactly what the battle of Verdun is like. I shall know whether the man who is I, the man who has already been through so many ordeals, the poor tired, discouraged man, with despair eating at his heart, is going to be able to endure this battle of Verdun.... What is it that fate has in store for us? The dead, I think, have settled accounts with her. But when will she say of those who have endured till now: "This is enough. They have had their fill of pain. I ask nothing more of them"?

"Here we are, sir," said the guide in a low voice. "In ten minutes we shall be in position. The Boches are very close, and it would be just as well, sir, if you told your men to make absolutely no noise. The Boches'd be only too glad of a chance of peppering the relief."

A whisper ran down the column:

"We're there. Complete silence. Pass it along." A little farther on, the guide called a halt.

"I think the captain of the company you're relieving is waiting for you just about here, sir. Follow me. Will you tell your men to wait?"

"Not too long, I hope. The poor devils are just about done in. You don't seem to realize that it's close on one o'clock."

The captain was waiting for them in the merest apology for a shelter—a shallow hole in the ground beneath a covering of brush-wood, very small, and full of all sorts of odds and ends. A lantern standing close by him showed a face white and ravaged with fatigue. When he had completed his handing over and had furnished a guide to show the men to their quarters while he went on chatting with Jerphanion, the latter asked rather anxiously:

"Is this company H.Q.?"

The other smiled.

"No...it's the company dump. H.Q. is a bit farther on, but it's not much better."

"Hot spot?"

"You've said it! But not particularly so. The whole sector's pretty hot. It's a little less bad here than higher up on the right, towards the Ravin de la Dame and Douaumont."

"Many casualties?"

"A goodish few, but, oh well, not more than you'd expect…

Today I've had only one man killed and three wounded; yesterday two killed and two wounded—no, three. The day before that—Oh I've forgotten, but somewhere about the same."

"I must say," remarked Jerphanion with sincere amazement, "that doesn't seem much to me, all things considered. . . ." He remembered that the daily casualty figures on the Champagne front had been much the same during what had been considered relatively peaceful periods…. "You surprise me….We had been told that the battle was terribly costly…."

"Let me explain. In a battle like this the front line's fairly soft…or so it seems here. I can't tell what it's like elsewhere….I'm not speaking, of course, of the opening stages. On the contrary, I'm told that when the business began, the front line was completely flattened out. Casualties were fifty or sixty per cent of the effectives engaged, in a single day….But now there's practically no shelling of the front line. The Boche trenches are too close. Their artillery is too frightened of hitting their own men."

"Are they really very close?"

"Fifty yards or so—a little more in your particular sector…. Owing to the shifting nature of the fight, their guns haven't been able to register properly. It's more or less impossible for them to fire. Behind us, at Froide-Terre, they've been getting 105's and 150's—which is lucky for us. We can see them going over. Not more than one in a hundred falls this side of the ridge. So far we've not even been trench-mortared—I don't know why, unless it's because they haven't got any, or because there's nothing here they want to destroy….They worry us a bit with bombs and rifle grenades….And then, of course, there's the parrots, and a damn nuisance they are too."

"Parrots?"

"Same as what they call squirrels in other sectors. The

ground's just made for 'em here, with all these high trees. Some of them get a sort of sporting kick out of it. They crawl along to the foot of a tree, climb it, and ensconce themselves comfortably enough in the branches. It's not always easy to pick them out even with glasses....But the worst thing you'll have to put up with here is fatigue....One never gets a chance to close one's eyes....Something plaguing one the whole time. Always having to watch out. There's no end to the patrolling and counter-patrolling, to the thousand and one jobs that have got to be done at once, to the alarms and the local raids. The Boches are always up to some dirty trick. And then at the back of one's mind there's always the thought that at any minute they may start a big attack. It's bound to come sooner or later. Obviously the battle's not going to become stabilized on the present line. That's quite clear from the number of shells they're sending over to our rear....Well, good luck. I must be off; I'm all in."

Jerphanion went back to his men. He found them in the depths of gloom.

"Have a look here, sir, and here. This is what they call a trench!"

"Don't talk so loud. The Boches are only fifty yards away."

"Then all I can say is it's damned decent of them not to have killed every man jack of the lot who were in here before. Look at this shelter, sir!"

Jerphanion, his arms crossed, looked. He was as depressed as the rest of them. The position he had just taken over was so much like a bad joke that he half believed the guide had made some mistake. It consisted of a few hollows scraped in the ground just deep enough to protect a man from grazing splinters if he knelt or squatted. Between these hollows ran a ditch, about half as deep and with widely sloping edges. Unless one crawled along it on all fours it afforded no cover at all. Here and there a few bays had been scooped out of the sides big enough for two or three men to lie flattened against the earth. The whole thing was like one of those ground plans of field-works which a company may be set to trace in the course of an afternoon's training.

All the weariness of six hours of marching through the snow, among the dead horses and the shell-holes, all the accumulated exhaustion of the last few days, seemed concentrated in an unendurable load upon his back while he gazed on these ridiculous scratchings in the mud which the next army order would no doubt tell him to hold "to the last man and the last cartridge."

"They couldn't do any better"—with some such thought he tried to keep himself from unjust comment. "They" were his immediate predecessors, whose fate it must have been, as the result of some retirement, to take over the position just as God had made it—bare earth, grass, brushwood, the only holes those made by bursting shells.

But what about the people on whom had been laid the responsibility of defending Verdun, of covering Verdun, of organizing a series of defensive positions in depth? An irrefutable intuition told him that everywhere the conditions were the same, that wherever the wretched troops had been forced to retire, whether they had halted a little nearer, a little farther, they would have found just the same ground awaiting them, earth, grass, brushwood, and as "works" nothing but the holes obligingly made by the enemy shells.

"Well," said Jerphanion to his men, moving in front of them from one scooped-out hollow to another, "we're fresh to the place, and the only thing to be done is to get it into some sort of shape as soon as possible."

Among the various instructions and recommendations handed over was one which suggested putting out knife-boards and wire immediately "wherever there are gaps," in view of an enemy attack which "might take place any moment." That "wherever there are gaps" was in the best staff style of humour. A supply of knife-boards and wire, it was added, would be found in a shelter near company H.Q.

Rather nervously Jerphanion announced to his N.C.O.'s that it would have been advisable to get a few knife-boards and a few lengths of wire out that very night, but that he realized how tired the men were. A few minutes later two sergeants appeared with the news that they had got together a dozen or so men who had volunteered for the work.

"They said they'd as soon do that as stand look-out, and that they certainly didn't want to sleep. If you like, sir, we'll take the necessary party out of the number of look-outs detailed. They'll be able to keep an eye open just the same, and in that way we shan't have to dock anyone of his sleep."

"Good. Please thank them....They're good fellows. I'll be along to see them in a moment."

The night was cold, though without the edge of frost. The brushwood lay all about in a tangled mass like bundles of old string. The place gave one a feeling of being a stray dog.

"How wretched it all is!" thought Jerphanion. "How squalid!" He repeated the words to himself as he tramped through the snow along the little zigzag ditch, the ground level of which reached now his knees, now only his ankles:

"How squalid!"

CHAPTER SIXTEEN

A Luncheon in the Public Interest

"Well, Octave, what do you advise?"

Octave assumed a confidential air. "I have some very nice partridges today, sir."

"What, has the season opened?"

Octave smiled. "For us, sir, it is always the season."

"I should not have thought," said Haverkamp, turning jokingly to his guest, "that there were any poachers left. I'm told that all the apaches have vanished from the big cities. It must be true, for one never hears nowadays about gang fights or hold-ups after dark."

"The poachers may be few, sir," said the head waiter with well-bred facetiousness, "but the gendarmes are even fewer. They've got work to do elsewhere."

"All right, then, partridges let it be, since you guarantee them."

"That I can do without any hesitation, sir.... The trimmings you can leave to me. How about a little fish to start with, sir?"

"Why not? You like fish?"

"Indeed I do."

"Have you any preference?"

"Well, no, I like almost all fish—except cod."

"Good. What do you recommend, Octave?"

"May I suggest our *quenelles de poisson à la niçoise*? Our chef makes a speciality of them. But perhaps the gentlemen know them already?"

"No...I think not."

"Then try them, sir. If by any chance you do not like them, I will bring you something else. But I feel quite confident, sir. And for the other gentleman too, sir?"

"Yes indeed....I adore southern dishes as a rule, when they are not too heavy."

"Yes, sir....A few oysters to begin with, sir?"

"Well—"

"May I recommend our Marennes special, sir? They are magnificent. We have never had better Marennes than since the war. The demand is so much less than it used to be, you understand, sir. They are at their best just now. In another month they will be nearly over....I will send the wine-waiter, sir."

"That seems all right," thought Haverkamp; "not too ostentatious. I'll order a Chablis or a Pouilly...to be followed by a good red Burgundy...not one of the great growths, nor one of the outstanding years."

He was anxious not to give the impression to his guest, Cornabœuf the Controller, nor to feel himself, that they were "making a splurge" just at the moment when the battle of Verdun was at its height. Nothing was more natural than that two busy men should arrange to meet at luncheon ("you must lunch somewhere, eh?") to discuss a matter of public interest. There would have been something of affectation in deliberately choosing a bad restaurant or a sparse meal just because the boys at the front weren't getting the food one would have liked them to get. Still, a certain moderation must be observed. Simply a question of tact. Partridges.... Quenelles....Well, after all, that was no more than the two courses to which most people thought it right to confine themselves. Nothing very excessive about that. The oysters didn't really count. If nobody ate oysters what would happen to the cultivators? There was quite enough poverty as it was. The oyster beds were a source of national wealth and must be encouraged.

It was, in fact, to oysters that the two men at first confined their conversation, and to the question of the enormous losses that the breeders must have had for the last eighteen months. The idea that they were doing their little best to keep ruin from the Marennes beds allowed them to begin their meal with a clear conscience. From that subject they passed to the early vegetables of Normandy and Brittany, which the English were no longer buying. Then to the bad time that was afflicting the watering-places, a fact to which Haverkamp made only a discreet allusion, almost as though he were referring to a family bereavement.

It was only when they were starting on their second helping of quenelles—the merits of which they fully endorsed ("There's nothing like French cooking. When the Boches can produce a dish like that they can start talking about their *Kultur*—not before")—that the real reason for their meeting emerged like a pea from its pod.

"I have been over my calculations again," said Haverkamp, "and I can tender at once for three million grenades, with delivery of a million at the end of the present month, a second million on April 10th, the balance on the 20th. Should the necessity arise, I could guarantee to deliver another five million at intervals between the end of April and the beginning of June. The rate of production, I think you will agree, is worth careful consideration. I am willing to be penalized in the event of my failing to keep to my dates, unless, of course, such failure is due to *force majeure*. I had already worked out my prices pretty carefully, but I have been into them again, and I can now offer you a flat figure of 0 francs 93 each, provided the order is for not less than three million. For eight million I might be able to get it down to 0 francs 91 net."

M. Cornabœuf remarked that certain firms were offering grenades at 0 francs 80 on a basis of five hundred thousand.

"Must be bad stuff, then," replied Haverkamp with a shrug. "Don't think I don't know all about it. I could quote you a similar article at 0 francs 70. But I bet you could crack them between your two hands like nuts."

M. Cornabœuf, who had just been served with a sound Beaune of 1911, condescended to smile. Where national defence was concerned, he agreed that saving on quality might very rightly be held to be ill timed, if not actually criminal.

But that was not the chief difficulty.

"You must, I think, be aware that the Ministry is bound by an undertaking entered into before Parliament not to treat, in the matter of grenades, with middlemen."

"In principle—eh?"

"We are very closely watched."

"I could quote you a number of cases in which it has been done....But, in the first place, I am not a middleman. If anyone raises the point you can reply that I have already tendered as a manufacturer for a hundred thousand grenades, and delivered them, as I think you will agree, to your complete satisfaction."

M. Cornabœuf smiled politely and bowed.

"You can prove that I have my own factory at Grand Montrouge."

M. Cornabœuf continued to smile. "Oh, of course…but you've no idea how pernickety they are. It's open to them to reply that your factory at Grand Montrouge (a little too close to Paris, between ourselves…your competitors and ill-wishers, you see, can check their facts so easily)—well, it comes to this —they'd say, in fact, that this factory of yours might be capable of turning out, say, a hundred thousand grenades in two and a half months…but hardly three million in five weeks, much less eight million between now and the beginning of June. From which they'd argue that you'd have to subcontract for the greater part of the order, and that consequently you'd be acting chiefly as a middleman, and that we must have known this when the order was placed. Insinuations might even be made that your factory was—how shall I say?—nothing but a screen."

"Oh, come!"

"I can only repeat that you've no idea of the lengths they'll go to embarrass us. There's always some deputy or other ready to complain to the Minister, or, if need be, to threaten to ask a question in the House. The old-established manufacturers are always on the look-out. They go through the orders with a fine-tooth comb. They get the details of the tenders from government clerks in their pay."

"All I can say is it's perfectly scandalous!" cried Haverkamp, quite forgetting that he had frequently employed the same methods. "It comes perilously near to divulging secrets concerning national defence!"

"Very near...but what can we do to prevent it? Do you know their latest demand? That the market should be closed not only to middlemen, but to all businesses started since the war—yes, to all those manufacturers who were not operating in the same branch of industry before 1914! So, you see, the fact of your having a factory at Montrouge wouldn't really be accepted as an argument."

"They've got a cheek, I must say! Were they turning out grenades before the war? If so I'd like to know where!"

"Not grenades, perhaps. What they mean is that a metallurgist or an ironmaster is qualified, but that, say, a rubber-manufacturer is not. We've already had a hell of a row over a rubber factory."

"Damned cheek!" repeated Haverkamp, waving a leg of a partridge on the end of his fork. "The whole precious crew have been quite incapable of meeting the demands of national defence in this tragic hour of the nation's history, whether in the matter of shells, grenades, or anything else. They've not been able to develop their plants sufficiently to deal with the present situation. They've failed to build new factories when new factories were necessary. As a matter of fact, even with the start they've had, they can't manage to compete with the so-called 'improvised' plants. What it comes to is that they're trying to prevent other people from doing the work, from turning out the stuff, and those people in particular who've shown initiative and the necessary enterprise. And here are our ministers, our members of Parliament, letting these gentlemen treat them like a pack of schoolboys. There's always some deputy ready to bring their demands and their grievances up in the House—that's to say, to fight for a monopoly of private interests over national necessities. It's quite obvious what those talebearers are after. No one's got the slightest illusion on that point. But the effect is the same. And our Parliament of shivering cowards hasn't got the guts to say: 'To hell with all that! What matters at the moment is not your private interest but the salvation of the country!' No, to please these gentlemen our soldiers can go without shells and grenades. There's already a shortage at Verdun. I know that perfectly well. It's one of the causes of our retirement. Well, we shall go on suffering from shortage, and so much the worse for us. We shall let our men be slaughtered, we shall lose territory... maybe we shall end by losing the war. But our fine pre-war manufacturers will have succeeded in defending their monopoly. That is the one essential point, is it not? What a state of mind! It's just as though I, simply on the grounds that I had been running my Limoges factory for years before the war, were to insist that all orders for boots must be given to me or to my colleagues in the trade. Have I ever put in such a claim? I can keep my end up without that!"

"The case is not quite the same," observed M. Cornaboeuf "It's easier for you to keep your end up. It's more difficult to improvise a boot factory than a grenade plant....The latter does not require such special machinery nor such skilled workers."

"I stick to my opinion," insisted Haverkamp with the pride born of the sense, at that particular moment, that he could claim to be an "old-established manufacturer of boots." "And let me remind you that everybody, ironmasters included, have had to improvise plants for the production of grenades, since none existed before. That's all the more reason why they shouldn't be allowed to put a spoke in our wheel like this...."

He paused to allow a tray of cheese to be passed. While M. Cornaboeuf was helping himself, Haverkamp let his gaze wander towards the rue Royale which was visible in the space between two curtains. There was not much traffic, but, for all that, the thoroughfare looked charming; there was about it a delicate hint of melancholy. The sky held still the colours and the light metallic glint of winter, but now and then a sudden ray of sunshine struck through the cold stillness with a message of warmth from the still invisible spring. Elegant women were passing along the pavements, some of them with bunches of violets pinned to their dresses. Others, clad in deep mourning, sometimes relieved with an edging of white, showed handsome faces discreetly touched with rouge, sad red lips, sad eyes in which a smile yet lingered, set in hoods of the severest black trimmed with pure white. "War widows," they were called. They roused the sense of the men of middle age, including those many foreigners drawn from distant continents by the mingled odours of the European charnel-house. Many of these "war widows" usurped a title to which they had no right; but not all.

Haverkamp found the scene vaguely touching and full of charm. What a fair country was this land of France! Nothing could steal her grace from her. He turned again to M. Cornaboeuf.

"Well," he said in a tone intended to rouse his companion's curiosity, "I shall discuss the whole thing—the general question, I mean—with my friend Gurau, the Minister. It'll be well worth the trouble."

CHAPTER SEVENTEEN

Haverkamp Provides Boots for the Armies of the Republic

The opening of the battle of Verdun had suddenly disturbed Haverkamp's peace of mind. He read with emotion the communiqué and the comments of the war critics. He went about collecting rumours. He became restless.

A number of confused intuitions jostled one another in his mind: "This is going to be the toughest struggle of the lot; maybe the decisive struggle. It won't be over in a few weeks, as the Boches think, nor perhaps will it turn out quite as they expect. But the one certain thing is that the war won't go on very much longer. I'd give it roughly until the autumn. The Boches are putting all their eggs into one basket because they're beginning to feel the strain....In six months' time it'll be too late to cash in, but at the moment the chances are excellent. The government are about to ask the country to make an enormous effort—and that goes for the contractors, too. No arguing about trifles. Rules and regulations will take second place when it comes to delivering the stuff."

Not that Haverkamp had altogether wasted his time since mobilization, but he was not the kind of man who makes the most of opportunities. He reckoned that others, given the same chances, and starting the war with the kind of hand he had been dealt, would have been able to show by this time very much more brilliant results. He tried to explain the situation to his own satisfaction: "The war caught me at a bad time. Life's like that: no one's always at his best. My returns were diminishing and my health wasn't any too good. Two or three speculations had just turned out badly. Put baldly, I was on a dangerous slope. Perhaps the war saved me. But since at the moment it broke out I was not in a position to take the

initiative, I have not been able to turn circumstances to
account with the necessary energy and speed."

The first few weeks—those of August 1914—had left with
him a memory of which he was not very proud. He had
reacted passively to the stimulus of events, his will immobi-
lized, his intelligence blunted. He had allowed himself to be
called up as mechanically as the dairyman opposite. He
belonged to the class of '94, and he found himself drafted into
the Army Service Corps. Luckily, about a year previously, and
for no obvious reason, he had had the idea of getting himself
transferred from the fighting to the auxiliary service (he could
no longer remember clearly why; probably in order to avoid
the boredom of having to do his period of training, which
happened to be imminent). Thanks to this, he never left the
Versailles depot. But for this accident, he would have allowed
himself to be sent into the battle area with as little resistance
as he had shown to mobilization; and then later, when he
would have awaked from his lethargy, he would have found it
the very devil to retrace his steps.

He remembered the deplorable and utterly unworthy way
in which his mind had worked during that first period.
Although he realized quite clearly that the war would do that
most necessary thing: "wipe the slate clean," and that doubtless the general economic and social situation of the country
would emerge from it healthily stimulated, he had been weak
enough to regard it as inevitable that he should be among
those who would be the war's victims rather than its heirs.
"My particular piece of bad luck is that the war happens to
have caught me just as I am involved in a kind of speculation
which it cannot possibly benefit. That my business may profit eventually, in the distant future and well after everything
else, from a general return of prosperity is not the question.
Between now and then I might well be ruined ten times over.
I should have to start again from zero, and that, at my age, is
neither amusing nor easy. The mere threat of war during the
past two years has been enough to diminish demand and to
begin bringing prices down. The real-estate market flourishes
only in periods of calm when people can plan ahead and

prosperity is on the up grade. At the present moment," he thought also in those early days of August '14, "if there was any business at all it would be at knock-down prices. People are no longer paying their rents, and you can't get a bailiff to distrain on tenants, shopkeepers, or farmers who have been called to the colours. No one will rent vacant flats or shops, especially those above a certain level. Things will go from bad to worse. With the disappearance of rents, the value of real property will go to nothing. Land, whether built up or not, is due for a worse crisis than it has ever known. If there should happen to be a sale, it would be a forced sale, and there would be no buyers. It'll be possible to barter title deeds for a loaf of bread. Now's the moment when a man should have plenty of liquid capital, so as to be able to take advantage of such bargains. Obviously, things will get right again some day—quietly, of course, and little by little. Real estate isn't like other forms of property, it doesn't blossom at the first touch of the sun. It's none of your wild plants that grow like weeds in any soil. It needs ground that has been plentifully manured and has shown what it can do. What it comes to is that those who have been able to take advantage of the drop in prices and wait for the rise will some day make a fortune....But the trouble with me is that I have no liquid capital. On the contrary, I'm worried by debts on every side....What money I have is all tied up, and I can't realize. No good either talking about what profits I might make as a middleman. In the first place, I've been called up. Besides, no one will need a man like me to put him on to the few good things that may still be going. The middleman can only act efficiently in an over-stocked market where the investor runs the risk of getting lost among all the various opportunities and of missing the best chances because of all the amateur speculators. But when there are only three lots of vegetables offered for sale, and one buyer, he thinks he can manage the business for himself...." The pessimism that afflicted him during those August days of 1914 was not confined to such general arguments. "Where I'm concerned, there's one more than usually irritating circumstance. What looked like being a magnificent enter-

prise has turned out to be a stone round my neck which will
end by sinking me completely: my bathing-establishment, of
which I was so proud—and with such good reason. What
could possibly be more hopelessly exposed to the shocks of
war than a bathing-establishment recently opened? Already
Vichy, Plombières, and Contrexéville are feeling the draught.
But they are built on solid foundations. What chance is there
for my poor Celle? Who would be so absurd as to go and
bury himself there now? There may still be a dozen visitors or
so left who had made their arrangements well in advance, but
whatever happens we must close down definitely by the 1st
of September in order to save expense on heat and lighting.
If only I had managed to sell off all my villas and building
plots! But there are several still on my hands which no one
will take now at any price. What makes it even worse is that
for the last few I got rid of I had made arrangements for
deferred payments, which means that, what with the morato-
rium and one thing and another, I shall never see a penny of
my money. Meanwhile I must shoulder all the running
expenses of the place—the upkeep of the buildings, the gardens, and the roads. I can't abandon everything to the weeds
and the rats. I've got my work cut out already to keep pace
with damp walls, faded fabrics, and damaged roofs. For my
colleagues who are old-established capitalists all that is no
more than a tiresome detail. For me it is the knock-out blow."
And like the unfortunate artist or inventor who, despite
everything, remains enamoured of his work, he sighed: "Perhaps in ten years' time Celle will once again be a first-class
establishment, finer, more widely favoured than it ever was in
the past….But where shall I be by that time?"

And then one day towards the end of the month, when he
was brooding among the unemployed crowd in barracks on
these sombre thoughts that were gradually turning to a sour
spirit of resignation, a sudden inspiration dawned:

"My Limoges factory!"

By reason of the many latent thoughts that this gleam of
imagination brought to the surface of his mind, and the creative
emotion which it released within him, he found himself pass-

ing through the same sort of experience which marks the turning-point in the lives of artists, inventors, and mystics.

"My Limoges factory!"

Secretly, obscurely, the illumination had been coming to birth during those sombre days when he had felt inclined to abandon himself to circumstances, brooding over what might have been, reading the papers, listening to talk most of which was of an infectious stupidity. In particular, he must, unknown to himself, have caught the first signs—already visible to the general public—of that stampede of contractors of every description to mop up the orders of the military departments. But it might have seemed that the phenomenon would affect him as little as it affected any little tradesman or petty official, caught up like others in the machinery of mobilization, with the prospect of receiving no more than his daily pay for the duration of the war, and of being released, for that reason, from the necessity of keeping his end up in the growing struggle of greedy self-seekers.

Why had he not put two and two together— "I own at Limoges a small boot factory which up to now has been nothing but an expensive whim. Isn't this just the moment to turn it to advantage? Orders will be placed in their thousands, and quite blindly. Can't I make boots for the army as well as another? Perhaps other leather articles too—equipment, for instance, which can't need much technical skill....After all, I have some influence!"

If any such thoughts had occurred to him, he had been blissfully unaware of them.

But once the idea had emerged into consciousness, he entirely threw off his previous lethargy.

Within a week he had collected a whole library of documents on the needs and intentions of the Ordnance Department. He knew at which doors he would have to knock, what forms must be filled out, whose favour to woo in the various grades of the hierarchy, what outside pressure to bring to bear. He realized that he knew a number of people capable of giving him a helping hand, from ministers to friends mobilized like himself in the second-line troops, clerks in the

Ordnance office, whom he met at restaurants and cafés and military canteens both in Paris and Versailles. At that period of the war the men of the back-area services, concentrated, for the most part, round the Military College of Versailles, formed a solid mass of several tens of thousands of men, submitted to a very loose discipline and with duties of the vaguest, scarcely withdrawn from civil life, feeding and sleeping as the fancy took them, and always in a position to get two hours or half a day whenever they wished for reasons of "private affairs," with no more ceremony than that involved in a whispered word in the ear of some corporal. They could pay visits where they would and invite to their canteens some friend from a neighbouring formation. The orderlies stationed at the gates had long ago given up trying to keep a record of all who went in and out. The number of visitors was beyond all reckoning at every hour of the day, and each had an apparently valid excuse which it was impossible to verify. On the occasions when the local administration, in a fit of indignation at the happy-go-lucky manners of the Paris garrison, spurred the guard to an access of zeal, it was usually quite enough to present a scrap of paper adorned with the signature of some entirely unknown individual.

A constant movement reigned in this confusion of soldiers, semi-soldiers, and civilians who made up the garrison of Paris and of the military district of which it formed the centre, a continuous flow from barrack to barrack, staff room to ministerial department, public building to public building, with all sorts of delays, and many diversions into unofficial and private localities, such as restaurants, editors' anterooms, the offices of big businesses and large industrial enterprises, where the first gurglings of the money fountain were beginning to fill all hearts with an anticipatory emotion.

This world full of movement, but no less full of darkness and difficulty—made up of men almost all of whom were doing things they had never done before, meeting unusual people, looking different from what they had done, who often found it hard to recognize old acquaintances, who ran into one another unexpectedly or sought one another in vain—

had a sort of curious charm, was alive with the intoxication of the unpredictable. The general atmosphere was reminiscent of that of old-time carnivals, minus their grace. The individuals concerned moved about more or less in disguise. Not one but had, to a greater or less degree, broken with former habits, with the deadening weight of duties, to take on others, no less irksome perhaps, but seeming to bear less heavily on the conscience, and leaving the spirit with a feeling of more abundant peace. Many took advantage of this freedom from their adult pasts merely to recapture the joys of their irresponsible youth, to steal a couple of hours from office duties for a game of cards in some staff canteen where nobody would think of looking for them; to arrange with the other members of a detachment of six, sent on some mysterious job of inspection in a distant factory, a system of reliefs which would give all the men in turn an opportunity for a good time; to get themselves detailed for an errand at the other end of Paris, and then to idle away the afternoon with two or three pals under the tarpaulin of a regimental truck, with an occasional halt at convenient bars in discreet side-streets. On the other hand, a few of the men caught up in this bustling life had very soon managed to create new interests for themselves. This carnival of regimental overcoats, fancy caps, and tunics seemed to them to open new roads into a world of intrigue and enterprise and profitable business. The very objects to be attained had the merit of novelty, and more than one, by reason of the vast prospect that it opened up, had much the same power to thrill as the big prize in a lottery.

As soon as Haverkamp had shaken off his lethargy he took his place in the ranks of this industrious minority. He became one of those soldiers to be seen in good-class restaurants seated at the same table with men of obvious importance, or haunting streets and government offices at hours when men in uniform, even in time of war, are not usually free.

He managed to land his first commission during the wave of prosperity that followed the battle of the Marne. In itself it was nothing very grand: a matter of twenty thousand regulation boots to be delivered not later than the 15th of October.

He was not sure how far his "Limoges factory," which had been more or less shut down since mobilization, was capable of turning out that particular type of article, nor in what quantities. But he made up his mind not to be checked at the outset by considerations of that kind.

He got leave in order to go and see to things for himself. Once on the spot, he quickly realized that by adding a few more machines, and provided he could get back a few of his skilled hands (the women were still at work), he could transform his small factory, till then used only for delicate footwear, into a plant capable of producing a hundred pair of "great clodhoppers" a day, which meant about three thousand by the 15th of October. This left him with seventeen thousand to find elsewhere.

The problem of costs was another matter to be decided. To get the order he had had to quote a figure rather below the normal rate. A simple calculation showed him that for each pair produced by his factory he would have to pay a franc more than he would receive. On the other hand, there could be no question at the moment of enlarging his premises or of embarking on heavy expenses in the matter of equipment. He had not got sufficient capital available, and the order was too small to attract a partner.

He got a second period of leave and went to Romans, in the Drôme country. There he made contact with a local manufacturer, who agreed to subcontract for the seventeen thousand pairs at a price which would give Haverkamp a profit of 1 franc 75 on each.

The whole business brought him in no more than just over twenty-five thousand francs (actually rather less, taking certain expenses into account). But, as he said, it enabled him to "get his foot in." He was delighted. As he rushed from one Ordnance office to another he never ceased saying to himself: "Splendid little factory! How right I was to hang on to it! What a sound instinct I had when I bought it! Who would ever have guessed then that some day I should owe everything to it? I must have been almost stunned by events last month not to think of it at once!"

His first order was still uncompleted when he got a second, this time something worth looking at: a hundred thousand pairs to be delivered in three months. Two additional advantages made this windfall all the more acceptable: he was to get sixty centimes more on each pair, and he was relieved from routine duty in order that he might give his personal attention to the factory. Dear, darling "Limoges factory" which thus assured its master a full and happy life!

In order to mark the importance of the commission which he had solicited, and to justify his release from regimental duties, he thought it wise to install a new work-room, to buy a few extra machines, and to engage more hands (women). The rosy future opening before him led him to consider asking for Wazemmes, who was serving with a dragoon regiment somewhere in the north. Wazemmes, duly sounded, declared that he did not want to be given a "soft job." Besides, he belonged to the 1912 class, had been called to the colours in October 1913, and was now, if not actually at the front, at least precious near it. There was very little chance of his being released. Haverkamp quickly got over the disappointment. For nearly a year now he had learned to do without Wazemmes. He was not the kind of man to find the absent indispensable.

Twenty thousand pairs of the new order he ear-marked for the Limoges factory. For the other eighty thousand he had recourse to his Romans manufacturer, and was honest enough to share with him the bonus of sixty centimes which he had wangled out of the Ordnance people. A little later he learned indirectly that his Romans colleague, finding it impossible to produce more than fifty-six thousand pairs within the stipulated period, had handed over twenty-four thousand to one of his local competitors at a discount of a franc per pair. Haverkamp was nothing if not a realist. He found nothing to complain of in the arrangement.

While the order was going forward, he had another stroke of luck. He learned that in certain cases, where large orders were concerned, and especially when the manufacturer had to invest money in machinery, the State was willing to pay a certain amount in advance. Just for the sake of principle, he put in a claim for two hundred thousand francs, feeling quite certain that it would be refused. Half of what he asked was granted without a murmur.

The deal left him with a profit of about a hundred and sixty thousand francs. Moreover he now had at his disposal a brand-new plant, better suited than the old to turn out military boots. The cost of installation was already almost paid off, and he would henceforward be in a position to work with a much larger margin of profit.

The year 1915 saw the progressive extension of this field of activity. Haverkamp continued to provide boots for the armies of the Republic. In the course of the twelve months he produced an additional four hundred thousand pairs. As he was up against the same difficulties as his competitors in the matter of obtaining leather, he got official permission to use hides tanned by a special rapid method (the qualities of which were compared by the men in the trenches, who were better placed than most to know what they were talking about, to those of blotting paper), and chemically stained skins. Nevertheless, in a period marked by its great commercial temptations, he did maintain a reasonably honest standard of workmanship. Unlike many of his competitors, he resolutely refused to substitute for soles made in one piece soles made up of two thin slices of leather packed with scraps. The troops were duly grateful.

At the beginning of spring—that is to say, just as Ordnance was setting about refitting the armies in view of the forthcoming offensive in Champagne, he landed an order for a hundred thousand sets of leather equipment. He contented himself with making only a hundred of these in his own factory, for the sake of the experience and to learn the technicalities of the operation. He found it simpler to pass the other ninety-nine thousand nine hundred to subcontractors. His profit on the transaction was therefore very small, working out at twenty-two and a quarter centimes per set.

In September, while the aforesaid offensive in Champagne was in full swing, his attention was drawn to winter supplies.

An official who was devoted to his interests communicated to him, the day before it was issued, a circular dated September 22nd, in which the Minister called upon the Ordnance Department to submit requirements in the matter of warm clothing for the next six months: knitted jerseys, woollen socks, flannel body-belts, blankets, etc....Haverkamp, therefore, was among the first to have no illusions about the results to be expected from the Champagne offensive (the first shots were fired on the same day as the circular was issued—the 22nd of September) and to abandon all hope—or fear; it depended on the point of view—of seeing the war end before the beginning of winter.

The same official let him know what the answer of the services concerned had been. Ordnance, having reckoned its needs, was demanding, among other articles of warm clothing, five million four hundred and twenty-three thousand knitted jerseys, fifteen million four hundred and sixty-one thousand pairs of woollen socks, and fourteen hundred thousand sheepskins.

Haverkamp set his mind brooding on the five and a half million knitted jerseys and the fifteen and a half million pairs of woollen socks. He foresaw various difficulties. He would have a hard tussle with long-established competitors, who would look on him as an intruder and might, in revenge, try to make difficulties for him even in his own chosen field of leather goods. In short, he showed signs of timidity. He fell back on the sheepskins, for two reasons: one (on general lines) because there was an obvious connexion between sheepskins and leather; the other deriving from special circumstances. In negotiating a purchase of leather abroad (for which he had been granted a licence), he had chanced to get wind of a consignment of sheepskins, a trifle moth-eaten but quite good enough for the troops, which was lying in a warehouse at Liverpool. Thanks to the rapidity with which the information had reached him through the good offices of his official friend, he was able to put in his tender before the rush began, with the result that he received an order for a hundred and fifty thousand. Relatively speaking, it was the best stroke of business he had yet done. It cost him a few telegrams, three or four days spent in formalities, twenty thousand or so francs expended on various commissions, and it brought him in, net, rather more than two francs per skin, which represented a small fortune.

Meanwhile he had been successfully negotiating another enterprise. The wounded were beginning to flow into the convalescent centres, and the Army authorities were renting for their use a number of big hotels in the watering-places. Haverkamp got his Celle stockholders moving, pointing out that if only they played their cards well and made use of their friends, who were many and influential, they could easily get the authorities to pitch on Celle, which had all the requirements needed by a healthful and modern convalescent establishment. The results were exactly as he had foreseen. The whole business of negotiation was left to him. He was careful to ask only a relatively small rent, but he stipulated that when the war was over, the whole place should be restored before being handed back. There was no difficulty about getting this clause accepted. The military authorities were concerned only with immediate economies and did not bother their heads about future budgets which would have to be faced by civilian members of Parliament when the time came. Besides, victory would settle that, as well as a great deal else. Haverkamp even succeeded in slipping his casino into the prize packet which he was handing over to the Army. The casino was his especial nightmare. This masterpiece of Turpin had not stood up well to abandonment. Cracks were showing in the walls; the plaster was bubbling and flaking. The mosaic paving was bulging in several places. There were spots in the walls where the cement had sweated and effaced the mural paintings. The furniture, deprived of proper ventilation and heating, was beginning to exhibit traces of mould. Nothing could be more acceptable than an entire overhauling of the casino at public expense as soon as peace was declared. Haverkamp "threw the casino in," pointing out that it would make an ideal club-room for convalescent officers.

CHAPTER EIGHTEEN

The Boom in Grenades

Until then a vague sense of decency had kept him from tapping two other sources of wealth—Supplies and Munitions.

So far as Supplies went, the sense of decency was genuine enough. Haverkamp had no wish to make money by providing canned tunny fish, horse sausage, or frozen meat from the Argentine. What was the use in having climbed, in time of peace, to the higher levels of respectable business, if he was now to degrade himself by touching dirty money? For Haverkamp the term *profiteer* was reserved solely for those who made fortunes out of food. He regarded it as a title of disgrace. He would not willingly have heard himself referred to as a profiteer for all the money in the world.

The same taint did not attach to Munitions. On the contrary, Munitions were closely allied to Metallurgy, to Blast Furnaces. There was something of the ironmaster about the man who dabbled in Munitions. His hesitation proceeded rather from a sort of childish fear. "I shouldn't like them to think I was making a fool of myself." In this connexion "they" were not just anybody, but certain specified individuals, the most important of whom was Count Henri de Champcenais. Their relations had never been close, and had become even less so since M. de Champcenais, lured ever higher towards the peaks of International Industry, had tended to regard with a rather distrait eye the whole Celle enterprise and the paltry million which he had risked in it. But the point now was that the aristocratic dabbler in the metal market had become a large-scale provider of weapons and munitions for the Army (of gasoline, too, by way of the cartel in which Sammécaud, though much against the grain, was still the central figure). Haverkamp imagined him one day learning—as he most certainly would—that the former real-estate agent had taken to turning out shells, like so many others who in civil life had been hatters and shyster lawyers; the sort of trashy, imperfect, cracked, and porous shells which burst in the gun-barrels and were loaded by the gunners with a constant sense of terror. What a world of meaning would M. de Champcenais have put into his words when he said: "That fellow? Well, of all the odd creatures!…" thus ranking Haverkamp summarily with the inefficient. Ah no! To be thought inefficient was as bad as being thought a profiteer, particularly when the thinker happened to be the aristocratic ironmaster. By a curious method of exclusion, to appear in the sight of M. de Champcenais as an inefficient workman seemed to the founder of Celle the worst thing that could happen to him.

Then came the great period of grenades. There was no tradition about grenades; they were nobody's special preserve. There might not be anything particularly glorious about making grenades, but at least there was nothing obviously absurd about trying. One could always save one's face by adopting a more or less detached air: "The government asked me to try to get a grenade factory going….It was my duty to help them if I could. If I refused they'd have had to go to some German-Swiss firm!—and that, I think you'll agree, would have been a bit too much. Anyhow, it's the merest child's-play."

Of course, in this field, as in every other, there was the danger of running up against rivals, of provoking jealousy, anger, and spiteful litigation. But such rivals would be pretty small men, none too sure of their own legal standing. Their hostility was not much to be feared. Their contempt? Why, it wasn't worth worrying about. M. de Champcenais certainly wouldn't bother his head about who was making grenades any more than about who was turning out fireworks. If the worst came to the worst, one could always answer (Haverkamp staged a thoroughly satisfactory piece of dialogue in his imagination): "Oh well, yes, I make a side-line of grenades as you might of gasoline drums."

And then, of course, the war was getting on, was growing old. One of these days it would end. All the sources of golden wealth would suddenly dry up. So much the worse then for those who had been too fearful or too scrupulous to make the going while the going was good. They would have to look up from their lower levels at the arrogant fortunes of their fellows. They would regret, when it was too late, the hey-day of the grenade boom as farmers might regret the hey-day of the cherry harvest.

It was about the middle of November 1915 that he got his first order for grenades: a hundred thousand, for delivery in two months and a half, at a price of 0 francs 98 each. It was in connexion with this order that he first made the acquaintance of the Controller, Cornabœuf.

Before signing the contract, he had made the elegant gesture of improvising a workshop at Grand-Montrouge out of an old garage. The whole installation had cost him but a couple of thousand-franc notes.

True to his former policy, he set himself to produce a fifth only of the stipulated quantity, farming out the rest at 0 francs 70 each. His own cost-price worked out at roughly the same figure. The margin of profit was highly satisfactory. Despite its modest proportions, the grenade stood revealed as one of the most potentially profitable sources of wealth produced by the war. The only problem was how to work in big enough quantities.

All this was well known to the Controller, Cornabœuf. He had instituted a system—unofficially of course—by which all the producers with whom he dealt agreed to pay him a bonus of two centimes on each grenade. Two centimes were little enough, and he quieted his conscience by the thought that he had saved the State far more than he got, by the zeal with which he beat down the manufacturers' prices. But the soldiers at the front used a very large quantity of grenades. They did not all pass through M. Cornabœuf's hands—far from it. Nevertheless, in the one month of December 1915, four million were guided into that channel and paid the toll of two

centimes. M. Cornabœuf had no sons at the front. But he had
daughters for whom he had got to find husbands. Besides, the
thought had occurred to him, as to others, that the war would
not go on for ever.

But the point to be noticed was that, according to his lights,
M. Cornabœuf was incorruptible, as Haverkamp was not long
in finding out. The two-centimes clause had to be accepted,
but, that done, there was no question of any hanky-panky in
the matter of quality or price. As he was fond of saying himself, he was always "ready to put up a devil of a fight for the
public's pennies." On the occasion of a meeting in February
'16 when a new contract for grenades was to come up for discussion, Haverkamp, in the hope of keeping the price to 0
francs 95, hinted that M. Cornabœuf's two centimes might,
perhaps, become three. He was severely snubbed for his pains.

At the end of December '15 Haverkamp had worked out
his balance-sheet on the year's business. His calculations
(some of the items brought forward as well as certain estimates were a bit arbitrary) showed a profit amounting to one
million forty-two thousand and two hundred and fifty francs.
This was no small sum at a time when, in spite of premoni-
tions of a change to come, the franc still maintained its face
value. If Haverkamp had thought it worth while to compare
this result with what he would have made over a similar period as a mere second-class private in a front-line formation, he
would—quite apart from questions of personal danger and
bodily comfort—have had every reason to congratulate himself. But such an approach to the problem would have seemed
to him trivial in the extreme. Not that he wasn't perfectly
ready to give himself a pat on the back. It was the first time
in his life that he had been able to reckon his profits in terms
of a clear and tangible million. But his delight was overshad-
owed by a further consideration which may be summed up in
the following words: "When a man's made a million like that,
he has no excuse whatever for not having made five or even
ten. What it comes to is that he has been lacking in energy."

The practical conclusion was that he must do better next
time. Haverkamp promised himself with no little vigour that

whatever the total of his profits at the end of December 1916, he would not have to reproach himself on the score of having confined his plans and enterprises within too modest a limit, or of having been guilty of that false shame which too often serves as a mask for laziness. He decided that, if need be, he would snap his fingers in M. de Champcenais's face and take to making shells; but in no "inefficient" way. Oh no. If he did it at all, it should be on a grand scale. Grenades would have served him as stepping-stones. It's difficult to laugh at a man with an order for a million shells in his pocket.

The "grocery business" was the only one in which he was still resolved not to get himself mixed up. He realized that this was to be guilty of weakness. But he could not see any way in which a profiteer could be made to look like a merchant prince.

CHAPTER NINETEEN

The Problem of Wazemmes

To this mood of high enthusiasm the battle of Verdun gave an added fillip. Haverkamp had set himself as his first objective "a really big order for grenades." Eight million were not to be sneezed at. At 0 francs 91 each, even allowing for the deduction of two centimes as commission for M. Cornabœuf, the total profit would show as a net figure of one million five hundred thousand francs.

Meanwhile the supply of boots—which he regarded henceforward as the legitimate basis of his activities, something rather like an employment under government—would jog along comfortably, or, rather, would develop in a perfectly normal fashion. Nor must he lose his hold on the rights he had acquired in the matter of leather equipment and sheepskins. But above and beyond all this, he would be free now to turn his attention to the possibility of fresh outlets and the capture of difficult markets.

But for all these various tasks he needed colleagues. He had recruited two or three, but he couldn't feel that confidence in them that he would have liked to. Wazemmes had again come on the scene. This time it was he who had approached his old employer. He had had time to sow his patriotic wild oats. He had spent the winter of 1914–15 as a dragoon, on the banks of the Yser. He had even had a short spell in the trenches—but in cavalry trenches, which meant that they had been comparatively comfortable and far removed from the heat of battle.

Meanwhile a letter which he had received from Lambert had given him a bit of a shock. Lambert was covering himself with glory in the infantry, Lambert had taken several prisoners with his own hands. Lambert had been mentioned in dispatches in the following terms: "Showed on more than one occasion a remarkable gift of initiative, and a courage that earned the admiration of his comrades." Lambert's letter, which could scarcely be suspected of lying about the more important details, was written in the heroic strain of the back areas. Jean Richepin, Henri Lavedan, and General Cherfils would have recognized in this young soldier a lad after their own hearts. "See!" they would have cried, "our unworthy countrymen accuse us of forcing the note and of making a parade of conventional sentiments which would not stand up to five minutes of real trench experience. Well, you can't say that this fellow's talking about what he doesn't understand!" Maurice Barrès might have smiled, but the smile would have been kindly.

As to Wazemmes, his feelings on reading this letter from Lambert, which concluded with "Long live France! Long live the King!"[1] had been those of humiliation and jealousy. His position as a dragoon, of which he had been so proud in time of peace and even in the opening months of the war, seemed to him now intolerable and liable to expose him to much sar-

---

[1] It may be well to point out here that Lambert of the rue des Gardes, salesman at the Maison Dorée, had, since his affiliation with the Camelots du Roi, been made the victim of a particularly irritating practical joke played on him by his fellow shop workers. The proprietor of the Maison Dorée, a man who was feared by his employees of both sexes for the stern discipline which he had instituted, and regarded by some, especially by the women, as a "damned nuisance," was called Leroy. (Hence the nickname of Galleroy, a portmanteau word probably made up of Gale [nuisance] and Leroy, which was freely used in the departments.) A colleague whose political opinions could be summed up in the cry of "*Vive le Roi*" naturally became the object of facile punning. The trick adopted in this case by Lambert's friends, both men and women, was to murmur in his ear, whenever they met him, in a tone of incredulous amazement: "*Vive Leroy*? Do you really mean it?" which had eventually become shortened into "Do you really mean it?" accompanied by a glance of stupefaction. Lambert had kept his end up pretty well in face of this persecution. He had gone so far as to substitute a Y for an I whenever he had occasion to exclaim: "*Vive le Roi*!" and to the "Do you really mean it" of his tormentors, he had got into the habit of replying: "Certainly I do—with a Y."

casm in the future. Already the infantrymen whom he met on the roads or in billets showed a complete lack of respect.

Wazemmes put in a request to be transferred to the infantry with the rank of corporal. (His senior officers, while showing themselves willing to accede to his wish to make closer acquaintance with the furnace of war, had pointed out to him that a cavalryman who became a foot soldier could wipe out the disgrace only by insisting on an extra stripe.)

Both his demands were granted. He became a corporal of infantry and after a fairly long term at the depot, followed by a period at an instruction school, was sent to the Champagne front. Two months later, in June, he was wounded by a machine-gun bullet in the Pompelle sector.

The wound, which had not seemed serious, took a long time to heal. Complications set in at the top of one lung. The senior doctor mentioned the possibility of tuberculosis; and, since he liked Wazemmes, took no immediate steps about returning him to duty. The boy, on his side, did all he could to prolong his convalescence. The hard work he had had as an infantryman, his period of residence in "real" trenches within shell-range, and his wound had completely assuaged his appetite for military glory. An added cause of bitterness was that he had not been mentioned in dispatches. All that hero stuff for nothing!

He had got into the habit of saying to his fellow-patients, with the blasé air of a disabled veteran who is merely waiting for his pension and his military medal: "Oh, the war's over so far as I'm concerned!"

Still, there was no chance of his getting his discharge. Partial return to duty, which would have meant all the dirty jobs, he didn't want, even if he could have got it. His new ambition was to be transferred to the Administrative Branch as "unfit for war service by reason of wounds," and later to be attached to the Paris establishment.

In his spare time in hospital he had written more than once to "the boss" and had kept him posted on his state of mind. He had told him of his wish to be transferred to the Administrative Branch and had asked him to back his application when the moment came. He added astutely: "Once I'm in the rice-bread–salt business, you'll merely have to ask for me. The rest'll be plain sailing." Meanwhile it was borne in upon him that the infantry does not willingly let go of a man once it has got him. He was granted two periods of sick leave; he was offered a temporary discharge of three months, which he was foolish enough to refuse; but of the Administrative Branch there was not a word.

He continued to hang about the depot. He was set to training recruits, but recurrent weakness made him continually report sick. He was temporarily transferred from the front-line to the auxiliary services. But the infantry held him fast. The Administrative Branch still remained for him a Promised Land.

He repeated his application and this time attempted to make his case seem more deserving by offering to hand in his stripes. What was more to the point, Haverkamp, when next he visited the big-wigs of the Administrative Branch, took it upon himself to drop a few words about a certain Wazemmes, "a young fellow who had once been in his service, excellent in every way, who had behaved very well at the front, where he had asked to be sent from the cavalry, but had been seriously wounded, and had refused a discharge, though he was quite unfit for duty with the infantry and would be much better employed in an office." The particular big-wig in question made a note of the details, and three days later Wazemmes was informed in writing that he had been attached, as a simple private, to the Messenger and General Utility Section of the Administrative Branch. (The attitude of his comrades caused him a momentary anxiety, but he soon discounted it: "Bah, they'd be only too glad to be in my shoes.") His new employers would have been perfectly willing to take him, stripes and all, but since he had been foolish enough to offer to resign his rank, the infantry which had bestowed it, now withdrew it. Taken all in all, Wazemmes's flirtation with the infantry had not turned out any too well.

Haverkamp, informed of the result of his intervention, thought: "Better wait a few weeks before claiming him, so as not to seem too greedy all at once."

In the meantime Wazemmes, who was free to do what he liked from six to nine, put himself at his boss's disposition during those hours. Haverkamp did, in fact, give him one or two jobs to do.

CHAPTER TWENTY

"It's Appalling!"

In spite of its immediate anxieties in connexion with the battle of Verdun, G.H.Q. at Chantilly by no means abandoned the various inquiries and surveys which it had in hand. Some of these were directed to thwarting the further plans of the enemy, who, though for the moment he seemed to be pinned down to the Verdun salient, was quite capable of preparing a surprise elsewhere. Others were directed towards amassing a great deal of fresh information in view of the offensive which the Allied armies had by no means abandoned. In particular, all commanders of armies and army groups were invited to submit periodic statements and suggestions relative to conditions on their fronts. Although it was no business of theirs to meddle in the general conduct of operations, it was open to them to make proposals for diversions which might have the effect of relieving pressure on the Verdun sector, in accordance with the military principle which holds that just because the senior officer can rely on implicit obedience to his orders, his junior officers (at any rate those above a certain rank) must be left free to express their views before those orders shall have taken final shape.

Consequently, for the last few days Duroure had undertaken, in Clédinger's company, a series of visits to various points on the front held by his group, his object being to collect as much fresh evidence and up-to-the-minute information as possible in support of a report, voluminous in extent and startling in its range, which he proposed submitting to Chantilly. These tours, which were long and detailed, led to considerable disruption of his normal time-table. He got back to his headquarters when he could—sometimes well after dark.

On the particular evening with which we are concerned he was driving rapidly, followed by his second car, along a road which would take him back to L—, after having made a detour towards the rear to visit a reserve artillery park. He was still about fifteen miles from L—. It was pitch dark, though the sky was clear but for a few patches of cloud. His head-lights were full on.

"We shan't dine before eight o'clock—a quarter past, prob-ably," said the general. "After dinner, if you're agreeable, we'll go to my office and work till about eleven."

But Clédinger had just then been listening with lifted head.

"What's that, sir?"

He pointed with his finger at a long, dark shape which was travelling across the sky in almost exactly the reverse direction to their own movement.

Both men exclaimed simultaneously:

"A Zeppelin!"

"Switch off your lights; quick!" said the general to the dri-ver. The second car overhauled them in a white glare of illu-mination. "Switch off! Switch off, there! don't you see the Zeppelin?" The road became almost invisible. "Go on slowly. If you're afraid of an accident, pull up.... You there, behind, don't you go overrunning us!"

Then, turning to Clédinger:

"What are they doing here? It's very annoying. I only hope the fellows up the line saw it cross and remembered to tele-phone! It's probably on the look-out for stations or depots. If all lights haven't been dimmed there'll be a pretty mess up! ...Why aren't the gunners trying to get him? I haven't heard a shot. Well, I hope Radigué's taken the necessary steps."

As soon as the Zeppelin had disappeared they switched on their lights again and continued on their way to L— at high speed. They met only two convoys. The first had seen the air-ship but had no more to report; the second had seen nothing.

When they reached the outskirts of L— they were con-scious of a degree of animation unusual at such an hour and on so dark a night. All the lamps had been extinguished except two which had been reduced to a glimmer—proof that the Zeppelin had been sighted and the alarm given.

A little farther on, Duroure thought he could detect a mingled smell of rubbish and explosive. "I wonder," he said to himself.

The house in which the general was quartered stood with one or two others on the summit of a small rise. It was the "smart" district of L—. The two cars started to climb the slope which led to it. They had to round two more bends before the house would come into view. The number of people in the street, civilians and soldiers alike, was decidedly greater than usual. The smell seemed to become more accentuated. Passers-by were stopping to peer at the two cars in the darkness. Their faces wore a look of strained curiosity as though they had never seen anything of the sort before.

They swung round the last bend; the beam of the headlights flooded the corner of the house with dazzling whiteness, then slid over towards the left and the entrance to the little square.

"Gosh!" exclaimed Duroure. Clédinger said nothing.

The general's house was in ruins. Not entirely, however. The main block, standing parallel to the square, behind a small strip of garden, appeared to be intact. It was the farther wing, at right angles to the main block, and giving on to an interior courtyard, in which the general's room was situated, that had received the bomb fair and square. The whole building had been split open from roof to ground level. The torn ceilings hung over a gaping void. Scattered rubble lay about. The general's room had not collapsed, but the side wall had been carried away, and it was clear that everything inside had been reduced to smashed debris.

A small crowd was jostling inside the courtyard. Men were moving about with lanterns, hurricane-lamps, and large acetylene flares. Some staff officers were examining a mass of papers which had been recovered from the ruins.

"It happened at seven ten precisely, sir. It must have been the Zeppelin that passed you, judging by the time and the course it was steering. Nobody saw it arrive. It was navigating with lights out. By the time we could hear the engines it was on top of us. It was entirely unexpected. We were warned by telephone of its approach, but by the time the messages came through it had come and gone. How that happened I don't know. When it got over the town it reduced speed. We got the impression that it made a half-circle....All the lights here were full on. You see, nobody was expecting anything. Not that there are many of them or that they're particularly bright. It dropped two bombs in all; one full on the house. The other hit a row of alders by the river. I don't know what they were aiming at there...but it's pretty obvious they were aiming at something, sir. The extraordinary thing is that they hit the target so plumb. Mere chance of course."

Duroure, preceded by a young staff officer and followed by Radigué, Clédinger, and several others, had succeeded in climbing to his room by a small staircase at the far end of the building, which had remained intact. The party was equipped with a variety of lamps. They could only just see their way.

"Look out, sir...Let me go first. I don't think everyone ought to come at once. I believe the floor supports are still standing, but one never knows."

One of the four walls of the room looked as though it had been sheared away by the vertical blow of a great knife, and on that side there was nothing but open space. On the same side, at the inner corner, a large piece of ceiling had collapsed, and a mass of rubbish and debris, mixed with various odds and ends which had fallen from the floor above and from the attic, lay on the general's bed, three quarters of which was entirely covered.

Duroure stared at his bed. He seemed stunned as by some sight that staggers the imagination, and deeply moved.

"If I'd been there, I should have been killed as sure as fate," he said.

A moment later:

"It's fantastic!...absolutely fantastic!"

Then he fell silent, still gazing at his bed beneath its covering of brickbats.

At the end of a minute one of the officers ventured to make a remark:

"Luckily, sir, you wouldn't have been in your room in any case just then."

"Nonsense!" replied Duroure sharply, without turning his head. "I frequently went up to my room for a moment just exactly then, a minute or so before dinner, to brush my hair or wash my hands…or take a pill.…There used to be a dressing-table just over there…" and he indicated the abyss that yawned to the right of the bed.

He added, in the same tone of solemn pathos and profound disturbance:

"All my things must have gone down there."

It was clear that he meant his toilet articles.

He glanced round the rest of the room. Most of the furniture was in its accustomed place. But the chest of drawers, the armchairs, the wall table, and the carpet were all covered with white dust and rubbish.

Duroure, nodding his head several times, spoke again:

"It's appalling!" he said.

CHAPTER TWENTY-ONE

Complaint at G.H.Q.

Lieutenant-Colonel G. was in his office, where he was in the habit of working every evening until a late hour. He was preparing a number of drafts on which a decision would be taken next day by the Commander-in-Chief after consultation with his most intimate advisers. Most of them had to do with the battle of Verdun, which had just entered on its second month. The lieutenant-colonel had before him various reports either issued by the Army of Verdun or having reference to it. He examined them one by one with scrupulous and at times anxious care.

There was, first of all, the battle-strength state just rendered for the 11th of March. According to it the IInd Army on that date comprised 13,120 officers; 471,606 other ranks; 164,644 horses and mules. In other words, since February 21st—that was to say, in nineteen days—in spite of negligence in some quarters and opposition in others, the Army of Verdun had grown from less than 150,000 to slightly under 500,000 men. The artillery, especially the heavy batteries, had increased in much the same proportions. Not too bad, especially if one took into consideration the losses over the same period.

For there was also, lying on the lieutenant-colonel's desk, a casualty return. The first official statistics went no further than the 5th of March, the thirteenth day of the battle: "Killed, 243 officers; 7,714 other ranks. Wounded, 794 officers; 27,189 other ranks. Missing, 560 officers; 32,939 other ranks. Total, 1,607 officers; 67,842 other ranks." Provisional figures for the subsequent period, up to March 21st, brought these totals to 1,900 officers; 80,000 other ranks. Reckoning the daily average, therefore, on this basis, it looked as though by the 31st of

March the inclusive losses in the two categories would stand at 2,200 and 90,000 respectively.

"But by that date," said the lieutenant-colonel to himself, "we've got to have in line at Verdun 520 or 530,000 men with their due complement of officers. Pétain insists, and Pétain is right; all the more so, since things seem to have come to a standstill on the left bank, which looks as though we may have to reckon with a renewed offensive there."

For the tenth time he embarked on the difficult game which he had to play unaided there at his desk, which consisted in shifting about the various units, withdrawing from the Verdun front exhausted divisions for a period of rest, and bringing up others, first into reserve and later into the line. These he had to take either from general reserve, from the local reserves of the several army groups, or, at a pinch, from other sectors which could be denuded without too grave a risk. The problem was made all the more difficult by the terrible rate of wastage, which on the Verdun front—taking into account not only actual casualties but also the exhausted condition of the survivors—amounted to one whole division in every forty-eight hours.

To help him, he had before him numerous scraps of paper marked with the numbers of corps, divisions, and even brigades. Marginal notes gave such additional information as the names of the generals in question, the date and nature of each formation's previous move and employment, with such other details as might seem relevant. These scraps of paper were destined to form a row of small heaps, or, rather, of tiny fans in which the separate pieces overlapped like the cards in a hand. Each fan-shaped group was arranged under a cardboard label with a written designation, these proceeding from left to right in the following order:

In line: (units in battle order, or in group reserve)
In army reserve
On the move
Withdrawn from the line (in process of reorganizing)
Available on March 20th in other sectors

Available before March 31st in other sectors in case of extreme necessity.

What he had set himself to achieve was the most rational arrangement of the first four groups on the 31st of March. The raw material of his work, even certain suggested decisions, had been furnished by the lieutenant-colonel's colleagues. He had also, available for immediate reference, two maps filled in by the Intelligence people in consultation with the Operations staff. The first of these, inscribed in a bold, round hand: *Order of Battle on the Verdun Front up to March 20th, 1916, with Appendices*, gave the arrangement of formations under the first four headings (in line, in army reserve, etc.) as it had been on the 20th of March. Of this the lieutenant-colonel had been forced to make use in building up his first four heaps. The other map gave the redistribution proposed by the Intelligence and Operations sections, taking into account the demands made by the Army of Verdun as well as the general situation of the front, as due to come into effect on the 31st. The lieutenant-colonel might have been content merely to examine this scheme (which in all probability was very sensible), improving a detail here and there. But, being on his guard against mental laziness, he preferred to make his own solution of the problem first and then compare it with notes furnished by his staff. The disadvantage of this method was that it took a long time and demanded great concentration in the midst of constant interruptions caused by the coming and going, the entrance and exit, of a crowd of persons, by telephone calls, and by the constant threat of diversion. Consequently, it was his rule to take in hand this particular piece of work between dinner and midnight, when he could rely on a period of relative tranquillity.

Once more, after a good deal of shuffling, he had arranged before him the pack corresponding to the rubric *In line*, and was now giving his attention to each separate piece of paper, being careful not to lose sight of the marginal notes: "EM 13…N.B.: attached to IIIrd Army"; "EM 20…N.B.: can't be in the line before 30th"; "EM 33…N.B.: in the line on 20th;

relieved EM 21, due for army reserve...." Just then there was
a knock at the door.

"Come in."

Captain Maynard appeared, with a guilty look on his face.

"I'm sorry to interrupt you, sir, but General Duroure has
just been on the telephone. He was very insistent, sir. I told
him you couldn't possibly speak to him, that I didn't even
know where you were…But I had to promise to have a word
with you at the first possible moment."

"What does he want? Don't tell me the Germans are
attacking on his front."

"No, sir, it's not that exactly....It seems a Zeppelin has
crossed his lines...."

"A Zeppelin, ah!…"

"We knew that already, sir. A telephone message came
through earlier from S——, where it seems to have dropped two
bombs on a dump...."

"Much damage?"

"Not much, sir. One or two wounded, and a certain
amount of material destroyed. After that the Zeppelin turned
back, but, you'll never guess, sir"—the captain had to make an
effort not to smile—"on its way there, the Zeppelin dropped
a couple of bombs and scored a direct hit on the general's
quarters—smashed the place up, sir...."

"Badly?"

"Yes, sir."

"Was General Duroure there?"

"No, sir…he was going round the line."

"So much the better for him. Any casualties?"

"By some miracle, not one. But the general sounded in a
terrible state. I could hear him trembling with rage at the
other end of the wire. He wanted to speak to General Joffre.
He wanted…"

"A declaration of war to be sent to the German government? He's a bit late in the day...."

The captain felt at liberty to release the guffaw of laughter
which he had been holding back since the beginning of the
interview.

"He wanted in any case to speak to you, sir, and to know at what time tomorrow he could see the C.-in-C. He said that his quarters had been carefully registered and deliberately attacked…that there must be spies in L— and its neighbour-hood…that the incident was extremely serious…that every-thing must be held up while the necessary measures were taken…that he might have to consider the immediate shifting of his headquarters…and I don't know what else, sir.…He was unbelievably violent…I'm not sure I remember all he said.…For two pins he'd have blackguarded me…he did blackguard me.…I swore by everything I hold sacred that I would report the whole matter to you as soon as you were back in your office, and that first thing tomorrow morning you would explain the full gravity of the situation to General Joffre."

"I see. And did you take the opportunity, may I ask, to point out that we too had our minor worries in connexion with a certain place called Verdun?"

"No, sir; but you'll be able to do that yourself. He's quite certain to ring up again in the morning."

"You did quite right to warn me!"

"He even spoke of coming to Chantilly himself tomorrow."

"What, all the way from the Vosges? You're joking!"

"I certainly am not, sir."

Lieutenant-Colonel G. gave himself up to a moment or two of amusement; then:

"What a pity we've got other things to think of.… It won't be without its comic side.… And now please forgive me"—he nodded towards his scraps of paper—"I want to get this done tonight."

Next evening Lieutenant-Colonel G. went into Joffre's room.

"You won't believe it, sir, but he's come."

"Who?"

"Duroure."

Joffre raised his eyebrows, opened his eyes wide, and allowed a comfortable smile to spread over his face while deep laugh-ter shook his stomach.

"The man's mad!" he said.

G., also smiling, made a gesture indicative of polite contradiction.

"If you'd rather not see him," he said, "I'll try to edge him off, sir."

Joffre thought for a moment.

"He won't be turned away so easily after a journey of nearly two hundred and fifty miles....What on earth time can he have started?...Bring him in. But tell him that I can spare exactly five minutes."

"Good evening, Duroure; having trouble?"

"You know what's happened, sir? ...Perhaps they didn't tell you...."

"Yes, yes. They're rough customers, these Germans, eh? This is the first time they've done a thing like that. What have you been up to?"

Joffre joked away quietly, all the while watching Duroure out of the corner of his eye.

For the first time since the beginning of his expedition, Duroure, whose nerves were not in the best condition after his interminable motor drive, was visited by a moment's doubt.

"Don't you think it's serious, sir...as an indication, I mean?" he said rather shamefacedly.

"Oh, to be sure," replied Joffre, still on a light note. "I can't have them going about killing my generals...." Then suddenly his tone changed. He stopped laughing and shot a brusque question at his visitor: "What do you want me to do about it?"

"I don't know, sir....Of course, the house was very badly situated...."

"Then you must find another!" said Joffre. In a voice in which dignity, harshness, and mockery were subtly mingled, he added:

"My advice is that you don't change your headquarters. At the present time it would make all sorts of complications for you—and for us. We've quite enough to bother us without that. Besides, the moral effect would be bad. The men, you know, are very simple-minded. I'm not saying that they want to see bombs falling on our heads, but when one does happen to come our way, they rather expect us to practise what we preach, and not desert our posts."

He reverted to his former air of cordiality, and held out his hand:

"Good night, Duroure. You must forgive me for not asking you to stay to dinner. Verdun's giving us a lot of work just now. The Germans are beginning to exert considerable pressure on the left bank. They took the Bois d'Avocourt and the Bois de Malancourt the day before yesterday. They're pressing me as hard as they can on what remains to us of the Forges stream …and this is only a beginning!…They mean to get across at all costs.…Good night. You'd better get back at once. So many things may happen.…You'll be a bit tired, but you'll sleep all the better for the trip.…You'll have forgotten the whole business by tomorrow morning."

CHAPTER TWENTY-TWO

Jallez Also Is in the Boot Trade

Jerphanion looked at Jallez, who was wearing a very odd sort of uniform: an old-pattern great-coat with the skirts turned back; a pair of shabby and faded red trousers tucked into leather gaiters; and a rather newer cap, obviously turned out by a good maker, and worthy of a sergeant of reserve in time of peace.

"You're wondering about my cap? The one they issued me was awful, and much too small, so I bought myself this one."

"It's terribly smart. But I don't mind telling you that those trousers make you look as though you'd stolen it....You hadn't finished telling me what you're doing."

"Oh well, let's get that off our chests, and then we can talk about you....I am in charge of boot repairs."

"What?"

"Don't misunderstand me. The post is not a very exalted one. I'm really a sort of scrutineer. I sit all day behind a black, greasy bench, passing through my hands, one by one, a large number of boots of various ages—most of them extremely old. These boots reach me from the workshop where they have been undergoing more or less extensive repairs. I have beside me an assistant—yes, I mean what I say, an assistant...a lad less well educated than I, and, in a general way, regarded by the authorities as less robust....This lad holds a paper which has become greasy from much handling. It is a statement of all the repairs put through, and might, in fact, be termed a nominal roll, since each boot appears on it as a separate item. I seize a boot. My assistant reads out the list of relevant repairs, as, for instance: one invisible patch; twelve nails; twenty-four nails; vamp resewn; resoling; half-heeling—I spare you the various technical phrases—at which I run a professional eye over the sewing, the twelve nails, the new piece of sole, and I say: 'Two centimes,' 'Seven centimes,' 'Thirteen centimes'—and my assistant enters the amounts. It's an odd sort of process, which passes through a great number of stages. The master cobbler, like the master tailor, is a man who lives on commission. His 'hands' are provided by the State, and so, I suspect, is his raw material—though I'm not yet up in all the mysteries—and he has a right, in respect of each repair executed, to a sum of money of roughly the value I have indicated. He is paid for his position as supervisor, for his initiative, if you like, his power of making others work. In the ordinary course of events he earns considerably more than a Sorbonne professor or a general. He is a big man in his way. I have never met him in the flesh....I have nothing to do in fixing the tariff; I merely refer to a ready-reckoner. But I must have a sharp eye. Where I think a job has been scamped I can refuse to accept it—if, say, only eleven nails have been put in instead of the twelve contracted for....You don't find me passing a thing like that!"

"Did you tell them who you were?"

"When they were considering what sort of work to put me to, I just mentioned that I had been through the École Normale Supérieure and held a degree in Philosophy. They made a note of it."

"And you don't find all this in opposition to your principles?"

"Not too much so. If boots are sinews of war, it's only very indirectly....Besides, I don't do the repairing. Even if I did, I should find the work less—how shall I put it?—disturbing than if I were a hospital orderly. For, shut one's eyes to it as one may, one can't help realizing that most of the nursing done in hospital isn't primarily in the interests of the wounded, isn't really dictated by motives of charity or humanity. ...The object of getting them well is that they may be sent back to the front as soon as possible. All I send back to the front is boots."

Jerphanion hesitated a moment; then he said: "And your

views are still the same as those you expressed, do you remember, in one of the letters you wrote me?—that it's important there should be a sprinkling here and there of men like you, men who refuse, as far as possible, to get mixed up in the 'universal crime'? You think it makes a difference, however small?"

Jallez did not reply at once. He weighed his words before uttering them.

"In my heart of hearts, as you may guess, I go a great deal further than that. If one could bring it about that millions of men on both sides should refuse to get mixed up in 'the universal crime,' then I should agree with you that the 'sprinkling' was not worth bothering about, was a mere childish makeshift. But in the absence of those millions, it is still worth while to give one's mite to the cause of saving, if only symbolically, the dignity of man, the invisible seed-ground of the future...of that future about which you have become so sceptical. I am convinced that at all periods of the world's history, particularly in the blackest, this role played by a handful—no matter how small—has been inestimably precious, yes, necessary; far more necessary than the other duties called for by the times. When, for example, human sacrifices were the common rule, I believe that those who managed not to take part in the feast, not to take their share of the body, their platterful of blood when the victim was parcelled out among the onlookers, were not working against the interests of humanity, were not out of sympathy with the future, were not without a value for the ages yet to come. I know that there have been times when you too thought along such lines....You know the dogma of the Communion of Saints—a very lovely conception? While the barons and the robbers of the Middle Ages at their height were pillaging, burning, and slaughtering, while the whole world was more or less given over to a career of mutual massacre, don't you think that the men who shut themselves up in remote monasteries in an effort to keep the hands of their fellow-men pure and undefiled were working for the salvation and the absolution of all? There's no lack of people to do the rest of the world's work—but for that particular duty there are few enough....There are priests, I know, who boast that they are sharing the dangers of the trenches. ...All the more reason, then, for a 'sprinkling here and there' to think of what is due to God....But enough of me and my concerns. I want to know how you've been getting on at Verdun. I've thought about you such a lot! I breathed so much more freely when I got your letter saying you were coming on leave. I do hope you're not going back. Surely you've done enough....Naturally I don't expect you to go into details. But, you see, there's one thought in particular from which I can never get free, one thought that torments me continually: How can human flesh and blood stand it? How can you, of all men, carry on?"

Chapter Twenty-three

At a Café on the Boulevards.
The Miseries, the Pride, and the Contemptuous
Superiority of the Fighting Soldier

They were seated in front of a café on one of the Boulevards, between the rue Drouot and the faubourg Montmartre, almost opposite the Variétés. Jerphanion had grown thinner. His eyes were brighter than of old. He was bronzed by life in the open air, but the colour of his cheeks had an odd look of being superimposed upon a basis of flesh which had been eaten away by some corrosive poison.

"This leave of mine doesn't mean that I've sneaked out of anything. We were in the line for nineteen days at a stretch, from the night of the 11th and 12th to that of the 29th and 30th."

"The 29th and 30th? Why, that was the night before last."

"Yes. I was propelled straight here, like a trench-mortar bomb. But do you realize what nineteen days bang in the middle of the battle of Verdun means? I find it almost impossible to believe that it all happened."

"Were you in the same place the whole time?"

"Yes; in that Haudromont Valley I wrote to you about."

"And all the time you were there you didn't retire?"

"Not a step."

"Were they attacking?"

"Not in a big way—just local raids; some of them so local that they didn't even involve the whole of the sector. And we weren't sent over the top either during that time—there was nothing in the full-dress line—assault, zero hour, and all that. But don't run away with the idea that we had a nice quiet fortnight."

"I'm not such a fool."

"We didn't actually have many casualties.... They'd told me

we shouldn't, but that didn't prevent my being surprised when I came to make up my returns—not many more than in a so-called 'quiet' part of the line. I know, of course, that our effectives were reduced to almost nothing. A company reduced by fifty per cent can't, other things being equal, lose as many men as a company at full strength. But, for all that, it's a curious fact—and rather deceptive. People at a distance, judging our situation from the casualty returns, would probably have said: 'Well, they've not got much to grumble at.' But they'd have been wrong, for all that!"

"But, tell me, wasn't your comparative freedom from losses rather abnormal? The figures we've been given for the battle as a whole have been so huge."

"It's like this: In the first place, you've no idea how little one bothers about losses not one's own when one's in the line. If one's own lot gets the worst of it, one feels it like hell; if someone else, well, it all depends. If you've been in a show with another company, and it's come off worse than you have, you condole, more or less for appearance' sake, but deep down you're conscious of a sort of pride: '*We* know how to look after ourselves; even danger is frightened of coming too near us.' If it's had losses as a result of being detailed for a job which you might have had to tackle instead, then you're secretly— sometimes not so very secretly either—delighted, though your conscience may be slightly uncomfortable, and you may be aware of a touch of anxiety about the next time. You're afraid that luck may turn, and that you may have to pay later for your immunity….As to the more remote companies, the other battalions, the rest of the regiment—you aren't really aware of them as living entities. You don't, of course, want to see them sacrificed for others. You'd hate to find, after some offensive, that your regiment had had heavier casualties than other regiments….You dislike the feeling that the unit to which you belong is out of luck. There may even, if you insist, be a sort of feeling of sympathy for the chaps who wear the same numbers on their collars as you. But there's not much more to it than that. When it comes to thinking about the losses on the whole Verdun front…well, you feel about as much concerned personally as you would in some problem of metaphysics. You just don't bother about them, except when you're out of the line, and then only in order to impress civilians. Nowhere in the world is there such a close, clannish feeling as in the front line....Well, that's that. But you were asking me a question, weren't you? Why, you wanted to know, were casualties so light in my particular corner of the battle-field?... The explanation's quite simple. Up to the 20th we'd hardly been shelled at all. The big and medium stuff was going over our heads to burst more or less far to the rear. The Boches were afraid of hitting their own men who were lying very close to us."

"How far?"

"About fifty yards."

"Then you could see one another perfectly easily?"

"You've said it. We were near enough even to blackguard one another. Some of the Boches used to shout insults at us at night. Nothing very serious—rather like the rude jokes that fly about between two gangs of boys, two classes at school, two dormitories. Since there was a good deal of foliage still left in the wood (it was eventually thinned out a good deal by gunfire), some of the Germans had a way of climbing the trees and sniping into our trenches. Our fellows paid them out by crawling out after dark on all fours and throwing grenades into their lines. You remember at school, how we used to shout at each other from our study windows? Well, it was all rather like that. In Haudromont Valley the game used to result, as a rule, in a few dead on either side. But that was because the two gangs of boys concerned happened to be playing with real rifles, with live grenades, and with bombs that could blow a man to pieces. What one's apt to forget in thinking about this war is that, for the most part, it's being conducted by very young men. A few fathers of families pull it back to a serious level, contribute a bit of humbug, but they're the exceptions: they don't set the tone. The young fel-lows soon get used to the dirt, the crudity, the lack of comfort. They don't bother about the future, and they're not easily moved to compassion. They can be fierce with a grin on their

lips. But I don't want to give you a false impression in this
matter of casualties. After the 18th or the 20th we did get a
few shells, 77's and 105's, those of us especially who were on
the far side of the valley. The Boche gunners no doubt
thought that they could drop stuff on us there without hitting
their own men. But it was the fatigues that copped it worst.
The poor devils used to start off between six and eight to go
down for rations, and they had to pass through the area where
the heavy shells were falling. They had to move almost completely in the open; the communication trenches made practically no difference at all. Of every eight that set out only
about five or four returned. Sometimes none of them
returned at all. One day the ration parties of I don't know
how many units were blown to bits with the limbers round
which they were waiting for the night's issue. That was the
beginning of a frightful time. Movement of any kind became
almost impossible. We were three days without food, and we
had practically no reserve rations to fall back on. Men don't
die of hunger, I agree, in three days, if they're spending the
time in bed. But just think what it's like for fellows in the last
stages of exhaustion, who get hardly any chance to drop off
to sleep, and when they do, can't, who spend every day and
every night in bitter cold and damp, with their nerves continuously on the stretch because of the day-to-day risks
which they have to face, with a corresponding expenditure of
nervous energy, and then think what they must feel like when
there's not a bite to eat or a drop to drink except what they
can scrape out of the bottom of their mess-tins and collect
from dirty pools of water, for twenty-four hours at a stretch,
and then for another twenty-four hours; and then a third day
dawns which there's no reason to think will be any different
from the days that have gone before. Why are you looking at
me like that?"

"I'm thinking of my poor old Jerphanion going through all
that…and then, yes, I just stare and stare."

"Your poor old Jerphanion, true to his character as a careful and cunning old man of the mountains, had stowed away,
for just such an eventuality, two big bars of chocolate, a dozen

or so lumps of sugar, and a flask of crème de menthe. And though, as you well know, he is an incorrigible optimist, he had got into the way of never expecting anything good of the morrow, with the result that during the first twenty-four hours he ate only one bar of chocolate and five lumps of sugar and drank a third of his flask; and during the second twenty-four hours, half a bar of chocolate, three lumps of sugar, and little more than another third of his crème de menthe. So well had he managed, indeed, that he began the third day with half a bar, four lumps, and more than a third of his little flask still in hand. Not that that would have gone far. But what do you think we did? Not I, but my men, and they were decent enough to let me go shares. They crawled out at night to where they had noticed a lot of dead bodies, Boches and French alike, most of them old and rotting, lying out between the lines, and rifled their pockets and mess-tins of anything they could find—bits of biscuit, scraps of chocolate, even sausage. Do you realize what that meant?—sausages that had lain cheek by jowl for weeks with corpses, pickled in a stench of decomposing flesh. We ate them. Doesn't that disgust you a bit?"

"My dear fellow, how can you say that?"

"I should understand if it did. I sometimes find myself wondering, in a sudden panic, whether I'm not in the way of developing great numb patches in my sensibility of which I shall never be cured—even if I do come through this war. Delicacy of feeling. What a wonderful expression! Shall I ever again know what delicacy of feeling is? I may be nervous, irritable, exasperated by trifles, but shall I ever recover that sensitiveness which is the mark of civilized man? I sometimes see myself in the future transformed into a sort of invalid who has suffered an amputation of all his delicate sentiments, like a man who has lost all his fingers and can only feel things with a couple of stumps. And there will be millions of us like that."

"No, no, you re wrong. You'll soon get well again. After two weeks of peace there'll be nothing left of what you describe. The human spirit is like that, as you very well know. In next to no time it lets forgetfulness swallow up the times that have bruised it too heavily, that have seemed too unworthy of its destiny. It joins itself up to the days that went before all that. It's just like what we do when we wake from sleep and suppress a whole series of stupid nightmares, beginning again in thought precisely where we left off the night before."

"These last nineteen days at Verdun have stunned me like a knock-out blow. Looking back on it all, I'm inclined to think that until then I might have managed to come through unscathed, and that's saying a good deal!...But now something's been broken that can never be replaced....I feel it in my bones....I confess that if you asked me, I should be hard put to it to say why. Except for the three days I have just told you of, I saw nothing and endured nothing that I hadn't already more or less seen and endured. I'm not sure that I haven't even been through worse times. Of course, we were longer in the line than usual. But, all that apart, it's no use trying to find logical explanations of what one feels living that kind of subhuman existence...trying to reduce things to their proper proportion. What was it that so particularly demoralized me during that period? Not just going three days without food. No, I think it was the general condition of the sector we had been given to hold, the awful look of those scratches in the ground which they had the cheek to call trenches...the sordidness of everything, the absence of all organization, of all thought for the future; and the hasty digging we had to put in, under continual shell-fire, to get some sort of reality into the second- and third-line positions which those slackers of the Fortified Zone had had six months, a year, to get ready, and without the added terror of bombardment—digging that came on top of everything else, the exhausting job of mounting sentry, constant alarms, working parties....You've no idea how one comes to value, to rely on, the organized routine, the human element, in a sector, especially when one has got used to it over a long period, when one has got into the way, each time one goes up the line, of finding the little habits, the trivial round of duties, which one had left behind at the end of one's last tour. Even when it's a new part of the line, the habits, the little ways, of one's predecessor form a foundation on which one's own can be built up. The place can at least be lived in, even if the sky is raining shells. But that valley of Haudromont was hideous; no man could have lived there....And then somehow, when I first got there, I was under the impression that I was about to make my entry into what the journalists call 'the furnace of Verdun'; you know what I mean—shelling from every side, battles in the woods, advances, retirements, attacks and counter-attacks —an avalanche of dangers, all on the heroic scale...something, anyhow, that should be more terrible than anything we had known before...emotional storms more violent and more continuous than at any previous time.... And that's one proof the more of the deadening of one's sensibility about which I was speaking just now. Do you see what I mean? Whenever we front-line fighters, intoxicated as we are by the heady draughts of war, remain for any length of time in conditions that can be called comparatively peaceful, without, that is, having to undergo any particularly violent shocks, we feel worried, unoccupied. We are conscious of a sensation of emptiness. Don't read into my words what isn't there. We don't want to get back to a state of terror. We aren't looking for danger, oh no! But it is a fact that when each violent shock ebbs, it leaves behind it, deep down in us, a void, the hideous kind of void that follows a demolition; and nothing comes to take its place. Life seems like a roadway between two walls that have collapsed in ruin....We just wait. We are terrified, horrified, at the thought of what may be coming next, but if nothing comes, or if what comes is less convulsive, less tense and taut with violence, our nerves are, as it were, left in the air. They had got ready to face the next shock, and no shock comes—only the hateful, grim necessity of sticking it. One had prepared oneself for the most staggering blow of the lot, and there's no staggering blow. Do you see what I'm getting at? One gets used to the paroxysm. It's a kind of vice. The opium addict is ill unless he has his ration of pipes. It gives you some idea of the degree of deterioration to which we have all come when a man like me can quite honestly feel that the valley of Haudromont, bang in the middle of the battle of Verdun, is no longer a paroxysm. What progress I must have made in the descent into hell! I begin to wonder whether, when peace comes, I shall be capable of living in a world where I shall have to go for months without trembling from head to foot because a shell has burst twenty yards off."

"But just now, don't you see, you're still feeling the effect of those three awful weeks. You're like an overtired man who says to himself: 'I shall never be able to sleep again; never.' But as night succeeds night he slowly learns once more to sleep."

"Perhaps, perhaps. But, all the same, I'm afraid of what may happen. To become that—a piece of wreckage thrown up by the catastrophe; a wretched creature so inured to violence that he finds normal life a bore, finds that it has no more hold on him than a cogwheel with blunted teeth. If I was given the chance tomorrow of taking up my old job at Orléans, I should jump for joy, but my reaction would be only a reasoned reaction. I should be pleased because I ought to be pleased...and for my wife's sake. But I can't see myself settling down to correct exercises. At the first tiny difficulty with my superiors or with the family of one of my pupils, I know I should exclaim: 'Oh hell! No more hanging around for me! I'd rather be sitting down under a barrage.'"

Jallez listened, pondering what he heard.

"Something of the sort's bound to happen," he said quietly; "otherwise it would be impossible to keep the war going...impossible to get men to face it afresh again and again—for that's what you're doing, all of you—being sent in, taken out, sent in once more. You're waging not one war but several....I'm not suggesting that you go back to it each time with cries of joy, but you do go back. Obviously the idea of a goal, of moving towards a goal, may bolster up the spirits of some, but not of all, and not all the time. I imagine that when you're in the line, you don't waste much time thinking about the general situation....Do you even read the communiqués?"

"Only sometimes, I admit, and then very superficially. But there are other reasons to account for that. We dislike communiqués because they are cold and distant. They distort the life we know. When we read: 'A certain amount of artillery fire in the Tahure sector. Night comparatively calm on the rest of the Champagne front,' we know it to mean that our pals round Tahure have been sitting for hours under a damned tornado of shells, and that from one end to the other of the Champagne front the night has been made hideous with grenades, flares, trench-mortar bombs, and raids. Similarly, when we've been conducting a God-awful operation which made our eyes jump out of our heads, and set the fellows all round us throwing up their guts, we don't get much of a kick from reading in three quarters of a line that 'a minor adjustment was carried out in our positions to the left of the Nth Army.' As to the general situation, you're quite right. We in the trenches bother about it a good deal less than the folks in the back areas, and not a great deal more when we're in the back areas ourselves. When we've been on leave, too, or out of the line at rest, it's not by thinking of the general situation that we screw up our courage when it comes to going back."

"How do you screw it up, then?" asked Jallez in the same quiet tone.

"Difficult to say....Perhaps by thinking of all the pals we're going to meet once more...of the monastic life we lead— because being in the trenches is like being in a monastery, shut away and isolated, a monastery with walls of fire. We're helped, too, by the idea that we're getting away from all the degradation of the back areas—putting a wall between us and the men behind, a wall that they won't dare to scale. We've barely time to get a whiff of them as we pass by. We guess what they're like rather than know. But the few hints we do collect are enough to fill us with a sort of exaltation at the thought of escaping contamination. You mentioned the monks of the hey-day of the Middle Ages. Don't you think they found it less difficult to go back into their monasteries, no matter how hard their rule of life might be, when they had taken a good look round at the contemporary world and seen from what it was that their monastery walls protected them?"

"What it comes to," Jallez ventured to suggest, still speaking thoughtfully, "is something very like pride."

"Oh rot!" answered Jerphanion. "That's ridiculous!"

But it was his turn to ponder.

"I'm not so sure, though," he said a moment later; "perhaps you're right."

Very slowly Jallez brought out his next question:

"Tell me…when you're here, for instance, sitting outside this café, what do you feel about all these people round you, enjoying the sun, drinking…all of them, my God, as though such places as Verdun and the valley of Haudromont didn't exist?…"

Jerphanion felt that Jallez was putting him to the test; he wanted to show that he was still capable of intellectual honesty.

"Yes, you weren't so far wrong," he said; "we are touched by a sort of pride, and we're most conscious of it, naturally, when we're with other people, people like these. Of what does that pride consist? The armchair windbags would say: 'a glorious sense of duty accomplished.' Duty my eye! There may be a touch of that kind of thing, but it's not the main ingredient. Our pride is the pride of the explorer. We feel that we have returned from an incredible country, a country at which the imagination boggles; that we have managed to live our daily lives there in conditions which are the very antithesis of living; that we have borne hardships, terrors, and endurances which to those here have seemed since childhood things worse than death. Well, we've come through, and here we are, seated peacefully with our fellows, enjoying the sun in front of a café, condescending to take a glass of beer or an apéritif, enjoying the trivial pleasures of the rear, just for a few days; for we're bound to go back, as a sailor goes back to the open sea.…Obviously we can't regard these folk as our equals, for if they were our equals"—and here Jerphanion's voice trembled slightly—"that would mean that we'd made an awful mistake, and that would be harder to forgive than anything.…"

After a pause he continued:

"You see in what a detached way I'm trying to explain it all. It's not so much what *I* feel as a general sort of feeling in which I can't help being soaked, even though my reason repudiates its validity. In spite of myself I've caught something of the infection, and honesty bids me make a clean breast of it all."

"It's very natural—almost, I'm inclined to say, inevitable," replied Jallez.

"Perhaps....Look at that fellow over there. He's on leave too, straight from the trenches; I recognize the type. For all I know, he may be from Verdun. If we met somewhere at the front, I should mean nothing to him and he would mean nothing to me. But here there's a bond between us. We've been through the same 'ordeals,' in the ritual sense of the word. There's a freemasonry of front-line fighters; they form a sort of order...."

For a moment he sat silently smiling at his thoughts.

"Taken by and large, you know, this feeling develops in odd ways, ways of which we're not really conscious. One's not aware of it unless one does a bit of self-examination, as I'm doing now....It's something very deep down in human nature that's working up to the surface again. That's because the conditions that produced it long ago are recurring, are taking root and becoming permanent. What we're seeing now is the re-emergence of the warrior spirit in the bosom of society. I don't mean the spirit of the professional soldier. That's something comparatively recent; no, it's the warrior spirit as it existed centuries ago, the spirit of the man who fought from year's end to year's end while the others didn't...while the others cultivated their gardens, herded their cows, and looked after their children. The warrior knew all sorts of hardships which he kept at a distance from his neighbours, but in exchange for that he was spared the toil of every day and the cares of home. He had the right to be maintained and to be regarded with honour. The others, those who didn't do the fighting, had to make a shift to provide him with the necessaries of life. Such workaday problems were not for him. He looked down on the rest of the world—on women, craftsmen, peasants, all of whom seemed to him to live the lives of slaves. Yesterday, when I was passing a fruiterer's stall, I suddenly realized that I was thinking (you mustn't take this too seriously): 'He ought to think himself damned lucky that we don't relieve him of his pots of jam and his vegetables.' (Probably the memory of my three days' fast had something to do with it.) But there's something in that whole attitude that is pleasurable and stimulating. Isn't that exactly what went to make up the sense of belonging to a noble caste in the great days of aristocracy? The noble fought, let himself be killed, but, apart from that, didn't do a hand's turn. He expected the villein to bring him the tithe of his crops, a proportion of the yield of his wretched industries, the virginity of his female children. My men don't think of themselves as aristocrats, don't address one another as 'Sir knight,' or 'Baron'…because in their eyes those terms have a glamour of age which disguises their real significance. But they are passing through a comparable stage of evolution. Many of them will feel badly let down when, one of these days, they are asked to take up once again their base, mechanic trades. All will accept as their right a pension which shall assure them a means of life when they're beyond work. Put yourself in their place. They've entered into a compact with the nation, and that compact has two main clauses, no less binding for being unspoken: 'You must protect me, even at the cost of your life,' says the nation. 'All right,' replies the soldier, 'but in that case you must make yourself responsible for my life so long as it continues.' The trouble is that there are too many of us, whether it's merely a question of our pride or of the privileges which we claim from the future. It's difficult to be overweeningly proud of a state of life which one shares with millions. It's difficult to expect the nation to keep its warriors indefinitely, when those warriors are no less than 'the nation in arms.' Aristocracy is only an effective doctrine when it's applied to a limited number. The ennobled should not amount to more than a hundred thousand."

"It's an odd situation," said Jallez, "but I like the realism of your approach. The same argument holds good of heroes and martyrs. There's something unsatisfactory about having to admit that four million men in any given country have suddenly become heroes and martyrs."

"You've no idea," went on Jerphanion, "how the mere thought that one has a right to the means of existence, without having to give in exchange the labour of one's hands or the product of one's industry, automatically breeds in one a deep, instinctive pride. Are you amazed to hear me speaking like this? No doubt you will ask what there is to prevent the merely leisured in times of peace from sharing in this sense of pride. The fact remains that they don't. If they are proud it is of the advantages that leisure brings them, and not of the leisure itself. Of recent years many of them have actually felt embarrassed by it. They have been haunted by the thought that they are parasites. The warrior, the noble—and I don't mean the man with his name in the Social Register, the man who merely takes delight in the consciousness of an ancient lineage—feels himself to be anything but a parasite. He thinks: 'It's only because of me that everything goes on as it does.' It wasn't only in front of the fruiterer's stall, but in front of theatre posters, too, and advertisements of concerts, that I've been recently reflecting—or, rather, that the simple soldier who lurks deep within me has been reflecting. 'They ought to consider themselves damned lucky that I'm at Verdun, so they can go on enjoying their lives.' Odd, eh? You see what I'm getting at?"

"I see."

"I'm not trying to justify the common soldier. I'm merely trying to explain to you the feelings—legitimate or absurd—which help him to carry on; feelings which I glimpse occasionally deep in my own heart, feelings which I encourage and recognize, without, for that reason, becoming their slave. Why should I refuse the assistance of anything that saves me from despair? I shouldn't refuse a quart of wine or spirits in the heat of battle. But that doesn't mean that I should become a slave to wine or to spirits, does it? You're to blame, you know, for setting me off like this. You started it with all your talk about pride."

"Please don't apologize.... There's something so genuine in what you've been telling me, something so racy of the soil, and, in an odd way, something so characteristic of yourself. I shall never be able to thank you enough for this proof that our friendship is as it has ever been, this sign—how shall I put it?—that you're not keeping me at arm's length. But there are still one or two questions I want to ask. My excuse must be that I'm for ever asking them of myself, because I do want to get things clear, and that I can never find a satisfactory answer.

"Fire away, old man! It's such a pleasure being able to talk to you about all these things. There's nobody else with whom I could discuss them so freely."

"Honestly? Not even with your army friends?"

"Not even with my army friends."

"Not with your great friend Fabre?"

"Least of all with Fabre, who, if it comes to that, isn't a great friend at all, but a good pal forced on me by circumstances, whom, when the war is over, I doubt whether I shall see more than once every two years. I should be much more likely to discuss things of this sort with Griollet, the leather-worker, but in his case there are certain difficulties of language. It's too much effort to explain to him what I mean, and there's always a danger that he won't quite understand."

"I can't tell you how fine it is to hear you talk like that. But now, tell me this: You were speaking awhile back of the contempt which soldiers feel for the civilian. How does that square with the fact that one's always hearing the men from the front, talking of some friend who's got a soft job, saying: 'Lucky devil! I wish I was in his shoes!'…"

"It's all rather complicated. You've led me perhaps to stress the feelings that help us to face things. But there are others which get us down, which knock us sideways. The front-line soldier always pretends to despise the man with a soft job, but he envies him just the same. How many times haven't I said to myself: 'Isn't my life as valuable as another's? My preservation as important as his—more important for my country than letting myself be blown to pieces in a trench—a service which any man of normal courage could render as well as I?' And then, too, our contempt is very unequally distributed, and in accordance with laws whose secret springs are known only to us. If you were to ask me who it is we despise and hate the most, whom it would give us the greatest pleasure to punish, my answer would be: First of all, the war profiteers, business men of all kinds, and, with them, the professional patriots, the humbugs, the literary gents who dine each day in pyjamas and red leather slippers, off a dish of Boche. Why, only yesterday I was reading an article on Verdun by that swine George Allory, on 'the holocaust of Verdun'—the 'heroes of Verdun'! I needn't quote it; you must know it all beforehand. I even started a letter to him, in which I rubbed his nose in his own beastly excrement, signing with my rank in full and a statement of my qualifications. But I tore it up. A letter is too tame a retort. Stuffed figures like that ought to be killed, stabbed to death with the bayonet, that bayonet which they celebrate so eloquently and christen 'Rosalie' with such a sickening parade of sentiment. The fools! Do you remember that article of Lavedan's which you showed me at the time of the explosion on the *Latouche-Tréville?* He's another who's lived up to his beginnings.... Next in order come the soldiers who have worked themselves into nice safe jobs, officers for the most part. They form a very special category—fellows who are lucky enough to have been posted to some back-area town, twenty or thirty miles behind the line, where they are in no greater danger than you are in your boot store, but play the brave soldier and say: 'We in the trenches.' Those are the men who put in a claim for decorations, and who get them—before we do. They'd be perfectly happy if the war went on for ten years. Never in their lives have they touched so many perquisites as now. And don't they love one another! Their time is as much taken up with intrigues, backbiting, and plots as in the most squalid of peace-time garrisons! The worst offenders are the regulars, the men who deliberately chose the army as a calling in the days before the war, but who, now when we civilians are asked to spill our blood, just take to cover. Their fellow-soldiers hate them as bitterly as we do. Whom else shall I mention? Certain ambitious generals, with hearts of stone, to whom the lives of thousands or tens of thousands mean nothing if, by sacrificing them, they can assure their own advancement or, moved by slightly less selfish motives, carry through pet schemes of their own. These are the men whom we at the front regard as the exact antithesis to Pétain....As to those in soft jobs who lie low and want nothing so much as to escape notice, who probably think of us with feelings of kindliness and compassion, saying: 'After all, it's damned hard luck on the poor bastards'; who look shamefaced when they meet us; who really do want the war to end as soon as possible, if only to avoid the danger being combed out—they don't really get our goat. They are the back-area fellows we envy when we are tempted to envy anybody. I don't suppose there are any of us—with the exception of a few mystically inclined or fanatic men—who have not more than once longed to share the luck of those securely placed individuals; most of us would jump at the chance if it was offered us....Oh, but I was forgetting perhaps the most symbolic of all these back-area figures—the well-set gentleman of a certain age, in a nice warm suit, freshly bathed and pomaded, who sips his chocolate and reads the communiqués, and says: 'Damn slow progress. Trouble is the Staff's too timid. The important thing is to know when to make sacrifices.'"

Jallez laughed.

"The awful thing is that there are so many like that," he said. "I come more in contact with civilians than you do, and I'm always meeting them, always hearing them holding forth. In the lower middle class they're legion. They may not be so well dressed, but their stupidity, their selfishness, their insensitiveness, are just as appalling. My own family, for example, my parents!...You've no idea of the kind of things I've heard them say."

"Oh, mine are just the same, though perhaps not quite in the same way."

"Surely not. People of peasant stock are less prone to that kind of idiotic intoxication than the members of the middle class."

They proceeded to a rather disillusioned discussion. Jallez said that, for the comfort of his soul, he would have liked to be able to regard the vast crowd of soldiers in their horizon blue as so many pitiable victims who not only had had to pay the price of all the political idiocies of peace-time, but were now forced in addition to endure silently all the kicks that came their way as a result of the no less blatant idiocies of war. But certain simple truths were only too obvious. Hadn't all these soldiers been civilians once? And, as civilians, hadn't they taken their share in applauding the asinine antics of a policy which had been directed solely to maintaining national prestige? Hadn't they applauded Millerand's army-pension scheme? Hadn't they welcomed the advent of Poincaré to power? Hadn't they shouted with the rest that Caillaux and Jaurès were in German pay? Hadn't they, in their own fashion, and to the best of their ability, played a part in shaking the pillars of European peace? Was it for them to start whining now that the stones of the building were beginning to fall about their heads? What was the fifty-year-old chocolate-drinker but a soldier who had passed the military age? It wasn't fair to suppose that his selfish stupidity, his crude fire-eating, had been merely the result of his immunity. Ten years earlier he would have taken an honourable place among the heroes and the victims. He, too, would have been brave without illusion, would have shown, like the young men of today, a spirit of bitter resignation, a pride in sacrifice, a contempt for the hypocrisy of others.

"Certainly he would," admitted Jerphanion. "I've had indirect proof that what you say is true. When I was convalescing in hospital, I used to listen to the soldiers talking, N.C.O.'s and privates alike. For a time, at least, they were away from the atmosphere and the realities of life at the front, and they expressed themselves in almost the identical words of the fifty-year-old gentleman with his cup of chocolate. They too thought that things were moving too slowly. They too gobbled up the Boches at every meal with all the proper literary accompaniment of a Lavedan and a George Allory. They were all for big-scale offensives and great slap-up battles. Poor devils like that, lacking all imagination and power of judgment as they do, can only see the war straight if it gives them a daily kick in the pants. It's a pleasant prospect for the future. One of these days, presumably, the business will come to an end, and what'll happen then? Will they start at once just talking nonsense about it all? Will they take their impressions of battle and sudden death from the works of General Cherfils or Maurice Barrès?"

One had to admit, they agreed, that there was a conspiracy of misrepresentation which went deep and spared scarcely anybody.

"War," concluded Jerphanion, "claims many victims, but very few of them are innocent. For some time now, as I think I've told you already, the spectacle of my fellow-men has filled me with loathing. The trouble is that those who are most to blame are not, as a rule, those who suffer the worst punishment."

CHAPTER TWENTY-FOUR

How Verdun Managed to Hold Out

On leaving the boulevards, they wandered down to the quays beside the Seine and, as pilgrims might, moved slowly along the left bank towards Notre-Dame. Jerphanion thus found himself on his direct road home.

"Look here," he said to Jallez, "if you're free this evening, why not come and dine with us? Odette's made no preparations, but that doesn't matter. I'll buy something on the way. Odette'll be delighted to see you. She wanted to come with me to our appointment. It was I who asked her to let me meet you alone. I felt sure that we should talk frankly about all our concerns. As you know, she is very intelligent. There's nothing she can't understand, and in fact I never hide anything from her. But there are certain harshnesses of judgment, certain bitternesses, certain extremes of suffering, that I soft-pedal when I am with her, because they would rouse in her such a terror of despair that she would cry suddenly aloud: 'You mustn't go back!'"

Jallez was caught in a quick wave of emotion at the hint of tragedy which his friend's last words had disclosed.

"Of course I'll come," he said. "I have such happy memories of hours spent with you two when—there still seemed a hope of happiness for the world. We've spoken so much about the war that perhaps we can turn the conversation to other subjects before Odette, eh?"

"If you like…we'll see.…If you've anything in your mind that might offer a little comfort for the future, anything that might bring the prospect of peace a little nearer…it would be very welcome."

"I'll do my best, old man."

"But until we get there, don't put any constraint on yourself. Ask me anything you still want to know."

Jallez spoke with considerable hesitation:

"No...I feel that I'm raking things up unnecessarily...things that you'd much rather forget while you're here."

"Not at all....Just the reverse, in fact. I like getting it off my chest. During all this hideous experience I've become more than ever convinced that Epictetus, Marcus Aurelius...Pascal ...were right. There's only one really heroic remedy for an excess of misery: to think the misery through honestly to the end. I told myself that I would keep a journal, in imitation of the philosopher Emperor; but I lacked the strength of character. A conversation such as we've just had takes its place. Besides, I've never forgotten what you once said on the subject of 'bearing Witness.' Do you remember? It was on the day of our first walk together, our very first, in the neighbourhood of the rue Claude-Bernard and the avenue des Gobelins....The *Road to Emmaus*....The light striking the top of a wall....Doesn't it all come back?...What beauty we knew then! How lovely life could be!...And look at us now, creatures of shreds and patches!...Selfishly speaking, the greatest comfort I could have found in this war would have been to have you beside me in the trenches, as I have had good old Fabre...so that we might have 'borne witness' together...so that, at certain moments, I might have been able to say: 'Do you see this?...Did you see that?...' But fate ruled otherwise....It is terribly important, though, for me to be able, in spite of everything, to make you a witness...to think all these things with you beside me....One of the Disciples at Emmaus was absent from the room when the Figure appeared. His comrade, who witnessed all, could not rest until he had explained what he had seen, until he had made the moment 'live again' for him. That was what he was after—to make the moment live again for his friend....So please go on; ask away."

His face took on the expression of a man setting himself to listen intently. At the same time, in an access of melting tenderness, his eyes took in the magnificent pageant of the river, closed at its far end by the mass of Notre-Dame.

"You've told me much that I find thrilling," said Jallez in measured tones; "but there is a good deal that still remains obscure. I don't yet understand the nature of that strength which can support millions of men in the life of an endless purgatory. You have mentioned the trivial aids, the little thoughts that buoy them up....But are they really enough to account for what is happening? These men of yours are such as we all have known: men cradled, more or less, by civilization. It was not idealism that swept them along....Enthusiasm? For a few days, perhaps, but not for years. How does it come about that these coddled, these matter-of-fact homunculi can endure so much, and over such long periods?"

"The first step was what counted. Once you've begun a thing, it exercises a terrible authority over you. That is one of the laws of existence about which I have fewest doubts. But if one's honest with oneself, one's got to admit that there is yet another authority which governs everything else. One's always realizing that one has somehow avoided mentioning it. Why?...Because it's axiomatic?...Because one's shy about putting it into words?...Even when one does take it into account one disguises it in borrowed plumage that gives it an air more flattering to self-pride: one calls it duty, patriotism, and so forth....Its true name is something much cruder: nothing more or less than the pressure of society. Society today has willed that men should suffer and die on the battlefield. Well then, they just suffer and die. That's all there is to it. At other periods it has willed other things, and men have acted accordingly. The only disconcerting feature about what is happening now is this: that for a long time now men have been told that society no longer had this mystic power over them; that they had certain absolute rights as individuals; that no one could any longer demand of them anything that was not wholly reasonable from the point of view of their own personal existence. Now, from such a point of view, it does seem unreasonable that a man should be asked to give his life—in other words, his all—just to defend that part of the collective interest, often a very small part, which concerns him as an individual. Let him do it if he is moved to do it of his own free will, but no one can 'reasonably' demand it of him. Well, the only explanation to account for what we are seeing is that mankind has not yet learned to take this new theory at its face value. Certainly no one has been sufficiently assured to claim immunity as a right."

"Perhaps you're right. What seems so extraordinary to me is that this pressure should at all times be strong enough to overcome even physical fear."

"It might be truer to say that man's fear of society is still stronger than his fear of shells."

"I suppose that's it.... The soldier says to himself: 'If I refuse to go forward, if I run away, I shall be shot.'"

"That's not it exactly, either.... Some do have to think something like that; but for most of them such deliberate argument is unnecessary. Their fear of society is not a physical fear. It concerns the spirit rather than the body. Man is so made that usually fear for his body is less strong than fear that touches his spirit."

"Even to the extent of controlling his immediate reactions? ...You start going over the top...shells are bursting all around...you find yourself in a machine-gun's field of fire...."

"The point is that the mystical, the spiritual, fear of society can take forms which themselves produce immediate response. On one side of the balance is the fear of shells; on the other the fear of what your pals, what your officer, what your men, if you happen to be an officer, will think. In some ways it needs more courage to make the average man face being dubbed a coward than to get him to stand up to shell-fire."

They spoke of fear. Jerphanion maintained that at the front everyone was afraid, just as everyone is cold when it freezes, the only difference in the way fear manifested itself being due to variations in temperament. The constant presence of danger did, of course, harden men to a certain degree of insensitiveness, but not always. Often, indeed, it had just the opposite effect, screwed the nerves up to an abnormal pitch of exasperation, giving an added horror to anticipation.

"And then, you see, one never entirely gets rid of the fear one has had on previous occasions. The thought of the

advance in which I was wounded last year still terrifies me. If
I had to go over the top again, I should be far more frightened than I was the first time. Fear, too, has its periods; it goes
in waves. There are days when one trembles all over, when
one just can't control one's limbs, and other days when one is
almost indifferent. Why it's impossible to say. I've found out
that one of the best cures for fear is to say to oneself that it's
completely useless (the same holds true of courage). One goes
on saying to oneself: 'Don't be a fool. Is your stomach in your
boots? Are you all strung up? Do your teeth want to chatter?
Well, that won't make the slightest difference to the trajectory of the next shell or the path of the next bullets. It's merely so much fatigue the more.' On such occasions one tries to
behave as though it were simply a question of going out in
the rain, harmless, ordinary rain. It falls in big, heavy drops,
but one just thinks of something else, like a cop huddled up
in his cloak at a street-crossing....See the kind of thing I
mean?...Or else one tries to imagine that one is a pedestrian
stranded in a swirl of cars in the middle of the Place de la
Concorde. Each of them, dashing at full speed across the
square, is more than capable of killing a man; and since they
are all converging from different directions, it seems that
before five minutes are out, one must crush the poor wayfar-
er....And yet, if you're a hardened Parisian, you don't tremble,
your teeth don't chatter....You realize the guile of my system?
One just pretends to believe that each shell will miss one as
each car misses one, and that one can be killed only by the
particular projectile loosed with that deliberate object by
some mysterious power....You remember Napoleon's famous
phrase about the bullet that hadn't yet been cast? It's not
much of a self-deception, but it works. Little things like that
are all one has left in such situations....I'm not sure, if it
comes to that, that it is so little. It's just fatalism in a new dress.
'I've got a feeling that destiny has not willed that I should die
today. If it has, then there's nothing I can do about it, so why
worry?' When one's lived some time under the constant
threat of danger, one begins to realize that fatalism is a necessary drug, just as alcohol is a necessary stimulant to a man on

an arctic expedition. One of the secret virtues of fatalism is that it implies, against one's better judgment, a belief in the supernatural. 'If destiny has so far taken charge of me as to fix the moment of my death, it's not likely that it's going to leave me in the lurch afterwards. It will take me through to another stage. The adventure isn't finished yet.' Fundamentally all that man asks is that the adventure should not be ended. He doesn't want to know what happens next; he's perfectly willing to let the future remain a mystery. So long as the adventure is not finished, he can bear anything. The shells hurtling down on the trench, the advancing wave of which he forms a part, the storm of 77's and machine-gun bullets which will probably knock him over two yards farther on and leave him with his head smashed to pulp near that little tree—all these things become merely an episode.... You've no idea, my dear Jallez, of the depths of inherited belief that are stirred by such tornadoes of death."

"Yes, I have, and the thought moves me deeply." (Far ahead, but nearer now than it had been, rose Notre-Dame, with its gargoyles and its dreaming spires.)

"What I want to make you realize is the way that all these ideas swarm and jostle and come and go, quite arbitrarily, in a man's mind. That's why all formulas that try to generalize our reactions to life in the front line are false. There may be some men gifted with an abnormal strength of mind, whose attitude never varies...but they can't be many....I can look back now, for instance, and see myself as I was on the second of those foodless days in the valley of Haudromont, about ten o'clock in the morning. A good many 77's were falling. Heavy shrapnel was bursting high up between our trenches and the crest to our rear, which meant that the bullets had a good chance of coming straight down into what shelter we had. As a matter of fact, I had one killed and four wounded that morning. But my own mood was one of almost complete resignation. I could hear the snapping of the branches, the burst of shells in the damp earth. It was as though I were standing aside from my own destiny. What might happen to me seemed no longer to have any significance. I didn't even have to take refuge behind my little tricks of mental comfort. My attitude was something that had been produced without any conscious exercise of my will. 'This is marvellous,' I said to myself; 'this is how a man ought to feel. Let's hope it continues.' And then, two hours later, when, if anything, the shelling was rather less intense, I found myself in a mood of hysterical and undisciplined excitement. But note this: that these ups and downs of the spirit can often have very awkward sequels. A man may be perfectly impotent in the face of shell-fire; still, the care or the speed with which he takes certain precautions may result in his being killed within the next three minutes, or finding himself still alive at the day's end. During those periods of superb indifference he may scorn to crouch or lie flat, may carelessly show his head above the parapet. When he becomes excited, on the other hand, he may get himself killed as the result of a clumsy excess of precautions, such as changing his position every few minutes, and the like. But the body is wiser than the mind. It draws the necessary inferences, adjusts the balance, looks after its own safety. The man of calm resignation and the hysterical worrier, taking the lead successively in each one of us, perform almost precisely the same automatic movements of self-preservation."

They were walking very slowly. Every few moments they stopped, the better to pick out for scrutiny some particular idea, just as woodcutters pause to choose one log rather than another.

A little later, after an effort, which clearly showed in the expression of his face, to assemble his ideas, Jerphanion said:

"I've been pondering again that question of yours.…Yes, the great operative influence is, I'm quite sure, the sense of social pressure. A man's got to stay where he is. He's caught like a rat in a trap, in a tangle of intersecting threads—the fear of a firing squad, a sense of shame, of dishonour, the moral impossibility of doing otherwise, a sort of mystical terror—on all sides he is hemmed in. Naturally, he is free, if he pleases, to be transported by ecstasy, free to declare that he is where he is because he wants to do his duty, because he loves his country. He is *free into the bargain* to accept his presence there as an act of will....And that will may be perfectly sincere....If we were intent on splitting hairs, we could prove easily enough that even this free and sincere will to sacrifice was something that he would never have come by unaided, that it is the product of that silly nonsense called education, or, in other words, of society's most cunning trick to mould a man to its design. But never mind. That's not what I meant....No....My point is that man is like any other animal: when there's no alternative, he gives in. Even the wild beasts give in under such conditions....Men can screw themselves up to resist or to rebel when the authority that enjoins obedience shows signs of weakness. It may be all very depressing, but it's true. In the old days my 'optimism' wouldn't let me believe it. But the war has only too clearly shown me that I was wrong. Where now is man's vaunted spirit of revolt, of 'revolution'? Isn't it obvious that all such talk was never anything but a bad joke? The 'governed' make revolutions not when the governors most abuse their privileges, but when, having been guilty of abuses—not, perhaps, very grave abuses—they lack the courage to abide by their actions....As my friend Griollet said, just think of the revolutionary fervour displayed by men like Pataud, Puget, Merrheim, and all the working-class leaders when they risked nothing....Are they quite so keen now? Show me a single factory hand conscripted on war work, no matter how militant he was in days gone by, who refuses to turn out shells or agitates for a munition strike among his pals to stop the slaughter of the proletariat....If the governments of the world don't deduce from what's happening certain philosophic and cynically Machiavellian truths for use in the post-war period, that'll only be because they are incapable of digesting any lesson of experience. In short, man is an animal who does what he is made to do very much more readily than one is inclined to believe. But once he has realized that, whatever happens, he has got to do what he is told, he likes nothing so much as to believe that the initial order came from himself...."

Jerphanion paused a moment, then continued:

"To be fair, one must recognize that, in a sense, it does. No matter how strong or how cunning the collective will may be, it could not compel, and continue to compel, the individual to actions that were at complete variance with his nature. One must always reckon, for instance, with the love of destruction, which is deeply rooted in humanity. Man loves to demolish what he has himself created. Don't mothers say: 'Children are so destructive'? Think of the rows we used to make over the food at college. Most of us were only too delighted to discover once or twice a term that the stew was uneatable, because it gave us an excuse for throwing our plates on the ground and smashing them. Men are always ready to revenge themselves on the increasing complexity of material civilization. The ordered life of society forces us to give too much time to the making of too many things, and compels us to an over-nice exercise of care in using them. Bang, bang, bang, go the guns—partly to give release to the nerves of men who have heard nothing since childhood but 'Don't touch that!' 'Don't upset that!' 'Don't break that!'…Then there's an emotion of a totally different kind to reckon with—humanity's liking for sacrifice. I'm convinced that it exists, that it is no mere fantasy of a morbid literary taste. It's the only thing that can explain the success, the fanatical success, that cruel religions have always had. No matter how ferocious the inventions of their leaders, whether lay or priestly, there has never been any lack of willing victims. No master has ever succeeded in getting men to accept such things against their wishes. The most dearly loved leaders have always been the most bloodthirsty. There has never ceased to be a deep complicity between martyr and executioner. Certain German theorists—you know more about these things than I do—have assumed a connexion between this taste for sacrifice and sexual perversion. That is being unnecessarily ingenious. I have studied my own reactions and those of others in the course of this war. My impression is that, unless they are under the strict control of reason, men are an easy prey to the attraction, the lure, of great emotional thrills. For anyone in the prime of life there is no thrill comparable to the horror of being tortured and killed.…The anticipation of some such thrill does, of course, explain most perversions and the delight of the sexual act in general. And, apropos of sex, you must always remember that among the influences that conspire to keep the soldier in the trenches, exposed to constant shell-fire, sex is by no means the least...."

"Hm!" interrupted Jallez. "Isn't that a bit far-fetched? ...You can't have much time to think about sex, surely?"

"In the crude, carnal sense, no—except when we are in quiet rest-billets. But the thought of women never leaves us. I'm not talking of the girls in pink undies cut out of the *Vie Parisienne* and pinned up in every hut and every dug-out...though they are not without their significance. I'm talking of the idea that women exist, 'way back, out of the war zone...."

"Whom it's up to you to defend?"

"Well, yes, if you like to put it that way, but it's not quite that, not so sentimental as that....What I mean is that we're always conscious of them standing, as it were, on the walls of some ancient fortified city, watching and criticizing. . ."

"Isn't that all a bit literary? Aren't you rather modulating on a traditional theme?"

"No. When the common or garden poilu dreams of getting a soft job, one argument above all others makes him pause, especially if he happens to be young....I've used it myself, more shame to me, in talking to country lads; and that is: 'What'll the girls at home say? They'll never look at you again.' Carry that same motive a little further, think of it as animating the man going over the top with his rifle at the trail. 'The women are watching,' he says to himself; 'watching to see whether I'm making as good a showing as the rest...watching to see whether I turn tail...whether I'm going to sneak into a shell-hole while the others go forward.' And if that constant obsession is not enough, there are always the war 'godmothers'—that admirable invention of the people at home for keeping the soldier in a constant state of slightly amorous excitation which, it is supposed, will be ultimately translated into patriotic ardour. Think of all those 'godmothers' going to bed with their protégés when they're on leave, and kissing them goodbye at the end of it, with a 'Be brave, darling,' which merely means: 'Do the sensible thing and get yourself killed....' How thrilling it must be for all these women, many of them no longer young, to have such interludes of love with fresh, virile boys, always with the thought at the back of their minds that the lover is going from their arms straight to death....The purely sensual delight of the female insect. Sweep away all women—women in the narrow sense of the word—from the back areas; leave no one there but mothers, old men, and children (to make use of the categories beloved of the official mind), and I don't mind betting that the war would soon be over."

"It's certainly worth thinking about," said Jallez. "What it all comes to is that war touches springs that lie deep at the heart of humanity."

"Of course it does. In a way that's all it does. But even that's not the only thing I'm after. The frightful thing about war is that, as a subject, it's inexhaustible. One's eye is always being caught by some new aspect of the business. My real point is this: that for the men in the trenches—for all of them, that is, who are above the purely animal level, for whom, as you must see for yourself, it is most necessary to find an explanation—the idea that they must stay where they are and get on with their job because there is no real alternative is not enough to keep them in spirits, to prevent their moral collapse. Each one of them has got to find some effective suggestion that will touch him personally, some thought, some fixed idea, the secret of which is known to him alone, the essence of which he can absorb drop by drop. Sometimes he has several among which he can take his choice. No sooner does one begin to lose its potency than he can change over to others. Take my own case, for instance. For quite a while I managed very comfortably on the idea that I was the kind of man who could 'rise superior to circumstances'—the circumstances in question being partly composed of mental distress, partly of bodily discomfort. 'I'd like,' said I, 'to see those circumstances to which I could not rise superior!' While shrapnel pattered round me (it was at the time when a good deal of shrapnel was being used), I would recite to myself like a sort of magic formula, those terrific lines of Horace:

Si fractus illabatur orbis
Impavidum ferient ruinæ…

It really is a magic formula. And then, one day, it no longer worked. My mental distress became too great, my fear became too great, and I just wanted to burst into tears and cry 'Mamma!' like a little boy.…Then take the young second lieutenant fresh from Saint-Cyr, all innocence and splendid bravery, who says to himself: 'If France is conquered, life will be impossible. I shall feel personally dishonoured. Far rather would I have my name on a headstone with the words: "Died on the field of honour," than live on disgraced.' Another example is that of the reservist with a taste for serious reading and an equipment of large-hearted ideals, the kind of man who says to himself: 'This is the war that will end war. We are bringing peace to the whole world. Thanks to our sacrifice, our children will be spared knowledge of such horrors.' Standing next to him in the same trench will be some fellow who thinks: 'This is the end of the world. We're all in for it. What does it matter if I get killed a little sooner or a little later?' Another there may be who believes in a coming reign of justice, who is still convinced that victory for the democracies will mean freedom for the oppressed everywhere in the world, the end of the domination of money and social iniquity, who would be willing even to die if only he could be sure that his death would mean greater happiness for men yet unborn. Then there's the sentimentalist, for whom nothing counts but personal relationships, whose world is made up of just a few dear friends, who argues: 'Most of my pals are dead. If they all go, what is there left to live for?' There's the man whose wife left him as soon as he was called up, and ran off with someone else; who gets no letters and no parcels; who feels himself too old to start life afresh, who would just as soon be dead, for whom the very fact of danger is a distraction, because it gives him the illusion that life is still sweet. There is the man who exists in a world of dreams and takes things as they come. 'Everything is predestined,' says he; 'I always knew it. No use fighting against fate. We must just go with the tide.'

There is the man who has never had a chance, who has always felt himself to be the victim of injustice and insult, who has always envied the good fortune of others, who so relishes the taste of equality bred of a general misery that he pays but lip service to the desire for peace with all the bitterness that it will bring for him in its train. Close beside him is another in whom the war has waked a deep-seated strain of pessimism, who thinks sincerely: 'The universe is a foul absurdity. It was always pretty obvious, but the war has proved it beyond the shadow of a doubt. Why cling to a foul absurdity?' or: 'Humanity is the work of the Devil, a blot on the face of the earth, born for murder and self-slaughter. So much the worse for humanity (and for me, who am part of humanity and so of the whole putrescent mess).' There is the fanatical Catholic, who thinks: 'This is God's punishment wrought on a corrupt and faithless generation. If God has decided that I too must pay the penalty, even for the faults of others, who am I to question His will?' There is the gentle Catholic who carries tucked away in his pack a tiny edition of the *Imitation*, who, when night falls, says his prayers in his shell-hole, very quietly, so that no one shall notice him, and murmurs: 'Let me suffer, as You suffered, Jesu mine. Why should I be spared, since You suffered a thousand deaths hanging on Your cross? Give me strength that I may be not too unworthy of You.' Finally, there is the man"—and Jerphanion made a gesture towards Notre-Dame, which was now immediately opposite them, across the river, its pinnacles just touched by the fading day— "who says: 'All that matters to me in this world is the language of France, the cathedrals of our French countryside, the quays of the Seine, landscapes that can be found nowhere else in the world, a way of life that is unique. If all that is to be taken away, life has no longer any point. If, by dying, I can ensure that all these things will live on after me, then death is right and proper....' Picture to yourself trench after trench filled with men thinking such thoughts, and you will find the answer to your question.... That is why Verdun still stands."

CHAPTER TWENTY-FIVE

Wazemmes Rejoins the "Fighting Services." A "Lady Fair." A Bearded Gentleman in the Subway

Wazemmes put on his clothes again in the filthy little anteroom which was full of the smell of damp human bodies. His braces were twisted. One of his socks had gone astray. He found it at last in one of the legs of his pants.

"Passed for duty! And they didn't waste much time about it. I don't think the M.O. listened to my chest for more than three seconds....I wanted to explain that ever since I was wounded...but they shut me up as soon as I so much as opened my lips!....Got their orders from up above, that's what it is. They're passing all they can...told to pass eighty-five per cent, so the Q.M.S. said. So long as one's got two arms and a couple of feet they don't care. They say five thousand men a day are being killed at Verdun....Jolly look-out for me! They're going to get me there as quickly as they can. Easy enough for them. According to the Q.M.S. all infantrymen passed for duty are being sent up to the front at once. I might have made capital out of the fact that I used to be in the cavalry. But I didn't get a chance to explain; they wouldn't let me get a word in edgeways. If the boss had been a decent sort of fellow, he might have pulled a few strings and got me taken on in the dragoons again....That wouldn't have been shirking....He could easily have said that I wanted nothing better than to get back to the front, but that my wound had made it impossible for me to carry a pack....I suppose they'd have answered that there's not much carrying of packs in the trenches...adding that it would do me good to sleep in the open air, as the little M.O. with glasses told me the other day. They rather enjoy being sarcastic. I'm big, and I look hefty, that's my trouble. No one ever thinks of being sorry for me.

Wonder whether they'll give me my stripes back. Just like the swine to send me up the line as a simple foot-slogger! I'll damn well go sick....Lambert'll have the laugh of me all right. He's a sergeant now. Those damned Patriotic Association people haven't been any too polite to me since I had a back-area job. Nor, for that matter, has my precious 'godmother.' When I was in the trenches on the Champagne front she never missed writing to me every week. And what parcels she sent! To say nothing of the things she wrote—enough to turn a chap's head....That last letter of hers—whew!...But I've not heard from her now for over a month. She's probably taken up with some other fellow; she wouldn't just drop me like that without any reason....Why wouldn't she ever meet me? It would have been so easy with me in Paris. I expect she's as ugly as sin....She didn't look so bad in that photo she sent me, 'so you can have it to carry on you when you charge the enemy'—though her neck was a bit scraggy...but it was probably an old picture... she never told me her age...or perhaps she's got some deformity. Oh well, I'll be able to write now and tell her I'm off up the line again. That'll thaw her out perhaps."

In the canteen, where he had gone to drown his sorrows, Wazemmes sat down at the far end of one of the tables. By doing so he could manage to be fairly isolated in the half-filled room, without seeming to avoid his fellows.

He took from his pocket the last letter he had received from Mlle Anne de Montbieuze du Sauchet. He knew the contents almost by heart, but he took a certain pleasure in re-reading it and in being seen with it in his hand. For the blue-grey paper had a distinguished air, and the handwriting was bold and elegant.

March 17, 1916

My Dear Félix,
Don't scold me for having left you so long without a word. Knowing you to be safe I was less worried about you than usual. All

my time has been taken up with getting that workroom going which I told you about, in the rue Las Cases. It was started by a number of us, girls and older women who are members of a patriotic association; but it's not been easy, chiefly because it gets harder and harder to make any money.[1] After a lot of talk we decided to specialize in knitted helmets. It appears that the nights are still very cold at Verdun, and that the winter woollies issued to the dear fellows in the trenches are beginning to wear out. The advantage of knitted helmets is that they can be put on over a knitted jersey, which really isn't warm enough without anything else. And we can turn them out in very large numbers. We hear that the dear boys are very fond of the helmets.

Of course I'm not angry at your wanting to see me. As a matter of fact I'm very touched. It was quite unnecessary for you to say that you would be respectful; I knew that already. But there are frightful difficulties in the way, and besides, I don't want your feeling for me to change. It is so chivalrous, and chivalry has always been the mark of the true Frenchman, whatever his social position. Do you know the *Princesse Lointaine* by Edmond Rostand? One of these days I'll send it to you if I can find a copy at my bookseller's. I'm sure we shall meet some time, if only you want to hard enough; perhaps at some party got up by our Association to celebrate the victory which isn't so far off, I believe, as some people think. The Boches want the war to finish; that's why they are hurling themselves against us at Verdun in a fit of Teutonic madness. But they will suffer for their rashness; and this time our dear boys will sweep them back over the frontier with their bayonets in their backsides.[2]

The best proof of what I feel for you, my dear Félix, is that I pray daily for your complete recovery from the effects of that horrid Boche bullet, so that you may soon be able to rejoin your comrades in that battle of Verdun which is already emblazoned in the pages of History. Verdun, as you must know, is a city dear to our Kings, and has always been loyal to them. How glad you will be in the days to come that you played your part in delivering it from the enemy. In that will lie your claim to glory. But don't delay, Félix. Remember what our good King Henry said: "Go hang yourself, my poor

---

[1] Thus Mlle Anne de Montbieuze. Her meaning, however, is clear.
[2] It seems incredible that Mlle Anne de Montbieuze du Sauchet should have meant precisely what she said. At that time the language of the trenches had penetrated into the best circles, where it was received with enthusiasm but not always with discretion.

Crillon. I conquered at Arques, and you were not there."

If you go back to the front, you will take my photograph, won't
you? It will bring you luck as it did before. Why do you ask me
again if I mind your kissing it occasionally? You know I don't.

Always, my dear Félix, your loving and faithful friend

Anne

After reading it through again, pondering its message, and
even sighing with a sort of manly melancholy, the cause of
which he did not much mind his neighbours from guessing,
Wazemmes penned the following epistle:

April 2, 1916

My dearest Anne:

I have already replied to yours of the 17th, and trust you've received mine, though not acknowledged. I can't wait now to tell you
I've succeeded at long last in getting taken for the fighting services
in spite of my wound which still causes me acute suffering and what
the medical officers can't make head nor tail of. I told them my
place wasn't here while the boys was fighting at Verdun and covering theirselves with glory and reaping laurels. All I want, my dear
Anne, is to give the Boches a smack in the jaw that will take away
any taste they still have for any longer defiling the soil of France.
There's only one thing not quite so good. I gave in my stripes when
I was sent down the line and don't know I'm sorry to say whether
they'll give them back to me. You said you knew a very important
general who thinks like you and me. If you could speak a word to
him just one word his influence would be very grateful to yours
faithfully seeing I've no reason for not recovering my rank, on the
contrary as I've managed to recover myself. It would be a very sad
thing for me if I couldn't charge at the head of my men crying long
live France, come on let's chuck the enemy out especially when I
think that my friend Lambert is already a N.C.O. and I've done just
as much as he has.

Your picture will rest against my heart, you can be easy on that
point. I shall like very much to read the *Princesse Lointaine* especially
if it is by the same man that wrote *Cyrano*. A little reading's always
welcome in the trenches and as I've already read some political
pamphlets it will be nice to have something to take my mind off
and I don't mean smut either.

I kiss your portrait every evening respectfully. I will be kissing it just the same if the blood is running from my lips while the bugles sound the charge. It is with saying long live France, long live the King that I draw to a close now before hurrying off to Verdun always regretting you can't see your way to arrange the meeting that I asked of your high-born kindness. But perhaps you will change your mind seeing as how I'm just off again.

Assuring you, my dearest Anne, of my very very kind thoughts which only wait a word from you to turn my heart into a raging furnace,

I am your affectionate

Félix

Two days before his leave ended, returning from a walk through the streets at the heart of Paris, Jerphanion and Odette found themselves in the subway, somewhere between the stations of the Palais-Royal and Saint-Paul, seated opposite a very strange pair. The man had a long, black, carefully tended beard, in which there showed a few white hairs. He had a bald forehead and deeply set and very small black eyes. He seemed close on fifty and was wearing a morning coat. He held a derby hat on his knees and was talking with an air of extreme politeness to his neighbour, a plump woman of about forty with large, surprised-looking eyes. She looked like a "companion" in her Sunday best, and was listening to him with the respectful expression of someone who does not in the least understand what is being said.

Jerphanion caught one sentence spoken by the man:

"I am just back from Verdun, where I had to go on duty...."

He missed the next few words, but heard the following, spoken rather sententiously:

"...The situation there is serious but not desperate."

"An odd sort of cuss!" said Jerphanion to Odette with a smile, at the same time making a sign that they had reached the station of Saint-Paul.

Maillecottin the Munition Worker.
A Fly in the Ointment

Edmond Maillecottin came out of the Four-Ways factory. He was dressed just as he always had been, the only difference being that he now wore an arm-band indicating that he was employed on war work. This, on pain of severe punishment, he was forbidden to remove, and, indeed, in these gloomy times, the badge had its advantages. When he met occasional policemen they did not say suddenly to themselves: "Hullo, what's this young fellow doing in civvies?" and they never asked him to show his papers. Military regulations ordained, too, that he should wear his soldier's identification disk on his wrist, but he had observed this rule only for a few days during July when it had had the charm of novelty. He had soon removed it, however, and carried it now stuffed away in his pocket. To have a thing like that on one's wrist when one is in uniform is natural enough, just an item in the general rig-out; besides, it may come in useful if one happens to get killed. But when one is in civvies, the little disk on its string bracelet made one feel like a convict or a tame dog. One had quite enough without that to remind one that one was no longer free.

Edmond had not got his bicycle. It was not much use to him now that he and Georgette were living quite close in one of the big new blocks in the middle of Saint-Ouen. The walk did him good. He needed the exercise. He was eating too much, and his food was over-rich. He had pointed that out more than once to Georgette, but whenever he did so, she flew into a rage: "I suppose you think you aren't making enough to afford decent stuff! Becoming a miser, are you?" Georgette was a great eater. She would have loved to spend

all day cooking fancy dishes, but she could spare only a short
while for her kitchen when she got back from the works in
the evening. At midday they had to make do with a scratch
meal which demanded next to no preparation. It was something that they had managed to get their times off at the same
hours, thanks to the kindness of Georgette's foreman, who
was rather keen on her. ("If it wasn't for that," she said when
they discussed him, "you'd have to tighten your belt.") But a
hurried meal did not mean a careless one. It was with these
picnic lunches in view that Georgette, whenever she could
spare a moment or two to visit one of the big grocer's, laid in
a store of various tinned foods, all of the very highest quality:
mackerel in oil, tunny, salmon, lobster; tins of foie gras from
Marie's, of ham from Olida's; pots of prepared food from
Poinseul ("five minutes on the gas-ring, and you have a hot
meal worthy of a first-class restaurant"). A few days ago she
had even bought a whole imported American ham, which
was much more tasty than the Paris variety, and was now
hanging from the ceiling of her kitchen. But it was over their
evening meal that she really exerted herself. No matter how
tired she might be after a day at the works (checking grenades
was probably more exhausting work even than making them;
it meant paying attention to more and different details, and
the finished articles were whisked by so quickly that after a
very little while one's eyes seemed to be starting out of one's
head), she threw herself with a fine courage into the task of
preparing some full-dress dish, something from the recipe
book; and it was a matter of pride with her to ring the
changes as often as possible. (Luckily, her two children were
not there to get in the way. She had planted them on her parents, who lived in the country. "Now that I'm employed in a
factory, a war factory, I shan't have the spare time I had when
I was at Pleyel's. I simply can't look after them. If they stay
with me they'll just run wild. People have got to help one
another at times like these. Of course I'll make you an
allowance." She had taken her mother into a corner before
adding: "Edmond's a decent enough fellow. It was his idea to
make a home with me. But I can feel that the kids get on his

nerves. You must put yourself in his place: it's not as though they were his children, is it? If you want him to marry me—and he's quite capable of it one of these days—the kids have got to be got out of the way. That'll keep him from having to think about it now. Later, we'll see.") She kept for Sundays the dishes that needed really lengthy preparation, hours of cooking on a slow fire, or the ones that proceeded by carefully calculated stages, with successive additions of sauces, gravy, seasoning and condiments, etc.—such things, for instance, as stuffed chicken, sweetbread *financière*, and pickled venison, were never long absent from their table. But on weekdays they had to fall back oftener than Georgette liked on comparatively simple dishes: roast chicken, pigeon and green peas, leg of lamb, and the modest roast beef.

This régime rather worried Maillecottin, all the more since Georgette had decided that she couldn't put up with a simple table wine at ten or twelve sous the litre. She had substituted a vintage variety which she got from a wine merchant on the Place de la Mairie. Not that Georgette knew as much about wine as she did about food, but common sense told her that wine at a franc or one franc twenty the bottle (she never went beyond that reasonable figure) was a worthier accompaniment than a coarse working man's tipple for her leg of lamb or chicken *cocotte*. Her taste naturally led her to clarets (she had discovered a sound Médoc and even a drinkable Saint-Émilion within her price limit), but she developed a liking also for an excellent Corsican variety, Sciacarello, which was to be had at her dealer's. Edmond's disquiet sprang from many causes. He was worried about his health. He had grown noticeably fatter during the past year; his digestion was out of order, and he suffered from heaviness in the head. He was not sleeping well. His face had grown puffy, and sometimes he was surprised by his own appearance in the mirror. But, apart from questions of health, he was not altogether easy in his conscience. This continual guzzling seemed to him not far removed from what he had most disliked when he had come across it in pre-war bourgeois circles. Being a decent-minded man, he could not help feeling that it was more than

ever disgusting in view of the general situation, and especially when one considered whence the money came that made
it possible. He could not explain the nature of his scruples to
Georgette, who would not have understood what he meant.
All she thought was that he grudged her the money, and,
because she did not want him to run away with the idea that
she was extravagant, she was for ever excusing herself: "Have
you even reckoned up what's coming in in the way of hard
cash each month?" No, he hadn't, was even careful not to do
so. "Well, then, I'll tell you. Last month, including overtime,
we earned nearly two thousand francs." She had no difficulty
in persuading him that two thousand francs represented at
least six times what a working-class couple like themselves
would have thought reasonable before the war. "It's true, of
course, that a lot of prices have gone up, but very few have
been doubled." She pointed out one curious fact: that really
good things, like luxury foods, showed a tendency to be
cheaper than they used to be. In the early months of the war
this economic peculiarity had been strongly marked. The reason probably was that the middle-class customers were cutting down expenses, while the restaurants and the large hotels
were no longer filled by rich foreigners. More recently prices
had begun to show an upward trend, since, that is, hundreds
of thousands of men had been drafted into the factories, and
women had begun to be employed at salaries undreamed of
in earlier days. "Your pal Pouchard explained it all to me,"
declared Georgette with an air of rather pathetic pride, "when
we met at the cinema. He put it like this, I remember: 'My
wife and I are making more than a general of division.'
…Well, then, I don't suppose for a moment that the
Pouchards are earning more than we are." Maillecottin had no
very clear idea what a general of division got, but he was willing to take Pouchard at his word. The only difference was that
he seemed considerably less elated than Georgette at the idea
of getting more than that functionary. She made him go mar-
keting with her. "You will see for yourself," she said. She got
the shop people to tell her in his hearing the price of chickens, of crayfish, of whiting by the pound. Maillecottin was

forced to agree that Georgette, even when she fed them on the best obtainable and paid for cinema tickets twice a week, was still well within her housekeeping allowance. "We can't be for ever saving; we're not misers. I've already invested in Defence bonds. What are we risking?"

Edmond was forced back on reasons of health. "You make me laugh!" she said. "A lot they'd be bothering about your health if you were in the trenches! Since you're not, you'd better make the best of it. Wholesome food never harmed anybody, and the food I give you is always that. You were always too thin, and so was I." Georgette was certainly not thin now, but Edmond had to admit that she had suffered neither in appearance nor in health from the change. A rich diet has the further advantage that it keeps a couple in a constant state of amorous warmth. The damned bourgeois have long ago learned that lesson. A woman who has fed well isn't likely to say, like her undernourished sisters: "Oh, I'm too tired tonight!" (It was convenient too, where those highly important distractions were concerned, not to have a lot of children running round in a not too extensive flat, and refusing to go to bed in the next room.)

Besides, if it was a matter of having one's conscience clear, there were more troubles than that to keep a man wakeful. Maillecottin did as little thinking as possible. He kept silent before others, and he kept silent in the privacy of his own mind. He even did his best to forget the short time he had served as a combatant soldier at the front, probably so as not to have to remember that others than himself were there still, and that conditions had grown worse since he knew them. He was cautious in his general attitude, in his words, in his least act and gesture. When the war was discussed in front of him, he assumed the airs of a man who, though of course he has as much right as another to think his own thoughts, is not going to give himself away by making hasty judgments, sweeping criticisms, and indulging in wordy, bombastic oratory. When he was with his fellow factory workers, there was a something about his expression, about his very silences, which seemed to say: "We, who know what war is, have little enough reason to complain." He no longer made a show of reading the newspapers of the extreme Left; no longer even bought them. (For that matter, they were no better than the rest, these days!) On his way to work he studied the *Petit Parisien*. Nothing in that for the boss to bring up against him or his pals…or that third type of colleague, so hard to identify, informers.

It was not that he felt himself to be particularly threatened. He was as secure in his job as it was possible to be. His technical qualifications were such as no one could question, and his work was excellent. From the moment that the Bertrand factories had accepted contracts for shells (it was hardly fair to accuse the boss of having gone all out for war profits; as a matter of fact, the Government had gone down to him on bended knee: "With your plant and your experience," they had said in effect, "it's your duty"; and he had agreed only under considerable protest), the first concern of the board had been to put in a claim for lathe hands, and Maillecottin's name had headed the list. Since that time there had been considerable outcry against men with soft jobs in factories, bogus specialists, and even bogus work-men. The workshops had been visited by Government commissions which had narrowly scrutinized the efficiency and the past history of all the hands employed. But as soon as Maillecottin's name had come up for consideration, the foreman or the engineer in charge had always exclaimed with an air of triumph: "Oh, he's one of our best pre-war men. If he wasn't here already we'd have to get him back in double-quick time!" In reply to which statement there was always a general nodding of heads and an exchange of understanding smiles, and Maillecottin, who had been politely waiting to answer questions, returned to his lathe. He was not even to be numbered now among the younger men. Besides, since the opening of the battle of Verdun, the only thing that seemed to matter was the speeding up of production. Every factory was working overtime, and numerous metal-workers, considerably younger than Maillecottin, had been brought back from the front. He would be returned to duty only if the authorities lost their heads, or if he himself happened to be guilty of a more than usually gross piece of imprudence. More than once he had regretted what he had done in the matter of Guyard Romuald. Once again it had been the fault of that bitch Isabelle. She had kept on begging him with tears to do something, had wheedled and cajoled, with that air of saying: "It's not natural for a brother to refuse his sister—still, of course, you must have it your own way...." During the winter of 1914–15 Romuald had been passed for service and sent to Morocco with other blackguards of his kind. Apparently he had got bored there, and the climate had disagreed with him. What chiefly counted, however, was that Isabelle could not do without him, and was afraid that he might pick up some bit of skirt in Africa and decide to stay there permanently. "If only you would, Edmond darling, it would be so easy. I know that heaps of men are being brought back, I've got it for a fact, and you're such a favourite of your foreman's. It's only a question of getting Romuald's name put onto the right list. Who's to know that Romuald didn't work at Four-Ways before the war? No one's going to bother to look up the records. And he's as clever as you make 'em. He learned all about handling machines when he was training as a dentist. He'll soon get into the way of things. He certainly won't bring you into bad odour." Isabelle had enlisted Georgette's assistance, and Georgette had espoused her cause, no doubt with an eye to the future, so that, should the day come when Edmond might begin to wonder whether he would not be doing a stupid thing in marrying her, his sister might say: "Why, of course you're not! She's just the kind of woman you need. She'll make you happy. Women know these things about each other."

The upshot of the business had been that Edmond had put in the necessary word with his foreman, who, to please him, had entered Romuald's name on the list of men wanted, and, thanks to the general confusion reigning at the time, Romuald had been duly taken on. Edmond had even been good-natured enough to give him a few hasty lessons in working the lathe, and Romuald had become a shell hand. He

had turned to the job with a will. No one in the whole factory was more punctual, no one more obedient. He knew
perfectly well that if he was turned off he would be sent, not
back to Morocco, but to the front with a special "recommendation" attached to his name. He knew more than one case in
which such a recommendation had had the effect of getting
fellows sent up to some listening-post from which they had
not returned.

But in due course had come the combing-out process. Specialists had had to be individually safeguarded, committees of
inquiry had made the round of the factories, etc. Edmond had
definitely refused to lift a finger for Romuald. He never wanted to speak to him again, nor even to see him. But Romuald
had managed to scrape through, God knows how!

The memory of all this still had the power to give Edmond
a nasty feeling in his stomach. "Trust a woman to start that
sort of trouble," he reflected. "If the boss had got into trouble
because of Romuald and had taken it out on me by getting
me sent to the front with him, that would have been a fine
look-out for Georgette!"

Then there had been that business of the separation
allowance. The immediate military consequences had been
less serious, but it might, all the same, have had an important
effect upon his future.

Shortly after mobilization, Georgette had lost her job at
Pleyel's, where there was no longer any work. She was left
without a penny, and Edmond, at that time serving in the
infantry, had been in no position to help. She had written to
him as follows: "If you don't want me and the two kids to die
of hunger, get me entered for a separation allowance on the
ground that I'm being supported by a man who's been called
up. My concierge, who's a decent sort, will swear that we've
been living together. You won't have to bother about anything." Georgette had drawn an allowance for herself and the
two children until Edmond had been brought back to the
factory, after which only the allowance for the children had
been continued.

As a result of all this, Edmund had set up house with

Georgette. He could hardly avoid doing so after her declaration and the evidence of the concierge. The arrangement had the added advantage of giving him a home within easy distance of his work. In the middle of 1915, thanks to Edmond's influence, Georgette had been taken on at a grenade factory. From that moment had started their period of joint prosperity. In a very little while they moved to a small but elegant flat in one of the new blocks in Saint-Ouen. By doing so they snapped their fingers in the face of fortune, since they ran the risk of losing the advantages they enjoyed under the law protecting pre-war tenants. But Georgette was anxious to start an entirely new chapter with Edmond.

More than once he said to her: "Now that everything's going well, don't you think you ought to go along to the registrar's and discontinue the kids' allowance?" To which she replied: "Certainly not. Are you out of your senses? Do you want them to think we're a couple of millionaires?"

While he negotiated the last crossing before reaching his home, lifting his face towards the rainy sky already dark with approaching nightfall, he suddenly said to himself:

"If somebody asked you: 'Would you really like the war to end tomorrow, would you really like it if the men at the front stopped killing one another with the shells that you are turning out, and all started to come home—if that meant that you would have to begin working again at your old wage of ten or twelve francs a day…what would you say?'"

He searched his conscience; then "I should say yes," he thought.

From Souilly to Vadelaincourt.
Pétain, The Flying Officer, the Big Gun, and the
Priest

Geoffroy, afraid that he might be late, ran up the steps at the entrance to the Mairie of Souilly, reached the first floor, entered the large room the door of which stood opposite Pétain's office, and asked that word should be sent in to the general that he was there and waiting for orders.

"The general's just gone out. He's at the Maison Janvier. He left word that you were to follow him there."

Geoffroy went downstairs again and descended the front steps, which, with their grandiose hand-rail and great balls of stone, never ceased to amuse him.

The main road was a roar of traffic. On the maps it appeared as the highway Bar-le-Duc to Verdun. The men of the sector already knew it as The Road.

It groaned beneath the weight of its double line of trucks packed with troops, moving in contrasted directions like two chains composed of huge links, extending in either direction to the opposed extremities of the village and indefinitely beyond them. The trucks, nose to tail-board, moved at half speed, with much jerking and grinding of gears and rattling of steel plates. Their human load maintained a stolid silence. The noise was so overwhelming, was made up of so many contributory sounds of the same kind, that it was impossible to trace it to any one vehicle more than another. The whole township seemed to be shaking like the crank-case of an engine. In front of the left-hand wing of the Mairie, on the slope in front of the church, as high as the Maison Janvier and beyond, stood great mounds of stone like beads on a rosary, and close to each mound a territorial armed with a large shovel with which he scattered, from time to time, a load of stone beneath the wheels of the trucks—a short jerk for the climbing file, a longer sweep for the file descending. The air was full of the smell of hot oil and crushed pebbles.

The Maison Janvier stood on the opposite side of the road. It was recognizable from a distance, and a stranger would have known it, not from any detail of its architecture, but from its size. It was the "big house" of the place. It resembled its neighbours in the matter of solid, dingy masonry, low-pitched graceless roof, and front bare of all ornament. But it had two storeys instead of one, and more windows to each floor than the houses among which it stood. It looked like a police station.

"What a gloomy part of the world!" thought Geoffroy for the thousandth time. "War can be no new thing here!...But how odd, how mysterious it is that whether here or in Touraine or in Provence, France is always recognizably France."

He pushed hurriedly through the ascending, then through the descending file of trucks which kept piling up in a solid mass, like so many blind animals, the newly spread rock crackling beneath their wheels.

He entered the hall and put a question to the orderly on duty:

"Do you know where the general is?"

"No, sir. He may be still on the first floor; that is, if he's not in the drawing-room. All I know is he's not come out since he went in."

To satisfy himself, Geoffroy gave a hurried glance through a door on his left into the dining-room, where a large number of plates stood glinting on the sideboard and the buffet. It was empty. Before stepping across the threshold of the large drawing-room, the door of which stood open, he listened for the sound of voices from the neighbouring small drawing-room, which was Pétain's favourite place for interviewing visitors. He could hear nothing. But the general might be there alone, reading. Geoffroy tapped on the door, stepped in, and took a hurried glance round the two rooms, both of which were overfull of furniture, some of which was old, some merely old-fashioned, and the general effect of which was that of a good middle-class provincial interior typical of the French nineteenth century. There was no one to be seen.

He climbed to the first floor, where his own room was situated. It was the second of a pair of tiny apartments which stood at the end of the corridor opposite the general's office and were known as "officers' rooms."

He knocked at Pétain's door.

"Come in."

The voice seemed to come from a long way off.

As a matter of fact, there was no one in the room itself, nothing but a mild radiance which entered from the garden and the landscape beyond and played a little fitfully over the great canopied bed of dark wood, and the huge rustic press of blackened oak. The hubbub of the road could be heard, but much as the machinery of a mill by the miller who lives within its walls. For all the roar and the rattle, peace seemed to reign in the room.

Pétain poked his head from behind the door of his dressing-room, which opened in the left-hand corner of the far wall.

"Ah, it's you."

"Am I disturbing you, sir?"

"Not in the least. I was just having a gargle. I don't want to get another cold." (He had spent the first week of his new command at Verdun shaking with fever in this very room, directing the battle from his bed.)

He went over to his work-table, took from it a pile of folded notes which lay there all ready, and handed them to Geoffroy, who arranged them methodically in his document-case, glancing at the addresses as he did so.

"There. You know what to do with them. But something's suddenly occurred to me. When you've finished at Bois Bourrus, why not spend the night at Mort-Homme? You can get a shakedown in one of the brigade H.Q.'s. I'd like to have you out there tonight. If anything happens you can send back word to me at once and give me your view of the situation. If nothing happens, you can come back tomorrow morning. I shan't want you before noon."

As he was working his way back through the rumbling traffic of the road, preparatory to picking up a car in the "park" which was situated above the Mairie, on the left-hand side, he was overtaken by a young captain of the air service who had a strongly marked scar on his cheek.

"Where are you off to?"

"As a matter of fact—" began Geoffroy with some hesitation, "I was going in the direction of Senancourt and the Meuse Valley."

"Passing anywhere near Ancemont?"

"I shall go through it."

"In that case I'll beg a lift. Put me down at Ancemont and I shall do nicely. My camp is just this side of Dugny."

"I'm going through Dugny as well, and can drop you wherever you like."

Geoffroy and the flying officer started off. They left the village by narrow lanes, with the intention of reaching the main Senancourt traffic artery without having to make use of The Road, where they would have had considerable difficulty in edging their way into the stream of trucks.

The flying officer was a high-spirited young fellow, and very talkative. He had been attached to the army of Verdun, he said, only a short while. He was part of the reinforcements demanded by Pétain. Formerly he had spent a considerable time on the Champagne front, between Soissons and Reims.

"That was the place for a good life. I got my promotion there. When the war started, I was a sergeant. The way things were run there was A1. For instance, they used to say: 'Like to take on a long-distance reconnaissance tomorrow, to spot this, that, or the other? Dangerous job, because you're sure to be chased. If you get back alive, you can have a couple of days' leave.' And off one went. Interesting work. Back one came (if one didn't crash, that is), and then off to Paris by the first train. Two days on the spree, with all the women one wanted, and there were plenty, too, willing to pay for drinks and hotel rooms as well. In the fighting squadron to which I was attached, we had a regular tariff: three days' leave for every Boche brought down, and even at one time, when sport was slow, four. All on the up and up, too. No cheating, and cash down. It was all right, believe me. If one wanted a bit of a spree in Paris, all one had to do was to get up early and have a squint at the weather. The old crate was always in the pink of form. The mechanics made it a point of pride to keep it always just so, and there was nothing they wouldn't do for us. One ran over the machine-gun to see it was working properly, and then one just chose the right moment to start off. No one to bother you. Up one went, got height, and cruised about for a bit over the lines. Suddenly one would see the little black speck one had been looking for: a Boche plane. After that it was merely a question of sport—and luck. The whole business might be over in twenty minutes, landing-time included. Once on the ground, one just let everything go to blazes—didn't even bother to see the crate into its hangar. Bang into one's glad rags, and off to the station in the little car. I've made up my mind sometimes at six a.m. and found myself at Prunier's in front of a dozen of oysters by half past twelve."

"But there must have been times when the Boche wasn't so easy to deal with?"

"Of course, but one could always turn tail before he caught one. The great point in flying is to be able to recognize at once the quality of one's adversary and to have no false pride. I never took on a plane when I had reason to suspect that it was faster or better armed than myself. In that way I could always be sure, in a fight, of having to deal with pretty harmless birds, and I never took risks with a chaser." He pointed to his scarred cheek. "The only time I got pretty badly hurt was when I crashed as the result of a misjudged landing. I was pretty well thought of—quite well enough. I'm not ambitious."

He talked of his women correspondents. In those happy days when he had time to write plenty of letters and arrange a number of meetings in Paris, he had sometimes carried on as many as eight "affairs" at a time.

"I really didn't know what to do with all the stuff they sent me. I used to share it with my pals, starting with the mechanics, naturally."

Here, at Verdun, there was no fun at all in being an aviator.

"One's a little less tied than the infantry, I'll admit, and one has better quarters, but that's about all...."

It was no longer a question of choosing one's day and hour for a little scrap with all the odds on one's side. The kind of jobs one got here were always very dangerous, and the time as well as the objective was strictly laid down by authority. What made matters worse was that for some time past the Boche had got on top in the air.

"We've nothing to put up against their two-gunned Fokkers. But as one can't just let them maintain their mastery of the air during a battle—and don't think I'm complaining, I see the staff's point clearly enough—we've not only got to stand up to attack but even to take the offensive with machines which are completely unfitted for the job. Take my own case, for example. I've got a squadron of Nieuport scouts—good enough for what they were built to do, but they've turned me into a fighting group. I'm flattered by the compliment, but just think what it means. So far I've been pretty lucky...touching wood. I've only lost two machines. But the other day, between the Côte du Poivre and Douaumont—that's to say within two and a half miles—five Caudrons were brought down in flames in the course of a few minutes."

As they were leaving Ancemont, Geoffroy, who had just delivered one of his notes to its addressee, turned to the flying officer.

"Would it amuse you to see a 305 firing from the siding? There's one close by, and it's probably in action."

The visit meant making a slight detour, but Geoffroy took a childish delight in watching these monstrous weapons at work, all the more so since the opportunity rarely came his way. What particularly delighted him was the gigantic recoil of the barrel on its sliding platform immediately following the discharge, and its relatively slow and calm return to the initial position.

They watched two shots from the 305. The operation was performed with a certain air of solemnity. The truck was stationed in a bend of the railway from Saint-Mihiel to Verdun.

The officer in charge was quite unhurried and looked like a peace-time engineer in uniform. His life at the front was not so very different from what it would have been had he been engaged in building a dam in Upper Egypt, or constructing a tunnel under the Andes: a matter of open air, splendid machines, simple but spectacular problems awaiting solution; an absence of all official meddling. He pointed out to his visitors the map reference of his target—a road-junction between the Côte du Poivre and the Bois des Caures, on the highway from Vacherauville to Ville, precisely where it cut a secondary road, a little to the left of a spot marked Hill 210. With luck he ought to be able to catch about a hundred yards of the thoroughfare in enfilade. Information of a good deal of concentration and much movement of troops had come in since the evening before.

"...Air reconnaissance, of course," said the gunner officer, with a polite nod towards his colleague of the flying services.

"Yes," said Geoffroy, "there's a lot of movement going on in the back areas all along the northern sector, on both banks of the Meuse....Looks as though they were preparing a new push....What range are you firing at?"

"Twelve miles, 300. I've already fired two rounds this morning at twelve miles 200. I've lengthened a bit, as a result of aerial spotting. We've got to be terribly accurate. Our shells are so limited in effect, you see."

Consequently Geoffroy was able to enjoy twice running the sight of the monster's recoil. The flying officer declared of his own accord that it was that particular movement that most excited him. It gave him, he said, such a feeling of "magnificent power."

Geoffroy smiled. "There must," he thought, "be something sexual in our delight. Without realizing the cause, we poor little male creatures are thrown into an ecstasy by this familiar movement carried out on a supernatural scale; and also by this miraculous organ which is appeased, but never exhausted, by its formidable release of energy." But he was careful not to explain the nature of his thoughts to the flying officer.

They bade a joint farewell to the officer of the 305, with

many thanks, and parted a little farther on, firm friends.

Geoffroy paid a very rapid visit to Dugny, where he had no desire to linger. He took the road to Vadelaincourt, which was the great hospital centre of the Verdun area. He had to make sure that certain instructions, sent from Souilly some days earlier, had been carried out, and was to deliver some fresh ones. H.Q., which had reason to fear an impending renewal of the German offensive, and, consequently, a sudden increase in casualties, wanted to speed up the evacuation of all convalescent cases to the rear.

He spent only half an hour at Vadelaincourt, which had become a little city of white overalls, dressings, and iodoform.

On leaving Vadelaincourt by the Rampont road, his car had to brake suddenly to avoid knocking down a priest who was hurrying across the road without looking where he was going. Geoffroy, who had a vague impression of having seen him before somewhere in the neighbourhood, gave him, on the chance, a friendly nod.

CHAPTER TWENTY-EIGHT

The Abbé Jean and the Badly Wounded Case.
Germaine and Another Wounded Man

The Abbé Jean was hurrying because he had just received a message which had caught at his heart-strings.

"There's a badly wounded man asking for you at No. 2 casualty clearing station. He knew you were here. He says he made his first Communion with you. He's been very badly hit in both legs. They'll probably carry out a double amputation this afternoon."

The Abbé Jean made his way towards the bed which had been pointed out to him. He did his best to recognize the face that lay on the pillow. But it was one of those faces often to be met with in Paris, the kind, too, that manhood transforms, by coarsening and enlarging the features, so that the peculiarities observable in childhood are hard to trace. A heavy moustache hid the line of the mouth. But what did it matter! He was not going to be called upon to swear to identity in a court of law. The wounded man's name had been given him: Devaux, Amédée. For purposes of recognition that was not much to go on.

The Abbé advanced:

"Hullo, Devaux, you here!"

"Yes, Father; do you recognize me?"

"Of course I do! I won't say you haven't changed, but I recognized you at once."

"Same here, Father; I knew you the moment you came in."

Devaux's voice was almost normal; his colour was high.

"What year was it you made your first Communion?"

"1899, Father. I'm twenty-seven."

"1899?…ah yes.…Are you a family man?"

"I'm married, with two children.… You might easily have

seen me since then, Father; I've always been a regular church-goer. But my parents left Montmartre; they ran a dairy, per-haps you remember? They bought a little grocery business in the rue Jeanne-d'Arc. I've hardly ever been back to Mont-martre since.

They spoke of Notre-Dame de Clignancourt, and of Mont-martre, in the old days. Devaux said he had worked for the gas company, but that a little earlier, when he was sixteen or sev-enteen, he had gone through a religious crisis which had been so violent that he had seriously thought of becoming a priest.

"A little because of my memory of you, Father."

"Indeed!" said the Abbé, deeply moved, and studying more attentively the very ordinary face before him. "Indeed!...I really am sorry that we never met again....But now that we have, we mustn't lose sight of each other...we must keep up our new friendship when we've both got back to civil life. ...It will be a great pleasure for me. Mind, I mean it!"

All the time he was speaking, he registered a feeling of plea-sure in the moral serenity, the freedom of spirit, which he thought he could detect in this seriously wounded man, who in a few hours' time was to undergo an operation which might well prove mortal and must, in any case, be dreadful.

Devaux's tone changed.

"I wanted to see you because there are things I want to talk about. My memory of you is so vivid....I don't know whether you've been told, but there's no hope for me."

"Nonsense! They told me just the contrary. They said they might have to operate, but that you would almost certainly recover."

"It's not much of a prospect—to go through life without my legs."

"But they may save them! The surgeon will do his very best, be sure of that. Surgery nowadays, you know, can per-form miracles. I see them with my own eyes, almost every day."

"No....I'm quite sure....Besides, I shouldn't like my poor wife to be tied to a cripple like me for the rest of her life."

"I'm certain that your wife loves you. She would rather a

thousand times have you back a cripple than not have you at all....You must know that!...She'd give you a fine blowing up if she could hear you now!"

"But that's not what I wanted to talk to you about.... There's a question I want to ask...Anybody else would put me off with a lot of humbug...but not you....Let me think a moment...Not that I need to think; what I'm going to ask has been going round and round in my head for a long time now; but I want to find the words to put it....What's going on is too frightful. I know what you'll say: that God wants to punish us or try us....I suppose the Boches say the same thing too....Well, I admit that He may have very good reasons for making us suffer like this...although—well—But what I can't understand is how making us do evil can possibly lead us to salvation....Do you think, Father, that what we are all doing now, both us and the Boches, is good?"

"My son, don't you think you are wrong in comparing the two cases—in treating them as analogous?...*You* are defending your country, which has been unjustly attacked...."

"Father, you know perfectly well that if it had been us who had unjustly attacked the fellows over there, I should have been in it just the same, and that you would be telling me, just as you are now, that I was doing my duty."

"Well, that's what it all comes down to. You are doing your duty."

"Oh, I know well enough, Father, that if I do wrong in the circumstances, there is much to excuse me....But I was talking of God."

The Abbé did not reply at once. The question put to him was of a sort to trouble him deeply. Had he not often put it to his own conscience, in spite of himself? He, no more than the man before him, found it easy to imagine Christ taking a hand in all this business ... the Jesus of the Gospel finding no other way of bringing men to Himself than by setting them to murder one another.

Devaux spoke again:

"My own feeling is that God can't do anything about it."

"You mustn't say things like that, my son. They show lack

of respect for God's almighty power....But there is, maybe, in your thought something that is not entirely wrong....Perhaps it is not altogether absurd to imagine that for this once God has been content, without actively intervening Himself, to leave men to the working of their own madness...their own human nature, alas!...For we must never forget that He created us free. To punish mankind it was not necessary to decree these horrors....He had only to withdraw Himself and leave men to their own devices....Yes, that I believe is the answer to your question."

"But then, Father, what comfort have we left?"

"I have sometimes asked the same question, my son...I tell you this to prove that I am not answering you thoughtlessly...Our comfort must be to think that Christ hates this war as much as we do ourselves."

"Do you really believe that?"

"Certainly I do."

"You don't think he likes to see his priests blessing guns and flags...chanting *Te Deums* to Him?"

"I think, rather, that such things must put Him out of patience, and that He will never be really happy until peace comes."

At about the same time Germaine and Mareil were seated close to each other, she in a nurse's uniform, he in that of a second-line soldier with the cross of an officer of the Legion of Honour, in a small house situated in this same village of Vadelaincourt, a charming miniature affair standing at the corner of a street, rather like a sort of doll's inn, in which the nurses had installed for their own use what they called a tearoom, which was known in official language as a "co-operative canteen for hot drinks."

"So you're really getting used to it all?" said Germaine. "You're not too exhausted?"

"It is pretty exhausting. It's the vibration of the wheel, after a while, that is so awful, and the appalling way in which one just can't alter the speed. My ankle gets quite numb with maintaining precisely the same pressure on the accelerator. I told you, didn't I, that the other day, when my truck had a breakdown, we had to push it into the ditch to avoid blocking the road.... Well, that was a real relief."

Although Mareil had been free of all military obligation, he had enlisted a month earlier, on the 10th of March to be exact, in the motor transport service, with the request that he be sent to the area immediately behind Verdun, and, so far as possible, somewhere on the famous Road. He, like many others, had fallen a victim to the Verdun fever, had felt the place drawing him to itself. The idea that he might find Germaine there—she had been acting for some time now as a nurse attached to the Vadelaincourt group of hospitals—or, at least, that he might feel himself to be near her, had certainly not weakened his decision.

"They're all extraordinarily nice to me," he went on; "so really attentive. I've only got to say I feel a bit tired and they offer me two days off at once."

A little later she said to him:

"I must introduce you to that Canadian officer I was telling you about. He was on the Somme. But he was determined to be sent to Verdun, to fight in front of Verdun. He had a frightful wound. He's a real hero. He insists that it was I who saved his life, but of course that's all nonsense!...You'll be awfully interested in him."

CHAPTER TWENTY-NINE

At Brigade Headquarters.
Polish Prisoners

About ten o'clock that evening, Geoffroy, after having spent some time visiting the new defensive positions at Bois Bourrus on which he had got to render a report, and after dining with the officer in command, decided to follow Pétain's advice and to seek hospitality for the night somewhere in the neighbourhood of the Mort-Homme at one of the brigade headquarters—to be precise, at that of the 84th. Studying the map of the sector, he saw that he could get there without difficulty by going down No.3 communication trench. By telephone he gave notice of his arrival to the general commanding, who expressed great delight at the idea of having him as a guest.

The walk would take about an hour. The night was marvellously clear, with a moon in its first quarter. From the military point of view it was perfectly quiet. All the way there Geoffroy did not hear so much as two gun-shots.

He kept up a steady rate of progress, and it was scarcely eleven when he reached the 84th brigade headquarters.

The general received him very cordially, and since he knew perfectly well for whose eyes Geoffroy's report was intended, he did his best to answer all the questions put to him, and volunteered several remarks of his own.

"In my opinion they're getting ready for something here. Will their main thrust be made against the Mort-Homme, which is obviously a thorn in their side, or against Hill 304, which is scarcely less so? Or will they attack both? It all depends on the size of the effort they're going to make and on the number of effectives they have available. In any case, I'm pretty sure, and I'm not the only one, that having butted their heads against the defences of the right bank, they're going to try to force the left, if only to take in the rear our batteries at Vacherauville, Marre, and Bois Bourrus, which prevent them from advancing as they would like to do on the other side of the river....When will they be ready to take their chance? That's difficult to foresee. But from what we've been able to judge of their movements, I should say it would be soon."

At this moment the telephone bell rang. The general, who had been called personally to the instrument, listened for some considerable time, emitting a number of interjections the while:

"Good, good, excellent....Send them along."

He went back to Geoffroy.

"It seems they're sending down two Boche prisoners—one of them's an officer—who've just been mopped up by a patrol of the 151st. They've given a lot of important information. Apparently they say there's to be an attack tomorrow, and they've got the details. Well, we'll see what they've got to tell us."

"Do you know, sir, whether they were taken unwillingly or whether they gave themselves up ?"

"I rather got the impression that they gave themselves up."

"That adds considerably to the value of what they have to say....The eve of an attack is the time usually chosen by deserters....They probably know pretty well what's going to happen, especially when they're officers...."

The arrival of the two prisoners was announced shortly afterwards. The officer in charge of them entered first. He was a great, hulking lieutenant of reserve, wearing pince-nez, and with hair that was too long over his ears. He spoke in edu-cated accents, but very simply, and without any show of excitement. One got the impression that he would have used precisely the same tone in addressing Pétain, Joffre, or one of his own men.

"It was I who took them, sir—not that that's much to boast of. They were trying to get to our lines with the idea of sur-rendering. One's a *Feldwebel*, the other a private. They've given us a lot of interesting details, which they'll repeat to you, sir. I think they're pretty genuine. The *Feldwebel* is a man of some education and speaks excellent French. But there's one thing I ought to warn you about, sir. The colonel I took them to in the first place listened to what they had to say and thanked them for the information; but he thought it his duty to read them a pretty sharp lecture. He told them, for instance, that he suspected their *bona fides* because they were deserters and cowards and traitors to their country. I'd already told him, and I repeated what I'd said, that both the men were Poles, called up against their will to serve in the Prussian Army, and that the first thing they were careful to say to me, as soon as they had surrendered, was that they'd been planning to desert for a long time because they hated Germany, that they'd chosen to take their chance today, in spite of the considerable risks involved, in order to do a service to the French, who have always been friends of Poland, by revealing to them the plan of attack. The colonel didn't seem to attach any importance to these details, with the result that all the way here my two Poles have done nothing but complain bitterly of their reception, and say how much they regretted that they hadn't just given themselves up without opening their lips. I thought you ought to know that, sir."

"Good....Thank you....I must say that colonel of yours does seem to have been lacking in tact....Have them brought in, please. I should like you to stay here, of course, while I question them."

The two prisoners were led in. The *Feldwebel*, a small, stocky man with a round head and a short nose, saluted with an air of stiff correctitude, but from his expression it was clear that he was still boiling with indignation.

"You understand French, I believe?" said the general in a very friendly tone.

"Yes, sir. My friend here doesn't know much of the language, though."

"Never mind. If necessary, I'll talk to him in German. I realize that you are both of you Poles, and that you have made your way to our lines out of friendship to the French, and with the intention of giving us information of the utmost importance. Allow me to offer you my thanks. I will give orders that you are to be treated with special consideration. France and Poland have been friends for centuries."

The *Feldwebel* seemed suddenly transfigured, and asked with much respect to be allowed to translate the general's words to his companion.

Then the questioning began. The general, Geoffroy, and the lieutenant, all had a working knowledge of German, but it was not necessary for them to make much use of it.

The *Feldwebel* confirmed what he had already said elsewhere, merely adding a few fresh details. He had managed to furnish himself with a copy of the German operation orders. The information he had to give was perfectly definite. The artillery preparation was timed to begin at eight o'clock the next morning and would work up to a maximum of intensity. Guns of all calibres would be employed, as well as aerial torpedoes and even flame-throwers used at long range. The infantry would be sent over the top at midday. If the assault was held up, the bombardment would start again and continue, if necessary, until the evening. The *Feldwebel* added that he had reason to believe that another attack would be launched on the right bank of the river in conjunction with the main offensive. The general order covering both movements was to the effect that the Mort-Homme must be taken at all costs.

He gave a few more details about the effectives involved, the position of the various units, of the reserves, and of the batteries. What he said agreed sufficiently with information already received to make it clear that he could be relied upon.

"Well," said the general to Geoffroy, after the two prisoners had been dismissed with repeated thanks, "your coming here this evening was certainly not a waste of time. Since there's not a moment to lose, I should be enormously obliged if you'd give me a hand with what's to be done. I'll warn the division and carry out the arrangements that immediately concern me, if you'll get in touch with Souilly. Can you manage that? Do you think you can get a word personally with General Pétain at this hour of the night?"

"I know I can."

"Get him to send us all possible assistance; we're going to be up against it!...And my brigade's already had a pretty rough time of it! What makes it all so particularly hellish," he added, with a sudden note of sadness in his voice, "is that I've just had a draft of poor little devils of the '16 class.... They've never been under fire...For the moment they're in reserve. ...But—I only hope to God I don't have to use them tomorrow!"

Counter-Attack at Mort-Homme

At one p.m. an encouraging rumour began to circulate among the companies in reserve on the slope opposite Mort-Homme, to the west of brigade headquarters:

"The Boche attack has failed."

The bombardment had, in fact, ceased with dramatic suddenness. There was no reason to suppose that this cessation was the prelude to a fresh assault, since at midday, when the German infantry had started to move forward, their guns, so far from being silent, had worked up to a still greater degree of fury, contenting themselves merely with lengthening their range. Wazemmes, who since midnight had run the whole gamut of emotions, was now conscious of an entirely new one. Its elements were a sincere relief, which he did not allow to appear, and a flicker of disappointment, of which he made considerable parade.

"Damn nuisance," he said to his young comrades of the '16 class. "What's the matter with 'em?"

His disappointment was, in fact, perfectly genuine. Since, obviously, something had got to happen sooner or later, the sooner the better. Wazemmes felt that he was in just the right mood to face a crisis, worked up to a state of unprecedented excitement.

But what a day it had been! About midnight, just when they had all dropped into a sound sleep, had come the fall-in. "It seems the Boches are going to attack tomorrow. Since we're in reserve, you can let your kids sleep a bit longer." (The kids were the members of the '16 class who had been drafted into the regiment a few days earlier.) "But see that they're all ready. The older men, and the N.C.O.'s of course, must take over sentry duties." At seven a. m., just when Wazemmes, his rifle between his legs, was snoozing against an angle of the trench wall, someone had shaken him by the shoulders.

"Hey! Wake up. The lieutenant's asking for you."

The lieutenant commanding the company, who had joined the regiment a few days before Wazemmes, was a very young officer who, in the eyes of the latter, shone with all sorts of reflected glory. His name was Comte Voisenon de Pelleriès. He had been due to start his career at the Military College in 1914, but had been introduced to the school of war before he had known the discipline of that other, more normal school (he and his class-mates had not even had time to sit for their oral entrance examination). Among his companions had been many who had fallen in great numbers during that first winter "advancing in dress uniform." the Comte de Pelleriès was a slim, not very tall young man, who maintained a standard of quiet elegance even in the trenches. He had fine grey eyes, the hint of an auburn moustache, and spoke with so cordial a tone of friendliness that his voice at times took on a warm and tender timbre. Each one of his men felt that he was enveloped in an aura of confidence and affection. He had been wounded three times, once seriously. As a result of his last wound but one, he had been left with a slight limp—quite temporary, he maintained—which he disguised with easy grace.

"My dear Wazemmes," he said, "I understand that you were formerly a corporal. I am pleased to be able to tell you that, as the result of my personal representations, your stripes have been restored to you. Your squad will be composed entirely of young fellows of the '16 class. You will probably have to lead them forward under fire in the course of today. I know that you are brave enough to face any call upon your courage, and that you will give your men an admirable example."

He held out his hand and shook Wazemmes's as though it had been that of an old friend.

At eight a.m.—"Boom, branranran, bang, bang...." Wazemmes, drunk with sleep and with the prospect of glory, spent his time walking up and down among "his men."

"That was a 77...those greeny-yellowish bursts up there are

105 shrapnel....That noise? That's probably trench-mortars firing on our front lines."

The poor little devils were both delighted and appalled, now pink with emotion, now green with terror. Since the bombardment, violent though it was, was not falling on their position, they gradually grew in confidence, and more than one was heard to say that the guns' bark was worse than their bite. Without wishing to shatter their illusion on this point, the N.C.O.'s repeated various bits of advice about how they should behave in open ground in order to avoid unnecessary risks.

The information given by the Polish prisoners had turned out to be perfectly correct so far as it concerned the preliminary bombardment. It was felt, therefore, that it would probably be no less correct in its other details, and it was expected that the enemy assault would take place at midday.

About half past eleven, the Comte de Pelleriès assembled his boys of the '16 class and, to the amazement of more than one of them, among whom Wazemmes was certainly numbered, made them a little speech in his kindly, cultivated voice, the gist of which was as follows: "My dear friends, we are probably going to take part in the coming action. We shall not be called upon to receive the first waves of the German assault" (he never let the word "Boche" pass his lips), "but since it is possible that our comrades in the front line may be forced to yield a little ground, we shall be called upon to bar the way to the attacking enemy, or perhaps to counter-attack with the purpose of recapturing the lost trenches. If we have to counter-attack, we shall carry out our duty bravely, shall we not, my friends? We are soldiers of the Republic. We are here to defend Verdun, because the fall of Verdun might mean the defeat of France. We do not want our country, which is a democracy, a republic of free men, to be conquered and enslaved by the men opposite, who are not free men, but live still in feudal conditions. Not far from here, at Valmy, a little over one hundred and twenty years ago, your ancestors drove back the foreigners who had come to crush the Great French Revolution. One of my ancestors, the Comte Voisenon de Pelleriès, was present on that occasion too, with the rank of captain. He was not one of those who had emigrated. …When, therefore, we move forward, I should like you, my friends, to shout with me: '*Vive la nation! Vive la République!*' as our ancestors shouted at Valmy, and then to advance on the enemy singing the *Marseillaise*."

In five minutes Wazemmes's political convictions had undergone a radical change. And since the portrait of Mlle Anne de Montbieuze had already been replaced on his heart by that of a charming typist of no marked political views, but probably sympathetic to the Left, whom he had met on the evening of the 2nd of April, he had no difficulty in feeling now that he was a soldier of Valmy and a corporal of the Republic.

Suddenly, a rumour passed down the ranks.

"Seems we've got to counter-attack. The Boches have advanced again. They're going to come down this side of the Mort-Homme….The chasseurs have been driven from their trenches….We've got to retake them."

There followed a period of intolerable waiting. The bombardment, which had started again, was spreading now on every side. Shells with all the names in the vocabulary, with all the magic, terrifying numbers which served to identify them, with their noises, none of which were really alike but which no ear could distinguish, so overwhelming was the uproar, with their bursts of smoke which looked like different species of poisonous fungus, with their smells which united into a single stench, gave the impression that they were all detonating at one and the same moment in the air, in the earth, in the interior of one's own stomach. The country which one could just glimpse through a breach in the parapet (strictly forbidden to show one's head) looked sad and comfortless. Though the sun was shining, a melancholy exuded from its bare, grey distances, which dwindled away towards the enemy lines in a series of slow undulations. That slope in front was the one to be climbed, there where each moment the earth was torn by some great shell. Smoke came from the ground as though a hook were drawing wool from a mattress with insistent regularity. The attacking line would have to move along the whole length of that slope so torn by shells, so witheringly swept by machine-gun fire. If only it needn't happen! If only the order to advance never came! Things do happen like that sometimes, luck does turn at the very last moment. Perhaps the Boches, too much exhausted by their own efforts, too badly mauled by our artillery (for our guns were hard at it, 75's, 155's, and all the rest) would retire of their own account. Perhaps the chasseurs might have sufficient self-pride to want to retake themselves the trenches they had lost. Perhaps, for some reason or other, the Staff might change its mind. . . . It was well known that Pétain did not like sacrificing men's lives.

Lieutenant Voisenon de Pelleriès could be seen putting on his gloves, smoothing his tiny moustache. He drew his sword (for, since this morning, he had taken to wearing it). In a voice of marked politeness he cried:

"My friends, it's our turn now!"

Then he clambered over the parapet, shouting:

"*Vive la nation! Vive la République!*"

The lads behind him shouted too, as men shout in dreams, without being quite sure whether their lips were uttering any audible sound. They leapt forward without, as yet, much difficulty, since the objective was still far away and the machine-guns were not, so far, concentrating on them. The lieutenant began to sing the *Marseillaise*. They did their best to sing it too. From time to time, interrupting his singing, the lieutenant shouted to them:

"Do as I do! Lie down!"

But he only half lay down. He watched them from the corner of his eye. They flung themselves down at once.

A few of them began to fall. Sometimes their friends did not notice what had happened; sometimes they saw but could not believe their eyes. They took up a verse of the *Marseillaise*, shouting the first words that occurred to them. They had no idea whether it was the same verse as the one the lieutenant was singing, or their pals on either side.

"Careful, boys. We've got to get through an artillery barrage.

...Do as I do....Bend as low as you can, and jump to it....Don't lie down again until you're fifty yards further on."

Wazemmes swallowed the scrap of the *Marseillaise* which stuck in his throat to pass the order back to "his men":

"Do as I do....Jump to it!"

He threw himself forward, bending his body as much as he could, and going as fast as he knew how. The noise was staggering.

"Ho!"

It was all over in a second. He had hardly time to realize that he had been hit, that the pain was hideous, that he was done for.

CHAPTER THIRTY-ONE

Order of the Day

"There you are," said Pétain to Geoffroy, holding out the sheet of manuscript which was still wet. "Have it run off and distributed at once to all units....I'd have liked to say something rather special about those lads of the '16 class, but I was afraid it might be too painful for their poor parents....Do you know how many of them actually reached the trench lost by the chasseurs? Ten, out of a total of two companies engaged in the counter-attack. Ten, just think of it! I'm told that de Pelleriès was magnificent. He made those boys sing the *Marseillaise*. He was killed half-way up the slope. I'm going to see that he gets a posthumous award of the Croix de Guerre."

Geoffroy took the paper and read the general's rather large, angular script, to which the shaping of certain letters gave a curiously feminine quality (the ink of the last few lines was not yet dry):

To the Men of the IInd Army

The 9th of April is a glorious day in the annals of our military history.

The furious attacks delivered by the German soldiers under the command of the Crown Prince have been everywhere broken.

Infantry, artillery, engineers, and flying men of the IInd Army vied with one another in heroism.

Honour to them all!

The Germans will undoubtedly attack again. Let every man

work and watch to the end that future successes may fall in no way short of yesterday's.

Courage.... We shall beat them yet!

Ph.Pétain

"Not bad, no, not at all bad," said Geoffroy to himself as he made his way down the staircase. "If only this could be the last order of the day to be issued in connexion with the battle of Verdun!"

He crossed the vestibule and stepped out of the front door. There before him the Road roared and rumbled, true to itself as ever, with its double line of trucks.